Praise for

JERI SMITH-READY's

EYES OF CROW

Book one in the Aspect of Crow series

"A spellbinding plot and smooth-flowing narrative draw the
reader into a world of myth and magic.... Lovers of fantasy
are about to embark on a great new series."
—*Romantic Times BOOKreviews*

"Smith-Ready's *Eyes of Crow* is just the first installment
in what could be an entertaining and profoundly moving
series. Jean M. Auel meets Mercedes Lackey."
—Barnes & Noble *Explorations*

"Mystical, magical, romantic, suspenseful and
action-packed, *Eyes of Crow* is an excellent example
of what a fantasy novel should be."
—*Coffee Time Romance*

"The first installment in this magical series is an emotional,
engaging, and appealing fantasy. Smith-Ready
is a born storyteller."
—*Book Loons*

"Jeri Smith-Ready's lyrical prose brings to life unforgettable
characters and a poignant story that haunted me long after

VOICE OF CROW

JERI SMITH-READY

LUNA™

www.LUNA-Books.com

LUNA™

VOICE OF CROW

ISBN-13: 978-0-373-80290-6
ISBN-10:   0-373-80290-0

Copyright © 2007 by Jeri Smith-Ready

First trade printing: October 2007

Author photo by: © 2006 Szemere Photography

This edition published by arrangement with Harlequin Books S.A.

® and TM are trademarks of Harlequin Books S.A., used under license. Trademarks indicated with ® are registered in the United States Patent and Trademark Office, the Canadian Trade Marks Office and in other countries.

www.LUNA-Books.com

Printed in U.S.A.

Dear Reader,

An intriguing challenge of writing a trilogy with a core love story is how to continue after the happy ending of book one. Things never stay perfect—not in real life, and certainly not in the world of the Reawakened.

In *Eyes of Crow* Rhia found the courage, with Marek's help, to accept her Aspect so she could aid her people in their hour of greatest need. Marek himself had to overcome his past to regain full Wolf powers and prove he was worthy of this sacred responsibility.

But doesn't it always seem that in solving one problem within ourselves, we create another, opposite problem? Even strengths like bravery and loyalty can turn into fatal flaws. Each of us is a work in progress. But when someone loves us for who we are, we can do anything, be anything. It gives us the ultimate freedom to be ourselves—and even recreate ourselves, if necessary.

That's why I enjoy following a hero and heroine throughout a series. In *Voice of Crow* Rhia and Marek's world takes them to the end of their strength and makes them grow and change in ways they couldn't have imagined a year ago. But their bond will never break, right down to the last moment of the next book, *The Reawakened,* and beyond.

Best regards,

Jeri Smith-Ready

To Aunt Maria, because I promised

Acknowledgments

Many thanks to my family, for indulging a little girl's love of nature that would provide the lifeblood of the Aspect of Crow series.

Much gratitude goes out to my critiquers, for their invaluable insights: Cecilia Ready, Terri Prizzi, Stephanie Smith and especially Rob Staeger and Beth Venart for giving me the "tough love" every author needs. Kudos to the hardworking folks behind the scenes at LUNA who helped bring the book to life: Tracy Farrell, Mary-Theresa Hussey, Tara Parsons, Adam Wilson, Amy Jones, Kathleen Oudit, Maureen Stead, Don Lucey, as well as artist Chad Michael Ward of Digital Apocalypse Studios.

Thanks to my editor, Stacy Boyd, for her unshakeable support; and my agent, Ginger Clark of Curtis Brown, Ltd., who keeps me sane in a crazy world. I wouldn't trade either of them for all the coffee in Colombia.

Thanks most of all to my husband, Christian Ready, for his love and inspiration, and for putting up with my bloodshot eyes, bad hair and dubious clothing choices during Revision Month.

In the torchlight surrounding the camp of a hundred Kalindons, Rhia could see the rope burns on Marek's neck.

The man who would soon be her husband slept quietly
for the first time in several nights. Perhaps exhaustion had
stolen his nightmares, or at least his body's ability to mani-
fest them in twitches and starts.

The humid air draped over her like a second skin. Far
above, the breeze murmured through the pines and spruces,
but did not deign to descend to the ground.

She kicked off the covers of the bedroll, rolled her sleeves
up to her shoulders and spread her limbs to dissipate the
heat. To no avail. Summer's strength had reached even the
high mountain forest near Kalindos.

Whispers came. Rhia's muscles jerked as if she'd been

stabbed with a pin. *Not again.* She covered her ears, as if that would help. *Please let me sleep.*

But the voices of the dead would strengthen in her dreams, rumbles of discontent forming incoherent words. When she was awake they would whisper, or even silence when she spoke out loud or sang a distracting tune. Her traveling companions resented the latter, since her crooning voice was as melodic as that of her Guardian Spirit.

Crow.

Only a few months had passed since the Spirit had bestowed her with His Aspect. Yet she had borne these dark gifts for a decade—since she was eight—when she first heard Crow come to carry a soul to the Other Side.

The whispers changed, and Rhia realized with relief that these belonged to the living. She rolled onto her stomach to peer through the darkness.

Beyond the torchlight, a man and a woman patrolled together, carrying hunting bows so naturally, the weapons seemed part of their bodies. Everyone's vigilance had heightened since the Descendants had invaded Rhia's home village of Asermos ten days ago. With the help of the Kalindons she now traveled with, the Asermons had repelled the Descendant invasion, but at a precious cost.

Rhia shoved back a sweaty brown lock that had fallen into her eyes. Cut above her nape in mourning, her hair was now too short to tie back.

The voices in her head returned, louder. A wave of nausea swept over her.

Rhia sat up. A hand grabbed her arm, snapping shut like an iron-jawed trap. She stifled a yelp and looked down to see Marek's blue-gray eyes staring up at her. He let go and blinked rapidly to rouse himself.

"Sorry," he whispered. "Where are you going?"

She wiped the cold sweat from her forehead. "I feel sick."

"From the baby?"

"Too soon for that."

"The voices again?"

"Feels like flies trapped inside my skull." She rubbed her ear, as if that would relieve the itch deep within. "Coranna said it would be like this the first few months, but I don't think I can stand another hour." She was only two weeks pregnant, with the voices the sole sign she had progressed to the second phase of her Aspect.

Her new powers required her to return to Kalindos to continue studying with her mentor. Right now she wished they were back at her father's farm in Asermos, instead of spending another night in the mosquito-plagued forest. Normally the journey to Kalindos took only a few days by horseback, but conveying those with battle injuries tripled the travel time.

She pushed away the blanket. "I'm going to the river to cool off."

He sat up. "I'll go with you."

"You should rest. I'll bring Alanka."

"I need a bath, too." He drew his legs out of the bedroll, wincing.

"You'll get your bandage wet."

"I'll stand on one foot."

She grasped his hand to help him up, secretly glad he would accompany her. He slung his bow and arrows over his shoulder as automatically as most people would put on shoes. They tiptoed out of the camp together, two sets of footsteps but only one sound. Even Marek's limp couldn't undermine his Wolf stealth.

His palm pressed warm against hers. With his left hand, he wiped the shoulder-length, light brown hair from his stubbled cheeks where sweat had adhered it. The gesture revealed a pale face contorting with the effort to hide the pain of every other step. Rhia pretended not to notice, but slowed her pace nonetheless.

She fidgeted with the leather cord around her neck, from which a crow feather hung. When they returned to Kalindos tomorrow she would remove it. Each of that tiny village's three hundred residents knew the others' names and Guardian Spirits, so they saw no need to wear fetishes. In the much larger villages of Asermos, Velekos and Tiros, courtesy demanded one display which powers one possessed. As much as she loved the Spirit who had chosen her, Rhia sometimes wished she could hide her death-awareness. It tended to make people nervous.

Marek stopped short, throwing a glare to their right, where his Wolf-sister Alanka sat hunched in the dark on a fallen tree trunk with her former mate, Adrek. Rhia couldn't hear their words, but obviously Marek could.

"They're supposed to be patrolling," he said.

"Look." Rhia pointed to their left, where another scout—a Bobcat, she thought—circled the camp. "Maybe Alanka and Adrek's shift is over."

Marek's mouth snapped into a taut frown, and she knew what bothered him. "None of my business." He squeezed her hand and led her toward the river again. "But I hate to see her make the same mistake twice."

For the first time, Alanka felt true sympathy for the deer she hunted. Not just gratitude for their sacrifice, or respect for the life they had given. Now she knew how it felt to sense the stalk of a Cougar in the night.

"I miss you." Adrek shifted to face her on the tree trunk. "Fighting in that battle, almost dying, I realized what was important in life."

"I've never been important in your life." The catch in her voice betrayed her resentment. "And last I heard, sprained ankles weren't lethal."

He fidgeted with the hunting bow between his knees, eyebrows pinched. She almost regretted her retort. The battle for Asermos had been hard on everyone—even Adrek, who hadn't lost family. She turned away from his pout, knowing the effect it still had on her even after two years.

"I'm sorry," he said quietly. "I've done this all wrong. I just thought we could talk."

Alanka crumbled a shard of bark that had come loose in her hand. She needed to talk about the killing, too, with someone who had done the same, with someone else called by the Spirits to take the lives of animals, not people.

But not until she was ready.

"You never told me how you got hurt during the battle." She tried not to smirk—one of the Bobcats had told her what had happened, but she wondered if Adrek would invent a cover story to save face.

He slapped a mosquito on his arm. "I stepped in a hole."

"A hole."

His green eyes flashed at her. "I was too busy shooting arrows into Descendants to watch where I was going."

There it was again, the thing that turned her stomach and kept her awake no matter how tired she was. She pushed it away.

"Something snapped when I fell," he continued. "Next thing I know, someone loads me onto a skid and I'm in the healers' tent, covered in another soldier's blood." A corner of Adrek's mouth turned down. "But nothing compared to what you went through." He reached for her hand. She moved it away, pretending to test the tension on her bowstring.

Adrek's spurned hand scratched the back of his head. "Is this because of Pirrik?"

Her shoulders tensed at the name of her most recent mate. "You know I'm not with him anymore." She held her voice low, in case Pirrik lay awake in the camp.

"He should have been more understanding."

"My father killed his father. What's to understand?"

"That wasn't your fault. No one should blame you for anything your father did—that murder, starting the war with the Descendants. You're not him."

Her fingers trembled, vibrating the bowstring at the farthest depths of her hearing range. The sound made the memories flare in her mind, like wind over a campfire. She thrust the bow away. It toppled onto the needle-covered ground. Adrek gasped and lunged to pick it up.

"Are you two guarding the camp or reminiscing?"

Alanka looked behind her to see Endrus and Morran approach. Bobcat Morran had been her second mate, and the brown-haired Cougar, Endrus, who had just spoken, had followed soon after. She had loved neither man—Adrek had shown her that Cats were good for only one thing besides hunting—and had therefore remained friends with both.

Morran vaulted over the fallen tree trunk to land lightly beside her. "Good thing we weren't Descendants, or you'd be dead by now."

"If you were Descendants," she told him, "I'd have heard you before you saw me, and *you'd* be dead by now."

"They are loud, aren't they? Maybe they carry bricks in their shoes." Endrus perched on the trunk behind her and surrounded her with his legs, his left knee blocking Adrek. He squeezed her shoulders, and she groaned at the sudden release of tension. "Ooh, Morran, I made her purr."

"But can you make her scream?" The lanky Bobcat reached for her waist, his hand forming a tickling claw. By reflex, her foot shot out and swiped his legs from under him. Morran sprawled in the dirt with an "Oof!" Endrus pointed at him and stifled cackles that quaked his body.

"Boys," Adrek said, "we were trying to have a serious conversation."

Endrus snorted. "And we were seriously trying to keep her out of your clutches."

"I can take care of myself," Alanka snapped at him, with more annoyance than she felt. Her friends' interruption had broken the morose spell Adrek had begun to cast.

"It's our turn to keep watch." Morran rolled to his feet

and pulled a dead leaf out of his long blond hair. "So you two can get some sleep."

"Yes, *sleep*," Endrus directed at Adrek.

Alanka patted Endrus's knee and slid out of his grasp. "Good night."

Adrek followed her toward the camp. "So, back to my original question."

"And my original answer, which is no, you can't sleep next to me." She quieted her voice as they approached the slumbering Kalindons. "I need to be alone."

"What can you do alone that you can't do with me?"

"Think. Breathe."

He took her arm. "Alanka—"

"Remember what I did to Morran. You'll get worse."

Adrek dropped his hand. "Who taught you that move you used on him?"

"My brothers. Lycas, I mean." Her throat clutched her other brother's name, as if releasing it would kill him all over again.

Adrek's face softened at the sight of her grief—she had never been good at hiding her emotions. "You sure you want to be alone?"

"I didn't say I *wanted* to be alone. I said I *needed* to. Good night."

Alanka turned away, relieved that he didn't follow and not caring that he still held her bow. She never wanted to look at it again.

She found her bedroll where she had left it next to Rhia and Marek's. After clearing stones from a space on the ground, she spread the blanket and wrapped herself inside, using the next day's clothing as a pillow.

She stared at the shadows glimmering on the mossy gray boulder to her left, knowing that when her eyes closed, the same scene would dance on the back of her lids.

Her brother Nilo, sprawled in the mud and blood of the battlefield, giving his life to save hers.

She owed it to him to be brave, to be proud of what she'd done to defend his village. But her mind still flickered with the vacant faces of the dead.

Marek blanked his expression as he walked, showing far less pain than he felt. If Rhia knew how much it hurt, she would insist he stay behind at the camp. He would refuse, and they would have the same argument for the eleventh time.

He didn't understand how, after all the dangers they'd faced, she could call him overprotective. Protective, yes, but the *over* part was impossible.

"Let's slow down," she said. "I'm tired."

Marek knew she was shortening their strides to give his injured leg relief. It hadn't taken Rhia long to learn how to pacify his pride, and for that he loved her. That and approximately seven hundred and forty-nine other reasons.

He longed to tear the bandage off his calf and scratch the sword wound with a sharp stick. The salve Elora applied every morning was helping it heal, so that now the itching nearly outweighed the pain. He knew he was lucky to have a leg to itch.

Through the thinning trees, he could see the river's wide, calm surface glisten in the muted moonlight. The haze seemed to stretch from the dank ground all the way to the moon itself. Marek's skin yearned for the cool mountain water.

The bank sloped down, studded with tree roots. He let go of Rhia's hand and took her elbow. "Watch your step."

She glared at him. "I'm pregnant, not blind. Ack!" She stumbled on a root, waving her other arm to regain balance.

He helped her down the hill, then faced away from her as she undressed. Seeing her naked would torture him, since they had to abstain from lovemaking during her month of mourning. It was nearly all he could think about. It didn't matter that he couldn't twitch his leg without agony, or that his skin cracked from sun poisoning. He had survived, and he wanted to fill every moment with the woman he had almost lost.

A splash and a gasp came from behind him. He turned to see Rhia submerged up to the neck. "C-cold," she said, her jaw quivering. "Whose idea was this?"

He smiled as he took off his shoes, socks and trousers. Bandages covered the upper third of his right calf; in the dim light he was relieved to see the white strips free of fresh bloodstains.

A series of large rocks jutted out into the water to his left. He picked his way over these, carrying his bow and arrows, until he was near Rhia. This vantage point gave him a good view up and down the river, which he scanned for intruders. Seeing nothing unusual, he sat on the edge of the rough rock, extending his wounded right leg along its length and dipping his left leg into the cold water.

Rhia swam over, dark hair plastered against her scalp. "Want some help?"

"I'm fine."

She blew out a wet breath. "Stop it, Marek. You're not fine."

"Am I annoying you?"

"Yes. Now, take off your shirt and lie down."

He chuckled. "I should annoy you more often." He handed her his shirt and stretched out on his back. Rhia dipped the cloth in the water, then squeezed it over his chest. He hissed at the cool relief. She repeated the action, then gently wiped his skin.

"Close your eyes," she whispered.

A moment later, water cascaded over his face and ran through his hair, soothing his nerves and washing away three days' worth of sweat and grime.

He dropped his arm to dangle in the river next to Rhia. The back of his hand brushed her warm, smooth belly. "That doesn't tickle?" he murmured.

"I'm too tired to be ticklish." She squeezed the cloth over his hair again. "And at the moment, too content."

Marek eased his lips into a smile. It was odd to feel happy, after so many days of conflict and sorrow. Tomorrow he would return home, battered but victorious.

A scarce breeze blew over his body, cooling him and bearing a thousand scents of the forest he knew so well.

He sat up. One of those scents didn't belong here. One of those scents should have been a week's journey away from Asermos in the other direction by now.

He peered upriver. Nothing.

"What is it?" Rhia whispered.

He put a finger to his lips and closed his eyes. The human in him wanted to see to be sure, but the Wolf knew better. Truth lay in sounds and scents. The humid air hung heavy with the latter, carried by the fading wind. As the leaves on the trees hushed, the noise came to him.

A rhythmic slapping against the water, too precise and regular to be a leaping fish or frog.

He opened his eyes to check the riverbank beside them. No time to reach it without being spotted. He hid his bow and arrows behind a bulge in the rock, then slid soundlessly into the water.

Rhia gasped. "Marek, your bandage—"

"Shh. Hold still."

He stood behind her and wrapped his arms tight around her body.

Then he turned invisible, and Rhia with him.

The ship appeared around the bend upriver, near the middle of the waterway. It was long and low, its sails sagging in the dead air. Rows of oars protruded from the side like the legs of a centipede, but these limbs moved as one, back and forth, pushing the vessel through the calm waters. It floated past, for a moment blotting out the dim, distant view of the river's opposite shore.

Another ship appeared, identical to the first, then another. Nine Descendant crafts floated past as Marek and Rhia stood, unseen and unbelieving.

The enemy was leaving a place it never should have been.

Kalindos.

His home.

Marek clutched Rhia's waist and struggled to stay on the mare's back as they careened through the dark woods. Dripping branches hung low over the trail, making him dodge and duck at each turn.

Ahead of them, Alanka rode with Adrek, the Cougar's night vision leading them all. Elora hurried behind them on her own pony, and behind her rode two Wolverines, two Bobcats and a Bear on the other three horses. At their current pace, they would reach Kalindos by daybreak—less than an hour—but it couldn't be soon enough for Marek.

The rest of the Kalindons were following on foot, in two groups: one who could hurry and would reach the village by late the next morning, and one consisting of the wounded and their caretakers.

Soon the hill steepened, and they slowed their pace to an

urgent walk, the ponies huffing from the effort. In the pre-dawn glow Marek recognized the southernmost boundary of his hunting grounds. He knew each branch and rock as well as he knew the corners of his own tree house. The thought of Descendant swords polluting his peaceful forest home made his chest burn with rage.

The wind shifted, carrying the scent he dreaded.

Blood.

"Hurry!" he shouted.

They urged on their exhausted ponies. The path to Kalindos widened, then opened into the outskirts of the village as the sun's first scarlet rays oozed over the mountains.

They rounded a large boulder and pulled up short.

Shreds of tree houses lay like kindling, covering so much ground that it seemed as though the forest itself had fallen. The walls of nearly every house bore gashes and gaps, making the homes look like mouths with missing teeth.

No one peered from behind the busted walls. No one hurried down ladders to greet them. No one shouted or moaned.

No one lived here anymore.

"Let's go," Rhia said.

She and Marek took the lead, Adrek and Alanka following. Though Marek no longer had immediate family in Kalindos—his parents had died over a decade ago, when he was ten—his gut twisted in fear for his mentor, Kerza. The invaders wouldn't spare an old woman like her. Though they worshiped human-made gods instead of the Spirits, the Descendants understood how magic worked among people of the villages, how it peaked with grandparenthood.

The riders picked their way around the village's rubble,

shouting names of their loved ones. The fog swallowed their voices and muted all sounds except the muffled thump of hooves on pine needles. Not so much as a sparrow's twitter or a woodpecker's rattle responded to their calls.

Elora rode up beside them. "Maybe everyone escaped."

"No," Rhia whispered.

The Otter pushed back a damp strand of ash-blond hair and turned to face the village before them. She shrieked her sons' names again, her voice echoing against the hills and bouncing back, unheard.

"Wait." Rhia halted the horse and motioned for Marek to dismount. As soon as he did, she slid off and hurried into the trees. Marek handed the reins to Elora and followed as fast as his injury would allow. With a rush of scent, he understood what Rhia sought.

About a hundred paces off the path, a Descendant soldier lay pitched back in a clump of mountain laurel, as if he had decided to sit and rest awhile. The fingers of his left hand looped around the arrow protruding from his windpipe. He stared unseeing at the forest canopy, which dripped a steady stream of dew onto his forehead.

Rhia knelt beside the dead soldier. Marek wanted to yank out the arrow and plunge it again and again into the man's lifeless form.

With a steady hand, she shut the Descendant's eyes. Marek bit back a rebuke for her humane treatment of the enemy. They wouldn't have done the same for her. But she couldn't turn away from the dead any more than she could stop breathing.

"We should move on," he said. "There must be others."

"There are." She took a deep breath and closed her eyes—for the prayer of passage, no doubt.

A howl of anguish erupted from the far side of the village. Adrek.

"Go." Rhia kept her eyes shut. "I need to finish here."

Marek forced his injured leg to run. His bow and quiver of arrows slapped against his shoulder blades, and he wondered if he should be ready to fire, if danger yet lurked in Kalindos. Then Morran joined Adrek's cry, clearly not a warning, but a lament.

Marek's feet flew over the rocky terrain, and his hands fought back the underbrush that tore at his shirt. He followed the sound of the multiplying cries, and soon he burst into the small clearing that held the ponies' paddock.

He stopped and stared, his eyes trying to convince his mind that what lay before him was real. The morning mist shrouded everything but the three bodies in front of him.

Two men and a woman were tied to the paddock posts, throats slit, shirts blushed with the dull brown of dried blood. The hairs rose on the back of Marek's neck.

At the corner of the paddock, Adrek knelt at the feet of a fourth body, with a wide gash across its abdomen. His father.

Marek forced his ice-cold feet to move, circling the fence. The mist revealed more bodies tied to more posts. Zilus the Hawk, the village Council leader—dead, his throat slit. His wife, Dori, dead. Two more Council members, dead. All of the slaughtered were old.

Elora stumbled past Marek, perhaps searching for a spark of life she could fan into a flame. He scanned his neighbors' corpses for the long white hair of Kerza.

The Descendants had dispatched the most powerful villagers first. But where were the young people his own age? Where were the children?

A fury grew in him as he saw the grisly results of each death. These people had raised him, taught him how to survive in the unforgiving mountain forest. He had sworn to defend them. Instead he had abandoned them, and convinced the best Kalindon warriors to follow him to Asermos to fight in someone else's war.

A war that had come home.

Rhia ignored the stitch in her right side as she ran through the village. Shrieks of anguish filled the air ahead of her, but they all belonged to the living. Crow's wings were silent in Rhia's mind. He had passed Kalindos hours ago, taken what was His, and returned to His realm on the Other Side.

She forced her feet not to slow as she neared the paddock.

Elora stepped toward her out of the mist. "There's nothing left. Nothing for me to do." The healer's knees bent until she sat on the ground, head in her hands.

Rhia moved on, sealing herself into the same shell that had protected her during the battle. After so many had died in front of her, how could this be any worse?

It was worse.

The Kalindon elders dangled pale and purple from the tall paddock stakes. With cold hands she pushed the hair out of her eyes and examined the body of Zilus. His throat had been cut, but no blood pooled at his feet, which meant he'd been killed somewhere else and dragged here to be mounted like a trophy. The sight curdled her guts.

Her last moments with the old Hawk had been rancorous, for he had refused to send aid to her village of Asermos when they needed it. In a bitter twist of irony, those Kalindons who had defied Zilus's decree and fought the Descendants were the only ones left alive.

After speaking the prayer of passage, Rhia moved to the next body, another male elder. She wondered how her own mind could handle such a spectacle without shattering. Another of Crow's "blessings." With a few whispered words and an unflinching touch to the man's slick forehead, she released another soul to the winged Spirit.

Beneath the keening calls of the newly orphaned, someone spoke her name. She jerked her awareness back to this world. Marek stood at her side. He reached to touch her arm. She flinched, and he changed his mind.

"Adrek's father," he said. "Morran's, too. Twelve in all. Every third-phase Kalindon except Kerza, and she's not here."

"Where are the rest?" she whispered, dreading the answer.

"Gone. Maybe they escaped, or—wait." He drew a deep inhale through his nose. "Someone's alive."

They looked at the stable inside the empty paddock. It was large enough to shelter the seven Kalindon ponies, six of whom had gone to Asermos. A rope was tied to each of the paddock's four corner poles. The ropes led to the stable, disappearing under the door. Suddenly one of the ropes shifted in the dirt.

Rhia and Marek shouted, then hurried to open the paddock gate. Alanka followed. The two Wolves shot ahead of Rhia into the darkness of the stable. She stopped inside the door and waited for her eyes to adjust.

"It's Thera," Marek called from the middle stall.

Rhia stepped forward. The young Hawk woman's neck, wrists and ankles were bound by the ropes leading to the paddock posts. The Descendants had tied her up like a wild beast.

"Let's get her out of here." Marek spoke gently. "Thera, can you stand up?"

Rhia checked the other stalls and found nothing but the remaining pony, who snorted and shifted its feet, looking frightened but otherwise unharmed. Marek carried Thera out of the stable and lowered her onto the ground of the paddock. The young woman's hazel eyes stared into the distance without seeing, and her slack face seemed almost dead. Yet Crow's wings beat nowhere near—her life's essence was strong.

"Thera!" One of the other riders, a blond Bear man named Ladek, rushed into the paddock with Elora. They knelt beside Thera. Elora lifted a water skin to the girl's lips, but the liquid dribbled down her trembling chin.

Ladek took Thera into his arms. Rhia remembered, as if from another lifetime, that he was the father of Thera's three-month-old son, who was nowhere to be seen. She hoped the Hawk had answers, and would be able to speak them.

The young woman seemed not to notice their presence, but sat limp in her mate's arms while Marek cut the ropes that bound her. Elora stroked Thera's shoulder-length dark red hair.

"Can you tell us what happened?" the healer whispered. "Where is everyone?"

Thera nodded, her gaze distant and blank. The others had gathered outside the paddock, waiting to hear her story, but Thera just kept nodding, with short pauses. Rhia realized the Hawk was listening to voices in her own head.

"Give her time to come back to us," Rhia said.

"We don't have time," Adrek snapped. He gripped the fence post beside his father's body. "She might know where we can find the others, if they escaped, or if they were taken. We need to start searching."

"He's right." Ladek cupped Thera's chin in his thick fingers and turned her face to his. "Where's Etarek?" he asked her in a soft but urgent tone. "Where's our son?"

Thera didn't speak. A tear rolled from the corner of her eye, down her cheek and onto his fingers.

"No…" He pulled her closer, though she seemed as oblivious as a rag doll. "I never should have left you."

Rhia turned to Marek. They shared a look of remorse, then his shoulders stiffened. He moved to the edge of the paddock, his eyes gaining a faraway look.

He took a quick, deep breath. "Kerza!"

A baby's cry cut the air. A moment later, a white-haired figure appeared from the surrounding trees. Thera's aunt Kerza stumbled into the clearing, clutching an infant to her chest.

"Etarek!" Thera tried to stand, wild eyes fixed on her son.

Ladek leaped to his feet and dashed out of the paddock, nearly knocking the gate off its hinges. He took the squealing baby from Kerza and pulled him close, then delivered him to Thera's arms. She moaned as she laid the child's head against her shoulder, tears flooding her face.

Marek helped Kerza sit on a tree stump outside the paddock. Rhia moved toward them, listening for the rush of Crow's wings, which never arrived. The old woman was exhausted but strong.

"They came," Kerza said with a gasp, "in the dead of night. Our scouts called the alarm, useless against so many."

"How many?" Marek asked.

"At least a thousand. Almost ten of them for each one of us." She took a grateful gulp of the water Rhia offered. "Knew I couldn't fight, could only carry and cloak one person. No time to get food or water or put him in a sling. I came back hoping the soldiers would be gone. Couldn't watch him starve in the wilderness."

"You saved his life," Marek said.

"What about the others?" Kerza sat up straight. Her thin skin flushed, then paled when she saw the ghastly display. "Oh, no." She rose on unsteady legs and took a step toward the paddock. "This can't be happening. In all my years—"

"Get away from me!"

Rhia turned to see Thera scowling at Alanka, who stumbled back and put a hand to her paling cheek as if she'd been slapped. No doubt she was reaping the fruit of her father's treachery. Rhia entered the paddock and put her arm around Alanka's waist to comfort her and show her loyalty. The Wolf's chin trembled, and she rubbed it hard.

Elora stroked Thera's hair. "Your baby's safe now, and he'll be fine, a little dehydrated, that's all." She paused. "Can you tell us what happened? Start wherever you need, but we must know if we can save them."

Thera shuddered, then took a deep breath and wiped her

face dry. In a few moments, her demeanor calmed as she went into a memory trance. As a Hawk, she could recall everything she had seen and heard, whether she wanted to or not.

"They came at midnight," she said matter-of-factly. "Our scouts sent out the alarm. Cougars and Bobcats shot a few, but there were too many. We surrendered. They gathered us all in the big clearing, where we have our celebration bonfires. They brought out the elders and slit their throats. The ones who struggled were stabbed in the gut instead. They died a lot slower." She rattled off the details as if recounting the weather. "The ones who healed up right away, like Orias the Butterfly, they had their heads bashed in. We tried to stop them, but they restrained us."

Thera paused with her mouth open, as if waiting for her memory to catch up. "They brought the bodies here and tied them up. They asked for a Hawk to give their message, said everyone else would be taken away, so I volunteered. They tested my memory to see if I was lying, then they tied me up. They took everyone else—the children, the young people, the fathers and mothers—and they marched them to the river. They said they were taking them back to Leukos as prisoners."

"The White City," Rhia whispered. Next to her, Alanka shuddered.

"They said it was in revenge for helping Asermos," Thera continued. "They would have left us alone if we hadn't sent soldiers and archers to defeat them there."

Rhia's stomach went cold. Her worst fears had come

to pass. This death and destruction, this decimation of Kalindos, had happened because of her.

"It's not true," Alanka whispered, bending her head close to Rhia's shoulder. "They would have come here if they'd won or lost. Nothing would have stopped them."

But Rhia could feel the others' judgment, as heavy as a stone.

"Maybe some escaped." Adrek picked up his bow and quiver of arrows. "Maybe the Descendants couldn't keep track of all the prisoners. Or—or maybe they left behind the ones who couldn't keep up. Some of the children…" His fierce gaze darted among them. "We have to search."

Alanka was the first to shake the shock of Thera's story. "I'll go." She left the paddock and sprinted into the forest with Adrek.

Rhia turned to Marek and motioned to the corpses that surrounded them. They had to remove the gruesome spectacle before the others arrived. Marek pulled out his knife and reached for the rope binding the closest one. She glanced down to see a splotch of blood soaking through Marek's trouser leg.

Rhia looked at Elora, whose eyes were also focused on the reopened wound. The healer stood and approached Marek, mumbling, "At least there's one person I can help."

On her way out of the paddock, Rhia gave a last glance at the baby Etarek, quiet in his mother's arms. He had been named in memory of his grandfather, the first casualty of a war that had only just begun.

03

"Daria!"

Alanka echoed Adrek's call for his two-year old daughter as they ran through the dim forest. She added the names of other Kalindon children, the memory of each face stabbing her with regret. Her father had started it all, collaborating with the Descendants in their attack on Asermos. How could he have known it would bring so much pain to the village he loved?

No. How could he *not* have known?

Her ears strained for signs of others, but heard nothing over the sounds of their feet and the blood pumping through her head.

She grabbed Adrek's arm and pulled him to a halt. "Let me listen."

He obeyed, panting hard. Cats were sprinters, she reminded herself, and placed her palm over his mouth. "Shh."

Alanka closed her eyes to listen. Her pulse, accustomed to long runs, slowed and quieted. In a few moments, the world of scent and sound opened up to her.

She filtered out the background hum of the distant river and whispering pine branches. A squirrel shook the branches of a tree, claws scrabbling over bark in its haste to hide. From its scent she knew it was a female who had recently given birth.

She knelt on the forest floor and put her face near the ground. The damp dirt held the scent of people—so many, she couldn't pick out any individual. Many wore deerskin shoes, but some had been taken barefoot.

"They came this way." She sat back on her haunches and drew a deep breath. "But the scent is hours old."

"We already know they came this way. We need to know if they're here now."

"Not in that direction." She pointed to their right, off the path, toward the south, from which the wind blew.

"I'll climb." Adrek removed his moccasins and took off, racing for a pine tree whose lowest branch hung more than three times his own height.

She watched his lithe form speed up, long legs devouring the distance in less time than she could blink. With a graceful leap, he launched himself at the branch. Alanka gasped, certain he would miss and crash to the ground, but his hands seized the branch as deftly as if he had been standing next to it. Adrek arced his body to align his hips with the branch. He planted a foot on the limb, then stood up straight, with only a finger on the trunk to steady himself.

He surveyed the area, then shouted, "Nothing yet. I'll go higher."

He leaped to grasp the stub of a branch Alanka couldn't see, then used his bare feet to push himself farther up the trunk where he could get his arm around a longer limb. She watched him repeat the process until her neck ached.

She picked up Adrek's shoes and moved closer to the tree, hoping to glimpse his diminishing figure in the forest canopy. The breeze shifted to blow from the east, from the river itself.

A human scent struck her, too strong to be a lingering footstep. She closed her eyes again to isolate it. It was a child. Female?

As she turned to tell Adrek, he shouted, "I see something!"

He ran out on a branch too small for his weight, and Alanka tensed. Just before it snapped, he leaped to the limb of an adjoining fir. He slid down the smooth trunk, then hung from the lowest branch. Adrek let go and slammed to the ground beside Alanka. "I saw pink." He pointed toward the river, then grabbed his moccasins from her and shoved them on his feet. "The mountain laurel's stopped blooming, so it must be someone's clothes." His own face was pink from the exertion.

"I smelled a person in that direction," she said, "maybe a girl."

"Daria!" Adrek took off.

When Alanka caught up to him at the side of the path, he was kneeling over a small patch of pink. Her sweat turned cold.

She ran to join him and realized he was holding only a nightshirt. Its front was smeared brown in the center.

"It's hers. The stain is just mud." He heaved a wheezing breath and stood. "She could be anywhere."

"Give it to me." Alanka held the shirt to her face and inhaled the same scent as before. She shoved the shirt back into Adrek's hands and trotted off the left side of the path, to the north. As he followed, she said, "This is the one direction I couldn't smell before, because of the wind. Stay off to the side so I don't pick up the scent of the shirt."

But after a hundred or so paces, she knew it was futile. "Not this way. And not south." She looked at Adrek's face, taut with desperate hope. "We'll keep moving toward the river, and I'll track back and forth to see if she left the path, but—"

"She must have. She's always running off." His words tumbled over one another. "Turn your head for two blinks and she's gone. That's how they are at that age, right?" He twisted the pink cloth between his fingers. "She probably got hot and cranky in her shirt and made her mother take it off, then saw a rabbit or—or a flower or—"

Alanka put a hand on Adrek's arm. "We'll find her."

They ran. Alanka veered to both sides of the path, staying within the cone of scent the girl had created. Now that she had smelled the shirt, it was easy to pick out one person's trail among the others.

But the center of the cone never left the path. Alanka knew Adrek's labored breathing wasn't only due to the strain of the cross-country run. His anguish held an acrid scent of its own.

The light ahead brightened as the trees thinned. Her legs pumped harder, and in a few moments she burst from the trees into the blinding sunshine. She trotted up and down the riverbank, searching for a scent leading off to the side, some sign of a last-minute escape.

Nothing.

Adrek stumbled out of the woods and sank to his hands and knees in the mud. He coughed several times, then raised his head to look at Alanka.

She went to him. "I'm sorry."

"No…" His muddy hands grasped his hair as if to tear it from its roots. Alanka slipped her arm around his shoulders, slick with sweat and tree mist. He called his daughter's name again and again as if his voice could reach down the river and yank the child back to him.

"We'll get her back," Alanka murmured. "We beat them before—we can do it again."

"Not on their land. We don't even know if they'll keep her in the city. She could be—" He spit out the words. "She could be sold."

Alanka's grip on him tightened at the thought. "I swear on my Spirit, Adrek, someday we'll make them sorry they ever met us."

Rhia laid a blanket over the body of the last Kalindon elder they had removed from the paddock posts. Her chest ached at the sight of the woman's pale, wrinkled face. Though Rhia had seen people she'd known since childhood fall on the Asermon battlefield, these deaths somehow cut her more. So much wisdom and power, gone forever.

The voices of the dead still whispered. Now she knew they belonged to those who had perished here. She was almost glad she couldn't hear their words—surely they were accusing her.

Marek brought her a skin of water and placed a hand on her back. "How are you?"

She wiped the sweat from under her eyes with a clean cloth. "I feel responsible."

"You were protecting your home. It was the Descendants' choice to kill. You didn't put the swords in their hands."

"I put the targets in front of them."

Marek's gaze shot to the right, and his nostrils flared. "They're coming!"

Panic streamed down her spine. "The Descendants? Again?"

"No." His face broke into a near smile.

With a rustle of undergrowth, the forest gave birth to Wolves, stumbling under the weight of weariness and small children.

Rhia ran with the others to embrace the men and women—all second-phase Wolves like Marek, able to cloak another person with their nighttime invisibility. Ten had escaped, as Kerza had, when the Descendants invaded. Each had carried off a child to shield.

Rhia helped Elora deliver food and water to the returning Wolves and the children. The adults tried to muffle their mourning for the sake of the young ones, who seemed more dazed than frightened. Most were too small to grasp what had happened. Rhia almost envied them.

Not long after the Wolves' return, her mentor, Coranna, and the other nonwounded Kalindons arrived on foot. Coranna approached Rhia at the paddock gate, her pale blue eyes blank with shock. Most of her long silver hair had come loose from its braid, and her graceful gait had turned into a near stagger.

Rhia embraced her. Coranna's thin arms trembled against

Rhia's back, then she drew away and blinked hard. "Have you done the prayers of passage?"

Rhia nodded.

Coranna stumbled past her to sink onto a nearby log. After a moment, she sat up straighter and drew the heels of her hands over her temples. "I'll just rest a moment, then we'll get help moving the bodies to the pyre."

Good, Rhia thought. Keep moving, be useful. "How will we burn so many?" she asked Coranna. "There isn't enough dry wood for twelve funerals."

"We'll burn several at a time and have separate ceremonies away from the pyre. Each person should have their own tribute, especially since they—" Her voice caught, and Rhia waited to see if her composure would crack. These people were Coranna's closest friends. She and Kerza were the only remaining elders.

Coranna drew in a breath and pressed her lips together, as if trapping the onrush of emotion inside. "We'll hold the rituals as soon as the rest have arrived from Asermos."

Rhia had almost forgotten about the wounded and their caretakers. The scene of sorrow and discovery would repeat. The thought made the skin around her eyes feel tight and heavy.

"Why do they hate us so much?" she heard herself say. When Coranna didn't answer, she continued. "I can almost understand their invasion of Asermos. The lands there are rich. But here—" She lifted a shaky hand toward the line of shrouded bodies. "What they did to these men and women, it's—" She fell silent. Any attempt to describe the atrocity sounded feeble.

"I've never seen anything like it," Coranna said. "Never imagined."

"Where were the Spirits? Why didn't They protect Kalindos?"

"I understand your bitterness," Coranna said, "but it's not up to the Spirits to solve human problems. You're old enough to know that."

"I don't want Them to solve our problems. But a little help would be nice."

"Perhaps it's all part of a plan."

"Then it's a bad plan."

Coranna sighed. "Tell that to Crow."

"I will." She wished she could communicate with Him right here, right now, without waiting for a vision or dream. But the Spirits couldn't be beckoned like dogs.

A low croak came from the tree overhead. Rhia looked up to see a raven gazing down at them. She stood, ready to shoo the bird away from the bodies if it came any closer.

Coranna touched her elbow. "It has something."

The raven cocked its head, revealing a shiny silver object in its beak. It stretched its neck and opened its mouth. The thing fell to the ground in front of Rhia.

She picked up the object, which appeared to be a large flat button. It held an insignia in the shape of the sun, with tiny marks on either side.

"Must have come from one of the soldiers," Coranna said.

An idea dawned in Rhia's mind. She clutched the button in her fist and looked up at the raven. "Thank you."

Someone called her name. Alanka walked toward her, skirting the rows of bodies. The bitter set of her jaw told

Rhia the unwelcome news: no Kalindons had been found on the way to the river.

She approached Alanka quickly. "I have an idea."

"Our boats are gone, even the canoes, so we can't follow them. Adrek and I are going to Asermos to gather a rescue party."

"You're a step ahead of me already." Rhia showed Alanka the button. "Use this. It belongs to the invaders, so maybe it can be traced to a certain part of Leukos. Maybe that's where the prisoners will go first. It's not much, but it's a start."

Alanka examined the button. "Better than going in blind."

Rhia thought of the dead Descendant in the woods whose soul she had delivered to Crow. "Let's have everyone scour the village for pieces of the invaders' uniforms. The more clues, the better."

"And it'll give us something to do besides cry." Alanka put the button in her pocket. "We'll leave as soon as the horses are ready, before nightfall at the latest. Drenis and Ladek want to come. Maybe Morran, too."

The *shing-shing* of a sharpening knife drew their attention to Morran and Adrek, who knelt side-by-side at the feet of their fathers' corpses. The Cats stared straight ahead, fists clenched, as Endrus prepared to shear their hair in mourning.

"Now we're all orphans." Alanka fingered the ends of her own short black locks. "Time to grow up."

Whether we're ready or not, Rhia thought.

The darkness broke when he heard the screams.

Filip surfaced from a dense gray mind mist. A man was dying. Lights bobbed into the room and fixed themselves near the screamer, on the wall to his right. Pain and fear infused the shrieks, but Filip found neither of these feelings in himself. The gods had blessed him with fog.

Other voices mingled with the screamer's, shouting something about breathing or not breathing. A yellow glow flared like a ball of sunshine in the middle of the night.

The fog enveloped him, dimming the noise to a distant, meaningless cacophony.

When Filip woke again, light sifted through a nearby window. Birds chattered. He wanted to go back to sleep but couldn't remember why. Something waited for him there. Something good.

The sound of labored breathing came from his right. The man hadn't died, not yet. They were alone.

"Awake?" Filip whispered with dry, tight lips. No response. "Who are you?"

The breath changed rhythm and turned into a wheeze. "G-G—" The man's throat choked on his own name.

"Never mind. Sleep."

Filip tried to move his fingers. As they brushed the blanket to touch his hip, the light pressure sparked an itch that lay all over, everywhere and nowhere. When he scratched his nose, the skin felt rubbery, as if the nerves lay far beneath it.

Numb. Good.

Dark again.

In his dreams he ran—sometimes across fields, but more often in back alleys, through markets, dashing home in time for dinner to avoid the lash or racing his brother from one side of Letus Park to the other. *Loser gets a punch in the arm.*

Before the fog, what was there? Fire, he remembered. A fever inside him, raging up the left side of his body. Then came the sweet, damp cloth that held blissful release, and now...

He was awake, knew his name and knew he was staring at a white stucco ceiling with wooden rafters. He knew his older brother had died facedown in a flood of blood and bile, yet the memory did not skewer him today as it had before. A cloak of what must be opium cushioned his feelings.

His left foot itched. A great weight seemed to sit on his chest, keeping him from reaching down to scratch, so he tilted his right foot to rub the itchy spot.

Which wasn't there. Why? Curiosity followed him into his dreams. He ran.

That night the other man died in his sleep. One moment he was breathing—the next, not. Filip knew he should call out to alert someone, but his throat was too dry and sticky to utter more than a whisper. Instead he lay there, marveling that one who had struggled so fiercely should end his life so peacefully, like an old horse lying down in the pasture.

Sleep again, and when he woke the man was gone. Filip's stomach growled, a protest itself against death.

"Awake, I see," said a woman's voice from what appeared to be a door. He remembered now; this was Zelia, the Asermon healer who had treated him after the battle.

The battle.

"I'll bring you breakfast in a moment," she said, "but first there's something I need to tell you. Something hard."

Filip's mind flooded with memories of pain and fever—and the place they came from.

"No…" he said, in a voice too much like a child's.

"You're going to live." A blurry face appeared over him, framed by loose strands of brown-gray hair.

With effort he bent his right leg, angling his foot into the space in his bed where *it* should be.

He began to quake. "You should have let me die." He clutched at the blanket, wanting to tear it in half. "Why didn't you let me die?"

"You wouldn't be alive if your Spirit didn't want to stay. I've seen stronger men than you give up."

"Like him?" He jerked his chin to the right. "Why couldn't you save him?"

"He'd taken a sword to the stomach. Things inside were too mixed up to ever be put right again. It was a matter of time."

"Why couldn't you use your precious magic to save him? Why couldn't you use magic to save *this?*" He hurled off his blanket to see a scarred stump, all that remained of his left leg below the knee. He stared at the blunt monstrosity, laced with hideous black stitches that looked like sleeping spiders. He stared at it as if it belonged to someone else, someone he would spit upon in the street. "Where were your Spirits?" he whispered.

Zelia picked his blanket off the floor and held it in her hands. "I assure you, I did all I could, with Otter's help." She clasped the small carved otter hanging around her neck.

"Not as much as you would have done for one of your own." He couldn't blame her; an enemy's life wasn't worth much. "Your Otter Spirit is either weak or vindictive. Or both." Just like our gods, he thought.

"Otter loves all people under Her care equally." Zelia's brow lowered. "If only the same could be said for me."

"What do you mean?" he asked, though he could guess.

"Your people killed my nephew, my first cousin on my mother's side, my second cousin on my father's side, my brother-in-law, my neighbor two doors down, my best friend's oldest son—shall I go on?"

He tore his gaze from her harsh face. "I didn't kill anyone in that battle. It wasn't me."

She leaned closer. "I didn't kill anyone, either. Remember that, my boy, before you accuse me of negligence, and maybe we'll get along until you can walk out of here."

"Walk?" He yanked the blanket from her hands and covered himself. A lock of filthy blond hair fell in his eyes. "I'll never walk again."

"Not true. We can fit you with a substitute made of steel and leather. If you decide to stay, that is."

Decide to stay? A sea-size emptiness gaped within him. Everything he knew, everything he was, had been ripped away in one moment.

He could never return home.

A door slammed in an adjoining room. Heavy footsteps roamed the wooden floor, and Filip's defenses went on the alert.

A lanky, sandy-haired young man stomped into the room. "Are you one of them?"

Zelia stood between the bed and the door, arms crossed over her chest. "And who might you be, barging in here without my permission?"

"This is the Descendants' hospital, right? Then he must be one of them." His thin lip curled at Filip, who suddenly realized how weak the opium had left him.

"They have sanctuary here," Zelia said, "until Galen and the rest of the Council decide what to do with them."

"How about this—tie rocks around their ankles and dump them in the river."

"And who are you?"

"Adrek the Cougar. I've come from Kalindos to report the latest Descendant slaughter."

That name again, *Descendants*. Filip yearned for a dagger to slice the word out of this man's throat.

Zelia planted her hands on her hips. "You're in the wrong place, Adrek. You should give your report to Galen."

"I did. He told me you were harboring the enemy here, that I could speak to one of them."

"I'm not harboring the enemy. I'm treating patients." She widened her protective stance at the end of Filip's bed.

Adrek hardened his gaze on her. "They came to Kalindos, four nights ago. Killed our elders. Killed my father. Took everyone." His breath made his words shake. "Hundred and seventy people, gone, in the middle of the night."

Filip's face burned, and not from lingering fever. He'd heard of Kalindos—his army's intelligence had described it as a tiny, worthless forest village needing few defenses. It had nothing worth conquering, nothing worth stealing. Nothing but people. Filip's commander was as brutal as he was incompetent, and had now brought shame and dishonor to all of Ilios.

Zelia gave both men a look of astonishment, then turned back to Adrek. "Why would the Descendants attack your village?"

"Because we helped you win your battle against them. Turned out to be a mistake."

"Nonetheless, I won't let you harm one of my patients."

Filip almost laughed. She couldn't stop this Adrek person from killing him, and shouldn't. Better to die by an enemy's hands than live like an old man at twenty-one.

Adrek stepped around Zelia and brought forth a small leather bag. Before she could stop him, he dumped its contents on top of Filip. Several small pieces of metal rolled off to clang on the floor. "What are these things?"

Willing his hand not to shake, Filip picked up the rigid red-and-yellow ribbon that lay on his chest. It seemed like an artifact from a long-lost world. "They're nothing," he whispered.

"Nothing?" Adrek scooped up the pieces that had fallen, then tossed them into Filip's lap. "Your people left them behind when they massacred my village. They go on uniforms, right? They're not nothing."

"I didn't mean it that way." Subtlety was lost on this fellow. "Yes, you're right. They signify ranks and awards and—" He folded his fingers around the ribbon, though he wanted to toss it away "—it shows where they belong."

"So where do they belong? Where can we find them?"

Filip sifted through the medals and rank insignia until he found a silver button, the kind worn on the outside of the soldiers' sleeves. "Second battalion." He sneered. "Not mine." He tossed it back to Adrek, who snatched it out of the air.

"But you know where they're based, right?" he said.

Filip turned his head away and said nothing.

"They took my daughter." Adrek's voice cracked on the last word. "Where is she?"

"How should I know?"

"You know where these soldiers are from."

"Somewhere near Leukos."

"I know that already! Where?"

Filip stared at the cobweb in the corner of the ceiling. "I was first battalion. We wouldn't have bothered with defenseless, insignificant people like you."

Adrek held up the button. "These men bothered. Where are they based?"

Filip rubbed the ribbon between his fingers, contemplating what little honor he had left. "East of Leukos, not far. But they'll bring the prisoners through the city and process them there. They might not even be brought back to the base at all."

"What will they do with her?"

It took Filip a moment to remember who Adrek was talking about. "How old is your daughter?"

"Barely two." His jaw muscles tightened and bulged. "They won't take her from her mother, will they?"

He looked at Adrek's hands, stiff fingers opening and closing, and wondered what it would take to get them around his throat. Despite the man's overall leanness, his bare arms were well-muscled—perhaps he could snap Filip's neck before Zelia could get help.

"She's weaned," Filip said, "so yes, they will separate her as soon as possible. If she's lucky, well behaved and reasonably cute, they'll sell her to a wealthy barren couple to raise as their own. She'll be too young to remember her former life, and she'll grow up thinking she's an Ilion." He stopped, waiting for Adrek to beg for the alternative.

"What if she's not lucky?"

"Depends how pretty she turns out to be. If she's nice to look at, they might raise her as a house slave or a—" A twisted impulse of compassion prevented him from finishing the sentence. The thought of the children cowering in Leukos's high-priced brothels turned his stomach. "If she grows up coarse looking, though—" Filip raked a disdainful gaze over Adrek's appearance "—which seems likely, it's off to the fields, or more likely the mines."

"Mines?" Adrek looked ready to vomit.

"Children can crawl into little spaces that adults can't.

And they eat less, so they're cheaper to keep. Best of all, they take up less room in the burial pits."

Adrek blinked rapidly. "The *what*?"

"Individual graves would be too labor-intensive, so they use big pits for the slaves." He slammed the man's gaze with his own. "Along with the other beasts."

Adrek roared and seized Filip by the throat. Filip forced his own hands to clutch the blankets instead of fighting him off. His right shoulder throbbed—from an arrow wound he just now remembered receiving.

Adrek throttled him, slamming his head against the pillow while Zelia screamed and tried to pull him away. As the pain rippled through his neck, Filip realized the man had no idea how to kill a human. This death would not be quick.

Instinct shoved honor aside. Filip's body bucked. His right heel dug into the mattress, while the remains of his left calf scraped and squirmed. Stitches yanked loose, and he prayed that the warm liquid under his legs was only blood. Yet a vestige of purpose kept him from grabbing his opponent's neck.

Spittle dripped on his face from Adrek's incoherent shrieks. Thumbs squashed Filip's windpipe.

"Adrek!" shouted a woman too young to be Zelia. "What are you doing?" Filip couldn't see her behind the dancing black circles. The voice came closer. "He's a prisoner of war. You'll go to jail."

"I don't care," Adrek said.

"You'll care when Daria comes back." The woman was panting, and Filip could feel two opposing forces struggle over him atop his bed. Everything was going dark.

"She's never coming back." Adrek's grip tightened.

At last, Filip thought, and felt his body go slack.

"Let. Him. Go." Her voice, deep and commanding, had moved a few steps away.

Adrek froze. His hands stopped squeezing but didn't release.

"You won't shoot me," he said.

"I won't have to," she replied. "Because you're going to let him go."

The ceiling's wooden beams wavered and swam above Filip. He wanted to tell the woman to leave, let Adrek finish.

"I know you're in pain," she said, "but this isn't the way. You're better than this Descendant. Don't change that by killing him."

Filip tried to let go of life, to sink into the closest thing he could find to a warrior's death.

The hands left his neck, and breath came staggering back into his lungs through what felt like a pinhole. He gagged and coughed, gasping for air he didn't even want.

Zelia's soft hands touched his throat. He pushed her away and rolled to his right side. The arrow wound speared his shoulder with pain.

Filip dry-heaved over the side of the bed for what felt like half a day, but when he turned on his back again, the light in the window hadn't changed.

Zelia approached, carrying a cloth and a steaming bowl. "I've sent for more security. I can't tell you how sorry I am."

He shook his head and wiped his face.

"Don't try to talk." The healer sat on the bed and dipped the cloth into the bowl, which she then set on the nightstand.

"Suicide by crazy Cougar, huh?" She stroked his bruised throat with the cloth. "Bet you thought it'd be quick."

He shook his head again.

"Don't assume the future will be awful," she said, "just because it's not the past. It'll be different, that's all."

The warm liquid she rubbed on Filip's neck made his throat expand and relax. The next breath held half the pain as the one before.

"You can't make me live," he rasped. "I'll stop eating."

"How noble. An end fit for a warrior."

She had a point, unfortunately. "Who was that woman?" he asked her.

"Some Wolf from Kalindos. I was surprised she could sway him. Kalindons usually can't control *themselves,* much less each other. Still, it's unconscionable what your people did to them. It's my duty to protect your life, but I don't blame that man for wanting to kill you."

"Neither do I." Filip stared at the door, wounds throbbing, and wondered if the mysterious Kalindon woman deserved gratitude or contempt for what she had saved.

When Zelia left him alone again, he opened his right fist. The red-and-yellow ribbon stuck to his palm, its ridges leaving a fading dent in his pallid skin.

Just before sunset, Alanka found Lycas sitting at their brother's grave—at least, it was the spot where he'd decided Nilo was buried. The wheat field, scorched to the soil by the Descendant attack, had been turned into a mass burial ground, home to hundreds of dead Asermons and Descendants, as well as a few Kalindons.

She strode over the ruddy soil, pushing away the memories. She couldn't show her brother how the battlefield, even empty, scared her more than ever.

Lycas's head was bowed, and his chin-length black hair swept forward to hide his face. He poured an amber liquid from a clay pitcher into a mug.

As she approached, she noticed tiny seedlings of wildflowers—what the wheat farmer would have called weeds—thrusting up toward the sun, less than half a month after the battle. Soon the field would be a meadow of many colors, and within a decade or two the surrounding woods would reclaim it. No crops would grow here again.

She sat beside her brother without speaking. He gave her a grim smile and held out the mug he had sipped from. She nodded thanks, then took a long gulp of warm ale. It quenched her thirst in a way water never could.

Then she noticed the other mug sitting on the ground near them, filled to the rim. Nilo's ale.

"You're leaving tomorrow?" Lycas finally said. On the silent, breezeless evening his voice seemed to echo across the field, to the trees and back.

"In the morning. We need to get back to Kalindos and help rebuild." She paused. "You're staying here in Asermos."

"I don't want to." Lycas rolled a clod of dirt between his long, thick fingers. "I want to go to Leukos and get your people back. Our father's people, even though I never knew him. I want to kill Descendants."

She nodded, accustomed to his casual declarations of Wolverine aggression. "But you can't go."

"Not with Mali pregnant. Besides, a rescue mission needs

people settled into their second- and third-phase powers. I've only been second phase for a month." He took the mug from her. "You drink too slow." He drained the rest, then refilled it.

"I'm used to Kalindon meloxa. It's much stronger." Thinking of the fermented crabapple drink reminded her of home, and what had happened to it. "I wish I were second phase. Then I could be invisible at night, like Marek, and I could go with the rescuers. I dread going back to Kalindos. It'll be so empty."

"Hopefully not for long. Galen said the rescue party is picking up a third-phase Hawk in Velekos on the way to the Descendant city. Another one's coming from Tiros to stay here and receive her messages." He handed her the full mug. "Asermos will keep Kalindos updated as best we can."

"Didn't the Velekon Hawk just become third phase? Won't that make it harder to figure out what she's saying long-distance?"

"It shouldn't be too hard to interpret 'We found them!' or 'We're captured!' At least we won't be left wondering, feeling any more useless than we already do."

She took another gulp of ale. "Don't feel bad about staying with your family. Ladek's going back to Kalindos to take care of Thera and Etarek, and because he's our only Bear. So it's just Adrek going with the Asermons."

"At least it gets him out of your life, which can't be bad." He angled a black-eyed gaze at her. "Are you seeing him tonight before he leaves?"

She looked away and tried to sound casual. "I think so."

"Don't get pregnant."

She gaped at him. "Even if I were considering—which I'm not—it's still the month of mourning." She couldn't stop a glance at Nilo's mug.

"Good general advice, anyway. Don't wish you were second phase. Enjoy your youth while you have it."

Alanka nudged his shoulder. "My youth? I didn't know Asermons got old at twenty-four."

He didn't smile at her teasing. "Becoming a parent brings power, but it also takes it away. Mali and I should both be on that rescue mission, but instead we'll be here, driving each other crazy. Fulfilling life for a pair of warriors."

"But like you said, Asermos is only sending established second- and third-phase people, so if Mali hadn't gotten pregnant, you'd both be first phase and still not going."

"That's not my point—"

"And if you hadn't gotten your second-phase defenses before the battle, then you might have been killed—" She stopped before adding *too,* but not soon enough to avoid the meaning.

They looked at Nilo's mug for a long moment. Then Lycas slowly poured its contents onto the thirsty soil.

A child's scream splintered the night.

Rhia launched out of bed, stumbling over Marek in her dash for the door. He grabbed his bow and arrows on the way out.

They reached the wooden rope bridge between their house and Coranna's just as the Crow woman opened her own door.

"All clear!" called Olena, the Wolf woman from two trees over. "Just another nightmare." After a moment she added a soft "Sorry."

Rhia released a sigh, echoed by Marek and Coranna.

"Was that the third time this night or only the second?" he asked on their way back to bed. "I've lost track."

"The second. Better than last night."

He crawled in first to lie against the wall. "Were you asleep?"

"Almost." She sank onto her back and glared at the ceiling with wide-awake eyes. "You?"

"Sound." Marek lay his head on the pillow and sank back into slumber.

She envied his ability to drop off so easily, but knew his exhaustion came from patrolling all night, hunting before dawn, then chopping wood until dusk. In the five days since the attack, the Kalindons had repaired the homes of every remaining villager, of which there were only a hundred now. Tomorrow they would begin building a new stable and paddock. Nobody wanted to go near the old one and its grisly memories.

Rhia lay awake for what felt like hours, listening to the dead, unable to discern words among the jostling sounds. She drew her thumbs over her brows to relieve the dull ache behind her eyes. If she could talk back to those who had passed, maybe she could help them cross over.

She had to try or go mad. Rhia eased herself out of bed, not bothering to be quiet, since Marek would hear her anyway.

"Where are you going?" he mumbled.

"To Coranna's for chamomile."

"I'll get it for you."

"She'd rather have me, not you, creep in on her while she's sleeping."

"She won't hear if I do it."

"The baby needs fresh air."

He didn't argue. Outside, she trod over the rope bridge in silence. The cloudy night was pitch-black, but she knew which boards to step over to avoid telltale creaks. She lifted the rusty latch to Coranna's door, jiggling to release it, then reached inside to silence the hanging doorbell.

Rhia crept along the wall to Coranna's herb shelves. By touch she found the clay jar of chamomile and picked it up, so as not to make herself a liar. Then her fingers slid along the highest shelf until they encountered a smooth wooden box the length of her foot. She pulled down the box and opened it.

A white cloth lay in the center; she squeezed it to make sure the bundle of dried herbs was inside. Coranna had used it to speak with the dead—*thanapras,* it was called.

She took a cautious sniff of the bundle. The heady scent made her dizzy. She remembered the baby, and wondered how the thanapras would affect him or her. It might not be safe.

She sighed and closed the box, then set it back on the overhead shelf, a bit too loudly.

Coranna's snores stopped. "Who's there?"

"It's me," Rhia said. "I can't sleep, so I came for chamomile."

Coranna shifted in her bed. "How can you not sleep? You should be exhausted."

"Don't you hear them?"

"Who?"

"The dead. The ones we just buried."

Coranna sat up, or at least it sounded like she had. "You hear distinct voices? Voices you recognize?"

"No."

"Then how do you know who it is?"

"Who else would it be? They died violently, and they must want justice, like Etar did."

"You're probably right." Coranna's voice was muted, and Rhia remembered how stricken the older Crow had been when her friend Etar had died, then lingered instead of continuing to his peaceful rest. He had crossed to the Other Side only after Coranna had convinced him they would investigate what he knew to be his murder. "But their killers are far away. They might never find justice."

Rhia fumbled her way to the bed, banging her ankle on a chair leg. "Can we at least bring them peace? Convince them to cross over?"

"It's more complicated than that." Coranna shifted over to give Rhia room to sit. "On rare occasions, when people die, they take a piece of a living person's soul with them."

Rhia took a moment to rehear what Coranna had just said. "They take soul pieces to the Other Side?" The skin on her nape felt like it wanted to crawl down her back.

"Not exactly," Coranna said. "Crow won't let soul thieves cross over all the way. Such malevolence would pollute His peaceful realm."

"Why would someone do that?"

"Out of spite, often from a grudge or a heartbreak. It's a way to gain power over someone or take vengeance on them."

"Do the living know that they're missing a piece?"

"Sometimes they hear the voice of the dead person, but usually they just feel different, incomplete. The symptoms vary depending on which part of them has been stolen."

"They have to live that way forever?"

"Until the dead soul thief lets go. Sometimes they do it on their own, or a Crow person convinces them to give it back."

Growing up in Asermos, Rhia had known no Crows, and

it seemed as if every day brought a new awareness of their duties and powers. "Whose souls do the Kalindon elders hold?"

"Probably the soldiers who slaughtered them. Each man is no doubt lying awake now, hearing the voices of those he killed."

"Good." Rhia bit her lip, trying to quench an ember of bitterness. "Not good for the Kalindons, of course. Can the soldiers talk back?"

"No. Only second- and third-phase Crows can speak to the dead, and even then only with the help of thanapras."

"But I spoke with Nilo after he died, without thanapras."

"He was your brother. Sometimes loved ones can connect to us in a way others can't." She took Rhia's hand—an effusive gesture for the reserved old woman. "I'll speak to the elders, urge them to let go and cross over. But not tonight. Between the battle and the journey and the funerals, I've nothing left."

"I know you're tired." Rhia squeezed Coranna's fingers, which felt too cold for the warm weather. "That's why I want to help."

"Retrieving soul parts is exhausting, even dangerous. Besides, the thanapras isn't safe for the baby. You can help me after your child is weaned if, Spirits forbid, the elders haven't all passed on by then."

Rhia's shoulders sagged. "I hate feeling useless."

"You have many years to learn your second-phase powers." Coranna released a sigh that was half groan. "I wish you hadn't progressed at a time like this. It's such bad wisdom for one so young."

"Too late. What do I do with it?"

"Keep it to yourself."

Rhia thought she'd misheard. "We can't tell the survivors that their loved ones aren't at rest?"

"It would only trouble them," Coranna said. "Remember, your highest value is compassion."

"What about truth?"

"Truth brings pain. It's our duty to bring peace."

"Yes, to the dead."

"And the living."

Rhia wanted to protest, but she couldn't deny that the last thing the surviving Kalindons needed was more heartbreak.

"Get some sleep." Coranna squeezed Rhia's knee. "Tomorrow I'll show you some meditations to help quiet the voices."

A few minutes later, Rhia sank back into bed. Marek shifted and wrapped himself around her. She nestled into his embrace, hoping his presence would calm her thoughts.

As her breath slowed and deepened, the chorus of dead Kalindons faded at last. Sleep drifted over her like fog.

"Comfortable?" a deep voice said.

Rhia's eyes flew open. She must have dreamed it.

"Look at the cozy little Crow, lying in the embrace of my murderer."

Her muscles seized, waking Marek with their jolt.

He came alert at once. "What's wrong?"

Skaris the Bear, the man Marek had killed to avenge her own attempted murder, was in her head.

"Nothing," she whispered. "My foot cramped."

"Want me to rub it?"

"It's better now. Sorry I woke you."

Marek kissed her temple, then stroked her hair until he fell asleep again, his hand going limp against her head.

She waited for her old enemy to speak again. His voice hadn't stretched and distorted itself like the Kalindon elders; it had been as clear as a nightingale's call.

Did he hold a piece of her soul? Why did he haunt her and not Marek? She didn't dare ask Coranna, for fear of revealing Marek's guilt.

"I'll be sure to tell her," Skaris said.

Rhia jerked again. Marek grunted and sat up.

"What is it?" he said. "And don't tell me it's another foot cramp."

She reached out in the darkness. "I hear him."

Marek took her hand and kissed it. "Who?"

"Skaris."

His grip tightened. "Where?" he growled.

"In my mind. You don't hear him?"

"No. I thought you couldn't identify the voices."

"I can now. Just him. Do you know what that means?"

Marek put his other hand over hers. "Why would he hold a piece of you? Why not me?"

Skaris said, "He's not the cause of my death. You are."

Rhia slammed her palms against her ears. "Quiet!"

The Bear's voice was as clear as if he were sitting beside her. "Marek was just the instrument. You took a month of life from me, from all of us, when Coranna resurrected you. You caused all this death."

"No, I didn't!" She squeezed her eyes shut. "Crow doesn't work that way."

Marek took her hands. "We have to get Coranna. She'll help you."

"She can't, not now. If we tell her, she'll try, and she might hurt herself."

"Then what can we do?"

"Let her get her strength back. And pray to Crow that it works."

They lay down again, and Rhia welcomed Marek's arms tight around her despite the heat of the summer night.

"I wish I could kill him again for you," Marek murmured.

Skaris snorted. "That's not helping your cause."

"Shh," she whispered to both men.

Skaris didn't speak to Rhia again that night. Though his voice had silenced, in its place was the nagging siren of her own conscience.

He hated the birds most of all.

Half a dozen had babbled throughout the night near Filip's hospital window. With the first light of day, another set of nerve-jangling chirps and tweets penetrated his ears.

Soon the twittering was joined by another bird's rapid rat-a-tat. It felt like an awl against Filip's skull.

He drew the pillow over his head and squeezed. How could such a quiet place be so loud?

"You can't kill yourself that way," Zelia said at the door. Her feet scuffed the floor's wooden planks on the way to the bed. "As soon as you faint from lack of air, you'll let go of the pillow, and wake up alive, with a nasty headache. Ready for breakfast?"

He grunted and forced himself up onto his elbows. The

healer watched with a dispassionate gaze as he raised himself to sit against the wall.

"Talkative today, I see." She set a basin of steaming water on the nightstand. "I thought you might like to have breakfast outdoors with your fellows, get out of this stuffy room. But you need a bath first."

"I'll stay inside."

"No, you won't. It's a lovely cool morning, and your room needs cleaning. The other Descen—I mean, the other men have been asking after you."

"I don't want to see them."

"Well, it's all about what *you* want, isn't it?" She turned the covers down, exposing his bare torso. "Are you this contrary with your own mother?"

"Don't say *are*, as if I'll see her again."

"Excuse me. *Were* you such a little wasp with her, too?"

"Yes."

A smile tugged the corners of Zelia's mouth as she handed him a soaking hot cloth. "And did it work?"

"No." He cleansed his chest and arms, feeling only a shadow of pain in his shoulder from the two-week-old arrow wound. Either it had been shallower than he'd thought, or there really was something to this Otter healing power.

"It's too loud outside to think," he said, "much less eat."

"Loud? Whatever are you talking about?"

"Those stupid birds."

She drew in a breath, and he congratulated himself on finding a way to shock her.

"All night," he continued, "at least five or six outside my

window. Chirping and calling to each other, even though it sounded like they were sitting on the same branch."

Zelia took the cloth and motioned for him to turn on his side. "That wasn't five or six birds. It was one bird with five or six songs. A mockingbird."

"Oh." Now he was the stupid one. "We don't have those in the city." He shifted so she could wash his back.

Pain drove through the sole of his left foot, as if he had stepped on a spike. He grunted and clenched his hands against the blankets, imagining them grasping the neck of the man whose sword had ruined his life.

The healer reached over to touch his knee, then closed her eyes and murmured a soft chant. Filip wanted to punch her, as if he could relieve his pain by delivering it to someone else.

Within several moments, the agony dulled to an insistent ache under her touch. She did have magic, he had to admit, though not enough.

"Thank you," he told Zelia with a full exhale. "It's better." Filip hoped the others hadn't heard him cry out. He grabbed a clean shirt from the bedside table and slipped it over his head. "How can it hurt so much when it's not even there?"

"It's up here." She touched her temple. "One day your mind will accept what's lost."

"I can feel it." He closed his eyes. "I can wiggle my toes."

"No, my boy, I'm afraid you can't." The healer's voice was soft but strong as she touched his arm. "Come outside now."

He jerked away from her. "I won't."

"You will, or you don't eat. Breakfast is in the yard today

and nowhere else." She stepped briskly to the door. "I'll fetch my apprentice to carry you."

"No!" He threw back the blanket, knowing he was playing into her mind games. "I'll crawl before I let them see me cradled like a baby."

"You won't need to crawl if you can use these." She reached past the doorway into the examination room and brought out a pair of wooden crutches. The handrests were padded with brown fur. Zelia placed one on either side of him.

With more effort than he thought it would take, they got him standing for the first time since the battle. Though the crutches provided stable support, he found himself wanting to put his other foot down. He tried not to think where that foot might be. Perhaps it shared a mass grave with his brother and hundreds of other dead "Descendants." Knowing the Asermons, they'd probably fed it to their dogs, or prepared a feast of body parts for the hideous crows they worshiped.

Filip crossed the floor, his shoulder wound flaring from the effort. He welcomed that pain, since it came from a place that actually existed.

He passed through the exam room, then the waiting room at the front of the building. Filtered sunlight patched the floor with shifting yellow spots. He quickened his pace at the sight, longing to feel that sunlight on his own skin. He stumbled across the front threshold, then looked up at his surroundings.

Asermos. The village he had come to conquer for his country. For his gods.

Such a small, innocuous-looking place. From the hospital doorway he could see to the southern end of the village as it curved around the banks of the Velekon River. Modest buildings of stone and stucco sat adjacent to the sandy main road. Narrow streets branched off this road, leading three or four blocks up the riverbank. The entire village could have held no more than a few thousand people, including those on outlying farms.

They should have been easy to trample.

With Zelia's arm to steady him, he crutched himself off the porch, careful not to slip on the dew-slick grass. She led him around the building to the right.

A wooden fence extended from the side of the house at about the height of Filip's chest. On the other side lay a garden bulging with herbs and flowers. A flagstone path led through the garden and curved toward the back of the building.

Mother would have liked this, he thought as Zelia opened the gate. Her own garden had crammed their apartment's balcony, the flowers and ornamental plants leaving little room for people to sit and enjoy the view of the city below. Filip's mind veered from the memory of this view and the emptiness it carved in his gut.

Voices and laughter came from the back of the garden. He stopped in midstride, wavering. "How many?"

"Seven," Zelia replied. "All your people. The Asermons are at another healer's. We thought it best to separate the two sets of soldiers, seeing as you were trying to kill each other not so long ago."

He considered asking for a transfer to the other hospital. Better to be surrounded by enemies who scorn than friends who pity.

Zelia laid her hand against his back. "They'll be glad to see you."

"You don't understand."

She sighed. "And I'm a busy woman, with no time for your explanation."

Filip forced his leg and arms to move. He and Zelia came around the corner of the house, and the yard went silent.

He lifted his chin and looked straight ahead as he approached his fellow soldiers. With each step, the cuff of his half-empty trouser leg scraped the stone paving.

One of the figures stood. "Sir!"

Filip scanned the faces of the men around the long wooden table. Most were older than he was, in their mid-to late twenties. Rough-looking, brawny, with short hair. None would meet his eye; they studied the ground or the treetops or some fascinating object they had just picked out of their teeth. Only one didn't share their aggressive indifference.

Kiril Vidaso was saluting him. The earnest young second lieutenant, right arm in a sling, held his left fist to his breastbone in a backward image of the customary gesture.

Filip almost stumbled from the shock of being spoken to, much less honored, in his wretched state. Though he appreciated the show of respect, it was technically a breach of protocol. They weren't in uniform, which Filip would never wear again.

He cleared his throat. "At your ease."

Kiril pulled out the chair he'd been sitting in at the far

end of the table and offered it to Filip. He seemed to be trying to keep his glance away from his approaching superior's obvious injury.

"Thank you." Filip focused on keeping his balance while he turned to lower himself into the chair. His shoulder throbbed, but his stump bore only a dull ache. He wondered when Zelia's magic would wear off and the shooting pains would return.

Kiril took the crutches and sat beside him. "It's good to see you, sir."

Filip gritted his teeth. He had been promoted from second to first lieutenant only a month ago, and barely outranked his comrade, who was less than a year younger. "You don't have to call me *sir* anymore."

"I don't mind."

"I do," Filip said, then regretted his harsh tone. He gave his friend a curt nod. "Thank you, though."

Kiril's posture relaxed a little, but he rapped his fingertips on the table in an unsteady rhythm. "I see you cut your hair short," he said after several uncomfortable moments.

"I'm not an officer anymore. No sense in looking like one."

"Right." Kiril touched the ends of his own dark brown, shoulder-length hair. "Can I get you anything, s— Uh, Lieutenant?"

Filip slid a wary gaze over the soldiers at the other end of the long table. They had begun conversing again, ignoring the two lieutenants. "Who are these men? Some look familiar."

"Infantry, second battalion." Kiril's lip curled a bit, and

he lowered his voice. "All enlisted ranks, so they should have saluted you. Southerners, mostly. But they're all we've got."

"Got for what?"

"For escaping."

Filip looked around the garden, empty except for the patients. "I don't see any guards."

"Trust me, they're there. Corporal Addano, the one with the bandaged head, he tried to run two nights ago and came this close to getting an arrow in the foot." He held his thumb and forefinger apart to illustrate. "You should've seen his face." Kiril smirked. "Needed a clean pair of trousers after that, too."

"I can't go home and you know it." When Kiril tried to protest, Filip cut him off. "My wound can't be hidden, much less healed. If I go back to Leukos, I'll bring shame on my family and my city, remind everyone of the humiliation of their invincible army." He glanced at the enlisted men and lowered his voice to a harsh whisper. "My own parents will turn away, like these soldiers. I don't know why you're even speaking to me."

"I speak to you out of brotherhood. Not even death can take that from us."

"Death can't." Filip angled his chin toward his left leg. "But this can."

Kiril glanced down at his own feet, as if to confirm they were both there. "What will you do if not go home?" He glared at their surroundings. "Stay in this godsforsaken hole of a town?"

"Yes, and you should, too." Filip beckoned his comrade

closer. "Live among them, see and hear everything. When they let down their guard, steal a boat and go home. Take what you've learned for the good of Ilios."

"I can't stay any longer. This place is making me—" Kiril hunched his shoulders and threw a furtive glance at the others.

"Making you what?"

"Crazy," he whispered.

"It's not like Leukos, that's for certain."

"I don't mean *crazy* as in I'm having trouble adjusting. I mean, *crazy* as in—" He flapped his hand next to his head.

"Crazy."

Kiril nodded, fidgeting with the frayed end of his shirt-sleeve.

Filip didn't know how to respond. He'd been trained to handle his troop's battle shock on the field and in the barracks, but never expected to find himself a prisoner of war in a backwater bog like Asermos. "Crazy how?"

Kiril scratched the side of his jaw and didn't look at him. "I can do things."

"Breakfast!" Zelia appeared from around the side of the building, followed by two food-laden young male apprentices. She seemed at ease as the sole female in the company of ten men. In Leukos a woman would never risk such an insecure situation.

A yellow cur paced at her side.

"They let a dog come to the table?" Filip asked Kiril.

"That's Sunlight. She picks up things if we drop them, alerts Zelia if one of us falls or has a problem. Plus, she's good for morale." He smacked his lips and said the dog's name in a high-pitched voice. The beast trotted over, sat on its haunches, and lifted a front paw, which Kiril clasped. He flashed a smile at Filip. "I taught her that yesterday."

The dog leaned onto one hip and scratched vigorously behind its ear.

"Outstanding," Filip said. "It's got fleas, and soon we will, too."

Kiril chuckled. The dog shifted its weight, started to scratch its other ear, then grunted and returned to a sitting position. It looked up at Kiril, eyebrows twitching.

"Help," a female voice said. "I can't reach the top of my head."

Filip turned to Zelia to determine what, by the gods, she was talking about.

She wasn't there.

"My back isn't what it used to be," the voice chirped. "Please scratch my head."

Filip froze. The words were coming from— No, it couldn't be. He turned back to the dog, which was nudging Kiril's knee with its nose. The lieutenant ignored it in favor of the platter of eggs and ham in the center of the table.

Cautiously, knowing it could lead him over the brink of insanity, Filip reached toward the dog. It saw his hand and shifted to let him pet it. He scratched its wide yellow head.

Its mouth opened in what looked like a smile. "Ooh, that's good."

Filip screamed.

He looked at the others, eating unperturbed, and thanked his gods that he hadn't done it out loud.

The dog tilted its head under his hand. "A little to the left, by the— Now you've got it. Harder, please."

He obeyed, then realized he was obeying a dog. He jerked his hand away.

Kiril frowned at him. "Relax. She won't bite." The dog slid to its belly next to Filip's chair and rested its chin on his right foot. "See? She likes you."

Filip grabbed Kiril's arm. "You said you can do things that make you feel crazy. What things?"

Kiril's eyes flickered. "I don't know what you're talking about."

"You just told me."

"No, I never said that, sir." He took a bite of ham. "I heard you have an extra bed in your room. Would you mind if I join you? My room is full of enlisted."

Filip's mind spun. Perhaps he had imagined the dog speaking to him. Perhaps the painkillers had made him hallucinate. Besides the residue of opium in his body, Asermon healing magic might have strange side effects.

The other men had set upon the food like a pack of feral dogs, and Filip realized he would have to do the same to keep from starving. Fortunately the table was sturdy. He planted his hands on it and lifted himself to stand.

Pain spiked through his nonexistent leg. He tried to choke back his cry, but only transformed it into a gurgle. The others stopped eating and stared at him with undisguised contempt.

Kiril grasped his arm and helped him back into the chair. "Sit. I'll get it for you." Pity had replaced the respect in his voice.

Filip uttered his gratitude through gritted teeth. He had lost his appetite, but accepted the food and forced himself to eat. One more show of weakness could cost him his life. He wouldn't put it past these thugs to slaughter him in his sleep for their own entertainment. He picked up a chunk of ham.

The dog lifted its head and barked. "Drop it!" In his shock, Filip did. The ham bounced off the table, fell to the ground and disappeared into the greedy maw.

The others laughed, even Kiril. "Now who's giving orders?" said one of the infantrymen.

Filip's face heated, and he brandished his fork at the dog. "Get away from me!"

The beast backed away and sat, tongue lolling. "I like you," it said with a laugh. "You listen better than the others."

That night, Filip lay in bed, slowly going mad. It wasn't the loss of half his leg that propelled him in that direction. It wasn't his brother's death. It wasn't even the knowledge that he would never see his home or his family again.

It was the birds. The incessant, mindless chatter of birds.

On one level he heard the mockingbirds chirp and tweet, but only in the background. Overlaying that was, "Bad raccoon I'm a chickadee stay away stay away I'm a robin pick a fight berries berries grass is wet too many redbirds berries mine tree-to-take tree-to-take hee hee hee tell me a song fight on babies don't fly…"

Filip was about to search the hospital for a sword to plunge into his skull when a faint white glow came from the room's other bed. He turned his head to see Kiril lying on his back, staring at the ball of light he held in his hands.

The lieutenant illuminated the wall to his right. He

reached across with his left arm—the one not in a cast—and waved his hand in front of the wall to form a dancing shadow. His breath came hard, as if he were lifting a heavy stone block.

Filip intended to turn away, wanted to pretend that this, too, was a dream or a side effect of the medicine. But his voice leaped from his throat.

"Kiril—"

The man yelped and slapped his palms together, extinguishing the light. "Nothing. It was nothing, sir—Lieutenant, I mean. Nothing at all."

"I saw it. It wasn't nothing." He turned on his side to face the other bed. "Kiril, what are they doing to us?"

"Doing?"

"It must be a spell to make us think we have magic."

"Why would they do that?"

"To study us. That's probably what our people are doing to their captives right now, figuring out where these powers come from."

"What power do you have?" Kiril asked.

"I hear animals."

"I hear them, too. Especially those lousy birds at night."

"No, I hear what they're saying. In human words."

Kiril let out a low whistle. "Amazing. Have you told Zelia?"

"Of course not. I don't want them to know they've succeeded."

"You see now why we have to leave?" Kiril's whisper sharpened. "They're taking over our minds."

"*You* have to leave. I've told you I can't." Filip propped himself up on his elbow. "Do that thing again, with the light."

"I'd rather not."

"Consider it an order."

Kiril sighed, and in a moment his hands were full of light, a perfect white sphere.

"It's beautiful," Filip whispered. "Can you make different colors?"

"No, but I can make it flash. Watch." The light flickered on and off in a steady rhythm. Finally it went out, and Filip heard Kiril's arms thump on the bed. "It makes me tired."

Filip stared into the darkness, Kiril's sphere still dancing in his vision. "I think if I had that power, I wouldn't want to leave."

"I wouldn't mind being able to hear the dog."

Filip released a bitter chuckle. "It figures they'd give us the powers we don't want. They know us better than we realize."

"You're right," Kiril said. "But who's 'they'? The Asermons, or the Spirits?"

Filip's sweat turned clammy, though the night was warm. "The Spirits can't give us magic. The gods wouldn't allow it."

"Our gods have no power here," Kiril whispered. "That's why I'm going back to Ilios."

Filip sank back onto his pillow. First his brother, then his leg, then his home. All he had left was his fragile faith, and with nothing to place it in, soon he would lose even that.

Marek fought to focus in the thanapras fog. Thumping a quick, steady rhythm on the deerskin drum, his hands and wrists had fallen numb and felt detached from the rest of his body. He observed the sensations as if he were watching himself through the window.

It had been over a year since he last helped Coranna during the listening ritual, in which she would converse with the dead who had yet to cross over to the Other Side. He had forgotten how long it could take. The afternoon crept into evening, but he wouldn't let himself stop. It had taken over two weeks for Coranna to gain enough strength to do the ritual, and he was determined to see it through even if his arms fell off.

Once Coranna had stepped over the border between this world and the next, she had remained silent. He kept a close watch on the rhythm of her breath. It stayed deep and even as she lay on the thick brown rug in the center of her home.

He half expected her to start snoring. The thought made him want to laugh, and then the effort not to laugh seemed funny in itself, and then the fact that it was funny made him want to laugh even more, and—the thanapras was getting to him.

The Crow opened her eyes, and he stopped drumming. He knew better than to speak.

Slowly she turned to look straight at him. "Tell me your side of the story."

The truth poured out. "When Rhia said Skaris had tried to poison her, I ran to his home. Ladek was the house-arrest guard that day. I convinced him to let me speak to Skaris."

Marek closed his eyes, the memories as fresh as this morning's rain. "We fought. When Ladek tried to stop us, Skaris hit him with a chair and ran. I chased him to the edge of a gorge near Mount Beros. We fought again. He fell." Marek paused. "Because I pushed him."

After a long moment, Coranna spoke. "You were fighting hand to hand with a Bear. If you hadn't pushed him off that cliff, would he have killed you?"

"He could have." He opened his eyes. "Will he let go of Rhia's soul part?"

"Not yet." She sat up and rubbed her forehead with her thumb knuckle. "The only one who passed over this time was Dori."

"Without her husband?"

"Zilus was one of the worst. So bitter. Not that I blame

him." She held out a shaky hand, and Marek helped her to her feet. Coranna was lighter than he'd remembered.

"What do we do now?"

"About you? I haven't decided." She shuffled to the table and extinguished the thanapras bundle in a bowl of water. "I can't be your judge, since my testimony is all the evidence against you."

"Will you send for another judge?"

"I said, I haven't decided."

"If my punishment is the only way to convince Skaris to let go—"

"Just because he's dead doesn't mean he's right. To me it sounds like self-defense."

Marek forced his mouth shut. It may have been self-defense at the moment he pushed Skaris, but not when he chased him or when he barged into the Bear's house, bent on vengeance.

"Go now," she said. "Rhia must be waiting to hear how I did, though Skaris has no doubt already filled her in."

He returned home to find Rhia stretched out on the bed, looking paler than usual, as if the color had been scrubbed from her skin. Red-brown hair drooped against her high cheekbones and slender jaw, forming careless waves in all directions.

She glanced up when he approached but didn't raise her head. "He told me. It didn't work."

"I'm sorry." He sat beside her and brushed the hair off her cold forehead. "When was the last time you ate?"

"Breakfast. Food makes me ill."

"Because you haven't eaten. Elora told you to eat several small meals a day."

"She also told me my back wouldn't hurt for at least two more months, so she's not exactly infallible."

"Do the meditations help at all with—" Marek stopped himself. Saying Skaris's name out loud seemed to goad the Bear into talking.

"Some. I only hear him now when my defenses are down. When I'm tired."

"Which is all the time."

She nodded. "Elora said that was normal."

Marek went to the cupboard and pulled out a small stack of flatbread. He brought it back to the bed, then tore off a corner of a slice for her. "Food gives strength, or so I hear."

She munched a small bite of bread. "You made this?"

"With the flour from Asermos."

She chewed carefully, swallowed and hesitated as if waiting for a reaction. "It doesn't make me want to vomit."

"Why, thank you." He relished the sight of her brief, tiny smile. "Let's go home," he said suddenly.

She looked around. "We are home."

"Your home. Asermos."

"Why?"

"Think about it. Skaris died while you were in Asermos, but it wasn't until you came here that you started hearing his voice—or any of the others, for that matter."

"It doesn't work that way, Coranna says."

"Is Coranna always right?"

She chewed and swallowed another bite before shaking her head.

"What will it hurt?" he said. "You can get better care for the baby in Asermos."

"Elora's a good healer."

"But she's an Otter, not a Turtle."

She creased her forehead. "I don't need a Turtle. My pregnancy is normal."

"Having a voice in your head isn't normal."

"I can't leave Kalindos. These people are in mourning. I can't give up my duties just for—"

"What? Peace of mind? Just to be able to sleep at night or touch your husband without a dead Bear taunting you? How much misery will it take?"

"I'm not miserable." She sat up and crammed the rest of the bread slice in her mouth. "See?"

"Be careful. Don't eat too fast."

Rhia stood and grabbed the hairbrush off the nightstand.

"Where are you going?" he asked her.

"I have people to see." She shoved the brush through her hair and tried to pull it back far enough to braid. "People to help. I can't just lie around feeling tired and sorry for myself." She gave up and threw the brush on the floor. "Still too short. I hate it!"

"Rhia, it's all right. Don't—"

He stopped when he saw her gaze shift up and to the left, as if she were looking within. The muscle below her eye twitched.

"What is it?" Marek said. "What did he say this time?"

"He said the baby was—" Her hand flew to her mouth, and he heard a gurgling sound from her stomach. She stumbled to the bucket in the other corner. Just in time, as her snack abandoned her in a series of retches that sounded as if her body were turning inside out.

He brought her a cup of water and a cool towel for her face. She took them with shaky hands. "I feel better now."

"Don't lie." He helped her stagger to their bed.

"I should take that down." She pointed to the bucket.

"Don't be ridiculous." He pulled the blanket up to her chin and wiped her face dry with a clean towel. "Go to sleep."

He lowered the waste bucket to the forest floor using the pulley, then descended and emptied the contents in a nearby latrine. When he returned home, Marek found Rhia sprawled across their tiny bed, arms and legs covering most of the territory. Since he couldn't join her without waking her up, he formed a pillow out of the spare blanket and stretched out on the tattered rug next to the bed.

He fell asleep to the rhythm of her snores—another new development with her pregnancy—and hoped she didn't step on him in the middle of the night if she got sick again.

In a dream, his mind played back the evening's events, but this time when he dumped the waste bucket into the deep outhouse hole, it contained more than the remnants of dinner.

A tiny human form—no bigger than his thumb, yet with distinctive arms, legs and head—slid from the bucket and tumbled into the abyss.

"No!" Marek flailed for the child, but the more he struggled, the faster the little person fell, as if the earth were pulling it harder to spite its father's desperation. The hole winked shut, and the darkness was complete.

Marek woke with a soundless scream. After a long moment of staring into the dark, shivering, he sat up and reached for Rhia. She had stopped snoring, but he could hear her breath if he held his own. There was space beside her now, and he climbed into it. When he pulled her close against his chest, she stirred but didn't wake.

Rigid with vigilance, he held her until dawn leaked its hazy light through the windows.

"Shh! They're coming!"

Standing with Elora, Alanka watched the Kalindon children play Descendant Invasion for the hundredth time. They slunk across the forest clearing, hunched over, the little ones on the backs of the bigger ones.

The oldest, a boy of six, directed them behind a clump of honeysuckle. "Everybody be quiet," he whispered so loudly it might as well have been a shout, "or they'll get us."

At a seemingly random point, some of the children decided to become Descendants themselves, chasing the others and taking them prisoner. Once everyone had been captured, the game began again.

"When will they get tired of it?" Alanka asked Elora as they dragged another cartload of wood toward the village center.

"It's their way of dealing with what happened. I'd rather they act out their fears than keep them inside."

"I'd rather forget it all." They arrived at the growing woodpile and began to unload the cart. The palms of Alanka's gloves were wearing thin; she'd get a splinter soon if she wasn't careful. But then at least she would feel something.

"We'll never forget." Elora grunted as she lifted an armload of wood. "We can try to turn our minds away, but our bodies remember."

"What do you mean?"

"Every day someone comes to me with a fluttery heart or cold sweats or both. Or they can't sleep at night, waiting for the next attack." She brushed her hands together. "What about you, Alanka? I haven't seen you in my office. How are you holding up?"

Alanka shrugged. "Too busy. No time to fret over things I can't control. When I go to bed I'm too tired and sore from combat lessons to lie awake worrying."

"I told Ladek and Drenis to go easy on the nonwarriors. You'll get hurt."

If only, Alanka thought.

Elora turned the empty cart around. "At least the rescue party has made it to Leukos, according to the Hawks."

Alanka should have been encouraged by the news the latest troupe of Asermons had brought to Kalindos. In her mind, though, Leukos was a gaping maw waiting to swallow Adrek and the other rescuers along with the captives.

"How's the hunting?" Elora asked.

"Don't know." She scuffed her moccasins against the dirt as she walked. "I've been trapping mostly." She didn't want to admit she hadn't touched a bow in nearly a month. It would prompt questions she couldn't answer.

"Elora!"

They turned to see the Otter's young apprentice, Pirrik, trotting toward them from the center of the village. He slowed as he neared them.

"Don't worry, not an emergency," he panted. "One of the Asermon Otters wants to go over your inventory to see what to bring back on their next trip. Figured you'd be a better judge of that than I would."

Elora cast a wary glance between her apprentice and Alanka. "I'll be back shortly."

Pirrik stayed behind and lifted the cart pole Elora had dropped. "I'll help you with the wood."

Alanka nodded once and said nothing.

They dragged the cart in silence until they were in sight of the fire ring—or what would be a fire ring once the trees were felled and the ditch dug. Alanka could see Vara the Asermon Snake giving directions to the men chopping trees. Her first-phase Snake magic allowed her to control the spread of fire, making her an expert in such defensive endeavors. Once the fire ring was built, Kalindos could light it to stop intruders. Theoretically, at least.

"We should have done this years ago." Alanka indicated the ring. "Lorek could have built it." The Kalindon Snake had been taken by the Descendants like so many others. "With a fire ring the invasion might not have happened at all."

"People were too afraid of another blaze wiping us out." He glanced at her. "Sorry."

She swallowed hard at the memory of the forest fire that had taken her mother's life over a decade ago. "This reminds me of then, how empty the village was. Did we play the fire game? I don't remember."

"The fire game?"

"Like these children, reliving the whole thing, over and over."

"Oh. I think Thera did. She was only five."

"I can't believe your sister's sixteen and already a second-phase Hawk."

"It's a big responsibility." He stopped, bringing the creaky cart wheels to a silent halt. "She's not angry with you. I know she lashed out when you first found her tied up in the paddock, but she was half-crazed then. None of us are mad at you."

Alanka examined the worn spot on her left glove. "Thanks for letting me know."

"I'm sorry for the way I behaved after I found out."

She pulled a splinter out of the glove's thick leather and waited for Pirrik to continue.

"You're not your father," he said, "and what he did to mine had nothing to do with you."

"That's not exactly true, is it?" She met the Otter's gaze. "He made a deal with the Descendants to protect Kalindos. To protect me, mostly. Your father got in the way."

"Doesn't mean it's your fault."

"I know that," she said.

He looked away and scratched the back of his neck, fingers rustling the strands of dark red hair that fell below his nape.

Was it only the last full moon when she had made love with this man in Deer Meadow, and they had talked about getting married? No, the last full moon the sky had been cloudy. Must have been the month before. The past was turning into one long haze of pain. She wanted to leave it behind.

"Anyway," he said, "I wanted to tell you I was sorry. I hope we can be friends again." When she didn't answer, he added, "Maybe someday we could even try—"

"No." To his startled look she replied, "I mean, yes, we can try to be friends. But nothing more."

"Alanka—"

"You turned away when I needed you most, after my father died." She gestured to the ditch ahead, where Morran and Endrus dug, shirtless and sweaty. "I thought you were different from all those Cats, not careless. I thought you were kind."

She'd rehearsed this speech weeks ago, before the battle, back when losing her mate made her feel as if she'd been stabbed with an icicle. Now it sounded hollow in her throat. She didn't care anymore. Nothing could touch her now.

A crack sounded, and the forest disappeared.

Arrows formed a wall of whistles around her, but they couldn't hold back the charging Descendants. They came, armor gleaming in the wheat field fire. She shot, again and again, hearing the snap-twang of the bow, the harsh song of an arrow's flight, the wet *thup!* of flesh parting at its point.

And the shrieks. Sometimes *Mother* or the name of a god or Spirit or no words at all.

The metallic tang of blood filled her nose and the back of her throat. Then vomit and waste as men died. Wolverines came, slicing flesh and smashing bones. The Descendants smelled like slaughtered animals, right down to the eyeballs. Their scents would drown her.

"Alanka!"

That voice didn't belong on the battlefield. Someone had her arms so she couldn't shoot. She snarled and raked her fingernails against soft skin. Alanka opened her eyes.

Pirrik sat before her, holding her wrists. The forest was back. She was kneeling in the dirt but couldn't remember how she got there.

"What happened?" she whispered.

"About to ask you the same thing." He released one of her arms and wiped a streak of blood from his cheek where she had scratched him. "The tree's all the way over there. It won't fall on you."

"Tree?"

"The one they just chopped down." He pointed to his left. Ladek the Bear stood with an ax by the stump of a small fallen spruce, watching her.

Everyone was watching her. She stood slowly.

"When the trunk cracked," Pirrik said, "you screamed and hit the ground with your arms over your head."

"For how long?"

He shrugged. "Ten seconds, maybe."

"It felt like hours."

He put a hand on her arm. "Let me take you to see Elora."

"No. There's a better way."

She broke away from him and strode toward the fire ring. On the other side of the ditch, Vara the Snake sat on a log nursing an infant. Her sharp gaze shifted to Alanka as she approached.

"Anyone afraid of trees shouldn't live in Kalindos." The wink that followed was the only indication of a joke.

"Can I ask you a favor?"

Vara tilted her head. "Sit."

Alanka settled herself on the log next to the Snake, then remembered her manners. "He's a beautiful baby."

"I know." The Snake flipped her long blond braid over her shoulder, away from the infant's face. "He'll be a heart-breaker like his father, no doubt."

"Aren't they all?"

Vara chuckled and threw her a glance of appreciation, and Alanka let out the breath holding her tension. Lots of Asermons looked down on Kalindons, but this one seemed friendly enough.

"You're second phase now, right?" Alanka said.

Vara's answer was an eye roll and a nod to the baby in her arms.

"Obviously," Alanka added. "So now you can burn away memories."

"Being able and being willing are two different things." Vara winced. "Ow, his teeth are right under the gums." After a moment, her grimace faded. "I've hardly had any training yet in memory burns. About all I can do is wipe out a person's whole life, and no one wants that."

Alanka felt an urge to shift away—maybe even run away—from the woman beside her. A Snake's powers were said to be so dangerous, only the strongest minds were chosen by that Spirit. Lorek the Kalindon Snake had frightened her even when they'd played together as children. But she missed him as much as any of the others who were taken.

"You can't help me, then."

"Not yet. I'm sorry." Vara's eyes softened. "What do you want to forget?"

Alanka sank her chin into her hands. "A simpler question would be, what do I want to remember? It's all so awful. Look at us." She motioned to the men working the fire ring. "We're willing to risk burning down our own village to prevent another invasion. That's how silly scared we are."

"You won't burn down your village," Vara said indignantly. "That's what I'm here to prevent."

Alanka barely heard her. "I wonder if this is how people acted before the Reawakening. During the Collapse?"

Vara scoffed. "There's no such thing as the Reawakening. Why do you Kalindons cling to that myth?"

"Because it makes sense. These Descendants are like the people before the Reawakening, believing they can take whatever they want. If that's what people are like without the Spirits, then that's what everyone was like back then, before the Spirits chose us."

Vara blew out a snort. "If that's true, then where were the Spirits before the Reawakening? Standing around doing nothing? Being weak?"

"Maybe they thought we could save ourselves. And when we couldn't, they had mercy on those who would listen to them. Who would be peaceful and live close to the land and trust the Spirits to provide for them."

"Like you Kalindons."

"Exactly. We don't farm or build roads—"

"Or plan for the future." Vara nodded toward the village. "Look where all that peace and trust got you."

Alanka knew she sounded naive, like her father. A new thought hit her. "But what if there'll be another Reawakening someday, when things get really bad again?"

"You think the Spirits will come rescue us from the Descendants?"

"Or help us rescue ourselves."

Vara gazed at the baby in her arms. "It's a nice dream." She blinked hard, then turned her attention back to the fire ring. "But I'd rather plan for the worst, just in case."

The cloud settled over Alanka again. She thanked Vara

and crossed the ditch to collect more wood, pulling on her gloves as she went.

Perhaps the Asermons were right, and the Spirits had always been strong, and things had always been the same. But everything had changed with the Descendant invasion, and if the future was one long decline into oblivion, she wanted no part of it.

08

"Wake up. It's time to go."

Someone shook Filip's shoulder. He rolled away from the urgent whisper, hoping to slide back into his dreams. It was the only place he could run.

"Sir, it's our last chance. Get up." Kiril gave him a shake that threatened to topple him out of bed.

Filip sat up and peered into the darkness. "Last chance for what?"

"To go home before they try to make us become like them."

Filip wiped the sleep sweat from his forehead and examined the faint outlines of Kiril's face. "What do you mean?"

"I heard Zelia tell her apprentice that Galen is coming tomorrow."

"Who?"

"The Asermon Council leader. But not just that, he discerns people's so-called gifts, like you with the animals and me with the lights."

Filip seized the lieutenant's arm. "I said never to speak of that."

"I haven't. But the other soldiers are having the same problem. Someone must have noticed."

"Have you seen them do magic?"

"No, but I know that look—the shifty eyes, the nervousness around each other, taking care never to reveal anything. You haven't noticed how quiet they've grown this last month?"

"I don't mingle much," Filip said.

"You'll have to mingle now. We're going."

"What about the archers?"

"Those weaklings won't kill unarmed men. Besides, even death is better than living here." He jerked Filip's blanket. "You hate it, too, so come with us."

Filip looked up at him, for a moment imagining the possibility. Home. Family. Hearing a dog bark and only hearing a dog bark.

"You know I can't," he said.

Kiril let out a gust of air, as if he wanted to argue. He looked at the door, then back at Filip. "I couldn't leave without asking."

"I know. Thank you."

Kiril stood up straight, snapped his heels together and saluted, fist to heart. Filip returned the gesture for the last time, then held out his hand. Kiril grasped it, and they stared at each other for a long moment.

"Good luck," Filip said finally. "If you see my parents, tell them—" He let go of Kiril's hand. "Tell them I died."

"I will, sir," he whispered.

When Filip heard the soft footsteps of the seven men pad through the front room, his own feet—the one that existed and the one that didn't—longed to follow. It was his feet that made him grab his shirt and yank it over his head, then seize his crutches. The feet that craved the smooth stone streets of Leukos.

As Filip lurched for the door, he heard a muffled but commanding voice yell, "Halt!" He kept moving. When he swung the door open, it banged against his right crutch, and he faltered for a moment.

He reached the porch and realized what that moment had granted him.

An eternity of exile.

His comrades' bodies lay sprawled on the grass in front of the hospital. Two writhed in agony, blood and foam spurting from their mouths. The rest lay unmoving. Arrows protruded from every back.

The crutches fell from his grip, and he clutched the porch railing with both hands.

A woman leaped to the ground in front of him, as if from the sky.

"Move no farther." She leveled an arrow at his chest, her bow creaking with tension. "Or you'll meet the same fate."

He looked up, past the arrow, into the pale green eyes of a hooded Asermon. Four others dropped around him, as lightly as cats, and he realized they'd been on the rooftop and in the limbs of a nearby tree. Two more raced down the street, bows in hand.

"Get inside," the woman said to Filip.

He reached for his crutches.

"Leave them," ordered one of the men. "We want you empty-handed."

"I can't walk without them."

"Then crawl."

Dazed with shock and fear, Filip obeyed, turning to place his palms on the porch. Then he heard a third guard snicker, and he stopped.

"No," Filip said, on his hands and knees. "Either let me walk or shoot me. Shoot me in the back, the way you did my comrades, like the cowardly beasts you are."

The woman gave a guttural oath and kicked him between the legs. Filip collapsed, his chin slamming into the wooden porch. The pain from the kick shot to his core, turning his vision black, then sparkling red, then black again.

Somewhere, beyond the haze of his agony, a familiar voice said, "What have you done?"

He wanted to tell Zelia he hadn't done anything, and ask why everything always had to be his fault. But he couldn't breathe, much less speak.

"They tried to escape," the first male said. "One got away."

"Who gave you authority to shoot them?"

"The Council. They said to take them alive if possible, but under no circumstances let them return home with what they know about us."

"We'll track down the last one." The female guard toed the sole of Filip's foot, sending an aftershock of pain up his body. "And this one isn't going anywhere."

"Don't touch him." Zelia knelt and lay a cool hand on Filip's forehead. His throat emitted a low whine with each breath.

"Hold still," Zelia told him. She placed her fingertips below his navel and began a deep, soothing chant. Filip's pain dulled enough for him to open his eyes.

"Who?" he managed to whisper. "Who escaped?"

"I'll see." Zelia's feet swished through the grass as she examined the bodies, all of which were silent now. "Kiril's the only one missing."

Thank the gods, he thought. If he made it home, Kiril could confirm Filip's parents' second-to-worst fear—that he, like his brother, had died of his wounds. They would be proud of him, and he would live in their memories as a brave warrior who had made the ultimate sacrifice for his country.

Somehow he would find a way to be something else.

"As you're aware, Filip, each of our people possesses the magic and wisdom of their Guardian Spirit animal. That magic and wisdom combine to form that person's Aspect."

Filip gave an almost imperceptible nod, his gaze switching among the three men who sat across the garden table from him. Two of them seemed close in age, late thirties or early forties, with similar short dark hair. But one of these two, the man in the center, had a presence of self-assured leadership—maybe too self-assured, Filip thought. This was Galen, who supposedly held all the answers. The other older man, Tereus, hadn't spoken yet. He looked as if he had spent many hours listening to Galen pontificate.

The third man could have been no older than Filip himself. His smooth blond hair grew past his shoulders, brushing against the braided horsehair fetish around his neck.

Filip had lived here long enough to know that these people sheared their hair to mourn the death of a close family member. This young man, Bolan, was only the second or third Asermon Filip had seen without short hair.

When the men had first arrived that morning, Galen confirmed Kiril's escape from Asermos. The rescue effort to bring back the Kalindon prisoners had depleted the Asermon police force of its best officers. Filip tried not to look as pleased as he felt.

"My Guardian Spirit is Hawk," Galen now continued, touching his red-tipped feather fetish. "My magic includes the ability to accurately recall events and words spoken, thereby making me an ideal messenger, either among humans, or between humans and the Spirits." He bowed his head at the last word. "I act as both a spiritual and political leader. My wisdom focuses on the discernment of others' gifts, which is why I'm here today."

Filip's shoulders tensed at the thought of his own powers, which was the last subject he wanted to discuss. He turned to Tereus, glancing at the dingy white feather he wore. "What about you? What's your Aspect, or whatever you call it?"

Tereus tilted his head with a humility that seemed more genuine than his companion's. "I'm a Swan. I interpret dreams."

"You make a living doing that?"

The man laughed, something he seemed to do often, judging by the creases around his mouth and the natural sparkle in his blue eyes. "Unfortunately, no. I have a farm where I breed wolfhounds and horses."

Filip's eyebrow twitched at the last word, and he looked away.

Galen leaned forward. "You have an affinity for horses?"

Filip stared at the stone paving next to his chair and felt his jaw tighten almost to the point of cramping. "I was a cavalry officer."

Bolan gasped. "You rode horses into battle?"

He glanced up at him. "It's an honor, reserved for the most intelligent men from the best families."

"Couldn't they get hurt?"

"Who?"

"The horses."

"They wear armor, like us."

"But they still get hurt, right? They still get killed."

"Bolan, not now." Galen held up a hand, clearly sensing that he was losing control of the conversation. He turned back to Filip. "I'll get to the point. I believe that you have the Aspect of Horse."

Filip's lip curled. "What in the name of all the gods does that mean?"

"The Horse Spirit has chosen you, given you the ability to hear the meaning behind the voices of animals."

A sensation cold as a knife blade trickled across the back of Filip's neck. "How do you know this?"

"Bolan, also a Horse, is Zelia's son. She knows the signs. The way you look at her dog, for instance."

"I don't look at her dog."

"Exactly." Bolan's eyebrows pinched in sympathy. "Ignoring them doesn't shut them up, does it?" He leaned in to speak in a conspiratorial whisper. "The birds are the worst."

Filip's eyes widened, then he looked at Galen. "So what good does it do me to know I have this Horse thing? The animals don't understand when I talk back. I can't even make them stop."

Galen spread his hands on the table. "You'll be able to return the communication when you enter the second phase."

"Outstanding," he replied, with a satisfying sarcasm. "How do I do that?"

"Before you can claim your first-phase powers, you must undertake the Bestowing."

"But how do I reach the second phase?"

"You must father a child. Bolan recently became a second-phase Horse." Bolan arched an eyebrow at Filip, a subtle boast of this proof of his virility. "He will help you learn to use your powers," Galen said.

"Use them for what?"

Galen motioned for Tereus to speak. The man who called himself a Swan set his elbows on the table and pressed his fingertips together. "Zelia tells me you're ready to leave the hospital. You'll come back to be fitted for your prosthesis when it's ready and when your leg is healed enough to—"

"It's not a leg," Filip snarled, "and it will never heal."

"When your stitches are out, then. In the meantime, you need somewhere to live."

Filip ground his teeth. Now he was a charity case—for the enemy, no less.

"As I mentioned," Tereus said, "I have a farm with dogs and horses. I live there alone, and—"

"You call those horses?" Filip snorted. "Those tiny, fluffy creatures dragging carts down the street?" He ignored

Bolan's glare. "Where I come from, the horses stand tall and sleek. Their beauty inspires great works of art."

"I know." Tereus shrugged off Filip's insults. "One of your horses lives at my farm."

Filip's jaw dropped.

Tereus continued. "Keleos, his master called him. Does that sound familiar?"

Filip's jaw dropped farther. "The colonel's stallion? How did you get it?"

Tereus waved his hand. "My daughter Rhia stole him, but that's beside the point. As I was saying, I live alone and it's difficult to handle all the farm chores myself. You can have room and board in exchange for helping with the animals."

Filip looked away, turning over the options in his mind. At least he wouldn't have to depend on handouts, and he could see Keleos, who had been off-limits to everyone but the colonel and his attaché. His fingertips tingled at the thought of touching the animal's gilded hide.

Then his nonexistent left foot stabbed with pain.

"I can't," Filip said to Tereus. "Not with—" he gestured to his leg "—this."

"I'm not asking you to do cartwheels. You'll groom, feed and water the animals. And you can ride, even without the prosthesis."

Filip looked up at him suddenly, trying to catch the lie in his eye. But Tereus's gaze held no guile. "I can ride?"

"If you want. Though our style might be different from what you're used to, and like you said, our ponies are—"

"Can I ride Keleos?" Filip heard the tone of his request, like that of a little boy pleading with his father. He cleared his throat. "That is, if he needs exercise, I could provide him with the sort of equitation to which he is accustomed."

Tereus looked amused, but not in a patronizing way. "Of course you may ride him, though not to the exclusion of the other horses. Are you coming?"

Filip hesitated. His father would have wanted him to be practical, and the alternatives—staying at the hospital or wandering homeless—would humiliate him more. Perhaps he should bide his time in Asermos until a better option presented itself.

Yet he suspected their generosity. "What do you want in return?" he asked them.

"Information," Galen said.

"I thought so." He sat back in the chair and crossed his arms. "I won't betray the land of my birth, whether it's still my country or not."

"I assure you it's for defensive purposes only. We have no desire and no plan to attack the nation of Ilios."

"You sent a band of warriors to my city."

"To liberate the prisoners your brigade stole from Kalindos. A thousand soldiers, ransacking an undefended village of a hundred. Was this an honorable use of arms, in your opinion?"

Filip held the Hawk's gaze for a long, silent moment. "No. It was unusually cruel, and unworthy of the uniforms they wear. My people are not so atrocious."

"They're not?" Galen leaned forward. "Prove it."

09

With strength she hadn't felt in weeks, Rhia ran across the forest floor into her father's arms.

Tereus clutched her tight until she gasped for breath. "It feels like four years since you left home, instead of only four months."

"It's been a long summer." She turned to Lycas as he dismounted the gray mare. "You actually came."

"I couldn't miss my little sister's wedding." Lycas lifted her high off the ground in a hug, then set her down. "I heard how hard Kalindons celebrate. I could use about a thousand drinks."

"I knew Mali would drive you crazy."

"Don't start." Lycas stepped back to examine her. "She's half a month more pregnant than you, but she's twice as fat."

Rhia grinned and wagged her finger. "I'll tell her you said that."

"Do it, and I'll stuff the words back in your mouth until you choke."

"Children, play nice." Tereus led the ponies farther into the village. "I'm not an expert, Rhia, but you do look small for four months pregnant. How do you feel?"

"Like I could climb Mount Beros in an hour." She swung her arms as she walked, the crisp autumn air filling her with excess energy. After three months of plaguing her sleep, the voices of the dead had faded, even the vindictive Skaris. They hummed in the back of her consciousness, like an infectious tune, but no longer made her ill. "Finally no more headaches, dizziness, throwing up—although that's probably more detail than you wanted."

She stopped when she realized she was talking to herself.

Behind her, Tereus and Lycas had come to a halt, gaping at the network of tree houses above their heads.

"It's incredible." Lycas lowered his gaze to Rhia. "But so empty."

Her face fell. For a few moments, her happiness at seeing her family again had overcome the daily dread of reality.

"Any word from the Asermon rescuers?" she asked.

Tereus shook his head sadly. "They left Velekos over two months ago," he said. "The Hawk sent a message when they arrived in Leukos."

"We heard. What about after that?"

"Nothing." His lips turned down. "The Hawk has gone silent."

Rhia's stomach seemed to drop. "Dead?"

"Maybe not," Lycas said. "She'd just gotten her third-phase powers, so that might cause a communication problem."

"There's another possibility." Tereus jutted his jaw to the right. "Galen thinks our powers might diminish in that land, so the Velekon Hawk could just be muted."

"Why would Galen think that?"

Tereus and Lycas exchanged a look. Her father said, "Let me tell you about Filip."

They led the ponies to the new paddock and stable while Tereus explained. Rhia was intrigued to learn about the Descendant who had acquired his own Guardian Spirit after a short time in Asermos.

"If our magic fades in Descendant land," she said, "does that mean the Spirits have no power there?" The idea worried Rhia. On the other hand, it was a more comforting explanation for the Hawk's silence than her death.

"We don't know yet," Tereus answered, "and without sending more third-phase Hawks, which we don't have, we have no way to test that theory. Filip has helped us in some ways, but I doubt he'll ever become one of us. He refuses to discuss the Bestowing."

They entered the paddock and tethered the ponies, replacing bridles with halters. "Tell her the bigger news," Lycas said.

Tereus glared at his stepson. "I said we'd wait for the wedding so everyone can hear it at once."

"What could be bigger news than the loss of the rescue party," Rhia said, "or the fact that our powers might fade in Descendant lands?"

Tereus put a hand on her shoulder. "Forgive me, Rhia, but first I need to meet with the Kalindon Swans."

She gasped. "Common dreams? A prophecy?" Her gaze darted between the two men. "Is it good? Bad? It's bad, isn't it?"

"No, it's good." Tereus gazed into the emptiness of Kalindos. "If it's what I think it is, it's exactly what our people need."

The following morning, in front of more people than Marek had expected, he and Rhia were married. Kalindon weddings usually attracted few guests, which couldn't be said for the feasts afterward, when most villagers would sidle up to the tables, pretending they had been there all along.

But today the ceremonial clearing was crowded with spectators, who whooped and wept when the bride and groom sealed their pact with a kiss. After the invasion and ensuing summer of struggle, the Kalindons needed to celebrate life—even if one of the objects of revelry was an Asermon.

The feast was the most raucous he could remember. There hadn't been time or the will to hold wakes for the elders killed in the Descendant attack, and the Kalindons' pent-up energy was releasing itself now in waves of defiant euphoria. It was as if they were trying to send a message to the Asermons, the Descendants and the Spirits themselves: Kalindos lived.

Marek sat at his new family's table with Rhia, who gazed up with amusement at her father's attempts to calm the crowd so he could make a toast. The revelers were slow to quiet, giving Marek several moments to do nothing but admire his new wife.

Rhia's pale, delicate features had bloomed with color these past two weeks as her strength had returned. Tonight her auburn hair was swept up in an elegant style that let her curls drape around her cheeks and jaw. The dark green dress brought out the vibrancy of her eyes, which seemed to reflect the life of the forest around her. His gaze traced the white lace edging the neckline. It swooped low enough to hint at the curve of her breasts, and he had a swift, sudden urge to leave the party.

Needing a distraction to keep himself from carrying Rhia off right now, he shifted to look at Alanka, who sat on his left side. She dragged her lips into a reluctant smile, which he knew would fade the moment he turned away. He'd hoped the party would break his Wolf-sister out of the shell she had sealed herself into the past few months. The possible failure of the rescue party, which included her former mate, Adrek, had added to her gloom.

Slouched over tree stumps and tables, the Kalindons gazed blearily at Tereus, waiting for the boring part to be over so they could go back to dancing.

The Swan cleared his throat. "I hope this will be like no other wedding speech you've ever heard. Partly because it will be short but—"

A roar of approval drowned out the rest of his sentence. Tereus laughed. Marek closed his eyes for a moment and reveled in the sound. It had been too long since he'd heard voices raised in anything but anguish.

The crowd finally humored Tereus, quieting to low murmurs.

"Thank you." He lifted his mug of meloxa. "First, to Marek and Rhia. If I prattled on about how I felt about them, they would die of embarrassment. So I'll just say that I've never known two people more willing to crawl to the ends of the earth for each other. May they never spend a day apart."

A jovial cheer rose from the Kalindons. Rhia widened her eyes at Marek. Apparently the work she had done to soothe and console the mourners had made up for her accidental role in bringing the Descendants' wrath upon Kalindos. Or maybe the villagers understood her devotion to Asermos, as fierce as that which they felt for their own home.

Tereus continued when the crowd noise had fallen lower than he could shout. "I also have an announcement, about something affecting the fate of our entire people." His words made heads turn and mouths silence. "Several Asermons have come to me recently with the same dream. I've conferred with your two Swans." He nodded to them, a man and a woman. They returned the gesture solemnly. "They tell me that a few of you have dreamed the same vision. Our interpretation is unanimous."

He paused, and Marek noticed that Tereus's mug trembled in his hand.

"What's the dream?" someone shouted in the back. A round of nervous laughter passed through the crowd.

The Swan did not smile. "Some elements change with each person, but the central image is the same. It starts with a flock of crows."

The tension around Marek thickened—he could smell it. Everyone's gaze shifted to Rhia. He squeezed her hand.

"The crows meld together into one giant black bird, which in turn transforms into an egg. The egg falls to the ground and shatters."

Marek shivered. His former mate, Kalia, had been a Swan; he knew enough about their interpretations to know that an egg meant a child. Such dreams were said to predict a person's future Guardian Spirit, since an animal usually emerged from the shell.

But if the egg smashed, it predicted a hard or tragic birth. Kalia had had such a dream of a flock of swans before she went into labor with their son. He had thought it nothing but a new mother's anxiety, but it had proven completely and fatally true.

Tereus waited for the murmurs of dismay to taper off. He took a deep breath, then another. "Out of the egg—" his voice hushed "—flies a raven."

Marek had never known such silence, not even in the dead of a winter's night. He heard nothing but Rhia's heartbeat, surging and skipping. He wanted to look at her, but couldn't tear his gaze from Tereus's face.

"It is well-known," the Swan continued in a near whisper, "that Raven has never bestowed Her Aspect. She is the Spirit of Spirits, the Mother Creator, the one who sees all times, all places. No human can hold such power.

"But they say that in dire times, when our people face great peril, perhaps even extinction, Raven will bestow Her Aspect on one young person who will be able to move through space and time and save us all." He looked at the crowd. "The dreams tell us that this Raven boy or girl will be the offspring of a Crow."

Marek looked at Rhia. Her green eyes glowed in the torchlight as she stared at her father. Her hand crept to cover her belly, but she otherwise looked strong, her jaw set, not half as frightened as he felt.

No one said anything for a long moment. Finally Rhia cleared her throat.

"Well, Father, at least you didn't embarrass me."

Laughter bellowed forth, as much from the relief of tension as from the joke itself.

Ladek the Bear stood and raised his mug. "To Raven!"

"To Raven!" the crowd echoed.

"To Rhia and Marek!" someone else shouted. More cries leaped forth and mugs clashed, spilling meloxa in widening puddles on every table.

Rhia looked at Marek, then they stood as one. Tereus sat, and the crowd quieted again.

Rhia spoke first. "Whatever the future brings, we have to face it together. All four villages must put aside their differences. We must be one people if we're ever to overcome the Descendants. We don't have to agree on everything, but it should be easy to agree on one thing—survival." She raised her mug of honey water. "To one people."

They cheered and drank.

Marek raised his own mug. "To the Reawakened."

They cheered harder.

He leaned over to kiss his wife amid the noise. "Congratulations, mother of the world's savior."

"The Reawakened?"

"You said we had to put aside differences. Including religious ones, right?"

She gave him a warning smirk. "I'll get you for that."

The Kalindons seemed to have decided the talking part of the feast was over, and launched into celebration with more intensity than ever.

After a long reel during which he and Rhia had to dance with everyone in attendance, Marek excused himself. Rhia waved to him, with more energy in her hand than he felt in his entire body, as another Bobcat swept her into his arms.

He saw his new father- and brother-in-law at one of the tables, and brought them fresh mugs of meloxa. He'd added extra honey, since the fermented crabapple drink was an acquired taste, he'd been told. He sank his wedding-weary frame onto the bench beside Tereus.

"This drink—" Lycas pointed in the general direction of his mug "—is amazing. I have to bring some back to Asermos."

"Absolutely not," Marek said. "We barely have enough here as it is."

"I'll pay any price." The Wolverine gazed into the liquid depths. "I'd trade a hundred barrels of ale for one flask of this."

"You have a deal." They clinked their mugs together, almost missing.

Tereus laughed. "So how are you holding up, Marek, with the baby coming in the middle of all this?"

Marek felt his lopsided smile disappear. "I keep dreaming the baby goes away." He covered his eyes with his fingertips. "What does that mean, Tereus? In all my dreams,

the baby either disappears or we accidentally throw it out."
He related the first nightmare, with the baby in the waste
bucket.

"Is this before or after it's born?" Tereus asked.

"Before. It's always tiny and looks more like a doll or a
little bird than a person."

"I see." Tereus grew somber, though he seemed to be trying to keep a calm face. "Excuse me for a moment."

Marek watched his father-in-law approach Elora, and
this time it wasn't to dance with the healer. Though he
couldn't hear their conversation through the crowd's babble,
their drawn brows and tight mouths gave him a chill.

"I have the same dream," Lycas said, bringing Marek's attention back to the table. "Except I have our baby—mine
and Mali's baby—on a leash, like a dog. The moment it pulls
on the leash, even a little bit, I let go."

"That's not the same dream at all."

"My point is, we all have nightmares about being a parent. We dream the baby will have two heads, or no skin, or
that we'll forget to feed it." Lycas took a long sip of meloxa.
"My child will be born to two warriors. What kind of life
is that? Even if it doesn't lose us in battle, it'll have to hear
us scream at each other. At least your baby will have a
quiet life. At least you and Rhia—" He gripped his mug and
rapped its bottom edge against the table.

"At least we what?"

"You'll never let each other go."

Marek looked across the tables, past the half-conscious
Kalindons picking at the meal's remains. Elora and Tereus
now sat next to Rhia, speaking to her with urgency.

Coranna sat down on the other side of Rhia and joined the discussion. He noticed that his wife's shoulder angled away from her mentor, betraying the chill that had overtaken their relationship in the past few months.

They often argued when they thought he was out of earshot, about those who lingered on the Other Side and what to tell their surviving loved ones. As Rhia matured into her powers, the two Crow women had increasingly irreconcilable ideas about how to serve their Guardian Spirit. Marek often felt caught in the middle.

Tereus and Coranna began to speak across Rhia, descending into argument. Her eyes flicked from side to side, following the conversation, growing wary and suspicious. She caught Marek's gaze. Awe and passion welled within him so hard it made his ribs hurt.

A slow smile spread across her face, and she stood, keeping the connection their eyes had forged.

"You're right," Marek said to Lycas.

"About what?"

Marek didn't answer. He stood and moved to meet Rhia at the end of her table.

When he reached her, she slid her arms around his waist. "They want me to go back to Asermos to be under Silina's care."

"The Turtle woman?" He held back an I-told-you-so. "Why?"

"Between your dreams, the Raven prophecy and the fact that I haven't gained much weight, Elora and my father think I should be cautious." She leaned her head against his neck. "Coranna thinks I should stay and continue my training, since the voices have faded but not stopped. No one's bothered to ask me what I want."

Marek knew what he wanted—to take her and the baby wherever they would be safe, regardless of Rhia's wishes. But it had to be her decision. He tipped her chin up to look into her eyes. "What do you want?"

"I want to stay."

A wave of fear washed over him. "But—"

"But I can't just think about my own desires anymore. So we'll leave tomorrow with my family."

He let out a long exhale. "Good."

She looked at Lycas, slumped over his mug, which Marek noticed was full again. "Maybe the day after tomorrow," she said, "if my brother keeps drinking meloxa like it's ale."

"I warned him."

She turned back to Marek. "You know what else I want, since you asked?" She tugged his shirt collar. "I want to take my husband to bed."

"Is it safe?"

"Of course. It was the first thing I asked Elora. After all, it's our wedding night."

He pulled her into a deep, long kiss that heated his skin and won catcalls from the wedding guests. The Kalindons stood and shifted to the ends of the tables and benches.

"What are they doing?" Rhia asked him.

"Moving the feast." He took her hand, and they walked from the clearing in the direction of their tree house. Behind them came the sounds of furniture being hoisted, as well as a few mugs and plates sliding off to meet their demise on the rocky forest floor.

Rhia glanced back. "Why are they following us?"

"Kalindon tradition."

"Are they coming to our house?"

"Below it. They'll keep playing and dancing and drinking all night." They reached the ladder to their home. "And all day tomorrow." He gestured for her to climb before him so he could block the view up her skirt. "And the next night."

From the porch they waved to the crowd below, who released a final, hearty cheer.

Once inside their house, Rhia reached behind her back to undo the dress. "You'd think there'd be a little less fuss in a village where hardly anyone goes to their marriage bed a virgin."

"Any excuse for them to be obnoxious." He batted her hands away from their task. "Let me do that."

With one slow tug, Marek untied Rhia's dress. He slid his finger under the white lace and drew the soft green fabric down over one shoulder, planting a trail of slow, biting kisses on the bare skin it left behind. Rhia shivered.

Without removing the dress he slid his hands over the curves of her waist and hips, wanting to touch her everywhere at once. It had been so long since her skin could bear to be caressed. Every night for four months he had held her, inhaled her scent, waiting for the pregnancy to give them her body back.

She turned and sat on the bed. He knelt between her feet. His fingers fumbled with the ties of her boots, but he managed to remove them and her stockings in little time. His hands glided under her skirt. The smooth skin of her thighs sent a rush of heat through his own body.

Lingering was out of the question. He grasped the soft undergarment and pulled.

Nothing happened. He pulled again, and met a firm resistance.

"It's attached," she said.

"Attached to what?"

"To the bodice." She pointed to her waist. "It loops up and around the back and over my shoulders."

He fingered the straps between the two segments of underclothes. "How do I get it off?"

"I have to take off the dress."

"But I like you in the dress." He reached forward and pulled her hips to the edge of the bed, tight against his. "I want you in the dress."

"I could take it off, then put it back on."

"That'd be ridiculous." Hands beneath her skirt, he tugged at the stubborn contraption again. "Whose is this?"

"It's mine."

"And you can sew, right?"

"Yes."

"Good." He ripped the undergarment in half. A gasp and a wicked laugh escaped Rhia's throat. With another snap of his wrists, he tore the other side, as well, then pulled the fabric down around her heels and tossed it aside. "That's better."

"Much." She leaned back on her elbows, then drew her toe over his ribs and gave him a heavy-lidded gaze. "Now what?"

"Now—" he leaned forward to kiss the tender flesh of her inner thigh "—I make you happy you married me."

Soon she sounded happy, and felt happy, and tasted happy. The music and chatter below them created a background hum that he hoped covered the noise of her rising moans. After they peaked, then faded, she let out a deep sigh tinged with laughter.

"What about you?" she said.

"I'm already happy I married you," he murmured against her leg.

"Then we can go to sleep, right?"

"Very funny." He got to his feet and untied his shirt, watching her watch him.

"Should I leave the dress on?"

"Oh, yes. It's not often I get to see you in one."

She passed a hand over her belly. "Soon I'll be wearing nothing but dresses."

He paused, and in the dim lantern light he saw her face turn horrified.

"Oh, no," she said. "Did I ruin it by mentioning the baby?"

"Of course not." Though to be honest, he would have to reconvince himself that they were alone in the room. "I just realized there'll be a good side to living in Asermos. You in skirts, for one."

"And more kinds of food, so I can get nice and fat." She grinned, but then her smile turned pensive. "Thank you for not telling me what to do. I know you're worried about the baby, more than most men would be."

He pushed the old images away. "I know better than to insist with you."

"I do tend to do the opposite of what people tell me."

"I've noticed that." He pulled his shirt from his trousers. "So I insist you close your eyes while I undress."

She smiled, openmouthed, so that when she laughed, he saw her tongue. "No."

He slid his shirt off, slowly, tossed it in the corner, then moved to stand within her reach. "I insist you keep your hands off me."

"No." Her palms started at his calves and slid up the backs of his thighs. They met in front where his trousers bulged, her fingers covering the length of his shaft.

He sucked in a sharp breath. "I insist you keep your mouth off me."

"Sorry." Rhia unfastened his trousers, then pushed them down along with his drawers. "But, no." She took him between her warm, wet lips, and his knees nearly gave way.

He had less breath than before, for fewer words. "Look away from my face." She ignored him, taking him deep and kneading the flesh of his buttocks with her strong fingers. "I insist," he somehow managed to add.

Her head tilted so that she could gaze up at him without taking him out of her mouth. The sight tightened his loins.

"Stop," he said. "I insist—I mean—please." He knelt between her legs. "I want to make love to you now. Not later, after I've recovered. Now."

Her eyes wide and playful, Rhia placed a finger over his mouth. "Don't insist. Just do it."

He slid inside her, bringing a sharp gasp from both their throats. She lay back on the bed and wrapped her legs around him, raising her hips to meet his. The skirt fell above her waist so that he could see where they joined. It was beautiful, and it took every scrap of control not to release himself at that moment.

He held her beneath him. "It'll be over too soon if we're not careful."

She smiled. "It's been a long time, hasn't it?"

In fact, it had been since the night they conceived the child inside her. Less than twenty-four hours later, he became a Descendant prisoner, and they'd almost lost each other forever.

Marek shook his head, releasing the regrets of the past and the fears of the future. He wanted to live inside the now that dwelled within Rhia, to feel every twitch of her tiniest muscle, to fill every breath with her scent.

"Much too long." He thrust deeper inside her. Their groans grew in pitch and volume, and in their surge of shared ecstasy, he felt, for the first time in months, hope.

Hope that didn't disappear after he collapsed on the bed beside her. It didn't disappear when she removed her wedding dress and joined him, naked, beneath the warm blankets. And when she woke him hours later to make love again, the feeling remained. Despite the cruelty of the Descendants and the eternal mysteries of the Spirits, he and Rhia would find a way to be happy, as long as they never let each other go.

10

"Alanka, will you marry me?"

She didn't reply, just scanned the forest from the deer blind that doubled as a guard station. It was tucked into the low, bare branches of a hemlock tree and allowed a clear shot of the path to the river.

Endrus hummed a short tune behind her, then tried again. "Alanka, how come trees aren't purple?"

His random questions had created a background hum in her head since before sunrise. Endrus's weird sense of humor used to leave her cheeks aching with laughter. When they were younger and training to be hunters, they would often try to ruin each other's shots with a well-timed remark.

"Alanka, what's the smallest spider you've ever eaten?"

She couldn't remember the last time she'd laughed. It

should worry her, but the same heavy cloak that kept her solemn also kept her safe.

"Alanka, where does bark come from?"

"I could hear intruders much better if you'd stop nattering."

"Just trying to cheer you up." The tip of his bow poked her shoulder blade. "Or get you mad." He waited, then poked again, harder. A year ago she would have broken the bow over the Cougar's head.

He blew out a gust of air. "Any reaction at all would be nice."

"Why?"

"We miss you. When are you coming home?"

"Don't know what you're talking about. I'm home."

"Right. Hold still." He reached out and drew forward a strand of black hair that had fallen from her braid.

She pulled away. "Ow."

"Told you to hold still." He held out a small spray of brown pine needles. "Looked like you were wearing a little hat. Rather jaunty, actually."

A strong breeze was blowing, and the air around them rained with pine droppings. "Lot of them this autumn," she said.

"Dry summer." They watched the thin brown needles twirl and fall. Endrus slapped his knee. "So Raven's coming. Pretty exciting," he added, as if he were talking about an upcoming feast.

"She's coming because our people are in terrible danger. That's not exciting. And if the Raven child is born to Rhia, that means at least fifteen years before it's bestowed with the

Aspect. It might not be this baby, it could be her second, or fifth, or someone else's. The Descendants could kill a lot of people between now and then."

"If you want to look on the dark side, yes."

"It's the real side."

Endrus scooted forward to sit next to her on the edge of the platform. "You should move out of that house."

"Why?"

"Get away from the memories. I'll help you carry your things."

She considered it for a long moment, deciding whether she cared enough to change her life. Finally she looked at him. "Maybe."

His dark eyes sparkled. "In return you have to clean my kitchen."

She glared at him with mock resentment, then turned back to the path. The breeze blew harder, making her shiver under her light horsehide vest. Soon it would be time to wear fur. She wondered if it would be indecent to find a better coat among the belongings of those who had been captured.

Alanka was about to ask Endrus's opinion on the subject when she heard the distant sound of footsteps. They rustled the dry leaves with a solid, regular beat—not a rabbit or bird. A deer?

"I hear something." Her nostrils flared, but the wind was blowing from the opposite direction.

Endrus readied his bow, nocking the arrow against the string.

She closed her eyes and listened to the rhythm of the footsteps. Human. A man, judging by the heavy tread. Not likely a Kalindon. They all knew that wandering through the hunting grounds at this time of morning could get them accidentally shot.

Besides, the steps were heading *toward* the village, not away. A stranger, then. A Descendant? No, surely not alone.

"I see him," Endrus whispered. He raised his bow.

A slim man with long black hair appeared. Though Alanka couldn't see what he carried on his back from this angle, the weight of his walk suggested a heavy load. Someone from a distance, then.

"Halt!"

Alanka jumped at the sound of Endrus's voice at her ear, low and commanding.

The man stopped and peered up into their tree. "Hello?"

"Who are you?" Alanka said.

He came forward a few steps, and Endrus shouted, "I told you to halt!"

The black-haired man held up his hands. "Don't shoot, please. I come from Velekos."

Endrus tautened the bow further. "I'm supposed to take your word for it?"

"Wait," Alanka told the Cougar. "I remember him." She scrambled out of the tree, scraping her arm and nearly falling on her head.

The man watched her, hands in the air, his long muskrat coat hanging below his hips. She approached him, his name stuck between her mind and her mouth. Then she saw the black feather fetish around his neck. "Damen?"

"That's right." He smiled and nodded at her, then shook his head. "I haven't the slightest idea who you are."

"I'm Alanka. You can put your arms down now, by the way."

"Alanka?" He gaped at her and held his hand waist high. "Little Alanka?"

"How long has it been? Ten years?"

"Ten long years." Damen grinned at Endrus, who had dropped from the deer blind, with much more grace than she had. "Greetings."

"Welcome." Endrus introduced himself and gave Damen the traditional Kalindon vigorous embrace. Damen reacted in typical eye-bulging non-Kalindon fashion. "What brings you here?"

Damen recovered his breath from the hug and straightened his crow feather. "At long last, I entered the second phase."

Alanka and Endrus shared a gasp. "Have you heard the Raven prophecy?" the Cougar asked.

Damen rolled his eyes. "It's all anyone talks about, especially now that Reni's pregnant."

"Your wife must be so excited," Alanka said.

Damen's glance darted away. "Well, we're not married, ya see."

"Ah." Alanka wondered why it had taken so long for Damen to enter the second phase. He must be twenty-seven or twenty-eight by now. It was rare even to reach twenty-five without becoming a parent.

"Go take him to Coranna," Endrus said to Alanka. "I'll stand guard alone, try to keep myself entertained." He winked at them, then leaped to grasp the edge of the deer blind. In a moment he had hoisted himself back into position.

Alanka and Damen headed toward the village. "Coranna will be happy to see you," she said.

"And more than a tiny bit surprised, I imagine."

"Funny you showing up now. Her other apprentice just left to go back to Asermos. She's having a baby, too."

"I did hear that from the rescue party, very good news."

"Coranna and I are going to be there next spring when it's born. You should come, too, and meet her."

"I'd very much like that," he said, "but no doubt she won't feel like getting acquainted in the middle of labor, heh?"

His lilting Velekon dialect extracted her first smile in weeks. "I remember when you were here before, I'd follow you around to listen to you talk."

"You find my accent amusing, do ya?"

"The way all your words run together in one long breath until you get to the end of the sentence and it pops up." Her voice pitched and plummeted over the last two words in what she thought was a perfect Velekon accent.

"Uncanny. You'd fit in nice there."

"Thank ya."

"So what did you turn out to be?" he asked her.

She held up her bow. "Wolf. Kerza's my mentor. You remember Kerza?"

"Yes." He paused. "She survived the attack, I heard."

"There's only about a hundred of us now." The dead feeling, banished for a few moments by Damen's appearance, returned. "Just the ones who fought in the battle for Asermos, and a few second-phase Wolves who disappeared in time."

He jammed his hands in his coat pockets. "Velekos is finally changing its shameful policy of neutrality toward Ilios."

"What took you so long?"

"We didn't want to be conquered, so we looked the other way when the Descendants invaded Asermos. We're a small village."

"Not as small as Kalindos. Especially now."

He brushed his hand against her elbow in an awkward motion that she nonetheless found sweet. "I heard about your father."

She groaned and covered her face.

"I'm sorry," he said. "But I don't understand why Razvin would spy against Asermos for the Descendants."

"Partly to bargain for the safety of Kalindos, for my safety. But also because he hated Asermos. A long time ago he was in love with Rhia's mother, Mayra. He wanted to marry her but the Asermons didn't want some Kalindon scum to marry one of their women. That's what he told me, anyway. He left Mayra with twin boys—Rhia's half brothers and my half brothers, Lycas and Nilo, who never even met him."

"I see. Go on."

"Last spring he made a deal with a Descendant soldier and gave him information on every Animal's powers. But he also made the mistake of showing off his third-phase Fox magic."

"He shape-shifted in front of a Descendant?"

"Who got scared and killed my father while—" her voice threatened to break. "—while he was in the form of a Fox." Alanka took a deep breath. Telling the whole story at once had loosened her chest.

As they continued toward the village, Damen asked her

about several Kalindons he remembered from his last visit. He gave up when it turned out most of them were dead or missing.

When they entered Kalindos, he fell silent at its emptiness, to which Alanka had almost grown accustomed.

A blue flag hung from Coranna's porch, signaling that she was home and accepting visitors, though Alanka knew it was no guarantee the Crow woman would feel sociable. They climbed the ladder to her porch and knocked on the door.

"Who is it?" came an irritated voice from within. "I'm busy."

Damen leaned close to the entrance. "Too busy for an old friend, heh?"

Rapid footsteps approached the door, which swung inward with a whoosh. Coranna's mouth dropped open at the sight of Damen. "I don't believe it." She moved onto the porch to wrap him in an embrace. Alanka stepped back; she'd never seen Coranna show such unrestrained affection to anyone.

"Come in, come in. You must be exhausted." She dragged him inside, beckoning Alanka to follow.

"I should get back to my post," Alanka said.

Damen offered her a slight bow. "Thank you for escorting me."

"Yes, thank you." Coranna started to close the door.

"Coranna, wait." When the Crow woman stopped, Alanka said, "With Marek and Rhia gone, do you need help?"

"Thank you, but now that Damen's here—"

"I mean, for practical things, like food and supplies, what Marek used to do for you. I could live next door in his house until they come back."

Coranna glanced behind her at Damen. "I don't think—"

"Please," Alanka said. "It's hard living in my father's house since he died."

Coranna's eyes softened. "I suppose I could use the help. Thank you." She gave a tight-lipped smile and shut the door.

"That's odd," Alanka murmured, wondering at Coranna's reluctance. Then she walked over the wooden rope bridge to what had been Marek and Rhia's home.

The tiny house was sparse but clean inside. Alanka opened the two windows to let in fresh air, then sat on the bed and dared a small smile.

Maybe if she left her father's house, he would leave her mind.

11

Birds again. Why was it always birds?

Filip frowned at the roost of pigeons that sat against the stable on Tereus's farm. They cooed to each other about sand and stone and fried bread.

A chill wind ripped over the hills, finding passage through his thin leather coat, which he pulled tighter around him. It was only the middle of autumn, according to the Ilion calendar he'd drawn on parchment and hidden under his pillow. Yet here in Asermos all but a few dry yellow-brown leaves had fallen from the oaks and hickories, and this morning he swore he could smell snow in the air. Perhaps if the Ilion generals spent one winter in this place, they'd end their plans for conquest.

The pigeons continued to converse, and he leaned closer

to the roost, as much for shelter from the brutal wind as to hear their bird words.

"Thinking of adding a little something to their food to knock them out?"

Filip turned to see Bolan rounding the corner of the small farmhouse, followed by Galen the Hawk. They wore no coats, of course. Bolan's long blond hair was tied back from his face as if it were midsummer.

The young Horse, whom he saw every other day now, walked up and gave him a friendly pat on the shoulder. Filip and Galen exchanged uneasy bows.

Filip indicated the pigeons. "What are they talking about?"

Bolan listened for a moment. "Sounds like Velekos. They're talking about home. They are *homing* pigeons, after all. Isn't that what you called them?"

"Have the others arrived yet?" Galen asked.

"Almost an hour ago. Fastest test flight yet." Filip pointed to the Asermon pigeons, two white birds on the right side of the roost, in a cage separate from the others. "They brought these." From his pocket he produced two small scrolls and handed them to Galen. Unlike the Ilion pigeon messages, these held pictures and maps but no words. Though these people could sound out letters and simple words, they had trouble grasping the syntax of complex written language, no matter how he explained it. But in this case it didn't matter, because the words came from the birds themselves. The Asermons had taken his people's military tactic, added magic to it and made it their own.

Bolan eased the smaller white pigeon from its cage. He

held it near his face but far enough to avoid getting pecked in the eye.

"When did you leave?" he asked the bird.

"Right after sunrise," was all Filip could understand before the pigeon's words turned garbled. It embarrassed him to have Bolan translate bird-speak. Dogs and horses were easier.

"Any further messages?" Bolan asked the pigeon. A few moments later he laughed. "Galen, next time you're in Velekos, Nadia the Horse woman wants to have dinner with you."

Galen coughed, then looked at the darkening sky. "It took the birds almost all day to get here, but it's faster than we could ride. Safer, as well."

Bolan set the bird on its roost and gave it a gentle stroke. "Hawks would be even quicker."

Filip latched the cage. "I told you they can't be trained to deliver messages. Our military tried, but hawks only work for hunting." The men looked askance at him, and he realized he'd said, *our military*. "The Ilion military, that is."

Since arriving at Tereus's farm three months ago, Filip had resigned himself to no longer being an Ilion. But he refused to help the Asermons any way but defensively. Even that aid was self-preservation, he told himself; if Ilios invaded Asermos, Filip would have nowhere to live.

"I suppose you're right," Bolan said. "Arma's trying to teach our hunting falcons to fly long-distance, but even third-phase Horse magic can't work against an animal's instincts."

From the corner of his eye, Filip saw Galen examining him carefully. If he didn't excuse himself with a farm chore, the Hawk would put him through another round of questioning. Galen seemed to regard Filip and his latent magic as a puzzle whose solution held the key to his people's survival.

"The horses need watering." Filip picked up the bucket and headed for the pump. "Release one of the Velekon birds if you want."

"Wait," Galen said.

Filip stopped short. He winced, not only because his prosthesis chafed his thigh when he made sudden moves. "What is it?"

"Have you decided what to do about your Bestowing?"

He hesitated. "Yes."

"Yes, you'll go?" Galen sounded surprised.

"Yes, I've decided. I've decided not to do it." He walked toward the pump and heard Galen's footsteps following.

"During the Bestowing," the Hawk said, "the Spirit of Horse will grant you your full powers."

"I tried telling him that," Bolan called.

"I don't want any more powers," Filip said. "The ones I have are bad enough."

"The Bestowing will help you control them." Galen caught up to him—an easy thing to do. "It's like taming a young colt. All his speed and power aren't much use until you can rein him in. The Bestowing gives you the reins."

Filip didn't answer. He wanted better control over his powers, but the Bestowing carried other, unacceptable consequences.

"When you undertake the ritual," Galen said, "you will become one of us."

"Exactly."

Galen stopped, and Filip moved on.

Rhia and her family rode to a fork in the wooded trail, with one path leading uphill. Tereus turned to her. "Do you want to go home first or visit Silina for an examination?"

"Home," she said, as the voice behind her said, "Silina."

She turned to glare at Marek, who held on to her waist even after they'd stopped moving. "I won't go into town looking like this."

"You look fine," he said.

"Smelling like this, then."

They continued uphill. As they neared the family farm, the rolling, sun-drenched fields seemed to want to yank her out of the dark woods. She could almost smell the hay and hear the melodic twitter of the red-winged blackbirds.

When at last the woods grew sparse, she could see the small farmhouse and its pastures below. The ponies were gathered at one side of the paddock, where the water trough lay. A figure walked toward them with an unsteady gait, carrying two buckets.

"Is that Filip?" Rhia asked her father.

"That's him." Tereus scanned the farm from their vantage point on the hill. "The place hasn't fallen apart." He turned to his stepson. "I told you we could trust him."

Lycas shrugged. "He probably trained the hounds to attack us when we return."

They rode toward the paddock. The sandy-haired Descendant acknowledged them with a nod as he emptied the water buckets into the trough. Rhia felt Marek's arms tense around her waist.

Tereus halted his pony next to the paddock and slid off with a grunt. "Filip, greetings. This is my daughter, Rhia, and her husband, Marek."

Filip started to bow, then stared at Rhia with recognition. "You gave me water," he said.

"Excuse me?"

"After the battle, in the healer's tent. We spoke." He looked away and ran his fingers over the edge of his coat. "I regret some of my words."

Her memory unclouded. "But at the time you weren't— that is, you had—"

"Two legs?" His face reddened, and she felt hers do the same. "An infection set in later." He looked at her pony's head, then back at her and Marek. "He's tired."

"No, I'm not," Marek snapped.

"I meant the horse." Filip glared at the Wolf. "And his right hock is sore."

"I hadn't noticed." Rhia nudged Marek, and he slid off the pony. She dismounted after him. "His gait was fine on the way here."

"I doubt that." Filip walked around the horse's right side, passing his hand along the dark brown flank until he came to the rear leg. The Descendant's limp was imperceptible now, maybe because he knew he was being watched. "Then again, with these ponies it can be hard to tell when their gait's off. They're not exactly the height of refinement."

She gaped at her father. Was this man insulting their

stock? Tereus just turned his eyes to the sky with a look of resignation.

Lycas dismounted and led his gray mare to the stable without a word for Filip. The tension among the men made Rhia uneasy. Only her father seemed at peace with the situation.

"Everything all right while we were gone?" he asked Filip, who was crouched beside the gelding's right rear leg.

The Descendant didn't answer. Rhia ducked under the pony's neck to see Filip's blue eyes unfocus as he ran his hand over the hock and down the cannon bone to the ankle. He seemed to be listening to another world. She knew the feeling.

"No heat, and the pain isn't sharp, so it's probably only a bruise." Filip stood and patted the horse's haunch. "We'll put a poultice on it and see how it feels in a few days."

"Thank you." Tereus held out the reins. "If you could attend to these two while we get cleaned up, I'd appreciate it."

"I'll help," Rhia said.

Marek placed a hand on her shoulder. "You should get something to eat and drink."

"Yes. Let me know when it's ready." She leaned forward to kiss him and added in a whisper, "Don't let my father cook."

She ignored Marek's frown and joined Filip to lead the ponies toward the stable. The swish-thump of hooves through grass was the only sound until he cleared his throat. "They come scruffier in Kalindos, don't they?"

Her neck jerked. "What did you say?"

"The ponies." He gestured to the piebald whose reins he held. "Smaller, with thicker coats. Because of the colder climate, right?"

"Oh." She thought he had been referring to Marek. "Yes, I imagine. Everywhere seems to be uphill there, so the horses are sturdier."

They entered the stable. Lycas stood at the far end, untacking his pony. He shook out the riding blanket and laid it over the door of a nearby empty stall without sparing them a glance.

A slim golden head poked from a stall door to Rhia's left.

"Keleos!" She crossed the stable to greet him, leading her own pony. The stallion's ears pricked forward, then pinned back.

"Wait." Filip reached to take the reins from her. "Those two don't get along. Greet him alone."

"Sorry." Rhia approached Keleos more slowly and let the stallion nuzzle her hand before reaching under his jaw to scratch him. "Does he remember me?"

Filip hesitated. "Not really. He likes you well enough now, though."

"He saved my life."

"I know." Filip's voice fell flat.

Rhia bit her lip and rubbed Keleos's sleek neck. No doubt her theft of the horse from the Descendant camp gnawed at Filip's pride. "Did Father tell you about me?"

"What specifically?"

"About my Aspect." She turned to him. "I hear voices, too."

He looked unimpressed. "Are the dead as talkative as animals?"

"You'd be surprised how much they have to say."

"Nothing would surprise me anymore. When I first heard an animal speak to me, I thought I was going insane. The second, third and fourth time I heard an animal speak to me, I thought I was going insane. Then I found out one of my comrades had magic, too."

"What was his power?"

"He could make light from nothing."

"Ah, Aspect of Firefly." She ruffled Keleos's silver mane, then took back the reins of her pony. "Useful."

"Kiril didn't think so. He left, hoping he'd shed the powers when he returned to Leukos."

Rhia put a halter on her pony so she could tie him to the grooming post. "Do you think our people would also lose their powers there?"

"Maybe. But like I told Galen, my people were born without magic, so Kiril would just be reverting back to normal. Your people grow up around the Spirits, so it's more a part of them."

"You believe in the Spirits now?" she asked.

"I don't have much choice," he said sullenly.

"Then you admit that your gods are false?"

"No!" His voice rang sharp. "There's no reason why the gods and the Spirits can't both exist. They have different domains. What's so hard to understand about that?" He currycombed the pony with more vigor than was necessary even for the thick-coated creature.

She approached him slowly, keeping the piebald mare between them. "Then if you underwent the Bestowing, it wouldn't be a betrayal of your gods."

"You don't understand." He rubbed harder, sending up clouds of dust and black-and-white hair. "I might not belong in Ilios, but I don't belong here, either, not in that tight, selfless way, like we're all part of the same body."

"We are. We need each other's gifts."

"I don't want to be needed." He tossed away the curry-comb and picked up the wood-handled brush. "You people make no room for what any person wants. The Spirits choose you and that's your destiny. There's no fighting it, no decision of your own."

Rhia couldn't argue, since those same thoughts had plagued her as she'd struggled to accept Crow.

Filip continued. "What if I don't want to talk to animals? I don't even like animals."

"You like horses."

"Horses were a way to get around, a way to gain advantage. A way to kill the enemy." He wiped his sleeve over his brow. "Now horses expect me to be their friend, to care about what they want."

"And do you care?"

"Yes. But I don't want to."

"What *do* you want, Filip?"

"I don't know!" He lowered his voice and kept brushing the pony's flank. "I don't know."

"Your Spirit can help you figure that out."

"If I get Bestowed." His lips twisted the word into something distasteful. "But then I'm trapped forever."

"You might not have a choice of gifts, but you can choose how to use them. Even after the Bestowing." She went back to her pony and removed the riding blanket. "When Crow gave me my full powers, I thought my trials were over. Then I found out I had to die."

He stopped brushing. "Die? As in, dead?"

"To lose my fear of death, I had to experience it. Or so my mentor, Coranna, claimed."

"What did you do?"

"I ran away." She picked up the currycomb he'd tossed aside, then stood and met his gaze. "But I didn't get far."

He nodded. "They tracked you down."

"No, I came back. It was my choice. I froze to death on Mount Beros, then Coranna brought me back to life. Third-phase Crows can do that, though there's always a price."

"Weren't you afraid you might not come back?"

"Of course. I had to trust in Coranna and trust in Crow." She saw him stare at her with new respect, as if she'd aged twenty years before his eyes. "But I'd spent my whole life believing that the Spirits want what's best for us. You don't have that faith."

He shook his head. "My magic has brought me nothing but lost sleep. The thought of spending the rest of my life like this…" He stretched back his shoulders, sighing, and stared up at the rafters. "Does it get easier?"

The lie sat in her throat, waiting to soothe his fears. "It gets harder."

"I figured." His mouth tightened, then relaxed as he looked at her. "Thank you for being honest. You're the first."

"I don't like secrets. And you need the truth to make your decision about the Bestowing."

"I've already decided not to do it." He turned back to the piebald mare and resumed his vigorous brushing. "For now."

12

Alanka cracked open the small square window, bracing herself against the bitter air, and waited for Damen to appear.

Most nights when it wasn't snowing, he would smoke his pipe on the bridge between her house and Coranna's. At first the pungent scent had assaulted Alanka's sensitive nose, but over the past month she had come to welcome the rich aroma of burning leaves.

Usually she left him alone in these moments, for his gaze seemed to wander to some distant internal realm. Perhaps he was thinking of the family he'd left behind, which she knew little about, only that he had parents and a sister in Velekos, and that the mother of his child wasn't even his mate, much less his wife. Though Alanka often shared meals with Damen and Coranna, she hadn't had a moment alone with him since his arrival. The dinner conversations could have veered toward the personal, but despite his amiable nature, something about Damen told her those parts of him were off-limits.

Tonight Alanka would cross that boundary, even if it burned her. It had been too long since she'd felt anything for a man but indifference. If she could connect with Damen, maybe she'd feel normal again. She undid her braid and drew a brush through the soft waves.

Damen stepped onto the porch. He shook the heavy snow off a pine branch hanging over the rope bridge, then moved to the center of the bridge, pulling the muskrat-skin coat tighter around his chest. His pipe was already lit, and he leaned against the railing to smoke.

The moonlight, nearly obscured by the trees but reflected by the fallen snow, lit Damen with a soft blue glow. As he drew the first inhale of the pipe, his sharp brown eyes closed in relief, and the tension flowed off his face like water over a rock.

Alanka hesitated. She should probably leave him alone, and leave herself alone while she was at it.

She shut the window and opened the door.

Damen jumped when he heard the latch click, then gave her a genuine, though distracted, smile. "Alanka, hello. I didn't hear you at first."

"Wolf stealth. Didn't mean to startle you."

"I was in another world." Head cocked, he examined her appearance. "Aren't you cold wearing that?"

"I'm used to the weather here." She drifted toward him, trying not to let her teeth chatter from the wind that cut through her knee-length, sleeveless shift.

He brushed a dusting of snow off the railing. "It only snows in Velekos maybe once every two or three years."

"Summers must be hot, though."

"But a breeze always blows off the sea, so it's tolerable. Tiros is the worst. Blistering hot in summer, freezing in winter. Nothing to see but dust and cattle. Don't know why anyone lives there."

His voice verged on the more clipped speech of Kalindos, and she wondered if he did it on purpose. Crows were adaptable, if nothing else. "I've never been to Tiros or Velekos. I never left home until the battle in Asermos."

He took a puff of his pipe and examined her face. "You fought, didn't you?"

She nodded and blinked away the wind that made her eyes tear up.

"How was that?" he asked, in his typical understated manner.

"Bad." She stared at the distant ground.

Damen shifted his feet. "Coranna told me what happened to your brother."

She tried to shrug. "It's what he would have wanted. He was a warrior. A Wolverine, born to fight and kill. Born to die, I guess."

"Born to protect the people he loves, you mean. Protect his home."

"That's what they say, but I could tell they enjoyed it. When my brothers killed, it made them stronger, not weaker."

"What do you mean, weaker?"

"Taking another person's life didn't carve out a hole inside them and make them wish—" She cut herself off, unable to voice the secret desire, even to a Crow. "At least, it didn't seem to."

Damen let out a sigh, and the sound reminded her why she was here—not to discuss the battle and the dead feeling it had left within her, but to find a way to make that feeling go away.

"May I try?" she said, pointing to his pipe.

"It's rather strong."

"So am I."

He handed her the pipe, a bemused expression on his face. "Be careful."

"Careful is one thing I never am." *At least, it used to be.* She smiled as she slid the stem between her lips. Her gaze fixed on his. She inhaled.

And choked. The pipe nearly flew from her hand as she heaved a violent, hacking cough. Damen took it back without so much as a chuckle.

"It's all right." He patted her back. "Happens to everyone their first time. Sometimes I still cough if I inhale too hard."

She tried to reply but couldn't get her voice past her tight throat, which spasmed like a dying snake. Damen led her to her house, and she needed his guidance, for the gagging had blinded her with tears.

Once inside, he poured her a mug of water. She grabbed it from him and took a long gulp.

A moment later, she spewed it out again. It was meloxa. Unsweetened meloxa.

"That wasn't water, was it?" he said.

She cracked open her eyes to see that she had spit the sour concoction all over his coat. "Sorry," she croaked.

"My fault." He sniffed another container. "Ah, water."

She grasped the flask and downed half its contents. Soon she was able to take a shallow breath without coughing. Damen pushed a clean towel into her hands, and she used it to wipe her eyes and nose.

"Better?" he asked.

She nodded, too embarrassed to speak.

"I'll go, then," he said.

"Why?"

He held up his pipe. "Don't want to stink up your house."

"No, I like it." She sniffled, not at all seductively. "Please stay. It's cold out."

Damen shrugged, then took off his coat, shaking out the drops of meloxa. "Thank you." He sat at the table while Alanka crossed the room to her bed. She scooted over the blankets to rest her back against the wall.

"Can I ask you a question?" she said.

He motioned to her with his pipe.

"You hear the voices of the dead, right?"

"Of course."

"All the time, in the background, like Rhia does?"

He tilted his head. "At first, but then I learned to suppress it."

"She can't always stop it."

"Coranna said it's because her pregnancy makes everything fluctuate. It's easier for a man, because our bodies aren't changing at the same time as our Aspect. It'll straighten out for her soon."

Alanka paused, realizing the similarity between Coranna's and Damen's matter-of-fact outlooks. Their powers didn't play havoc with their emotions, because age or experience had taught them to shut their feelings away. She hoped Rhia never developed that skill.

"What do they say?" she asked him.

"Who?"

"The dead."

"I can't tell you that." His mouth tried a smirk, but even in the dim stove light Alanka could see through it to something that troubled him deeply.

She drew her knees to her chest and rested her head on them, though her seduction attempt felt as if she was going through the motions. "What *can* you tell me about what goes on in there?"

His gaze flicked to the edge of her shift, which had risen midthigh, but his concentration didn't waver. "In where?"

"In your mind. You never talk about yourself. I see you every day, but I feel like I barely know you. I want to know you better." Her mouth curled into a half smile.

Damen glanced at the door. "What do you want to know?"

"Anything. Or, if you prefer—" she stretched out one bare leg "—we don't have to talk."

He stood slowly, and she leaned her head back, anticipating his approach.

"I need to leave now," he said.

She cursed inside but kept smiling. "Why?"

"Because I think you want something I can't give you."

"Why not? You don't find me attractive?"

He sighed and set his pipe on the table. She waited for him to prove her wrong, first with words, then actions.

Instead he crossed his arms over his chest. "No, Alanka, I don't."

She gaped at him, her face heating.

"Let me be clear," he said. "I like you. I think you're a wonderful person. But I have a mate waiting for me in Velekos."

"Oh." She straightened her legs and drew her shift down to cover as much skin as possible. "I'm sorry. You said the mother of your child wasn't your mate—"

"She's not."

"—so I thought there was no one else."

"There is."

"And you've never spoken of her—"

"Him."

"—so I assumed that—" She stopped and heard what he said, moments after he said it. "Him?"

"His name is Nathas. Do you understand now why I'm not attracted to you?"

She hesitated. "Only men?"

"Yes. And since you're a woman—"

"But nearly half the men in Kalindos will lie with men or women, especially when they're young."

"I know." He grinned. "Why do you think I have such fond memories of this place?"

"What about you?"

"Strictly men. Sorry."

She covered her face with her hands. "No, I'm sorry. I feel so stupid."

"Don't." He came over and sat on the edge of the bed. "I'm flattered. You're a beautiful young woman. Most men would give anything to trade places with me at this moment."

She tried to smile, but his words only made it worse. Suddenly curiosity stifled her humiliation. "You're second phase."

He looked at the floor and nodded. "It wasn't easy."

"But how did you—"

"I said it wasn't easy. In Velekos, people's views aren't as open as they are in Kalindos. With me having a rare Aspect, it was even more important to have children." The tips of his fingers rubbed together, as if they already missed the pipe. "Imagine my parents' reaction when I told them why I'd never be a father. Thus began the project."

"The project?"

"First, finding me a woman who'd be patient enough to conceive under exceptional circumstances, not to mention a woman who wanted children but not a permanent emotional commitment from a man." He shifted his weight. "Then came the obvious part. I had a lot of help from my mate with that."

"I see," was the only reaction Alanka could come up with.

"Reni lives in the home I share with Nathas. He's taking care of her while I'm here, and I'll return for the birth. If everything goes well, and Reni is willing, someday she'll have his child, too."

Alanka's mind spun at the odd arrangement. The thought of sharing a mate, even for such practical purposes, made her feel cold inside.

"I'll go now," he said.

Relieved, Alanka nodded. "Good night."

He gave her shoulder an awkward pat. She didn't watch him leave.

When Damen was gone, Alanka pulled on a pair of soft sleeping trousers and crawled under a pile of blankets.

Maybe men were more trouble than they were worth.

13

Marek rolled onto his left side and slipped an arm around his sleeping wife, who stopped sleeping.

"What is it?" Her voice pierced the darkness at full volume.

"Nothing. Didn't mean to wake you."

"It's all right." She covered his hand with her own and drew it over her bulging belly. "I have all day to sleep and do nothing else. You don't need any more scarves."

He smiled at the thought of the pile of wool scarves she'd knitted for him during her bed rest, which Silina the Turtle had prescribed a month ago.

Though Rhia had put on weight faster since they'd returned to Asermos five months ago, the Turtle woman was disturbed by the occasional spikes in Rhia's blood pressure. They occurred in those rare moments when Skaris's voice broke through the walls she'd constructed in her mind. She had told no one but Coranna and Marek about the Bear who haunted her.

Fortunately, Marek's baby nightmares had stopped. His sleep was still restless, however, due to the street noise outside their small house beside the hospital. He wondered if he'd ever get used to living in Asermos, a village ten times the size of Kalindos.

"At least held captive in here," she said, "I can avoid strangers who want to touch my stomach."

"Good. Only I'm allowed to pet you." He tried to sound casual as he asked, "Did he turn over today?"

"No." She quickly added, "Silina said that's normal with three weeks to go. If he's like this in another ten days, she'll try to flip him."

Marek fought to calm his breath. "What happens if you go into labor before he turns around?"

"Then we'll do our best."

"If he comes out breech—"

"Don't worry." She smoothed the hairs on the back of his arm. "It'll be harder that way, but in the end Nilik and I will be fine."

"Please don't say his name yet," he whispered. "It feels like bad luck. If something happens—"

"Shh. Nothing will happen. You're supposed to keep *me* calm, remember?"

"I'm sorry."

"I know why you're scared. It won't happen to you again." She pushed his hand behind her. "Forget your worries by rubbing my back."

He obliged, welcoming an excuse to touch her. As he

stroked the muscles around her lower spine, he nuzzled the back of her neck. She groaned deep in her throat.

"Marek, you know we can't."

"I know. I wanted to show the effect you still have on me."

"I should feel grateful you're not one of those men repulsed by their big puffy wives."

"On the contrary," he said, kneading the wide, strong sinews across her back, "I can't wait for you to have this baby so you can get pregnant again."

"Ha! He'll be an only child. I can't face all this pain and sickness twice."

He knew she would change her mind in a year or two, especially in light of the Raven prophecy, which they'd agreed not to mention again until after Nilik's birth. The more children they had, the more likely one would grow up to take Raven's Aspect. In these times of uncertainty, Marek wanted to increase their odds as much as possible, as long as it was safe for Rhia. "I see Arcas brought more art supplies today," he said.

"Clay," she said. "I made a vaguely dog-shaped blob and a vaguely bird-shaped blob."

"Is that what they are? I thought they were doorknobs."

She giggled. "You can tell I'm not a Spider. Thank you for not being jealous of my friendship with him."

"The wedding and very obvious baby make it clear which one of us you chose."

She shifted and sighed, and at first he thought the conversation made her uncomfortable, but the pattern of her breath turned quick and uneven.

"What's wrong?" he said.

Rhia held herself motionless for a long moment. "My back."

"I know." His palm tried to soothe the tight muscles. "It's no wonder you're stiff, lying here all day—"

"That's not it." Her voice held a new edge. "This is different pain." Her hand shot to her lower abdomen, and she drew a sharp breath through her teeth. "Marek, I think the baby's coming."

His hand froze. "No. No, it can't come yet. It's too soon. Maybe this is more false labor."

"I told you, this is different."

His mind blanked. "What do we do?"

"Go next door and get Zelia. She'll send someone for Silina."

"Right. Of course. Zelia." He tossed back the covers and leaped out of bed—unfortunately, not in that order. His feet tangled in the blankets, sending him sprawling face-down on the floor. "Oof!"

Rhia burst into laughter at the sound. "I wish I could have seen that."

"It's not funny." He extracted his feet from the blanket and reached for his boots. "Why aren't you worried?"

"It would only make things worse. Besides, that's what I have you for."

He grumbled an oath that was incoherent even to his own ears, then ran out of the house.

His knuckles were raw from knocking by the time Zelia came to the hospital door. "The baby's coming," he shouted.

The Otter frowned through her drowsiness. "Are you sure?"

"Rhia's sure. But isn't it too early? He hasn't turned over yet."

"We might be able to stop the contractions. I'll bring blackhaw tea. In the meantime, keep her lying on her left side, and keep her calm." He turned to dash back to Rhia when Zelia caught his arm in a surprisingly strong grip. "Keep yourself calm, too," the healer said. "If she's in labor, it'll be hours if not days before the baby comes. Don't waste your strength fretting."

Marek knew he couldn't obey.

When he entered their house, Rhia had lit the table lantern and was pacing the floor, her hand on the far wall to steady herself.

"No!" He ran to her and held her up, though her legs seemed sturdy. "You should be in bed. Zelia said we might be able to stop the contractions. She's making blackhaw."

"I'm sick of blackhaw. It tastes like bark."

"That's because it *is* bark."

She took his arm and made him look into her calm green eyes. "If I thought there was a chance of stopping it, I would. But I can tell it's too late." Her face shone with a new light as she stroked his cheek. "Let's meet our son."

He took a deep, ragged breath, closed his eyes and pressed his forehead to hers. I'm not ready, he thought. "Let's do it."

Several hours passed without incident. When the contractions came more frequently, Rhia moved to a room in the hospital equipped with a half-upright birthing bed, on which she now sat while Silina examined her. Despite the healer's demand that he save his strength, Marek paced the floor.

"Don't you worry." The Turtle woman lay a plump arm over Rhia's shoulders. "I've seen everything, and my powers are greater than when your mother and I worked together."

Marek's shoulders loosened a bit. Like Zelia, Silina had entered her third phase last year when she became a grandmother. Unlike Zelia, Silina's demeanor was pure softness and comfort. Between the two healers, Rhia had access to more sophisticated care here in Asermos than she would have had in Kalindos. But old memories plagued Marek's mind.

A knock came at the door, and he went to answer it, relieved at the distraction. It opened a crack before he reached it.

"Are we too late?" piped a familiar voice.

Rhia gasped. "Alanka!"

Marek's Wolf sister shoved open the door and threw her arms around his neck. The embrace was short-lived, as she rushed over to the bed to greet Rhia. "We thought we'd be early, but Silina said—" She stepped back. "You're huge!"

"Thank you. I think." Rhia crinkled her eyes at Marek.

Alanka's face reddened. "I mean, for someone so tiny, you're rather— I'll be quiet now."

"Who else came with you?" Marek said.

"Coranna, and our new Crow— Well, not exactly new. You remember Damen? He's back from Velekos for his second-phase training."

"Damen made his second phase?" He wondered if he remembered the wrong fellow.

"Another Crow?" Rhia's eyes lit up. "When are they coming?" she asked Alanka.

"They'll be here when the time gets closer. That's when I'll leave. I don't do well with human blood."

"I'm glad you're here." Rhia pulled Alanka to sit on the bed with her. "I want to hear about everything going on in— Aaugh!" She doubled over, or would have if her belly hadn't prevented her from folding in half. Marek rushed to her side. She motioned to him to help her stand, then pointed down.

"On the floor?" he said. "Why?"

"Just do as she asks," Silina said. "Wherever feels best for her. But put pillows under her knees."

Rhia's face twisted into a grimace, her breath coming too hard to speak. She grabbed his wrist and squeezed until he thought the bones would pop.

"What should I do?" Alanka asked.

"Keep talking," Silina said. "And get a cool cloth to wipe her face. She'll be working hard for a while."

Alanka fetched the cloth and began to describe in mind-numbing detail the past several months of her life. Marek was glad to see that his Wolf sister had regained some of her usual animation, though her voice was still shadowed. The cloud that had hung over her at their wedding seemed to have thinned, though not disappeared.

Morning passed into afternoon, and the contractions came and went with no discernible progress. Silina's assistant arrived, along with Zelia and one of her female apprentices. The four women's placid faces betrayed no sense of peril, but Marek knew the labor wasn't going well. Rhia was tiring, her muscles already weak from a month of bed rest, and her face grew pale and slack.

After a particularly hard contraction, they rested together

on the slanted bed, her back to his chest, while Silina examined her again. Rhia's head lolled back on his shoulder, and she moaned in frustration.

"You can do this," he whispered to her.

"Is it too late to change my mind?" she said.

"About going into labor?"

"About getting pregnant."

Everyone laughed except Silina. She seemed to peer through Rhia's skin as she lay her palms over the baby's body. Wisps of long blond-and-gray hair stuck to her sweat-soaked face.

"There's a slight problem," she said. Marek heard the forced calm in her voice, and suddenly the room reeked of fear. "His foot is extended. It's the toughest position to deliver."

Marek shuddered. It was Kalia all over again. He couldn't watch Rhia die, too.

"I might be able to change his position," Silina said, "get his legs up for a safer breech presentation." She looked at each person in the room. "This ritual requires everyone's silence and clear-minded focus. Rid your thoughts of fear and pain so the magic can flow like water, the element of Turtle."

"I need to speak to Coranna," Marek said.

Silina nodded to her assistant. "Bring in the Crows to help."

"I need to speak with her alone," he said. "Now."

Rhia stirred in his arms. "Marek, what's this about?"

"I'll be right back." He slid his leg from around her and got to his feet. "Alanka, hold her up while I'm gone."

"You're leaving me?" Rhia's eyes widened. "Now?"

"This is for you," he said, and slipped out the door.

In the waiting area, Coranna and Damen stood when

he entered. Marek approached Coranna so quickly she stepped back.

"Promise me you'll do it this time," he told her.

"Do what?"

"Take my life for hers and the baby's if they die."

"Marek, I can't."

"I won't let you betray me the way you did with Kalia. If anything happens, you bring them back, with my time on earth as Crow's ransom."

"You don't understand." Damen stepped forward. "She can't bring Rhia back to life twice."

Marek looked between them. "Since when?"

"Since always," Coranna said in a level voice. "Remember when Rhia revived on the mountain, then nearly died again as she recovered?" He nodded, and she put her hand on his arm. "I said I couldn't bring her back a second time, and that meant forever, not just that day."

Marek ran a trembling hand across his face. "Then trade my time for Nilik. If he doesn't make it."

"Marek, he's so young. If he's meant to live a long life, it could kill you."

"I don't care about my life."

"Rhia cares." Coranna's voice hardened. "How would she feel if I took her husband? You think she would choose the child over you?"

"She should."

"She wouldn't, and I would never burden her with that choice. I'll let Crow fly as He will today."

The door to the delivery room opened, and Zelia poked her head out. "Come now. We're ready to begin."

Marek turned to look at the front door, which seemed to beckon him away from the scene of blood and pain. No father should endure the sight of one son's simultaneous birth and death, much less two.

He wiped away the last tear for a woman and child long gone, then led the others into the delivery room.

14

This is harder than dying, Rhia thought. At least death had
a certain end. She imagined herself trapped for months in
this room with these well-meaning people, strength ebbing
until she became nothing but a dried-out husk containing
a stubborn little boy who would grow until he burst her
body like a moth leaving a cocoon.

Those weren't the kind of thoughts Silina needed for her
ritual, but Rhia couldn't help it. Serenity came and went,
fickle as the sun on a cloudy day. At least the voices had
stopped completely, either out of respect for the moment
or fear that her strength might resurge.

The door opened, and Marek returned, looking even
more troubled than when he had left. Alanka squeezed
Rhia's shoulders and moved aside for Marek, who settled
behind her again.

A woman appeared at the door. Coranna.

Rhia's eyes shed tears she didn't know were left inside her. She wanted to scramble out of bed and fall into her mentor's arms.

Coranna's face softened. She moved like liquid silver to Rhia's side and placed a cool, silky palm on her cheek. "I've missed you."

Rhia couldn't speak. Coranna moved aside, revealing a tall dark-haired man. Though Rhia had never seen him before, she reached for him as if by instinct, this honored and cursed cocarrier of the Aspect of Crow.

Damen stepped forward and spoke her name in a deep voice that soothed the ragged edges of her soul. "I'm glad to meet you," he said.

"I'm glad you exist." She took his hand as another contraction hit. His eyes bulged from the pressure of her fingernails into his palm.

"Hold on," Silina purred, mopping Rhia's brow. "After this contraction I'll perform the spell."

Blinded by the pain and pressure, Rhia couldn't even acknowledge her. She wanted to cry out for her mother, but could only close her eyes and focus on the memory of her strong, gentle face.

When the wave passed, Rhia opened her eyes. The curtains had been drawn, and the sole light came from three candles around a deep bowl of water on a nearby table. Silina stood next to the table, staring into the space above the bowl. The candlelight created three dancing yellow spots in each of her hazel eyes.

A chant began low in the Turtle's throat. She held her

palms down over the bowl. The others watched, faces blank with the same calm that Rhia felt at the sound of Silina's voice.

The water in the bowl moved—at first just a ripple, then a series of waves. Silina's voice rose in timbre and volume. The water lapped faster against the sides of the bowl. The blood and water in Rhia's body surged in response.

A tiny whirlpool formed in the bowl's center, then grew until it encompassed every drop. The rushing liquid harmonized with Silina's voice. She turned to face Rhia, who wanted to shrink from the immense power. Marek stroked her arms with strong, soothing fingers.

Silina held her hands apart as she approached. The space between her palms shimmered with liquid force, as if she had transformed the air itself into water.

She placed her palms on the underside of Rhia's abdomen, over the place where Nilik lay. Silina's chin tilted, and her young assistant joined the chant in a high, lilting voice. Rhia sank back into Marek's arms, floating and soaring on the sound that flowed like water over and within her. Shivers of bliss entered the base of her spine and trickled to the tips of her fingers and toes.

Nilik shifted.

The two women continued the chant, and Rhia felt another swell of motion within her womb. She gasped as a wave moved *up*, in the opposite direction of the birth. It felt wrong, but she had to trust Silina's Turtle Spirit.

Something slipped inside her, then sank into a place that felt right—and urgent.

"There!" After the ethereal chanting, Silina's mundane

speaking voice startled Rhia. The Turtle smoothed the skin over Rhia's belly. "He's ready when you are."

"Thank you," Rhia breathed.

Silina patted her leg. "Sorry, the hardest part's to come. But now you can let your body do what it wants."

What it wanted, very badly, was to expel the person it had carried for thirty-seven weeks.

The room cleared then except for Marek and Silina. A hundred people could have surrounded Rhia, for all she knew or cared. Her mind shut out all but the tiny space within. It reminded her of the day on the mountain when she had frozen to death, when the slowing rhythm of her breath became her whole world. The same peace draped over her now, even in the midst of heaving, rippling pain. But instead of the numbing lull that came between her and all sensation, Nilik's birth planted her deep within her own body until nothing else existed.

It was the opposite of death.

As if from a distance, she heard Silina say, "And there's half of him."

Rhia craned her neck over her belly to see, but another contraction slammed her head back onto Marek's chest.

"Not much longer," Silina crooned. "Good, his arms are down. That'll make the shoulders easy. There you go, little man. Nothing left but your beautiful face."

Rhia tried not to tense. The hardest part was yet to come, and if it didn't go quickly…

Marek smoothed back her hair. "Ready for us to call in Coranna and Damen?"

She nodded. Crows attended every passage from one

world to another, no matter the direction. Attending a birth was one of their sweeter duties.

She closed her eyes to rest for a few moments before the final effort. When she opened them again, Coranna and Damen stood near the door, along with Silina's assistant.

As her body moved with what she hoped would be the last contraction, the Crows began a soothing chant of welcome, Coranna in a smooth contralto and Damen in a bass so beautiful Rhia would have wept if she'd had the breath. She bore down hard but felt nothing move below.

"Hold on." Silina's mouth tightened. "The head's not coming. Stop pushing for a moment."

"I can't stop!" She wanted to throttle Silina. "Just make it happen. Please."

"We have to be careful. Stay calm. Only push when I say."

Marek held Rhia, whispering calm encouragement, and a distant part of her marveled at the strength he'd found within himself. Rhia focused on her breath and tried not to panic.

Until she heard it. Crow's wings.

Nilik was dying.

"No!" She clawed at the air as if she could fight off the Spirit with her own hands. "You won't take him from me!"

Damen's voice faltered. He heard it, too, Rhia realized. Coranna, however, kept as steady as ever.

The wings grew louder in their approach. Soon it would be too late.

"Now!" Silina cried, and Rhia drew on strength that flowed from nowhere and everywhere at once.

With a final effort, she gave her son a chance at life, and he slipped into Silina's hands.

"Good," the Turtle said. Rhia knew that the flat tone was not an understatement. He hadn't survived…yet.

"He'll be all right," Marek whispered. "He has to be."

Zelia entered and reached for the baby, who was eerily silent. Rhia had attended enough births to know he should have cried by now.

"Give him to me," Rhia said.

"We have to revive him." Zelia wiped Nilik's face, swabbing the inside of his nose and mouth.

"Revive him here."

The healers exchanged a quick glance, then Zelia placed Rhia's son on her stomach. His glassy half-open eyes stared at her.

Rhia reached inside herself and found one last bit of strength. The strength to see.

As the healers rubbed Nilik's chest, Crow soared, waiting. She held her breath.

The wings faded, and she grabbed Marek's hand. "He's going to live. He's—"

She was interrupted by a loud gurgle as Nilik took his first halting breath. His chest heaved and a moment later a scream ripped his throat.

Rhia laughed with all her breath at the ear-numbing sound. Marek's head fell onto her shoulder, and she felt his tears drip down her breast.

Perhaps she was too exhausted to prevent what happened next, or perhaps she forgot not to look. As she watched her son clutch at life, her mind's eye opened a little, and in the next moment, she flung it wide.

The vision sucked her into a tunnel of time, longer than

any she had traveled through before, though its journey lasted a moment. She came out the other side on a sandy beach, where waves surged green and white.

And red. The water receded, its foam tinged with blood, then flowed in again to lap the heels of a man facedown in the wet sand. A scarlet rivulet ran from under his bare chest and long, light brown hair. The hilt of a sword lay near his outstretched hand. His body was slim, like that of a young man.

Too young.

Nilik would never grow old.

She screamed at him to get up, to run, to live, but her shriek held no sound.

The vision turned as black as Crow's breast. The weight on her stomach disappeared, and she fell unconscious as she reached for the son who wasn't there.

The sunlight still spotted the wall when Rhia awoke, so she knew little time had passed. Marek appeared next to her bed as soon as she opened her eyes.

"Thank the Spirits." A bundle in a white blanket filled his arms. "How do you feel?"

She reached for the bundle. "Is he—"

"He's fine. There were a few scary moments right after he was born, but he's alert now." Marek's lips twitched. "And hungry."

She sat up, wincing. "He's not the only one."

Marek laughed. "I'll see if I can get you some bread. But first, may I present Nilik, officially the most beautiful baby in the world."

Rhia held out her arms, which shook from exhaustion. Marek placed the bundle on her, one end in the crook of her left elbow.

She gazed down into the face of her son, who already looked like his father, and felt one moment of perfect happiness.

Then she remembered. The vision yanked at her mind, as if longing to show itself again.

No. She closed her eyes at the sudden dizziness. He can't die.

"What's wrong?" Marek said.

Rhia felt her heart clench. She'd never kept a secret from Marek. But this one she could never share.

"Nothing's wrong," she said. "But his head will need to be round before we can proclaim him the most beautiful baby in the world."

"Silina said that was normal, for the birth to misshape his head."

"I know." She smiled at him and realized that it wasn't forced. Despite the vision, she was happy. "I was joking."

"Oh. Right." He scratched the back of his head. "I should get Silina now."

"And some bread."

"And bread. But I don't want to leave you."

"I promise I won't fall asleep and drop him on the floor."

He leaned over to kiss her softly, then kept his face close to hers as he whispered, "I love you." He turned his head to Nilik. "And you, too." After a quick kiss on the baby's forehead and a squeeze of Rhia's arm, he bid them a brief farewell, then left the room walking backward.

When he was gone, she tilted her head to the child. "I'll never let anything bad happen to you." She pushed the blanket down so she could attempt to feed him. "And we're never going to the sea."

15

Alanka disappeared, though not as much as she wanted to.

She tracked her prey through the woods without a sound, careful to stay downwind of its flaring nostrils. It quickened its pace, hooves thumping over the carpet of soft, dead leaves. She ran, too, letting its footsteps cover the sound of her own.

Alanka had gotten used to hunting alone, especially now that Marek was preoccupied with caring for his son. Fatherhood suited him well, at least for these first two weeks. She'd never seen him so tired, nor so happy. It drew a sharp contrast to the rancor in the home she shared with Lycas and Mali, who had taken to parenting like fire takes to water. The past few days of snow and rain had kept Alanka indoors with the pair of cranky warriors and their new daughter.

The morning sun angled warm and mellow through the bare trees, painting the snow patches a pale orange. Her prey angled to the left, and she realized it was heading for a nearby meadow. She frowned, for it would see her out in the open. Time to move in for the kill.

Alanka slipped behind a wide-trunked hickory and waited for the animal to turn to give her a larger target. As it did, she slid an arrow from her quiver and nocked it against the bowstring. She aimed, then drew back an empty right hand in a pretend shot.

"Got you!" she yelled. "You're dead!"

The golden horse snorted and wheeled. His tall blond rider spun in the opposite direction but almost held on to the nervous animal. At the last moment, he slipped and came crashing to the ground next to a fallen tree. Something snapped.

"Oh, no." Alanka dashed toward the rider, spooking the horse further. He whirled toward the meadow and cantered away.

The blond man sat up, emitting a string of curses, some of which she'd never heard before. He yanked on his left leg, bent at an unnatural angle.

She scurried up to him, hands outstretched. "I'm so sorry."

The man cut short his tirade. Large blue eyes glared under a heavy brow. "No, *I'm* sorry."

"Why?"

He struggled to reach his boot. "Women shouldn't hear those kinds of words."

She almost laughed at the notion. "Are you all right?" she asked, then winced at her question. "Obviously not."

His voice hardened. "Why were you hunting my horse?" He looked around. "Where'd he go? Keleos!"

"I'll get him," she said, though she doubted she could fetch an animal she had just frightened.

"Wait." The man held up a hand and listened for a moment. From the meadow came a low whinny. "He says he'll come back if you leave."

"Oh." She started to turn. "But don't you need help?"

He leaned back on his hands and scowled at her. "You can help by going away."

"But your leg is broken."

"No, it's not."

She squinted at him, wondering if the fall had made him delusional.

His left foot shifted, drawing her attention. The cuff of his trousers had slipped up, revealing not skin but hard leather. "Oh! You must be—" Alanka pointed at him as her memory flailed for the name, which he declined to offer "—the Descendant who lives with Rhia's father."

He crossed his ankles, hiding the prosthesis. "Which freak aspect gave me away, the fact that I hear horses talking to me, or the fact that I have only one leg?"

She cocked her head. "I heard you had one-and-a-half legs."

He gaped at her, and she realized she'd doubled her blunder. "I mean," she stammered, "there's a difference, right?"

His mouth closed slowly, then transformed into a crooked smile that snagged her breath. "A difference of half a leg, to be precise."

Alanka stood staring at him, then realized she was standing there staring at him. "Do you still want me to leave?"

He frowned at the meadow where the horse waited. Alanka could hear the impatient stamp of hooves. "Hand me that branch over there," he told her.

Alanka stooped to pick up the dead limb he was pointing at, and realized he was watching her intently. He could be as dangerous as his Descendant comrades, liable to kill at the slightest provocation. She whirled on him, brandishing the limb.

The man put up his hands to defend himself. "What in the gods' names are you doing?"

"What do you need this for?" she asked. "To knock me out when I'm not looking?"

"I need it to walk." He lunged forward on his good leg and grabbed the branch. A splinter of wood bit her palm.

"Ow!" She sucked on the wound. "No need to get violent."

"Violent?" He used the limb to hobble to the fallen tree trunk. "First you pretend to shoot me, then you nearly brain me with a piece of tree." He heaved a sharp sigh as he sat. "You're even crazier than the rest of them."

"The rest of who?"

He waved the branch at their surroundings. "The Asermons. My lovely hosts."

"I'm not Asermon. I'm from Kalindos."

"You're a termite?"

Her face heated. "We don't appreciate that name."

"It's what the Asermons call you. You live in trees, right?"

"How dare they call us that, after we saved their village against the—against you. My Wolf brother, Marek, snuck into your camp to sedate your war horses. He was captured and almost killed. Does that sound like something a termite would do?"

The man had gone silent, his lower jaw jutting to the side. She felt a strange, strong desire to make him smile again. Then she looked toward the horse, back at the man, and realized what had happened.

"You were one of those cavalry soldiers, weren't you? You couldn't ride into battle and had to walk instead."

He nodded. "As did my brother. It's why he died. It's why I was injured. Why I'm here now."

"Oh!" Her memory clicked into place. "You're the man from the hospital. The one Adrek tried to strangle."

He examined her. "Are you the woman who stopped him?" She nodded with what she hoped was modesty, and his gaze lowered to her feet. "Then I am in your debt," he said quietly.

"Not anymore." She pointed to the spot where he'd fallen. "I could've killed you just now. So we'll call it even."

"No, I mean it. Among my people, if you save a person's life, they owe you loyalty forever."

She waved away the notion. "Fine. What's your name?"

He looked up at her, eyes wide, as if she had surprised him. "Filip."

"I'm Alanka."

He gave a quick nod, then said, "Forgive me if I don't get up to bow."

"Kalindons don't bow in greeting, anyway. We embrace." His eyes widened further, and she held up her palm. "Don't worry, I won't hug you."

He failed to relax, and she wondered if she should leave.

Probably. She sat next to him on the trunk. "What does that feel like?"

"What?"

"The leg that's not your leg. The fake one."

"It's—" He hesitated. "No one ever asked me that before, so I don't know how to describe it."

"Didn't your healer ask you how it felt?"

"In a clinical way, yes. As in, 'Does it still hurt?' or 'Does it still chafe?' or 'Do you still feel like burning it, then pissing on the ashes?'"

She laughed. "Do you?"

"Every moment." He put on a grim smile, then opened his mouth as if to say something.

"What is it?"

"I have to take it off and fix one of the straps. It broke when I fell."

"Let me help you."

"No, I'd rather—"

"It's my fault it broke." She squatted next to him and grabbed his boot. "The sooner you fix it the sooner you can get your horse."

He yanked his foot out of her grip. "What do you think you're doing?"

"Helping you take it off."

"I have to undo the other strap first."

"Oh." She glanced at his thigh. "How?"

"I have to take off my trousers."

She held his gaze but kept her tone light. "I can help with that, too."

His face reddened, accentuating the short blond strands

at his hairline, and she realized she was flirting. *Flirting,* as if she wanted someone, wanted anything other than numbness. Flirting was something the old Alanka did, the Alanka she could barely remember.

"I'm just joking." She stood, backed up several paces and turned away. Then she smiled. "Unless you want me to."

He wanted her to. In the name of all the gods or Spirits or whatever he could call upon for strength, he wanted her to. But the thought of this wild, beautiful girl seeing him *that way,* the thought of her trying to hide her pity or disgust, cooled his ache to be touched by a woman.

Barely.

"I'll be fine," he said to her back, and unfastened his trousers.

He had grown adept at maneuvering in and out of clothes, and he only had to push the waistband over his hips to reach the leather strap that held on his prosthesis. Within moments he had the hateful thing in his hands and was dressed again.

"You can turn around now," he said.

Alanka came back to sit on the tree with him. She looked at the false leg without embarrassment. "It's smaller than I thought it would be."

Something a man always loves to hear. He tried not to laugh.

"So how does it feel?" she asked. "You never told me."

Filip held the prosthesis between his knees and examined the broken strap. "I had it adjusted because it was starting to hurt. It's too loose now, so it slips under pressure. That's why I fell off—I'm usually a better rider than that." He glanced at her face, the edges of which were damp with sweat and dew. She was paying attention, but how long would her morbid curiosity last?

"Where did it hurt?" she asked.

"What do you mean?"

"When I've had boots that didn't fit, sometimes they would just hurt my feet, but other times my whole leg and even my back would hurt if I wore them too long." Her gaze flicked up to his face, and he tried not to stare into her dark, animated eyes. "Is that what happens to you? Does it hurt all over or just in one spot?"

Everywhere, he thought. Especially right now.

He cleared his throat. "Mainly there, on—on my—"

"On your stump?"

He took a sharp breath through his nose and nodded, not looking at her. Was there a single thought this woman didn't utter out loud?

"I'm sorry about your brother," she said. "Mine died, too."

"I'm sorry. I mean it." He unbuckled the broken strap so he could tie it in a knot. "You have no idea how sorry I am we invaded Asermos."

"It's not your fault. And I know you didn't kill Nilo, because you wouldn't be sitting here if you had. My other brother, Lycas—he's a Wolverine, too—"

"I know Lycas." His tongue hissed his enemy's name.

"Oh, of course, through Tereus. Anyway, Lycas killed the man who killed our brother. There wasn't much left of him afterward."

"Much left of who?"

"Nilo's killer." She paused. "There wasn't much left of Lycas after that day, either."

"I didn't get any kills in that battle." He pulled hard on the ends of the strap to test the knot. "I never had a chance."

From the corner of his eye he saw her rub her hands together, then fold and unfold her fingers into interlocking fists. "I did."

Her voice was so soft he wasn't sure he'd heard her correctly. "You did what?"

"Killed someone. That day." She rolled the quiver of arrows between her hands. "Lots of someones, actually."

"They shouldn't let women on the battlefield."

"I was behind the field. I was an archer."

Filip wondered if she'd put the arrow in his own shoulder. "From such a long range, how do you know you killed anyone?"

"A platoon broke through and came after us." Her shoulders hunched. "We had to shoot up close."

She looked so shattered, so unlike the woman he'd met moments ago. "You killed to save your own life and those of your comrades. There's no shame in that."

"It's not shame." She blinked, and her voice's strength restored. "Lycas is proud of me, and everyone here tells me what a hero I was, defending a land that's not even mine."

"It is heroic. It's an honor to be a warrior." Hearing his own words, he wanted to fling away the false leg. How could he speak of a warrior's honor when he would never fight again, when he hadn't had the grace to die on the battlefield?

"I don't feel honorable," she said. "I feel…nothing." The

corners of her mouth tilted down for a moment, then bounced back up. "At least not while I'm awake."

"You have nightmares?"

"No. Yes. Sometimes. What about you?"

"My dreams are all good." He hefted the prosthetic leg and thought, It's life that's a nightmare. He was glad he hadn't said it out loud; it sounded melodramatic enough in his head. "I dream about home. I dream of running."

"You can't run with that thing on?"

"Not quickly. A bit of a trot, on level ground."

"Can you dance?"

"Dance?" He snorted. "I don't dance. Except at weddings, maybe."

She smacked her knees in a grand gesture. "Then we'll have a wedding, so you can dance." When he raised his eyebrows, she added quickly, "Oh! I don't mean us. Although, you seem like a nice person, but I don't really know you very well. Let's not rush things."

He gave a full, hearty laugh for the first time in nearly a year. It turned into a harsh cough from the unaccustomed effort.

Alanka handed him her water flask and continued, deadpan, which only made him laugh more.

"My brother and his mate might get married," she said, "but honestly, I think you and I have a better chance at lifelong happiness than they do." She glanced at his prosthesis, then at his face in a manner he could only describe as saucy. "Do you need to put that back on now?"

"Yes, and it'll take longer than it did to remove it."

Sighing, she stood and brushed the bark and dirt off her backside. "All right, I'll find a way to occupy myself." She picked up her bow and arrows, then turned back to him. "What if I watched you while hanging upside down from a branch? Would that count?"

"Yes. Go." He couldn't keep the amusement from his voice.

She gave a flounce of false indignation, then swaggered some distance away to sit on another log, her back to him.

He removed his trousers, replaced the prosthesis and got dressed again as quickly as possible, unsure that she would keep her promise to look away.

"Stay there," he said. "I'm going to call Keleos." He put his fingers in his mouth and sent a shrill two-note whistle toward the meadow. Alanka flinched and covered her ears.

The horse clopped into view, but halted at the edge of the woods, silver mane gleaming in the sunlight. Filip held out his hand at waist level, hoping Keleos would come to investigate its contents, of which there were none. Unfortunately, he hadn't packed any food that could tempt the horse, but Filip could probably fool him once. He'd hear about it all the way home, though.

The horse picked his way through the undergrowth and came to Filip without even sniffing his hand. Filip felt himself go soft inside. Keleos hadn't come for food; he'd come because Filip was his master now. He stroked the stallion's golden neck and murmured his name.

Keleos huffed. "I wasn't scared."

"I know. You're very brave to come back." He had long ceased feeling foolish for talking to animals. Even though he knew they couldn't comprehend his words, he thought they understood his intentions.

Filip led Keleos closer to Alanka, who was still sitting on

the log. Her hands were folded, in the exaggerated style of a prim little girl doing as she was told. "Would you like a ride," he asked her, "or are you in the middle of a hunt?"

"I wasn't hunting to kill—I was practicing my stealth. Not that Mali and Lycas would mind if I brought home dinner." She gave Keleos a wary regard. "I'm not much of a rider."

"He's easy and smooth, not like these Asermon ponies." He got Keleos to sidle next to the fallen tree, which he then used as a mounting block. The left leg felt a bit unsteady, but it would hold up as long as he didn't tumble off again. He turned to extend a hand to Alanka. "Come on."

She hesitated, then put her hand in his. He kept his face blank, not wanting to show the effect her touch had on him. It zinged through him like a tiny bolt of lightning, and when she mounted the horse behind him, he had to remind himself how to breathe.

Keleos pinned his ears back when Alanka settled in. Filip urged the stallion forward before he could start complaining.

"Isn't he a bit skittish for a battle horse?" Alanka asked.

Filip scoffed. "Colonel Baleb never rode into battle. He usually just sat on a hill and watched other men fight under his orders. As long as he looked good doing it, that's all that mattered. You were lucky he was in charge of your invasion. With a smarter commander, we would have crushed you."

She didn't respond, and he wanted to punch himself for mentioning the battle again. It accentuated the chasm between them. A woman of her people could never be seen with a "Descendant," no matter how many legs or how much magic he possessed.

A rustle came from the bushes beside the trail, and a rabbit dashed away to their right.

"Duck!" Alanka pushed him forward onto the horse's neck.

"What are you—"

Something whistled in the air above his right shoulder. A moment later the rabbit screamed.

Pain and fear washed through Filip's mind. He clutched his head and moaned.

Alanka gasped and put her hand on his back. "Oh, no, I forgot. Filip, I'm so sorry."

The rabbit uttered incoherent pleas that threatened to rip Filip in two. "Just—go kill it," he said. "Now."

Alanka slid gracelessly off the horse's haunches but managed to land on her feet. Her footsteps crashed through the underbrush. The rabbit's fear flared for an instant, then all was silent. Filip sat up and wiped his clammy brow.

Alanka was moving toward him, the rabbit dangling behind her back in both hands.

"I'm sorry. Usually I make a clean kill, but I'm out of practice. It's the first time I've shot an arrow since the battle." She stood next to his right foot and gazed up at him with wide brown eyes. "It was bad, wasn't it?"

He could do nothing but nod.

"When we hunt," she said, "we learn not to think about what it's like for the animal—otherwise we'd never eat. And we always honor their Spirit." She cleared her throat. "I have to sing now. That might be more painful than hearing the rabbit cry."

She laid the animal on the ground and knelt beside it. A plaintive song rose, and its sound was anything but painful.

Filip closed his eyes and listened to her mix mourning and triumph into a paean to Sister Rabbit, and hoped that someday she would hold *him* in such high regard.

After she finished, he pointed to a nearby tree stump. "You can remount over there."

She looked at him with disbelief. "You want to be around me after what I did?"

"I want to be around you." He tried to swallow the words. "Today, and another time. We could meet here. If you want, that is."

She smiled, and he was lost.

16

"What if she'd been a boy?"

Rhia ignored her brother's mate and focused on the face of her newborn niece, Sura, who lay sleeping in Rhia's arms. She didn't stir despite her parents' bickering and the night wind that rattled the roof of Lycas and Mali's home.

Mali looked over Rhia's shoulder. "If she'd been a boy," the Wasp continued, her breath hot on Rhia's temple, "she would have been named in memory of Nilo. He was Lycas's twin, but only your half brother, so why did your son get that name?"

"Mali, not again," Lycas growled from the small corner table where he sat across from a nervous-looking Marek. "We knew it would be a girl."

"What if the next child's a boy?" Mali snapped. "The name should have been saved." She threw Rhia a dark-eyed glare that a year ago would have left her quivering. Mali didn't scare her anymore, beyond the fear that she was making Lycas miserable.

As if to confirm this suspicion, he said, "Who says there's going to be a next child?"

The face of his Wasp mate reddened with rage. Moving much faster than her still-plump body allowed, she stomped out of the house, banging a hip on the corner of a chair and nearly slamming Alanka out of the way.

Lycas heaved a deep sigh but didn't move.

"You should go after her," Marek said.

"Why?" The Wolverine's voice dripped with hostility. "Then we'd be in the same place. This is much better." He examined his empty mug. "More ale?"

Alanka stepped close to Rhia and smoothed a lock of dark hair over the baby's forehead. "Isn't she beautiful? I wish you could've brought Nilik to meet his cousin."

"It's too cold for a month-old baby to be out. Coranna and Damen will take good care of him. Damen needs to learn how to change a diaper if he's going to be a father. Besides—" she showed Alanka a guilty grimace "—we needed to get away for a few hours."

"Spend some time with adults?" She watched their brother wrestle and curse a small barrel of ale. "Not that you'll find any adults here." She took the squirming Sura out of Rhia's arms. "She needs changing, I can smell."

"We're out of ale." Lycas stood, then groaned at the ceiling. "I'll have to go to the cellar."

"No, it's fine," Marek said quickly. "I don't need any more."

"I do." Lycas rubbed his chin, a look of dread on his face.

Rhia realized that he might have to pass Mali to get more ale, since the cellar entrance was outside.

He sighed and shuffled to the front door, where he stopped, as if gathering strength, before opening it.

When he was gone, everyone—even the baby, it seemed—let out a deep breath.

"Please come live with us instead," Rhia said to Alanka.

"I'd love to." Alanka wiped the child's bottom with a damp cloth. "But I'm afraid what might happen to Sura if I left. All Mali does is feed her. I do everything else."

"What about Lycas?" Rhia asked.

"He tries to help a little. Mostly he sits in the corner and wishes he'd gone with the rescue party. Sometimes he wishes it out loud."

Rhia felt a pang of sympathy for her old nemesis Mali. It was hard to live with any Wolverine, much less one grappling with the loss of his twin. Mali, a warrior herself, had missed the battle because of her pregnancy. Everything she'd trained for came second to the peculiar duty of motherhood. The Wasp had cause to be bitter.

Rhia's own emotions had swung in unpredictable directions since Nilik's birth, but Marek had shown inhuman patience and stamina. She looked at him now, enjoying a well-earned rest and mug of ale, and felt so lucky it hurt.

Later that night they walked home, arm in arm, recovering from the evening of acrimony.

"Think they'll get married?" Marek said.

Rhia groaned. "I doubt it. Then again, if you'd asked me a year ago if they would get this far, I'd have said no."

Marek took her mittened hand in his as they walked down the dark, quiet Asermon street. "Speaking of fathers—or fathers-to-be, rather—you and Damen seem to be getting along well."

"It's wonderful to have someone to share the burden."

"The burden of being a Crow or the burden of dealing with Coranna?"

She chuckled. "Both. But I'm a little jealous that he's gone further with his training than I have. He's conversing with the dead, but I can't use the thanapras until Nilik stops nursing. Even then, Coranna says she might make me wait. She doesn't think I'm ready."

"But Damen is?"

"He's almost ten years older than I am. And he hasn't been pregnant, with all the power instability that entails." They turned onto the street where they lived. The house next to the hospital would be their home for another month until they returned to Kalindos. She lowered her voice, in case Damen was outside smoking his pipe. "But I think it's because he's just like Coranna. He can separate himself from the people he deals with, both the living and the dead. He's practical."

"Cold."

"Marek—"

"I mean that in the nicest way, of course." He put his arm around her shoulders. "I love Coranna like a mother, and I consider Damen a friend, but promise me you'll never shut down like them. Your connection to other people is a strength, not a weakness." He drew her close and kissed her temple. "Always remember that."

She smiled. "You sound like Crow."

"Then I can't be too dumb, can I?" A bitter breeze blew down the street, and Marek's hand went to his neck. He heaved an exasperated sigh. "I left my scarf at your brother's house."

"You want to go back now and get it?"

"No, that place is poison. Besides, you made me a dozen—" His face froze, then his gray-eyed gaze fixed across the street, on the door to their home.

"What is it?" Rhia looked at the house, the window of which glowed with the same lantern light as when they'd left.

"Do you hear that?" He tilted his head. "It sounds like Coranna, but—"

"I don't hear—"

"Stay there!" He darted across the street toward the house.

Rhia couldn't obey. She dashed after him, her chest aching from a breath held too tightly.

When she neared the open door, the stench of blood slammed her nostrils. "Nilik!"

Marek was kneeling beside Coranna, who lay prone on the floor in a wide red pool. Blood streaked a trail behind her. She moaned softly. Damen was facedown halfway across the room, motionless. Nilik was—

Where was Nilik?

"He's not here," Marek said. "Give me something to stop the bleeding. And get Zelia."

Rhia grabbed a blanket, then ran next door and pounded on the hospital entrance. Zelia appeared within moments.

"Coranna's been hurt," Rhia said between sobs that brought no tears. "Bleeding, stabbed, I think. Damen's unconscious, and I don't know—I don't know where my son is." Without waiting for the Otter's answer, Rhia turned away. She had to find him.

"Nilik!" she shouted into the streets. "Where are you?" He couldn't have crawled away, but maybe whoever had taken him had left him outside. If he heard her voice, he might cry out. She screamed his name again. Neighbors across the street opened their front doors and looked out.

"My baby's gone!" she cried to them. "He's gone!"

"Rhia!"

She turned to see Alanka running down the street toward her, waving the scarf Marek had left behind.

"Rhia, what's wrong?"

She grabbed Alanka's hands and dragged her into the house.

Marek looked up from Coranna's motionless form, covered with a blood-soaked blanket. "Where is he? Is Zelia coming?"

"She's coming." Rhia tried to rein in her galloping breath. "Nilik's not outside."

Alanka ran to kneel beside Damen. "He's alive." She grabbed a flask of water from the bedside table and shook its contents over the back of his neck. He came to with a start and peered around with unfocused eyes.

Damen turned over slowly, with Alanka's and Rhia's help. "What happened?" Rhia asked him. "Where's Nilik?"

"Bandits," he murmured. "They knocked, and when I opened the door, they pushed their way in. I turned for Nilik, and something hit me." He put a hand to the back of his head and winced. "That's all I remember."

Rhia clutched his hand. "Did they say what they wanted, where they're taking him?"

"They took Nilik?" Damen's eyes widened. "Where's Coranna? Is she all right?"

The sound of wings answered his question.

Rhia dropped Damen's hand and turned to Coranna. Zelia entered with her healer's bag in one hand and a large roll of bandages in the other. Marek quickly moved out of the way. He went to the crib and spread his trembling hands over the empty mattress.

Coranna was dying. Rhia looked back at Damen, who had rolled on his side, transfixed.

Zelia worked with haste, but her movements held a sense of resolution. Blood that had been pumping from the wound in Coranna's side now merely seeped.

Rhia knelt beside her mentor, ignoring the warm red liquid that soaked her own skirt, and took her hand. Coranna's pale blue eyes opened for a moment and locked onto Rhia's.

"Don't…" the old woman gasped.

"Shh." Rhia lifted Coranna's hand and kissed her fingers. "Save your strength."

"For what?" Her voice was as ragged as a toad's croak. "He's coming."

Zelia held her hands over Coranna's gashes and molded a silver light into them. Rhia recognized it as a spell to kill pain rather than to seal wounds. The time for healing had passed.

Damen had crawled to Coranna's other side. He smoothed her long silver hair. "Crow will take good care of you."

Coranna blinked at him, her eyes crinkling into a look of fondness. Then her gaze returned to Rhia and sharpened. She drew a rough breath and forced out the words, "Don't ever tell."

Rhia descended into a deep, sudden trance. It pulled her against her will, blocking Marek's shouts and Zelia's determined ministrations.

A warm blackness surrounded her. Unseen walls pulsed with life. She sensed Coranna's presence, and Damen's, too, but couldn't see them, couldn't see anything but black.

They were flying, with no jolts, bumps or tilts, just straight ahead and true. No breeze touched her face.

Rhia was inside Crow Himself. She had never felt so safe, even when He had Bestowed her with His Aspect and enveloped her in an embrace of warm feathers.

Beside her, Coranna's breath had turned deep and smooth, while Damen's breath came as uneven as Rhia's. She wanted to reach out for him, to touch someone alive before Crow dragged them all down together.

"Coranna," Crow's voice boomed. "In your lifetime of loyalty and wisdom, you have honored me with your service. For that I offer you a place at my side for eternity."

Rhia's jaw dropped. A chance to live on after death? Rather than descend into the peaceful oblivion of the Other Side, Coranna could remain herself and serve Crow.

"It is you who have honored me," Coranna said, her voice firm. "Your offer is generous, one no human deserves." She paused. "But I must decline. My life has been long, and I wish to rest forever."

"As you wish." Crow spiraled into a descent.

"Wait!" Rhia blurted, knowing she was probably violating every unspoken Crow code. "Coranna, will you linger like the other Kalindons who were murdered?"

"No," Coranna said. "The pain and fear I felt lasted only a moment, but the Other Side is forever."

Rhia felt a lurch, and she wanted to grab Coranna and hold her fast to life. But she didn't have that power. The only one who did was about to die.

"Go with Crow," Damen whispered. "We wish you peace."

Rhia tried to echo his sentiment, but anguish blocked her voice, so she sent her thoughts. *Peace forever.*

Coranna and Crow disappeared.

Rhia jolted back into the real world, leaning against Damen. Trembling, they held each other up. A movement in the corner of her eye brought her back to the terrible reality.

"Nilik…"

Alanka and Marek flanked the door, bows and arrows on their backs. Alanka held up the tiny yellow shirt Nilik had worn the day before. "For the scent," she said. "We're going to find him."

Rhia stood and approached Marek on unsteady legs. "Be careful."

He traced the outline of her face and looked as if he were trying to memorize it. "I won't return without him."

She wanted to beg him not to risk his life, to come home if he couldn't find their son. But her arms ached with emptiness for Nilik, and she knew Marek would heed no call for caution. So she kissed him goodbye, then watched as her husband followed her son into the darkness.

* * *

"Slow down!" Alanka had to keep reminding Marek to stay focused. She knew all he wanted to do was run, to close the gap between himself and his son.

By questioning the neighbors who had heard Nilik's cries, they determined the kidnappers had headed southeast, through the less populated sections of Asermos, rather than directly south to the road to Velekos. That meant they had probably arrived by boat and docked somewhere secluded.

They reached the edge of town, where fewer human smells distracted them, and looked out over the rolling fields ringed with sparse woods. The trees' bare branches reflected the light of the half moon. The river lay somewhere over these hills; she wasn't sure how far.

"Think they'd risk cutting across open land?" she asked Marek.

"It'd be quicker." He shifted his bow. "Let's go."

She grabbed his arm, unaccustomed to being the cautious one. "Let's try both ways. You take the field, I'll take the woods. If one of us keeps the scent, we'll signal."

Marek nodded, his face like a pale stone, then took off.

Alanka drew another whiff of the child's shirt, then stuffed it into the back pocket of her trousers and entered the thicket of trees to her right. There were no trails here, and dead blackberry vines clawed at her trousers.

She had taken fewer than twenty steps when she heard Marek's whistle. She shoved her way through the brambles to the edge of the field. He stood at the bottom of the hill, flailing both arms at her. She waved back and headed toward him. When he saw she was on her way, he took off again.

"Slower," she muttered, "or we'll lose the trail."

Another thought occurred to her, borne from years of blundering into dangerous situations—from which Marek had often saved her. If the kidnappers thought they were being followed, they might wait in ambush. She wished Marek would turn invisible, but he was probably using his magic for speed and stamina instead of stealth.

She slowed her pace and stooped into a crouching run, refocusing her powers to soften her steps. The frozen grass made it difficult, shouting out her presence with loud crunches.

When she reached the spot where Marek had signaled her, she found a white blanket that reeked of the baby. Poor thing, his diaper needed changing. But it made Nilik's scent easier to trace. She followed the scent downhill.

The terrain turned to woods again. The presence of mottled, twisted sycamore trunks told Alanka they were nearing the river. Her ears strained to hear the flowing current, but a rising wind clattered the branches above her.

A trail cut through the woods, and she saw Marek ahead, plunging downhill with unusual recklessness. She could smell the river now. Were they too late?

A few steps later, she knew the answer. No. There were others here, and—

"Stop!" cried a booming male voice far in front of her.

Alanka dropped to her knees, then crept forward to take cover behind a thick arrowwood bush half her height. She peered over the top. Marek was trapped between two sword-wielding men, one of whom had taken his bow and arrows. They weren't wearing uniforms, but the curve of their swords and the arrogance of their postures marked them as Descendant soldiers.

"Give me my son," Marek said.

"We can't do that. Leave now or we'll cut your throat."

"I won't leave without my son."

Alanka crept to the edge of the shrub to get a better look. Through the trees she saw a small boat, part of which was enclosed. A scruffily dressed man in his late twenties stepped out of this section, followed by a young woman cradling Nilik.

"We're not here to shed blood," the man in the boat told Marek. "But we're taking the baby. Now, as the fellow with the blade at your neck asked so kindly, please leave."

"I said, not without my son."

Nilik wailed. The man scanned the riverbank with nervous eyes. "This is not a negotiation. Leave or die."

"Take me with you," Marek said.

Alanka put a hand over her mouth to muffle her gasp.

"Very funny," the man said. "You'll try to steal the child and escape."

"I just want to take care of him." Marek pointed to Nilik. "I can make him stop crying. Please."

The woman on the boat nudged her companion, who turned to confer with her in tones too low for Alanka to hear. She scooted down the trail on her elbows and knees, hoping for a clear shot at the man or either of the soldiers. She had to wait until they lowered their swords. If she could shoot one, maybe Marek could disarm the other and retrieve Nilik. Maybe he was waiting for her to do just that, and offering to come with them as a distraction to buy time.

Her left shoe scuffed a twig, and Marek tilted his head. He knew she was there. The others didn't react. She moved closer.

The man on the boat turned back to Marek. "If you come with us, you'll be taken to the city of Leukos as a prisoner like your son. Is that what you want?"

"If it's a choice between that and never seeing him again, then yes, it's what I want."

Keep talking, Marek. Alanka inched forward to a place where the trail dropped off steeply, giving her a clear view of the sword wielders' backs. She slipped an arrow from her quiver.

The man motioned to the soldier holding Marek's bow and arrows. "Leave his weapon behind and bring him. The price he fetches better be worth our trouble."

The guards each took one of his arms and lowered their swords to lead him to the boat. Now was her chance.

Alanka rose to her knees and nocked the arrow. She aimed with a surety born in the chaos of battle. The bowstring stretched taut.

The world grew bright with fire. Through the smoke of the battlefield the Descendants came, swords raised. She shot one in the shoulder, her arrow penetrating his armor like a needle through fabric. He laughed and kept running toward the archers' line. Someone else shot him again, in the stomach. His laughter mixed with a scream as he lifted his sword and lunged for Alanka.

When he was a few steps away, she shot him in the throat. He stopped laughing, stopped screaming, stopped everything, and stared at her. The light in his eyes, rather than fading, flared with a fear she'd never seen in the eyes of an animal—the fear of death. She knew she should turn away and defend the line, but something held her gaze. She waited and watched.

The soldier stood rigid, blood-soaked fingers fumbling at his neck. His mouth opened and closed twice, then twice again. His gaze pleaded with her to take back the arrow's flight, make it so that all this never happened.

A day seemed to pass before he fell.

When his body hit the grass, the ground shattered.

Alanka looked around. The battlefield was gone and the riverbank, empty.

"No…"

She lowered her bow and ran to the water's edge. The Descendant boat, with Marek on it, was swept away by the swift current at the center of the river. He was gone.

Alanka sank to her knees, releasing a howl of anguish. Marek had known she was there, known she'd abandoned him when he needed her. She clutched her hair, rocked forward, and pressed her forehead against the cold, hard mud. Arrows spilled from the open quiver on her back, raining over her head and onto the ground, useless. She howled again, wishing she could shoot each one into her own heart.

Rhia handed her son's last dirty sock to Medus, the head of the Asermon police force, a second-phase Badger. In the past hour, he and Rhia had organized the neighbors into search teams to comb the village streets, alleys and houses for her lost child, by scent, sound and sight.

One of Medus's officers ran up. "Two other infants were stolen, at the southern end of town."

Rhia gasped. "When?"

"About an hour ago," the officer said. "The same time as yours. The parents were injured in the abductions."

"Wake everyone," Medus said. "Red alert. We're under attack."

The hospital door opened. Rhia turned to see Damen, his face grim and his apron stained with blood from Coranna's burial preparations.

"Alanka's back," he said.

Rhia's stomach lurched at the absence of Marek's name. She entered the hospital, followed by Medus and his officer. Alanka stood in the front room, panting, her black hair bedraggled. She held two bows, one of them Marek's.

"No…" Rhia's throat constricted on the scream she wanted to hurl.

"Rhia, they're alive. They're safe." Alanka gulped a breath. "But they're gone."

"Gone?" After *alive* and *safe,* Rhia almost didn't recognize the word. She repeated it, as if to confirm its meaning. "Gone? Gone where?"

"To Leukos. I saw them. Descendants. They offered to let Marek go, but he wouldn't leave without Nilik. So they took him, too." She stepped forward and pressed Nilik's tiny shirt into Rhia's hand. "I couldn't stop them. They were all too close together and I couldn't risk shooting Marek or Nilik and even if I'd taken out one, the others might have hurt them." She clutched Rhia's wrists, and her voice cracked. "I'm so sorry."

Medus stepped forward and took Alanka's arm. "Sit," he said. "Tell us everything, from the beginning."

She rattled off the story with a series of shaky breaths. Galen the Hawk entered and stood with the others, listening silently. Halfway through Alanka's tale, Rhia's mind began to spin.

Marek and Nilik couldn't be gone. They couldn't leave her life empty. She couldn't go to bed tomorrow night alone, wake up the next day alone, and the next day and the next, stretching out until the day she died. They couldn't be *gone.*

Alanka fell silent, or maybe her voice had been drowned out by the shrieks in Rhia's own mind. The sounds shifted and sloshed, then her world tilted like a capsized boat. She grabbed the wall and felt it slide past.

"Rhia!" Damen caught her under the arms. She opened her eyes to see the floor much closer than she'd remembered it.

Alanka dashed for the hallway, shouting for Zelia. Damen helped Rhia sit on a nearby chair.

The Otter healer rushed into the room. "Let's get her into one of the beds."

"No!" She couldn't lie helpless while her husband and son were carried off. She shoved Damen's arms away, then staggered to her feet. "I have to find them."

"I'll get some valerian," Zelia said. "It'll calm her down."

"Don't you dare calm me down." Rhia wanted to claw the sympathy off the faces around her. "I'm going after my family."

"There might be another way," Galen said. "We'll send a bird message at daybreak to Velekos. If it arrives in time, the Velekons can stop the Descendants."

Rhia's mind raced. It took a full day to sail to the bayside village. The kidnappers would arrive tomorrow night. If the pigeons didn't make it in time for the Velekons to save Marek, she would go herself, even if she had to swim the Southern Sea.

Less than an hour later, Rhia paced the floor of Arcas and Galen's kitchen, resisting the urge to look over Arcas's shoulder as he worked at the table. She twisted Nilik's shirt around her fingers, binding them so she wouldn't smash every object in Galen's house.

"Why would they take our babies?" she asked the Hawk. "To torture us?"

"I think they have a plan. If they just wanted to hurt us, they would have taken older children who are easier to care for and less likely to draw attention by crying."

"So what's the plan?" she said.

"To study our people's abilities, I think." At the stove, Galen poured three mugs of steaming chicory. "If Filip can gain magic, then maybe the Spirits reside in a place, not a person, which means our people might lose power in their land. If so, the Descendants no doubt wonder what would happen if one of us spent his whole life in Ilios."

"They're using our babies to experiment on us?" Her skin felt covered in centipedes.

Galen rested a hand on Rhia's shoulder. "It means he's not in immediate danger, which gives us time."

She took a mug of chicory from him, grateful that he understood she needed something to keep her alert, not to soothe her. "Alanka said the boat she saw was small, probably not seaworthy. So the kidnappers will stop and change ships in Velekos."

"And if they dock at night," Galen added, "Marek can turn himself and Nilik invisible to help them get away."

Rhia thought of the other two Asermon infants on board. Would he leave them behind to save himself and his son? Spirits forgive her, but she hoped he would.

"If the Velekons don't stop them," she said, "I'm going to Leukos."

He held up a hand. "We'll send others. You're our only Crow."

"I'm also Nilik's only mother, Marek's only wife. I'm going."

"You have no experience in this sort of operation."

"Neither do you, but you'd go if they took your son."

They looked at Arcas, who didn't blink at their mention of him. His dark blue eyes stared through the wall in a Spider trance as his thick hand moved the sharpened charcoal across the parchment. Tall, broad and dark, he still held the demeanor of the Bear Spirit he'd coveted all his life, the Spirit who never appeared at his Bestowing.

Galen turned back to her. "I can't keep you from trying to save your family. But be sure to take support. You'll undoubtedly receive many offers of assistance from other Asermons."

She knew it had nothing to do with neighborly generosity. "Because they think Nilik's the Raven baby."

"It could be."

She shook her head. "I'll take those I know are helping because they love us, not because of some prophecy. That way I'll be sure of their commitment."

"Nevertheless, I'll make sure the Velekons know the importance of the child they'll be rescuing tomorrow night."

"How's this?"

They turned to see Arcas, out of his Spider trance, holding out the parchment. Rhia took it and wanted to weep. On the page was a perfect likeness of Marek's face.

"How did you do it?" she asked.

Arcas shrugged. "I know that face well. I spent many a night contemplating it in my memory, wondering how you could choose it over this." His fingertips displayed his own face, then he gave a grim smile. "Sorry. Not a time for jokes."

Galen examined the picture over Rhia's shoulder. "Can

you make three more before dawn?" he asked his son. "I'd like to send all four pigeons to ensure the message arrives."

"I'll do my best." Arcas reached for a knife to sharpen his stick of charcoal. "I wish I'd met Nilik more than once and could do his picture, too. Babies all look alike to me."

"Babies will be easier than Marek for the Descendants to hide," Galen said. "The Velekons will be looking for a ship with him on it."

When Arcas had settled into another trance, Rhia whispered to Galen, "How did the Descendants know where to find the newborns? There must have been a spy."

"Indeed. And I intend to find that spy." Galen picked up the tiny tube that would attach to the pigeon's leg, then reached out for Marek's picture. Rhia held on to it, searing her memory with the face she might never see again.

No. She would find him if it took the rest of her life.

Her fingers, no longer trembling, released the picture.

Nilik cried.

Marek shifted the boy from one aching arm to another to try to settle him, keeping his little face shielded from the night's bitter wind. The boat was rocking more, having hit a rapid stretch of river, and Marek had to concentrate to keep from sliding off the bench built into the stern.

He hoped the baby's noise would alert someone on the riverbank to their dilemma, assuming the sound of the water didn't smother it. But the soldiers—if that's what they were—shot Nilik a hostile glance every time he so much as gurgled. Marek wouldn't put it past the Descendants to throw a child overboard if it jeopardized their mission.

He crooned a nonsensical string of words to the baby, lilt-ing his voice the way Nilik seemed to like. But he knew that this particular cry, at this time of night, meant that nothing would soothe his son but food.

"Can't you shut him up?" asked the ugliest of the six sol-diers who flanked Marek—four on one side, two on the other, to balance the boat against the wind's pull.

"He's hungry," Marek said.

"So am I, but you don't hear me whining."

The other soldiers laughed, but silenced when the wom-an came out of the cabin below. She was dressed simply, in a long gray dress that covered her from neck to toes. When the wind tossed her dark hair across her face, she pulled a cowl over her head, making her look like a turtle with its nose poking out of its shell.

"I'll take him." As she reached for Nilik, her sleeves fell back to reveal slender wrists and hands. Marek reluctantly passed his son to her.

She sat beside him and unfastened the front of her dress so that Nilik could feed. Marek was half relieved and half dismayed at how willingly the child acquiesced. His tiny fist opened and closed as he drank. Two of the soldiers watched them, while the others scanned the riverbanks.

"I'm glad you're along," the woman said to Marek. "It will be less work for me. Four babies, one of them my own."

"What's your baby's name?" he asked in a whisper.

"Neyla. She's five months old."

"Pretty name. And yours?"

"Mila."

"Mila, I'm Marek. And this is—"

"Don't tell me his name."

"His name is Nilik."

She blinked hard. "Not for long."

"Is it easier for you not to know their names? That way you can't imagine the pain felt by the people who named them?"

"Stop it."

"His mother's name is Rhia. My wife. Think how she must feel." His throat closed for a moment. "Imagine if someone ripped your child out of your arms."

Mila trembled, hard enough that Nilik broke off and cried. Marek stroked his son's light brown tuft of hair. Soon the boy fed again, hunger overtaking fear for the moment.

Marek looked eastward to the lightening horizon. At this part of the river, a quarter of the way between Asermos and Velekos, the banks steepened. Memories from his trips south told him that cliffs would soon surround the channel, cutting them off from the stray hunters, fishers and trappers living between the villages. By the time the sun rose, if someone saw the abductors' vessel, there would be no way to reach them. The Descendants had timed their escape well.

Inside the boat, another child whimpered. Mila sighed. "Come with me," she said.

Marek helped her down the stairs into the cabin. One of the soldiers followed them, clasping Marek's shoulder tightly.

The close space felt suffocating, though it was warmly lit by lanterns fixed to the wall, one in each corner. An open doorway on the other side showed a small cockpit, where the captain, with one hand on the wheel, was leaning over a table to examine a chart. He didn't acknowledge Marek's and Mila's entrance.

One of the babies on the left berth was crying. Mila nodded to it. "See if she needs changing."

"She doesn't, I can smell." Marek pointed to the baby on their right, who slept alone. "That one needs changing."

"Then do it." She sank into a chair in the corner. "But first hand me Neyla. That's the crying one."

He did as she asked, exchanging Neyla for Nilik, whom he placed in the left bed. Then he found the babies' supplies in a wall compartment. Keeping one eye on Mila and the captain, he cleaned the squealing young Asermon.

"Did they kill this one's guardians?" he asked.

Mila looked at him, mouth open.

"They slaughtered an old woman to get Nilik," he told her. "Stabbed her in the stomach. Did you know that?"

She spoke to the captain. "Sareb, is that true?"

"Of course not," he said laconically, without looking up.

"Liar," Marek snarled. "What do you want from us?"

Sareb set down the chart with a sigh and turned to Marek. "We're just doing what we were hired to do, Mila and me. The others, they're following orders, like good little soldiers." He crossed his arms and leaned his shoulder against the door frame. "We don't want to hurt you, but we won't mind it, either."

Marek looked at the soldier by the door, who mirrored the captain's smirk. Swallowing the lump of rage in his throat, he reached for a clean diaper. He had to stay alive for his son. Based on how the Descendants had treated him in their army camp, Marek expected to be beaten or worse when they arrived in Leukos.

Whatever they had planned for Nilik would no doubt last the rest of his life.

For the first time, Filip heard Alanka coming before he saw her. Her feet scuffed the leaves as she shambled across the forest floor toward the edge of the meadow. Unlike the three other times they had met in secret, she wasn't trying to sneak up on him, nor did she wear her bow and arrows slung on her back.

She quickened her pace into a near trot when she saw him. A closer view revealed a face creased by the tracks of tears. He fought the urge to pull her into his arms. In the two weeks they'd known each other, he had yet to touch her except to help her onto horseback.

"Good morning," she said. Her gaze flitted to his face but didn't meet his eyes. "I'm glad you came."

He wanted to smile in response, but it didn't match her mood. "I'm glad you did, too."

She drew a loose strand of black hair behind her ear, tucking it into the braid that fell down her back, and said nothing more.

"I heard what happened to Marek and his son last night," he said. "I'm sorry."

"It didn't have to happen," she said softly.

"But Tereus said the kidnappers were armed."

She wiped at her face, though it was dry. "Let's go for a walk."

They crossed the meadow, their feet rustling through the brown grasses. Though their conversations usually flowed easily, hopping from topic to topic whenever a random thought entered Alanka's mind, this morning Filip couldn't think of a thing to say. He took her hand.

She stopped walking, and he cursed his mistake. Alanka turned to him and covered his hand with her other one, so that she was holding it in both her own. His breath quickened.

"Can I tell you something awful?" she said.

He nodded, unable to speak.

"Don't hate me afterward."

He shook his head.

"I could have stopped Marek's kidnappers. I followed him, I had a clean shot. I might have saved him." Her voice choked. "But I couldn't."

Filip tightened his grip on her hand. "Why not?"

"I aimed at my target, but I couldn't see him. All I saw was the battle. It was like I was there again. I could smell it, hear it, even taste it." Her mouth twisted, as though she had bitten rotten meat. "When it was over, when I could see Marek again, he was already on the boat. It was too late. I failed him."

"You might not have been able to save him if there were two soldiers. Or what if you'd missed and hit Marek?"

"I never miss. I mean, I never missed. Not when I had my Wolf powers."

A coldness seeped into Filip as he understood her words. "You've lost them?"

"Since that moment. I turned away from my Spirit brother in need, so Wolf left me." She rubbed her cheek. "I can't hear or smell very well anymore. I can't shoot a bow, I can't walk with stealth. I had just started getting better, since I met you. But now I'm back to— I'm just nothing."

"No." He lifted her chin to look in her eyes. "Whatever Wolf thinks, you have great power."

A tear dribbled onto her cheek. Instead of wiping it away, he pulled her to him, slowly, as though she could shatter. Alanka tucked her wet face against his neck and let him hold her close as sobs quaked her body. He stroked her hair, wondering how, at a moment like this, he could dare to feel so happy.

That night, Filip's dream of racing his brother through Letus Park ended in a new way.

At the head of the dock leading out into the man-made lake, where their races always ended with a leap into the water, stood a white horse. Not a spot of gray dappled its coat; not a strand of yellow sullied its mane. It gleamed pure alabaster in the afternoon sunlight, the breeze wafting its mane and tail like tufts of thistle. It wore no bridle or saddle and seemed untouched by humanity.

Filip stood alone in front of the horse. His brother had

disappeared. The mare's neck looked as soft as a cloud. He reached to stroke it.

"No," she said, "this cannot be yours."

His hands ached to touch her. "Not ever?"

"Not yet. You are not whole."

He lowered his gaze to his leg, which hung incomplete. "I know."

"Not because of that," she said, "but because you are alone. You don't have to be alone."

"But how do I—"

"They're waiting." The horse touched her velvet nose to his forehead.

He woke with a longing matched by confusion. Who was waiting? Had one of the gods sent the horse to his dream, or did the Spirits now control that realm of his life, too?

Tereus's snore came from the loft above. Filip found the sound comforting, for it meant he wasn't alone. It still felt odd not to be surrounded by hundreds or even thousands of men in an army camp or barracks.

His mind tripped over a sudden thought of Tereus, and his breath turned cold in his lungs. Third-phase Swans could alter a person's dreams. Perhaps his host had lodged the dream in Filip's mind to encourage him to undergo the Bestowing. Maybe the Asermons were waiting for him to become one of them.

Bolan had told him that some people wondered if Tereus had planted the Raven dreams to build up his daughter. But from what Filip knew of third-phase magic, it required exhausting amounts of power and held grave consequences even when used for good. And from what he knew of Tereus, the man preferred to persuade through heartfelt conversation, not devious manipulation.

Tomorrow night the Velekon pigeons would return with word of Marek's fate, which no doubt was taking place even as Filip lay here safe in his bed. If Marek and the baby weren't rescued, Alanka would leave the next morning for Leukos. She would walk the streets he'd trod since childhood. His home was part of him, one he wanted to share with her, one he had to share if she would ever understand him.

He rolled onto his side. The rough scars of his left leg scraped the sensitive skin behind his right knee, reminding him that no matter how much he longed for home, it would never be his again.

19

Just after Marek watched the last flickers of twilight fade into night, the village of Velekos appeared. About half the size of Asermos, it perched on the edge of Prasnos Bay. Lights glittered along its main thoroughfare near the docks.

The soldiers bound Marek's wrists as the boat entered the harbor. The sail flapped loud in the breeze as it was released to cut their speed.

Captain Sareb came out of the cabin, dressed in a long blue wool coat, the neatness of which accentuated his disheveled brown curls. "We're transferring to another ship," he told Marek. "One word or move on your part, and a baby goes in the harbor."

The boat slid closer to the dock, and Marek scanned the edge of the village for anyone who could help. The streets were empty for this time of night, and no one had entered or left a tavern in several minutes.

The hull hit the pier with a light thud. The captain and one of the soldiers scrambled over the deck, securing the boat to the dock posts.

Two soldiers flanked Marek, while the three others filed out of the cabin, Mila following. They each carried a baby basket. The baskets' covers had been drawn up, ostensibly to keep out the damp night wind, but Marek knew it was to keep him from knowing which child was his. If he got closer, he could sniff Nilik out of the group.

As if they understood this, the soldiers seized his shoulders and pushed him ahead. He stepped onto the dock, wobbling as he regained his land legs.

They proceeded down the long wooden pier. A larger, seafaring vessel sat several docks over, near the deeper end of the harbor. Ahead of him, Mila carried her basket close to her body, murmuring to the baby inside.

"We'll be home soon, Neyla," she whispered.

The three soldiers behind Marek held their baskets so that they dangled over the edge of the pier. He knew the children were too valuable to be discarded. But the thought of Nilik sinking to the harbor bottom suppressed Marek's itch to escape.

"Quickly," Sareb said once he and Mila had turned left off the pier. "I have a bad feeling about—"

A high-pitched zing sliced the air. Instinct made Marek duck into a crouch. A moment later, the soldiers flanking him fell to their knees with arrows protruding from their chests. Their mouths opened and closed as they clawed at the vibrating pieces of wood.

Mila screamed. Marek disappeared.

"Move!" Sareb yelled to the soldiers. "Let the man go. Keep those baskets over the water."

A teeth-gnashing, spine-rippling sound erupted from an alley between two taverns. Next to Nilik's first yelp of life, Marek had never heard anything as beautiful as this Wolverine war cry.

A band of Velekons emptied out of the alley and charged across the cobblestone streets. Marek reappeared before they could trample him.

"The woman carries her own child," he shouted as they passed. "Get the other three." One of the dagger-bearing Wolverines stopped to cut Marek's bindings before rejoining the charge. Marek vanished again and slunk closer to the soldiers, ready to dive into the water after any discarded infants.

The soldiers dropped their baskets, but on the dock, not in the harbor. They drew their swords.

The Velekons advanced, a half-dozen Bears in front with swords, flanked by several Wolverines, who cut off the three soldiers' paths of retreat. Marek crept forward and grabbed the closest basket, ready to reappear if any swords came too close. He carried it to safety two docks over, then turned to retrieve the next one.

Beyond the fight, Sareb pushed Mila ahead of him down the docks, their guard running behind them on the way to the larger ship. Marek wanted them brought to justice, but first he had to get his son back. He grabbed the second basket as its guardian's stomach took the sword of a Velekon Bear.

The last soldier turned to leap into the water, but he was yanked back by a dark-haired Wolverine, who shoved a long dagger up under his ribs. His feet kicked and twitched as he died.

Marek reappeared as he ran toward the soldier's basket. The Wolverine shoved the body onto the ground and turned to him.

"You must be Marek." He wiped his dagger on his trousers. "Can we see the Raven baby?"

Marek's mind boggled at the Wolverine's rapid change of focus. No doubt the prophecy had made it easy to gather forces for their rescue. "We don't know if he's the Raven baby, but yes, you can meet my son." He eyed the blood on the man's hands. "You can look at him from over there."

He flipped open the first basket. The Asermon boy stretched and gurgled, kicking at his blankets. Marek dashed to the second basket. It contained the Asermon girl, who had somehow slept through the chaos.

He ran down the pier to the last basket, the one he had grabbed first. His steps slowed suddenly.

That basket had been heavy.

A woman screamed from the ship. "My baby!" Mila cried.

Marek sank onto trembling knees next to the last basket. His blood seeped cold to his fingertips as he drew back the cover.

Neyla gazed up at him, then sneezed.

"No…" He crushed his hands against his eyes.

The Wolverine ran up. "What happened?"

"How could I be so stupid?"

He peered over Marek's shoulder. "That's not him?"

"This one belongs to the wet nurse." He stood and stared at the ship. "They still have my son."

"We got the wrong baby?" The Bear who'd led the charge stomped over to him. "I knew we should've taken them all, killed the woman if we had to."

The Wolverine scratched his head. "The captain must've switched the baskets without telling her. Clever."

Marek picked up Neyla's basket and walked toward the ship.

"Where are you going?" the Bear asked.

"To make a trade."

Behind him he heard the Bear order two of the men to take the Asermon babies into the tavern, and the rest to follow him. He caught up with Marek. Though he was probably in his midthirties, his stubbled, wind-roughened face looked much older. His clothes smelled of blood and pipe smoke.

"I'm Eneas. My sister Nadia's the Horse who got the pigeon message. Two birds came right before dark. We barely had enough time to gather these men, but it was enough, heh?"

"Not yet." Marek turned onto the long dock where the ship was anchored. "We don't have my son."

"I'm sure they'll trade. They won't leave one of their own behind." Eneas peeked at Neyla. "She's cute, that one."

Marek wanted to believe the Bear, wanted to hope that the woman's child was more important to the captain than the mission. But if Sareb had switched the baskets, as the Wolverine guessed, this was the scenario he'd planned for.

"Looking for this?"

Sareb stood on the deck of the ship, which loomed far higher than Marek could jump. The captain stepped forward with Nilik in his arms, suspending the boy over the water.

Marek's stomach froze. Sareb couldn't be shot without dropping the child into the harbor. The impact alone from that height could kill the boy.

"I'll trade you," Marek said. "My child for yours."

Sareb laughed. "She's not mine. You can keep her."

"No!" Mila ran to the railing and clung to it as someone tried to drag her away from behind. "Give me back my baby!" she cried to Marek. "Please!"

Marek forced out the words. "Only if you give me mine."

"Sorry," the captain said. "I get paid to bring home Asermon babies, not Ilion babies. Your son could be our one chance."

"Chance for what?"

"For whatever it is they want babies for. I don't ask for answers, just payment." Sareb shifted Nilik in his arms, and the boy shrieked. Mila joined in, clutching the railing.

Eneas leaned close to Marek. "We could try to overrun the ship."

"If we attack, he'll drop Nilik. Besides, look." He pointed to the other end of the ship, where a line of soldiers were taking their places at the railing. "There could be a hundred more down below. You might not even get to him before you're all killed."

"Then what do you suggest?"

Marek drew a deep breath and picked up Neyla's basket.

"Take the other babies back to Asermos. Tell my wife—" He stopped, combing his mind for a message that would comfort her. "Tell her I'll protect our son. Whatever it takes."

The Bear nodded, face grim, and clasped Marek's shoulder. "Good luck to you."

Marek stepped onto the gangplank and boarded the ship.

20

Coranna's funeral pyre sat in a clearing north of Asermos, a space usually used for celebration bonfires. The morning of the funeral, Rhia stood in a clearing with her father, thinking of the weddings, birthdays and solstices she had attended there. Her memories turned as gray as the rain-swollen sky.

Only Kalindons burned instead of buried their dead—due to their rocky soil, but also to their desire to unite with the trees and the air in one final act. For the sake of the Asermons, Damen had prepared Coranna's body as if for burial, wrapping it in strips of scented, ritually blessed cloth.

She lay now inside the pyre, which rested on flat stones to keep the blaze from spreading to the grass. A pile of dry juniper branches sat off to the side, and torches flickered at each corner of the pyre.

"Damen set all this up in one day?" Tereus asked.

"He's presided over many funerals in Velekos." Rhia heard her own reply as if someone else had said it. Her mind kept flying down the river to the bayside village where Marek had been rescued, or not, last night. She wanted to scream at the sky to speed up time, for the sun to sink and make it evening, when the Velekon pigeons would arrive with news of their fate.

Tereus spoke again, bringing her back to the present. "Did Damen send word to Coranna's grandchildren in Tiros?"

"Yes, we apologized for not delaying the funeral until they could arrive. But we have to be ready to leave in the morning."

"Are you?"

She nodded. If he asked her one more question, she would explode.

Tereus touched her arm. "Your band of rescuers is here."

The friends she'd gathered for the mission were climbing the hill to the clearing, walking together as if already bonded by the trials ahead.

Her brother Lycas approached first, giving her a strong, wordless embrace.

"What did Mali say?" she asked him.

"She said if I leave her now, I should never come back."

"Oh." Rhia's heart twisted. Without her brother's power and ferocity, how could they overcome Marek's captors?

"With any luck," he said, "she'll miss me so much while I'm gone that she'll change her mind by the time we return."

Rhia hugged him again. "I'm sorry."

"Anyone who respects family loyalty as little as that

woman does can—" He gritted his teeth. "Never mind. It was a bad idea from the beginning, me and Mali."

The rest of them approached her one by one with quiet embraces. Arcas had insisted on joining them, because even though he had turned out to be a Spider, he'd trained his whole life as a Bear and thus could wield a sword almost as well as a natural-born soldier. Koli the Bat owned the boat they'd be taking to Velekos. Her stealth powers, scout experience and sensitive hearing would help them gather information. She was also the fastest rider Rhia knew. Bolan would come, as well, bearing pigeons who would fly home to Asermos so the troupe could relay messages in an emergency. Finally, Alanka's skill with a bow had few rivals. She could hunt food for them on the journey and help ward off attackers.

Damen beckoned Rhia from the pyre. His dark eyes scanned the heavy clouds as she approached. "Everything's set," he said, "as long as the weather holds."

She picked up his white ceremonial robe from the top of the pyre, then held it so he could insert his arms. Its sleeves bore two rows of crow feathers.

He turned to let Rhia fasten the robe behind his back. "I'm going to miss her." His voice was flat, as if he were observing his emotions instead of feeling them. "She was a good friend."

"She never felt like a friend to me," Rhia said. "More like a mother, though she was nothing like my real mother."

"She worried about you."

"Why?"

"She said you could be one of the most powerful Crows in a long time, if you'd only follow the rules."

"Instead of thinking for myself."

"It's never that simple. You'll understand when you're older. You can't make the world the way you want it to be."

Rhia's lip curled. She wanted to slap him. "I'm learning that very well now, thank you."

He was silent for a moment, perhaps realizing the carelessness of his remark. "I think that more than anything, she wanted your trust."

"Which I never gave her, not completely. Now it's too late." She turned to the pyre. "How did you die?"

The question seemed to startle him. "I've never talked about that with anyone."

She waited, not taking back the question.

He touched the handle of one of the tall torches. "I froze."

"Me, too."

He nodded. "But you thawed."

She watched the flame flicker against the dark clouds. "Maybe I was never meant to."

Rhia stood with her family, listening to Damen's eulogy.

"Thank you for coming today to say goodbye to a woman many of you never met. You honor Coranna's Spirit with your presence." He paused. "The Aspect of Crow is one of the rarest. Like most third-phase Crows, Coranna had no one to teach her except the Spirit Himself. Few have adhered so tenaciously to their Spirit's principles. Kalindos—indeed, the world itself—has lost one of its most valuable citizens."

Damen glanced at Rhia. She should say something about the person Coranna was, especially after Damen's dry tribute. She stepped forward. "Many people found it hard to get close to Coranna. She acted proud of the distance she kept from others. She said it was the only way to fulfill a Crow's duty, to pretend to ourselves that we don't care, that we don't hurt.

"I think she hurt." Rhia's throat ached. "I know she cared. Cared so much about doing right by others that she shoved her own feelings deep inside her. She did it not out of pride, but love."

Instead of stepping back into the crowd, Rhia joined Damen at the pyre to sing home Coranna's soul.

They began to chant, a rousing song that would last until at least one crow came into sight, cawed and flew away, symbolizing the flight of Coranna's Spirit to the Other Side.

It appeared quickly, beckoned as it was by Crow's own servants. It cut a harsh shadow against the muted gray sky as it flapped low across the clearing.

Though the bird was alone now, it would soon fly home to its mate, perhaps feed a brood of hungry mouths. Tonight it would share a warm, safe nest with its family. Envy sparked inside Rhia.

They ended the chant as the crow flew away. It was time to burn.

Damen and Rhia each took a torch and touched it to the bottom of the pyre. The oil-soaked wood lit with a sudden wisp of dark smoke. The flames licked at the dry slats, and as they climbed to the top of the pyre, they seemed to form a living creature made of pure heat. Sparks snapped and popped, and Rhia blinked hard with each loud report.

As the flames crept closer to the body, the crowd edged backward. Now the juniper branches were ablaze, releasing a pungent scent that would mask much of the odor of burning flesh.

Rhia wanted to run forward and douse the flames before it was too late.

But it was already too late. Through the flames she could see the strips of cloth curling, blackening.

Tears swelled behind her eyelids. As she reached to wipe them, a voice inside her whispered, *No.*

She closed her eyes. *Is that you?* She reached out for her Spirit, fearing the voice was Skaris again, returning to haunt her now that her guard was down.

It's me, Crow said, His presence like a warm dark cloak around her. *You don't have to be like those who came before. Tears don't make a person weak.*

Her chest ached. *But Crows are supposed to turn off the pain.*

In the past, perhaps. But the Spirits' ways are changing.

Does this have to do with Raven? she asked. *Will Nilik have Her Aspect?*

He was silent for a moment. *I don't know. Of all the Spirits, only She can see the future clearly. She's told each of us, "make your people ready."*

A thrill coursed through Rhia's blood, part fear, part hope. *Ready for what?*

Crow chuckled. *Didn't I just say I couldn't see the future clearly?*

Sorry.

Stay who you are, Rhia. Only more so.

As she felt Crow's presence fade, her tears began to flow. She didn't stanch them or even wipe them away.

When she opened her eyes, Damen was staring at her across the pyre. His eyes shone, though perhaps they only watered from the sting of heat and stench.

Finally the fire smoldered and sputtered, and the flames receded to reveal what was left of Coranna's body—many small bone fragments amid a pile of light gray ashes. Damen turned and thanked the crowd in a muted voice. Most of the people headed back toward the village, some steadying their queasy companions.

Alanka hurried up to hug Rhia. "I'm proud of you both. That couldn't have been easy."

"It had to be done." Damen picked up an urn and a small brush. "That's all."

Alanka grimaced at Damen's stoicism. He knelt and swept a tiny amount of ashes into the urn. The ashes would return to Kalindos to hang from the tree where Coranna had lived.

Rhia turned back to Alanka. "I wish I could say I thought of nothing but Coranna."

"I worry about them, too." She rubbed her elbows and gazed southwest, toward the river. "It's hard waiting."

Rhia watched the last curls of smoke rise from the pyre and wondered what she was waiting for—the news of Marek and Nilik's rescue or the signal to rescue them herself.

By nightfall she would know.

21

Alanka scanned the pale gray evening sky above Tereus's house for any sign of the white birds. Rhia quickened her pace as they trudged up the hill to her father's farm.

Behind them, Bolan cleared his throat. "The pigeons won't arrive until almost nightfall, especially after the rain we had." He paused. "They might not come until tomorrow."

Rhia turned on him. "Don't say that!"

The other members of the rescue party fell silent. Even Lycas held back his usual teasing.

Alanka almost whispered a prayer to Wolf to keep Marek safe before remembering that her Spirit had abandoned her. She had to concentrate to maintain a Wolf person's graceful gait and not trip over her own feet. The air smelled as stale as a stone.

Tereus was pacing outside his front door when they arrived. Angry voices shot through the open window.

"Don't go in there," he told them.

"What's happening?" Rhia's voice snapped taut.

"Galen suspects Filip in the kidnappings."

"I knew it." Lycas slammed his fist into his palm. "Let me see him."

"No!" Alanka said. "It can't be him."

Tereus gave her a curious look before turning back to Rhia. "Galen thinks he might have been spying for the Descendants, telling them where the newborns lived."

"How would he know that?" Bolan said.

"He spent weeks in that hospital," Lycas pointed out. "He probably overheard Zelia talking about other patients."

"Father, is it possible?" Rhia asked. "Could he do this to us, after we helped him?" Her voice pitched higher. "How could he?"

"He didn't," Alanka insisted, but no one listened.

"I never would have thought him capable of such a thing." Tereus rubbed the back of his neck. "But he's disappeared on several occasions in the last few weeks, for hours at a time."

The noise inside rose. "Where were you?" shouted a rough voice. "If you weren't meeting a Descendant spy, then where were you?"

Bolan huffed. "Galen brought Badgers to question him?"

"I was riding," Filip told his interrogators in a loud, firm tone.

"He's lying," said another man, "but not entirely."

Galen spoke in a measured tone. "Filip, did anyone see

you on these outings? Did you meet anyone in town or in the woods?"

Alanka crept closer to the window to hear his reply.

"No," Filip said. "I was alone."

"That's not true!" Alanka pushed past Tereus and opened the door. The five men inside gaped at her. Filip sat in a chair between two Badgers wearing the armbands of the Asermon police force. One of them was Medus, the man who had listened to her story two nights ago. Next to Galen stood a man she didn't recognize, wearing an owl feather fetish. He'd no doubt been employed to detect Filip's lies.

"He was with me," she said.

"What?" Lycas followed her in, banging the door into the wall behind it. "You and him? My sister and a Descendant?"

"Your sister and an *Ilion,* yes." She squared her shoulders. "And why not?"

Lycas blinked rapidly. "Alanka, his people destroyed your village, slaughtered your elders."

"They're not his people. He's not one of them."

"She's right." Filip glared at Lycas, then stood and moved to the trunk at the foot of his bed. "And clearly, I'm not one of you, either." He lifted the trunk's lid.

Alanka went to his side. "What are you doing?"

"Packing."

Her stomach flipped and twisted. "You're leaving?"

He looked at her, then at Galen. "Are we finished? I'd like to speak with her alone."

Galen turned to Alanka. "Will you swear by your Spirit that Filip was with you on the days in question?"

She worried her doubt would show, since she couldn't

swear by a Spirit she didn't have. Nonetheless, Alanka recounted the instances when she and Filip had met, where they had gone and for how long. She ignored her brother seething near the door.

The Owl appraised her, arms crossed over his broad chest. "The facts she relates are true."

Medus sighed. "It must have been the other Descendant, then. The one who ran away." The Badger gave Filip a grudging nod. "Sorry."

Filip's jaw clenched, and he didn't reply.

Galen rubbed his chin hard, clearly vexed. "Filip, why would the Descendants want to kidnap the children? Is it to see how we develop powers? It's not for the sake of cruelty, is it?"

"Why not?" Lycas said. "They're capable of anything."

Filip spoke to Galen. "I've never heard of such plans, but I was a junior cavalry officer, not exactly privy to secret strategic planning. Besides, I haven't been home in over a year, and no, I haven't been meeting with spies."

The other man looked at the Owl, who nodded. "I sense no treachery in this regard."

"My apologies, Filip." Galen gave a slight bow, then turned to Alanka. "We'll wait outside for the birds to return."

They left Alanka and Filip alone, though it took both Badgers to drag Lycas out of the house.

She turned to Filip. "Please don't leave."

"I can't stay, no matter how much you make me want to."

"Why not?"

"They only accept me when I serve their purposes." He

jabbed his finger to his temple. "Peering into the depraved mind of a 'Descendant.'"

"Maybe that's true of Galen, but what about Tereus? What about Bolan?" She took his hand. "What about me?"

"You're different. So is Bolan. Maybe Rhia, too. As for Tereus—I thought he trusted me, after all these months living in his home. But I saw the doubt in his eyes today. He actually thought I might be capable of hurting children." His lips tightened, and he let go of her hand. "I can't forgive that."

"His grandson was taken. He's probably not the best judge of character right now. Remember, he wouldn't have brought you here in the first place if he didn't have good instincts about you."

"But the others—you didn't see the way they looked at me. I'll never be anything but a Descendant here." He turned back to the trunk and sifted through his clothes.

"So where will you go?"

"Tiros. I hear people there leave each other alone."

"Is that what you want? To be left alone?"

"Sometimes." He folded a pair of trousers and tossed them on the bed.

Alanka slammed the trunk shut. "What about other times?"

He reached to open the trunk again, but she kept her hand on it. He straightened and faced her. "Other times, I want other things."

The intensity of his gaze told her what some of those things were. "I don't belong here, either," she said. "Soon I'll go home to Kalindos, unless the birds bring bad news, in which case I'll go to Leukos." She moved closer, until they were almost touching. "Will you come with me?"

His eyes widened, then their corners drooped. "I'm not made to climb trees anymore."

"I mean, to Leukos. If we go, will you help us find Marek?"

"Why would I want to help Marek? He's the one who sedated the battle horses so I had to fight on foot. He's the cause of all this." He gestured to his leg and his surroundings. "If it weren't for him I'd be home with my family, or on another campaign, serving my country with honor."

"Or maybe you'd be dead, or still have one-and-a-half legs. You can't know the Spirits' plan for your life. Maybe there's a reason you're here." She laced her fingers with his and lowered her voice. "If you hate Marek, then don't do it for him. Do it for yourself."

"Myself?"

"Don't you want to prove that not all Ilions are ruthless and cruel?"

"That's what I've been trying to do, but I can't make these people believe what they refuse to see."

She combed her mind for another argument. "This would be your chance to leave Asermos and go home. That's what you want, isn't it?"

"Haven't you been listening? I can't go home."

"Maybe not as the man you used to be. But you can learn to be someone else. I'll help you. We all will."

He pulled away. "You ask too much."

"Fine!" The strength of her dismay shocked her. "Don't do it for yourself, then. Do it for me."

He turned to her, mouth open.

Alanka struggled to explain. "Ever since the battle, I can't feel myself. I can't remember who I am. But when I'm with you—I remember." She sat on his trunk and crossed her arms. "I don't know yet what we have, but I know I don't want you out of my life. I realize it's a lot to ask of a man. Call me selfish if you want, but there it is."

He stared at her for a long moment. "Not selfish, brave. Braver than I am." He sat next to her. "I don't want to lose you, either. But—"

"I see it!" Bolan shouted from outside. "It's coming!"

Alanka jolted but stayed put.

She turned to her argument of last resort. "Filip, you told me you were bound by loyalty to me, because I saved your life. Did you mean it, or were you just being polite?"

His head jerked up. "Of course I meant it. I'm in your debt forever."

"Then will you help us?" she whispered.

He looked at the window, his gaze far away, then nodded. "I'll do what I can."

"Thank you." She kissed him on the cheek. "Let's go."

They hurried out of the house and scanned the southwestern horizon. A white pigeon flapped toward them over the tops of the pines, like a tiny cloud skittering against the slate-gray sky. Filip and Alanka ran to the roost at the side of the stable. The others waited, peering up.

Alanka went to Rhia, who was twisting her fists inside the hem of her blouse.

The bird alighted on its cage and pushed its way inside,

where a tin of food awaited it. Bolan walked forward, holding up a hand to the others.

"Give her a moment," he said. "She can't think of anything but eating right now."

When the pigeon stopped wolfing down her grain and was pecking at it more judiciously, Bolan reached inside, grasped her and pulled her out. He held the pigeon up to his face and spoke somberly. "What happened? What did the Horse woman tell you to tell me?"

The pigeon cooed and clucked. Alanka glanced at Filip for a clue, but his brow creased as if he only understood half of what was said.

Bolan broke into a wide smile, and a gasp of relief flooded the small crowd. Rhia grabbed Alanka in a hard embrace. Alanka looked to the sky and whispered thanks to any Spirit who might be listening.

Over Rhia's shoulder, Alanka saw Bolan's smile fade. She let go of Rhia and turned her to face the Horse.

"I don't understand," he said to the pigeon. "Repeat that last part. He got back on the ship?"

"What?" Rhia said. "Why would he—"

"Shh." Bolan gave her a warning glance. "It's complicated, and the bird keeps mixing things up and putting them in the wrong order. I hope, at least."

Tereus pointed to the sky. "There's another one!"

A blue-gray pigeon with iridescent neck feathers flapped over the stable and landed on top of the roost.

Bolan handed off the white pigeon to Tereus, then grabbed the gray one. "I'm sorry, I know you're hungry, but tell me what happened. From the beginning. Slowly."

This time as the homing pigeon spoke, Bolan kept his expression flat. His face almost looked trancelike. Alanka looked at Filip, who pressed his lips tight, as if trapping a hard truth.

Finally Bolan set the bird in the cage, then turned to the others.

"I'm not sure of the particulars, but it sounds like two of the Asermon babies were rescued." He turned to Rhia. "But not Nilik. Marek went back aboard the ship to be with his son. The ship left for Leukos."

Rhia quaked, and instinct made Alanka step away.

"No!" Rhia advanced on Bolan. "How could they rescue the others and not Nilik? What went wrong? What happened?"

"I—I'm not sure," he said. "Something about baby baskets being switched."

"I'll find out myself when I get to Velekos." She turned to the others. "We leave at daybreak."

22

Late the following morning, Rhia knelt with Damen on a pair of brown woolen rugs in the tiny cabin of Koli's sailboat. Alanka was perched cross-legged on one of the two berths, a drum between her knees.

It was time to speak to the dead.

"The first time with the thanapras can be strange," Damen said, and Rhia sensed it was one of his typical understatements. "If you feel like you're floating away, concentrate on the drum and remember that it's here in our world, the world where you belong."

Rhia felt queasy at the thought of addressing the dead, but it may have been the rocking of the boat on the river's gentle waves.

Damen lit the bundle of thanapras and placed it in a clay bowl on the floor between the two rugs. Rhia lay on her rug and closed her eyes. Even before he began the chant, she could feel the controlled power pouring from him.

His deep voice made the air vibrate and dance against her skin. The herb had already swollen her mind, mingling the real and the unreal. Crow's presence loomed closer, but out of reach.

Damen finished the chant. Rhia felt the movement of air against her as he shifted to lie down. Alanka began to drum. Rhia's muscles and consciousness sank into the floor as she focused on the quick, steady beat.

The thanapras filled her senses, creating a scent she could almost see on the back of her eyelids, swirling, dancing to the drumbeat, carrying her to another realm.

She slid into a fog.

The fog thickened, then thinned to reveal a dry, dead valley. A single bare tree reached its black branches to the side like arms. An invisible sun poured a dull orange over the rocks, which seemed to hold no color of their own. Damen stood beside her.

"Where are they?" she thought to him. They would speak in their minds to avoid Alanka's ears.

"Call out one of their names and ask them to speak."

She decided to start with the Kalindon Council leader instead of the dreaded Skaris. "Zilus!" she shouted in her mind.

Zilus appeared, sitting on a rock half her height, about twenty paces away. Yellow-gray curls danced below his shoulders and around his head in a wind she couldn't feel.

In his hands he held a writhing snake. Rhia stepped back.

"Where have you been?" he asked her. "We used to sense you constantly."

She tore her gaze from the snake and found the breath to speak. "Early in my pregnancy I couldn't shut you out. Later it became easier, especially after—" She didn't want to say Nilik's name in this place. "After my son was born. I meant no offense in ignoring you."

"None taken." He stood and moved toward her, squeezing the serpent behind the head. Its contortions increased, as though it were in pain. "I wouldn't want to hear from me, either."

"You're in this place by your own choice," Rhia said, as gently as her horror would allow. "Do you understand that?"

"Yes." He shifted his hands until he held the snake by the tip of its tail, at arm's length. It wriggled and spun and gnashed its teeth at him. "I like it here."

"Who do you have?" she asked. "Is that the man who killed you? Is that his Spirit?"

"You like it? It's mine, but I'll let you share it if you stay with us." He dropped the snake in the dust. Before it could slither away, he stepped on its neck. Its tail slashed the air, and its mouth opened in a soundless hiss.

"No. Thank you." She fought to keep the disgust out of her voice. "I'm here to help you get out."

"Did I say I wanted to leave?" Zilus gestured to his surroundings. "It's not that bad. Not when I have something to play with." He picked up one end of the snake in each hand, let it fall slack like a rope and made a motion to tear it in half.

"Stop!" she cried. "Let me speak to someone else."

"Thought you'd never ask," said a deep voice to her left. She turned to see Skaris. Her old enemy stood before her as she remembered him—a dark, husky Bear who carried his bulk as though he needed no other weapon. His hands were behind his back. She knew what he held there but didn't want to see.

"Marek attacked you because you tried to poison me," she told him. "He was protecting his mate."

"I couldn't hurt you, locked up in my home awaiting trial. Marek acted out of vengeance. Everyone knew it, but they let him walk free." He took a step closer to loom over her. "I told Coranna and this one—" he nodded to Damen "—and they did nothing."

"There was no proof other than your word."

"Bears don't accidentally fall off cliffs. No one looked into my death because they were happy to get rid of me. I'd killed an elder, after all, but that wasn't my fault. Razvin switched the cups so that Etar would die instead of you."

"How did you know that? Who told you?"

"I did." The smooth-as-oil voice behind her could only belong to Razvin, father to Alanka and Rhia's half brothers.

Rhia turned to him. He held a sleeping wolf pup in his arms, scratching its scruff. His long black hair swept the gray fur, making the pup's ears twitch.

"I saw you die," she said.

"So sorry." The Fox's tone was as suave in death as in life. "Couldn't have been pleasant for you. Certainly wasn't for me."

She was glad Alanka couldn't hear even the Crows' side of the conversation. If she knew her father wasn't resting peacefully on the Other Side, she would sink further into the haze that had plagued her since the invasion of Kalindos.

Rhia looked at the wolf pup in his arms. "Is that the Spirit of the soldier who killed you at the river?"

"Soldier?" He turned the pup on its back and rubbed its belly. The wolf stretched and yawned, tongue curling over its triangular baby teeth. "Don't you recognize her?"

"Her?" Rhia looked at Damen, who shook his head sadly. "What's he talking about?"

"Not all soul theft is malevolent," Damen said. "Some people just want to hold on to those they love."

Rhia fought to control her breath, even as her pulse sped up. "Alanka?" she whispered to the pup.

"Of course," Razvin said. "Can you think of a better reason for staying in a forsaken place like this?"

She held out her trembling arms. "Let me hold her."

The Fox turned away, dark eyes flashing. "She's mine."

"Razvin, your daughter suffers."

"It was her choice to fight in that battle. I raised her to be peaceful. I raised her to be Kalindon. But no, she had to go and kill for you, for your degenerate village."

Anger boiled within her. "Don't you care what you've done to her?"

"Of course. I love her."

Damen stepped closer to Rhia. "We've found that pronouncing judgment gets us nowhere."

She turned on her Crow brother. "Oh, you've *found* that, have you? You knew he had a part of Alanka, and you didn't tell her. You didn't even tell me."

"Because you would have told her."

"Of course I would! She has the right to know." A thought dawned upon her. "Is that what Coranna meant when she said, 'Don't tell'?"

"Perhaps." He took her arm and led her away from the dead men. "I've been trying for months to convince Razvin to let Alanka go. I've made progress, which you're about to undo."

She shook off his hand and pointed to the wolf pup, who lay limp in Razvin's arms. "That doesn't look like progress."

"Maybe not to you, but once you learn the proper procedures—"

"There's no time. Alanka needs her strength. We all need her strength. He's stolen it, and I'm going to get it back." She stalked toward Razvin. "Give her to me."

"You can't make me."

"You're in my realm," she told him, "and you'll do as I say."

"Not so cocky, little one." Skaris stepped between them. "Even a Crow's wings can be clipped."

He took his hands from behind his back. He held a crow upside down by the feet. It flapped and struggled, small black pinfeathers scattering in a cloud around it. Its beak opened wide, trying to peck at the hands that bound it.

Rhia reached out, unable to form the words.

"Come and get it," Skaris said. He ran.

She chased him through the rocky valley, Damen's shouts fading far behind her. They ran for what felt like hours, but the landscape never changed and her legs never tired. With every step, the Bear pulled farther away. Her feet could move no faster than the drumbeat tethering her to the other world. She couldn't let go of that sound, had to hold it inside herself or risk getting lost here forever.

Skaris disappeared over the endless horizon, but Rhia kept running. He'd have to stop one of these days, one of these years. When he did, she would steal back the crow, and be whole again.

As she ran, the rocks began to feel like markers showing the hours and days passing. Was she moving through a place or through time? Only Raven could move through time, but what if Rhia had been in this place for years? What if when she returned, everyone she loved had died?

She stopped and listened for the drum. It came from her right. She moved toward it, following the beats like stones on a path. It drew her on, giving her strength to resist the pull of Skaris and the treasure he held.

The dark tree appeared again, its branches pointing to the fog between two boulders. Damen stepped from the fog and held out his hand.

"This way," he said. "I'll help you."

She swallowed her resentment and took his hand. The fog grew so thick, it was like breathing wool. She tried to pull back, but Damen yanked her arm.

Rhia opened her eyes to the pale ceiling of the boat cabin. The thanapras stung her nostrils.

The drumbeat stopped, and Rhia remembered Alanka. She sat up and clutched the berth in a wave of dizziness.

"Are you all right?" Alanka said.

Rhia looked at Damen through blurry eyes. "I have to tell her."

He crammed the smoldering thanapras in a bowl of water

to douse it. "Do what you need to do." He jerked open the door and went outside to the crowded deck.

"Tell me what?" Alanka said.

Rhia clambered onto the berth beside her, head swimming. She took a deep breath, wondering how to start. "You've been…out of sorts for a long time, haven't you?"

Alanka shifted away a little. "A bit."

"Now I know why."

Rhia explained everything while Alanka listened, wide-eyed.

"Thank you for telling me," she said when Rhia was done. "I thought I was crazy. I thought it was my fault."

Rhia took her limp hand. "None of this is your fault."

"Why didn't Damen tell me?"

"Maybe he wanted to protect you. Maybe he thought he could solve your problem."

"Can he? Can you?"

Rhia trembled inside at the thought of returning to the Gray Valley. "I'll try my best."

"When?"

"Tonight. Tomorrow. Every day until I get it back. See, you're not the only one missing a part of herself. Skaris has a piece of my soul."

Alanka gasped, then her face turned puzzled. "But you haven't been like me. Not as bad."

"I've been angry. Now more than ever. Maybe different people take different parts of others. Your father took your fire, your passion. Skaris took something else from me." She shoved her hair out of her face. "I'm tired of feeling nothing but fire."

"I'm tired of feeling nothing." Alanka sat for a long moment, running her teeth over her upper lip. "It doesn't explain everything. When I came to Asermos, I felt better, especially after I met Filip. I felt like myself again. Not all the time, but sometimes." Alanka swallowed hard. "But the night Marek was taken…I couldn't save him."

"Of course you couldn't." Rhia put a hand on her arm. "He was too close to the soldiers for you to shoot them."

Alanka hesitated. "I lied. I had a clear shot, and if I'd gotten one of them, Marek could've disarmed the other. He was probably waiting for me to shoot."

Rhia's skin prickled. "Why didn't you?"

"I aimed at the soldiers, and suddenly…my mind came loose. All I could see were the men I killed on the battlefield. It was like I was right back there with death and blood all around me. When it was over, Marek was already on the boat." She put her face in her hands. "I'm so sorry, Rhia. I failed you. I failed Marek. So Wolf took away my powers, and now I'm useless."

Rhia barely heard Alanka's last sentence. She wanted to grab her by the shoulders and shake her. "Why didn't you tell me before?"

"I was ashamed, and I didn't want you to feel guilty. It was your war that made me this way." She pounded her fists against her thighs. "But it was my choice to help. I don't blame you."

"Are you sure?"

"You didn't force me to fight. I came out of loyalty to you and my brothers. And maybe because my father was the one who caused it all. I wanted to prove I wasn't like him."

Rhia reined in her frustration, remembering the wolf pup in Razvin's arms. "I think that's why he's taken your soul piece. He wants a link to you, but he's also angry you went to battle."

Alanka's mouth dropped open. "*He's* angry with *me*? How dare he?"

"Exactly."

She drew in a quick breath. "If my father lets go of my soul part, will I get my powers back?"

"Maybe. But maybe not. Just because it's all connected doesn't mean there's one solution. What happened to you on the battlefield would have been enough to damage even a whole, complete soul."

Alanka nodded. "Filip called it battle shock. Sometimes it happens to real warriors, too."

"You're a real warrior, Alanka." Rhia sighed. "We all are now."

23

Alanka was grateful to leave the crowded boat that night when Koli anchored it in a calm tributary of the Velekon River. They made camp on the banks to avoid traveling the river's rocky portion in the dark, and to give each other much-needed space. In another hour, Alanka figured, Lycas and Filip would have thrown each other overboard.

Soon a fire was burning, and the eight travelers gathered around it. They roasted potatoes and ate fresh spring greens with the dried venison Tereus had packed. After dinner, Arcas led them in a series of songs to lift their moods and beseech the Spirits' goodwill. As he sang, he worked on his latest wood carving, which turned out to be a bat. He offered it to Koli, who did a poor job of feigning indifference.

Alanka sat next to Filip and stole glances at him when she thought he wasn't looking. The firelight glinted off his golden hair and ruddy skin, and created shadows in the hollows of his cheekbones and the sockets of his deep-set eyes—eyes that regarded everyone but her and Bolan with distrust.

He caught her glance and motioned behind him to indicate he wanted to speak with her alone. Or maybe he was just embarrassed because he didn't know the words to the songs.

They walked along the riverbank until they were out of range of even the most sensitive ears. Alanka sat on a mossy log. The dampness seeped through her trousers, and she wished she'd brought a blanket, though that would have spiked her brother's suspicions about what they planned to do upon it.

Filip sat beside her. "I was thinking about your power loss and other ways to remedy it. If this soul-capture procedure doesn't work."

"Soul retrieval." She hated to correct him and was flattered he'd been considering her dilemma.

"Have you considered a sacrifice to the Wolf Spirit? In my country, we slaughter an animal and dedicate it to the god we want to favor us."

"Before you eat the animal, you mean?"

"We don't eat it."

"Sounds wasteful."

"That's the whole point." He lifted a palm to the sky. "It's a tribute, showing the gods that they're so important, we'd in essence give them food from our own table."

"So they can eat it."

"No, gods don't eat." Frustration tinged his voice. "They're not human."

"I know, but—I don't understand. It seems so pointless, so impractical."

"Why should faith be practical?"

She rubbed her arms, which had grown cold. "You still believe in your gods? Now that you know the Spirits are real?"

He nodded, and she wished for enough light to read the emotion in his eyes. "My beliefs haven't changed," he said. "Except that I'm no longer certain that the Spirits are evil agents of chaos, like I was taught growing up." He turned to her. "What do you think of my suggestion?"

"Making a sacrifice?" She shook her head. "Even if I could catch a rabbit or a bird right now, Wolf wouldn't want it. He cares about what's inside me, and right now what's inside me is a mess."

"I know."

"Thank you for not denying it. Everyone wants me to be fine, so I pretend I am. That way I don't let them down more than I already have."

"Shh." He slid his hand over hers. "You don't have to pretend with me."

Her chest tightened with the ache of true connection. She wanted more than anything to kiss him, but something in his manner curbed her. She was confident he wasn't a lover of men like Damen, but Filip treated her so cautiously, it made her wonder at the level of his desire.

"I have another idea," Filip said, breaking her contemplation. "My people undergo initiation rituals when they become warriors."

"So do mine. The Wolverines and Bears and Wasps."

"But not Wolves?"

"Wolves are hunters," she said, "not warriors."

"Everyone's a warrior when their land is threatened, when their lives are at stake."

"That's what Rhia said, but it felt wrong." She tapped a fist to her chest. "Down in my blood it felt wrong."

"But think of Marek. He's a Wolf, and he killed a Descendant face-to-face, like a man."

She snorted. "As opposed to the womanly piercing of flesh with arrows?"

"Well…yes."

"Is that why your people don't have archers? Not manly enough?"

"Yes, but—" He waved his hand. "Back to the subject. The problem, as I see it, is that you've never honored the warrior in yourself. Not only that, you were never purified after the battle."

"Purified…" The word slid over her tongue like a pat of butter. "I wish we had been purified, instead of just going back to our lives."

"Which have no delineation from war. In Leukos, military uniforms are forbidden within the city gates. Before entering after a campaign, we lay down our weapons, then we're scrubbed clean with hot water and salts, so as not to taint our city's streets with the blood we've shed."

"How do you keep order if no one's armed? Asermos has a police force, mostly Bobcats and Badgers."

"I know," he said quietly. "Those Bobcats shot my comrades in the back when they tried to escape."

"I'm sorry."

"Anyway, in Leukos, we also have police, but they're

completely segregated from the military. Retired officers from one can't join the other. If I were to return home—" The muted hint of pain in his voice made her want to fold him into her arms. "Even if I were whole, I couldn't join the police force."

"Why not?"

"They'd think me too violent, too brutish."

"You don't seem brutish to me." She reached forward and swept an imaginary leaf off his shoulder. "You seem quite…restrained."

He glanced at the place where she had touched him, then returned his gaze to her face, more intense than ever. "Be assured, whatever restraint I show around you is merely a measure of the force it contains."

Her lips parted instinctively, the better to smell his desire and fear and see which was winning. But her powers were lost, so she would have to guess. "I admire your discipline."

"A warrior shows control when control is called for." He dipped his head and kissed her cheek. The warmth of his lips sent a shock snaking down her spine. "And shows abandon when…"

He grasped her face and melded his mouth with hers. She moaned, arching her back to demolish the distance between them. Desire sparked within her, a feeling so long unde-tected it felt almost foreign. For the first time since the bat-tle, she felt like she lived within her own skin.

She moved his hand to her breast as her leg slid forward around his. Her knee knocked into something unyielding. He pulled away suddenly, glancing down.

"It's all right," she whispered. "You know I don't care about your leg."

"It's not only that." He let go of her. "Where I come from, a man doesn't do such things with a woman he…"

"A woman he what?" She feared he would say "doesn't like."

"Respects," he said. "A woman he could imagine some-day wanting to—to have more than just her body."

She pondered this quaint notion. "Do you respect me too much to keep kissing me?"

He stared at her mouth. "I don't think anything would keep me from that."

"That's a start, then."

Alanka drew him close and reveled in the feel of his lips and tongue, in the novelty of a kiss that would lead to nothing further. It was enough, for now.

"This time, don't scare them off."

Rhia frowned at Damen as she knelt on the rug inside the boat cabin. "I'll try. This time they won't be a surprise. That should help keep my temper under control."

A small lantern glowed in the corner, giving them enough light to set up the ritual for Alanka's soul retrieval. Damen and Rhia had settled on a plan by which, working together, they would persuade Razvin to hand over his daughter's soul piece. Rhia was skeptical that anything other than force would convince him, but she was glad to have Damen to distract Skaris while she focused on the Fox.

"Why did Skaris want to kill you?" Damen asked Rhia.

"To get his time back, Crow's ransom, the amount of

other people's lives Coranna had to trade for resurrecting me. She told me it was roughly a month per person, if I lived to be her age." She set the drum on the berth. "Didn't people want to kill you after you were brought back to life?"

"Not that I was aware of. Then again, some say I'm a bit dense." Damen paused, thanapras in hand. "There's a way to force them to let go."

"Force them? How?"

"You can ask Crow to take them nowhere."

She stared at him. "I don't understand."

"These lingerers play a dangerous game, torturing the living. By not accepting Crow's release, they risk annihilation. No peace and rest on the Other Side. Just nothingness. Forever."

Rhia shuddered. "We can ask Crow to make that happen, and He'll do it?"

"Supposedly, yes. I've never asked for it, and I never will."

She sat beside Damen on the floor. "Why didn't Coranna tell me?"

"She said you weren't ready. She feared your emotions would lead you to do something you'd regret."

"I'd never do that to anyone."

"Not even Skaris?"

"No. I want to silence him, but not that way. I want to help him find peace."

"And spend the rest of your life missing a piece of yourself."

"If I have to." She ruminated on Damen's revelation. "What does it cost to ask Crow to annihilate someone's soul?" The words themselves felt foul in her mouth.

"The only price is living with what you've done. Such an

act can't ever be taken back. I'd think the regret would poison one's own soul." He sat back on his heels. "Ready to begin?"

She nodded. "I'll get the others."

Soon Alanka was lying on the floor next to Rhia. Koli stepped over them to sit on the berth. She set the drum in her lap, rolled up her sleeves and swung her dark blond braid out of the way. "Which tempo?" she asked Damen.

"Deep trance. Wait until I lie down."

Damen lit the thanapras, then chanted a high, potent keening that seemed as if it could smash the barriers between the Spirits' world and their own. Rhia could almost feel the sound tunneling through her mind.

After he finished, he sank onto the rug on the other side of Alanka. Koli began to drum.

A strange feeling crawled over Rhia's skin. She wanted to brush her arms and neck to check for spiders, but forced herself to remain motionless. Damen's chant echoed in her mind.

The fog between worlds appeared again, but this time lightning cracked its surface as though it were a thundercloud. When Rhia tried to pass through, painful tingles jumped among her fingertips. She backed up, and the fog seemed to pull her in and push her away at the same time.

She fought to keep her breath steady and focus on the drum. Perhaps this was a test. Alanka shifted beside her, and Rhia wanted to tell her to be still, but her mouth wouldn't move. She hovered, paralyzed, between two worlds.

Hands shook her hard. "Rhia, something's wrong with Damen."

She lurched to sit up, rubbing her face to banish the clammy, groping fog.

Her Crow brother was panting hard, lungs heaving as though he were running at full speed. He clutched at the front of his shirt, twisting the fabric. It tore in half down the center of his chest.

"Koli, stop," Rhia said. "This isn't right."

The Bat pushed the drum aside. "What's happening to him?"

"I don't know." Rhia touched his hand. It shook as hard as her own and was twice as cold. "I'm going to bring him back."

"No…" Damen grasped his hair and pulled hard. "Not everyone. Stop." His body twisted on the rug. "Where are you? Speak!"

Rhia took his other hand. "Damen, come back to us. You'll be safe here."

He screamed, a sound so long and loud it seemed as though it could reach the Gray Valley and beyond.

Alanka and Koli yelped and leaped to their feet. Her heart pounding, Rhia told the two women, "Go. We need to be alone."

They jerked open the cabin door and pushed each other through. When the door slammed shut, Rhia turned back to Damen, wondering what to do. If only Coranna were here.

His moans had softened, and tremors racked his body. She wiped his face with a damp cloth, figuring it couldn't make things worse. "Damen, can you hear me?"

"I hear you." He opened his eyes and let out a deep

breath. "I heard it all, and then nothing. Nothing." He struggled to sit up against the berth, then raised a wet gaze to hers. "I think my baby just died."

Rhia stared at him in horror. If a first child died before coming to term, its parents returned to the first phase. As if it weren't bad enough to miscarry, one's second-phase magic would be lost, too. But it was the Spirits' way of ensuring no one got pregnant for the sake of power, only to abort the child.

"I'm so sorry." She pulled Damen close and stroked his long black hair. He gripped the back of her shoulders, shivering.

Suddenly his body seized, and he pushed himself out of her embrace. "I hear them again!" He crammed the heels of his hands against his eyes. "But I can't block them out. I can't even tell them apart."

She exhaled hard. "Then your powers are fluctuating, the way they were when I was first pregnant."

"The child's in trouble." Damen wiped his face with his sleeve. "This happened to my cousin. His wife had a hard pregnancy. In the month before their son was born, their powers swung from nothing to everything."

Rhia nodded. As a healer, her mother had encountered several such cases.

With a shaky hand, he quenched the thanapras in the water bowl. "It's my fault. Crow is punishing me."

"He doesn't take innocent lives to punish us. What do you think you did wrong?"

He angled a wary look at her. "I can't tell you."

"Damen, this secrecy has to stop. You wouldn't have mentioned it if you didn't want to tell me."

He sat back against the edge of the berth and let out a long sigh. "I saw Nilik's death. When he was born."

"So did I."

Damen stared at her, then blinked. "You have an excuse. You were tired and weak after the labor." He hung his head. "I was merely curious."

"About what?"

"About the Raven prophecy. Because of my own child. I thought if I could see how Nilik would die, it would tell me whether he was the one."

"Did it?"

"No."

The image burned her mind, and she wondered if Damen had seen the same one. "I saw him die young," she said, "seventeen or eighteen, facedown in the sand holding a sword. There's blood everywhere. I think he dies in the land of the Descendants. Which either means we won't rescue him, or that someday our people will invade—"

"Wait." Damen held up his hand. "Nilik won't die in Ilios. He'll die in Velekos."

"Velekos?" Rhia grabbed Damen's hand so hard she thought the slender bones would break. "Are you sure?"

"I recognized the place. It's an hour's ride west of the village, one of the few beaches without rocks."

Her mind raced with the implications. "Then that must mean—"

"It doesn't mean anything. He could still spend his life in Ilios and travel back to Velekos as a young man." He grimaced as if in pain and drew his hand out of hers. "I shouldn't be telling you this. It breaks the sacred law."

"But there must be exceptions. Why else would Crow give us these visions if not to share them, at least with other Crows?"

"I don't know. To test us? It's not for us to question."

"But it's up to us to act the way we think is right."

"So we just make our own rules?" He rubbed his temples, glaring at her. "Coranna was right about you."

Rhia's blood heated. "She wasn't, because she never knew that my vision saved Asermos."

"What are you talking about?"

"When I was fifteen, Galen tested me on his sick brother Dorius, Arcas's uncle. Everyone thought he was dying, but I saw that he could live. Then—I saw his death."

"Don't tell me."

"He was bleeding in a pile of golden oak leaves," she said. "I thought it meant he would die in autumn."

Damen put his hands to his ears. "I don't want to hear it."

She pulled his arms down. "No one in Asermos knew when or where the Descendants would attack, until Arcas gave me the gift."

"What gift?"

"He'd changed the colors of the trees around the wheat field. He made a sunset for me." She let go of Damen. "The golden oak was the sun."

He drew in a short gasp. "So you knew the Descendants were coming soon."

"I didn't tell anyone how I knew, but they believed me. That was when I realized how much people respect the judgment of a Crow."

"Which is exactly why we can't abuse it."

"I agree," she said, though she wasn't sure they held the same definition of *abuse*.

He exhaled hard and lay back on his blanket. "I'm sorry."

"For what?"

"Now I know how you feel, knowing your loved ones are in danger. I've been so cold about it."

"Not cold. Realistic."

"I've turned into Coranna, only more brittle." He laid his arm across his forehead. "At least she was happy that way. She found peace in her stoicism. Me, I'm just...dead."

She tucked the blanket around his trembling frame. "Not anymore."

Marek awoke from his sea-sickened fog into a world so white it hurt his eyes. For a moment he wondered if he'd died and floated up into the clouds on Crow's wings. At least the endless pitching and rocking had stopped, and his stomach felt as if it was part of his body again.

"Get up." Mila's voice cut through the haze. "We're home."

Marek opened his eyes all the way. He moved to peer out the round window next to his bunk, rattling the chain that bound him to the bed.

He saw what had blanched his vision.

Leukos. The White City.

He craned his neck to see the tops of the tallest stone buildings. Though he had lived his life in trees, the sight gave him vertigo.

"It must look strange." Mila's voice softened. "I'll never

forget what you did, bringing Neyla back. My prayers will ask the gods' mercy for you."

He turned from the window. "Can you get me to Nilik?" Since his escape in Velekos, they hadn't allowed him near his child, hadn't even let him leave this room filled with the stench of his own sickness. "I need to see my son."

Mila glanced at the door behind her. "I—I don't—"

"Don't speak to him, Mila." Sareb sauntered in with the burliest of the soldiers, who unlocked the manacle that held Marek's chain to the bed.

"Please don't take him from me," Marek said as his wrists were tied behind his back and attached to another chain. "I'll do anything."

"Do you want to live? Then keep your eyes open and your mouth shut." The captain pulled a clean cloth from his belt and wiped Marek's face hard. "And look decent. If you're lucky, she'll make you a house or stable slave."

"Who?"

Sareb poked Marek's chest. "What did I say about speaking?"

They climbed two flights of stairs to get to the main deck outside. Marek squinted at the sun blazing off the tall white stone buildings. The strange sights begged his attention, but first he had to find his son. They couldn't have come so far together only to be separated.

A plaintive cry pierced the crisp morning air.

Marek turned to see one of the soldiers who had taken him from Asermos. He was holding a baby basket. Marek lunged, but the chain jerked him back. Sareb cursed.

"You're going to the same place," the captain said, "so calm down, or I'll send you to the mines."

"I want to see him now."

"When we get there, if she decides to keep you." He pulled Marek closer. "To make us all happy and some of us rich, try to pretend you're a good boy." He clapped Marek's shoulder and gave him a wide grin. "Understand?"

Marek nodded. Whatever it took, he'd stay with Nilik. As the line crept forward, he breathed deeply, straining for the scent of his son.

It occurred to him that if Rhia, Alanka and Lycas hadn't rescued him from the Descendant army camp last year, he would have been brought to Leukos a captive, as he was now. For the first time, he wondered if there was such a thing as destiny.

A horse-drawn cart met them at the end of the dock, at the side of a busy street paved with flat, pale gray stones. The soldiers helped Marek into the back, where two of them sat on either side. Sareb sat across from him, wearing a self-satisfied smile despite the wails emanating from the baby basket in his lap.

The cart clattered over the street, jarring Marek's teeth and bones. Nilik's cries subsided soon after the rocking movement began. As they moved between the buildings, Marek's throat closed with a trapped feeling. He peered around for anything familiar—a tree, even a shrub. No green met his eye.

They made their way uphill, where the buildings became shorter and wider. Many windows were bedecked with flowers of all colors, but he couldn't see the soil in which they were planted. As they climbed higher, more of the city itself came into view.

White buildings lay astride narrow streets in long, crooked rows, like bricks waiting to be mortared. On every street they passed, workers scrubbed the buildings' walls to maintain the pristine appearance.

Marek would have covered his ears had his wrists not been bound and chained to the seat. The rattle of cart wheels and the harangues of what seemed like a thousand pedestrians and drivers created a whirl of sound that set Marek's nerves on edge. A hundred scents assaulted his nose—scorched food, raw sewage and the sweat of too many humans in one place.

Soon they reached a wide driveway of richly patterned paving stones leading to an iron fence about three times his height. The soldiers helped Marek out of the cart. Two guards approached the gate from the other side.

"Here to see Petrop," Sareb said.

They swung open the gate. Beyond it lay a large open space, bordered on one side by a stable and, on the other two sides, by the back of a stone house—white, of course. Horses and humans mingled in the space, glancing at his passage.

Feet crunching on a surface of tiny pebbles, the soldiers led Marek to a door with no handle on the outside. One of the gate guards rapped four times and waited.

A wizened bald man opened the door, dressed in a smooth white shirt and black trousers. His uniform bore no insignia or other flourishes, but his upright bearing spoke of his status, at least within this household.

"I am Petrop." He cast a narrow gaze at Marek. "What's this one?"

"The child's father," Sareb said.

The man waved them away. "He can't stay."

"Let Her Honor decide that." The captain lifted his heels and displayed a crooked grin. "Perhaps she'll offer us all a token of her appreciation for this extra gift."

"Enter, then." Petrop sniffed. "If she's not pleased, you'll get a token of something else."

They walked through a large, busy kitchen. The scents penetrated Marek's nose and went straight to his stomach. He'd eaten little on the ship due to his seasickness; now his appetite had woken, ferocious.

On the other side of the kitchen, they entered a windowless stone corridor, lit by torches held in iron sconces along the wall. Marek glanced back at Nilik's basket, which emitted louder fussy noises with each step they took.

At the end of the corridor an open archway led to a room with a long table—enough space for forty or fifty people. Marek's mind swam at the size of this building and its chambers.

They passed through a room with a large stone staircase to the right, and to the left, an ornate wooden door—which Marek took to be the front door. Facing them was a smaller, cozier room that was nonetheless larger than his entire house in Kalindos. They stopped in the doorway, the soldier with Nilik standing next to Marek.

"Is it him at last?" cried a high, melodic voice. It came from behind the back of a long, cushioned bench.

A young woman rose to her feet and swept around the

end of the bench, a flowing white silk skirt swaying above her ankles. Even from halfway across the room, Marek could see the eager spark in her bright blue eyes.

"It is him." She came forward with a jerky gait, as if she were trying not to run. Her hands clasped and unclasped each other, and long golden curls bounced with each movement.

A few paces away, she surrendered to impulse, and leaped at the basket with such a predatory ferocity that Marek stepped back, startled.

The woman looked at him, just now noticing his presence. Her pale brow creased. "Petrop, who is this?" she asked without taking her gaze from Marek.

Her servant frowned. "The infant's sire, Your Honor."

"He reeks."

Captain Sareb stepped forward. "Your Honor, he is quite docile and cooperative." He gave Marek a subtle glance, no doubt warning him not to reveal the truth. "Despite his current wretchedness, his physique is strong. If it pleases you, he would make an excellent home slave." The captain jerked his chin toward Petrop. "He's certainly younger and more vital than some of your current household staff."

The woman circled Marek, twisting the end of one of her curls as she examined him. "How much?"

"Three thousand," Sareb said with a confident air.

"How amusing. Nine hundred."

"He's young and civil tongued, and he'll clean up well. Two thousand."

Marek fought to calm his breath. They were negotiating over his price as if he were a pony at auction.

"What skills do you have, boy?" she asked Marek.

He bristled at the word *boy*. She couldn't have been more than five years older than he was—twenty-six or twenty-seven at most. "I can cook, clean, repair things, handle the horses. Anything you require, just please let me stay with my son."

"Shh." The woman stepped close to his side, and he realized that even in her slippers she equaled his height. She placed her hands around his upper arm as though measuring the muscle there. "Hmm. Could be meatier." She ran her hand over his shoulder and across the top of his back. "And the hair would have to go, for certain."

Marek flinched at the idea.

"The beasts only cut their hair in mourning." Sareb inclined his head to her. "But if you buy him, you can do as you like."

She stood less than a handspan from Marek, examining his face. He kept his gaze straight ahead, on the horse-bedecked tapestry covering the opposite wall.

"Were you a soldier?" she said in a low voice.

"No. Never."

She made a small noise of surprise. "But you've taken a life, haven't you?"

He looked into her gleaming eyes, etched with kohl into a feline shape.

"Maybe more than one," she said. With the tips of her long fingernails, she tilted his chin down and away. "Don't look at me like an equal." She turned to the basket. "Let me see my child."

Instinct made Marek step between them. "No."

Her eyes flared. "Say no to me again, boy, and I'll have you killed."

Sareb cleared his throat. "With all respect, Your Honor, you can't kill him if he doesn't belong to you. Two thousand."

"Fifteen hundred," she said, her gaze locked with Marek's. "You'd only get five from the miners."

The captain chuckled. "Fifteen it is."

"Pay him, Petrop." She gripped Marek's chin again. "I'll take my child now. Step aside."

It was the hardest thing he'd ever done—harder than killing Skaris, harder than withstanding a day's beating in the Descendant army camp. He moved away and watched the soldier ease Nilik out of the basket and into the arms of the nameless woman.

Her face transformed in an instant. "Oh, he's lovely." Her eyes glistened, then she turned away with her new bundle. "How do they make them so beautiful?"

Marek's arms already ached with the urge to seize his son, who didn't even gurgle in protest at another stranger holding him.

The captain winked at Marek as he unbound his wrists and unlocked the chain. "Remember, be a good boy," he whispered. He exchanged coins and papers with Petrop before swaggering out.

"Fetch the wet nurse," the woman said to Petrop, then flicked her fingers toward Marek and her guards. "Have this one washed, shorn and fed, in that order, then return him to me."

Marek nearly fell to his knees with relief. He would stay with his son. He knew he should already hate this woman for making him a slave, but she had spared him the one fate that would have killed him as surely as a sword to the heart.

"Thank you, Your Honor," he whispered as the two men led him away.

As he reached the door, he looked back to see her staring at him in surprise.

Rhia hurried to keep up with Damen, trying not to stumble over the slick cobblestones that made up the Velekon streets. They had left the others at the dock to negotiate a price for Koli's boat. Damen, of course, couldn't wait another moment to make sure his child was safe.

Her Crow brother's powers had continued to ebb and flow throughout the day, and rain had slowed their progress to an agonizing pace, so that it had been nearly sunset when they arrived. Rhia didn't want to admit it, even to herself, but she still clutched the hope that a mistake or a miscommunication had occurred with the pigeons, that Marek and Nilik would be waiting for her here in Velekos.

Damen's pace increased as they turned down a narrow street, past a grizzled old man with a half empty fish cart.

From the directions Damen had given the others, she knew they were near his home.

He stopped before a rough wooden door, reached for the latch, then hesitated. Rhia caught up to him.

"It's odd," he said. "This is my home, but after all this time, I feel like a stranger."

Rhia knocked softly.

After several moments, a panel in the door slid open and a bright blue eye peered through.

"Damen!" cried a female voice. The latch clicked, then the door swept inward, revealing a pale pregnant woman.

Damen spread his arms. "Reni, thank the Spirits." He took her into a careful embrace, then pulled back to examine her. "You all right? The baby?" His breath came quick. "Felt it almost die."

"Listen to you, sounding like a Kalindon still, heh?" Her musical voice held a tenor of exhaustion. "I'm fine now. We had a bit of a struggle, but the Turtle woman says if I rest and take care what I eat, he should make it to full term."

"He? It's a boy?" Damen looked past her. "Where's Nathas?"

"He's at market, I imagine. The Horse woman told us to expect you, so he's buying food for everyone." She turned her wan, shadow-eyed face toward Rhia. "Is this the mother of the child that was taken?"

Damen held his arm out. "My Crow sister, Rhia."

"Welcome." Reni smiled and smoothed the loose strands of red-brown hair that had fallen out of her own braid. "You'll forgive me if I don't bow, right?"

"I understand." Rhia bowed. "It wasn't long ago that I was pregnant." Her throat tightened around the word.

Damen took Reni's hand. "You should lie down. The others will be here soon."

Reni beckoned them in and motioned toward the kitchen to the left. "Please, dry yourselves, make some tea." She walked to a bed in the far corner of the living space, eschewing Damen's assistance. Even in her current state, Reni held a sprightly energy. A bushy gray squirrel-tail fetish hung on a nail at the end of a narrow staircase. She looked about Lycas's age, maybe twenty-three or twenty-four.

Rhia moved to the adjoining kitchen to give them time alone, though her mind burned with questions about the failed rescue attempt. She lit the stove and filled a pan of water. When she came back to the living space, Reni was lying on the bed with Damen sitting next to her, his hand on her abdomen.

"I felt him move!" he told Rhia. "He's alive."

Rhia tried to force a smile, but didn't succeed.

"Well, of course he's alive." Reni gave his arm a light slap. "Soon he won't have much room to move in there, so enjoy it while you can." She shifted her head on the pillow. "I'm so happy you'll be here for the birth, Damen. I worried you wouldn't make it, but Nathas always believed."

The door swung open, and a brawny redheaded man backed in, dragging a small upright cart containing a crate full of produce.

"Reni, I hope you're hungry," he said without looking behind him. "I bought all the spring vegetables the Turtle woman suggested."

He turned and saw Damen, who had moved to stand an

arm's length away. They stared at each other for a long moment, then fell into an embrace as fast and hard as if they'd been yanked together by ropes.

"Damen…" Nathas's eyes squeezed shut. "Spirits, I missed you." He drew away to examine the Crow's face. "When did you get so old?"

"When did you get so ugly?"

They shared a laugh, then a long kiss—long, especially, for the reticent Velekons. Rhia wondered if she would ever reunite with Marek in such a way.

"Time for that later," Reni said. "We've got guests coming and Damen won't let me play hostess."

Nathas let go. He spotted Rhia, and his hazel eyes grew sad. "You must be…"

"Rhia," Damen said, "my Spirit sister."

"Two Crows in one house." Nathas gave a tight smile. "Good times, heh?" He bowed to her, a motion Rhia returned. "I'm sorry about your family," he said. "My friend Eneas is coming by after work to report his account of the rescue. He was there with your husband, who gave him a message for you."

"A message?" Rhia's heart leaped. Perhaps it held a clue to finding him. "What was it?"

"You'll have to ask Eneas. He'll be here after dark, once he's brought in his fishing boat." Nathas dragged the cart into the kitchen. "Help me with the food, heh?"

Rhia followed him. "The pigeons said the other two babies had been saved but not Nilik. That Marek went aboard the ship willingly?"

"I wasn't there, but that's what I heard." Nathas unloaded

a crate of leafy greens. "If it helps, the children who were saved seemed to be unharmed. They're on their way back to Asermos already."

Bitter envy stung her tongue. Soon those other parents would hold their babies again, while her arms would stay empty. She should be happy for them, but her heart filled with a scorched black hate.

She picked up a long-bladed knife and a handful of root vegetables and began chopping. The slice and *thonk* of the blade temporarily eased her need to strike out.

To distract herself, Rhia tried to make conversation with Nathas. "I've heard a lot about you," she said.

"No, you haven't." He tapped the Owl feather hanging around his neck. "Even if I couldn't sniff a lie, I know Damen doesn't talk about me or anything else inside that head of his."

A knock sounded on the door. Damen went to answer it. Rhia stepped forward, hoping it was Eneas with her message, but it was the rest of her rescue party. The house grew loud with introductions, and Rhia retreated to the kitchen where she could make herself useful and keep from screaming at everyone. She picked up the knife and a head of cabbage.

Soon Lycas and Nathas joined her. "I was hoping the pigeon message was wrong, too," her brother said, pouring himself a mug of ale. "But we'll find them in Leukos."

Nathas looked up from the stove. "Er, how are you planning to get there?"

"We'll charter a ship, of course," Rhia said.

"Oh, dear." The Owl replaced the lid on the pot of water.

"After the kidnapping, Velekos set up a complete embargo on Ilios. No one comes or goes there from our port."

Rhia gripped the handle of the knife. "We can't sail to Leukos?"

"It's long overdue," Reni added from the other rooms. "If Velekos had embargoed Ilios after the invasions, then your husband and child couldn't have been kidnapped, at least not so easily."

Rhia set down the knife, fearing what might become of it. "How are we supposed to get to Leukos?"

"Go around." Filip sat down on the stairs with Alanka. "That's how our battalion came to Asermos. We traveled around the sea, then west of Velekos and met the rest of the brigade outside your village."

"Before you invaded it," Lycas added bitterly.

"You're an Ilion?" Nathas asked Filip. "I wondered why you wore no fetish, but I figured you were one of those contrary Kalindons."

"Filip's not an Ilion anymore," Alanka said. "He's been chosen by the Horse Spirit." She lifted her chin. "I'm one of those contrary Kalindons."

Rhia approached Filip. "How long will it take us to get to Leukos if we go around the sea?"

"On horseback, about a month."

"A month?" Rhia put her hands in her hair, wanting to rip it out. "Anything could happen in that time." She turned to Nathas. "Won't someone be willing to break the embargo? A smuggler, maybe?"

"Eventually, yes, once the enforcement slacks off. But right now, there are police all over the docks, warning of hefty fines and even imprisonment. In a few weeks some of the ship owners will be desperate enough for money that they'll take a chance, but right now everyone's lying low."

"We can't wait for something that might not happen," she said. "We'll follow Filip over land."

"Follow *Filip?*" Lycas slammed his mug on the table. "Are you crazy? He'll hand us over to the Ilions the moment we step across the border. We'll fetch a fine price as slaves for his people."

Filip's jaw tightened. "They're not my people anymore."

"*We're* not your people, either," Lycas said. "You've made that clear, Descendant."

"Stop calling him that!" Alanka said.

Filip put a hand on her shoulder and stood to face the Wolverine. "Lycas, you're right," he said. "I've done everything to distance myself from the people who have helped me the most. If we get near the border and you still don't trust me, I'll leave you." He looked at Rhia, then the others in the living room. "In the meantime, I'll teach you what you need to know about Ilios. How to read the signs, how to use the money. Whatever I can do."

"Whatever you can do to get us captured, you mean." Lycas advanced on him. "You're all treacherous to the bone."

"He's not lying." Nathas put a hand out to stop Lycas and focused a long, steady Owl gaze upon Filip. "He may have doubts about his decision, but his intentions are sincere."

"We'll leave tomorrow." Rhia gave her brother a defiant glare, then turned to Nathas. "The Asermons donated money for our crossing, but we'll use it for horses instead. You'll show us where we can find some?"

The Owl smiled and gave a slight bow. "Not only that, but I've been told that Velekos will double what Asermos gave you, and throw in the horses, too. After all, you might be searching for the Raven boy."

"Maybe not." Reni put a protective hand over her belly, then looked at Rhia. "In any case, it's time we started acting like one people. I work at the currency exchange. I'll get you the best rate for Ilion coin and waive my commission."

"Thank you," Rhia said. The villages had never shown such generosity to each other's people in her life.

"You're welcome." Reni sat up in bed. "Now, let's eat."

The rescuers and their new hosts shared a supper of fish and vegetables. Though the food was fresh, Rhia could eat no more than a few bites. She wondered where Marek dined tonight, if he watched over their son and if he would ever accept his captivity.

She suspected not. Marek would sooner die than kneel to a Descendant, and that pride could get him killed.

From his window in the slaves' quarters, Marek stared across the skyline of Leukos. The sunrise glared pink over the white buildings, but his gaze fixed on the green. Basha— the woman who owned him—called it a park, a place set aside where Leukons could enjoy something they called nature. The trees, from what he could tell, were of five or six types, and they sat in tidy groups, like the crops in Asermos.

It was artificial, but it was green, and it was all he had. His powers were fading, as if Wolf couldn't find him in the midst of so much stone.

As always, he heard Petrop's footsteps approach his room, but this time the butler was nearly at the door before Marek's ears caught the sound. He turned from the window.

Petrop stopped at the threshold long enough to say, "Go to her," before passing on.

"And good morning to you, too," Marek murmured.

Two house guards flanked him the moment he exited the room. Before he reached the top of the stairs, he heard Nilik bawling. The guards led him down into the sitting room, the chamber where he had first met Basha.

She sat on the divan with Nilik beside her. The child kicked his legs and squalled, ignoring the brightly colored rattle she dangled over his face. Marek stopped in the doorway and forced his fists to unclench.

"Praise gods, you're here." Basha flapped her hands toward Nilik. "Make him stop."

Marek went to his son, circling around the sofa to approach him from the side opposite Basha. As he'd been ordered, he didn't speak to her or even look at her. He picked up Nilik and held him against his shoulder, whispering and swaying in the rhythm the boy liked best.

"What's wrong with him?" she said. "The healer says he's not sick. He's feeding fine, and he doesn't need changing." Her voice pitched up. "I don't understand. Why isn't he happy?" When Marek didn't reply, she added, "You may speak to me if you have an answer."

"Perhaps he misses his mother," Marek whispered.

"Wrong answer!" Basha stood and advanced on him. "I'm his mother now, and he'd better get used to it."

Nilik screamed at her approach, and Basha stopped.

"Oh." She pressed her palms to her temples. "I know it's hard for him. I just want him not to hate me."

Marek spoke as softly as he could over Nilik's howls. "He doesn't hate you. He's too young to hate." He looked around at the cavernous room. "Everything is strange here."

"But it's not!" She glided to a table and picked up a wooden carving of an eagle with outstretched wings. "My house is full of Asermon things. I love their art, so primitive and pure. So natural." She stopped and stared at Marek, and he glanced away. "Hmm, I wish I hadn't had them cut your hair. But it will grow back, long and wild."

Marek didn't want to think about how many months that would take. He had trouble just getting through the day in this place. But his short hair didn't feel wrong for the circumstance—he was in mourning, even though no one had died.

Nilik's wails softened, and Marek lowered him into the crook of his arm. The boy's face was red and wrinkled from crying. He looked like a tired old man. Marek offered his finger to suck, and it was readily accepted.

"That's better." Basha sighed, and picked the rattle off the sofa. "He doesn't like this one. What does he like? You may speak."

He wanted to tell her Nilik was too young to like any toy, but knew she hated to be corrected. "He prefers sounds, actually. I could teach you some of his favorite songs."

She gasped. "I would love that. I'll send for paper, and you can write down the words." She motioned to one of the guards, who bowed and left the room.

"I don't write," Marek said.

"Can you read?"

"No. My people don't have the need."

"Well, you'll have need here. I'll teach you."

He gaped at her.

"Don't look so shocked," she said. "I can't have my people incapable of reading street signs and vendors' placards. You'll get lost or taken advantage of."

Marek's thoughts raced. Someday she would let him leave the house, if he could earn her trust. Maybe then he'd find a way to escape.

"Thank you," he said, "Your Honor."

"We'll start now." She glided to a nearby table and pulled out a drawer. "I'll show you how to write your name, which I seem to have forgotten."

"Marek."

From the drawer Basha withdrew a bottle of ink and a black feather. "It ends in a *k*, so you're named in memory of someone. Who?"

Marek stared at the feather, which reminded him of the fetish Rhia wore around her neck.

"You may speak," Basha said in a tight voice.

He kept his gaze on the feather. "A great-aunt. Marca."

"And the child? Who is his namesake?"

"My wife's brother, Nilo." Marek looked at Basha. "He was killed in the battle with the Des— With your people."

Her gaze dropped, and she stared at the contents of the drawer as if she'd forgotten why she had opened it. "My husband also."

Marek held back a false declaration of sympathy.

"When they informed me," she said, "I lost our child, still in the womb."

"I'm sorry," he said, and meant it.

She approached him and gazed down at Nilik, who still sucked Marek's finger. "I've changed his name to Demedor, after my husband. I need people to believe he's mine." She stroked the ends of her blond curl. "I do regret erasing the honor of his uncle, however."

Marek kept his eyes on the child. "I know what it's like to lose two at once. My first mate died in childbirth and took our son with her."

She drew a finger along Nilik's pink cheek. "But you found another," she whispered. Then her lips twisted into a smile that chilled Marek's blood. "As have I."

26

Rhia and Damen stood at the end of the road leading out of Velekos while the others took a brief rest. Behind them, the village was waking to a new day, one much less profitable than those before it, due to the embargo. Ahead, tufted marsh grasses stretched to the flat horizon, their heads tilted rightward from the steady breeze off the water. To their left lay the rocky shores of Prasnos Bay. By midday they would reach the sea.

"I wish I could come with you," Damen said to Rhia.

"No, you don't."

"Maybe not." He cast a glance at Nathas, who was helping Bolan load a cage with two Velekon pigeons onto the back of his pony. "It'll be good to finally be together as a family." Without looking at her, he said, "I hope I see you again, Rhia."

"Of course you will." She forced cheer into her voice. "Marek and Nilik and I will stop by to meet your new baby on our way home to Asermos."

His thin lips tightened.

"You don't think we'll find them," she said.

"I believe you have a fair chance."

"Then why do you wonder if you'll see me again?"

He stared out across the bay. "There are over two hundred Asermons and Kalindons in Leukos, maybe spread across the Ilion territories by now. Do you think you'll be satisfied bringing home only two?"

"If it means keeping Nilik out of harm's way, then, yes, I'll have to be satisfied."

"Rhia, we're ready." Alanka sat behind Filip on the bay mare.

Rhia waved to her, then turned to Damen. "Send a message to Asermos letting them know we left."

"I'll visit the Horse woman the moment we get back into town."

She hugged Damen tightly. "I'll miss you."

"I miss you already," he said. "Good luck."

Rhia let go of her Crow brother and drank in the sight of his lean face. Maybe it was the last time she'd ever see him.

She mounted her pony, trying to remember the last time she'd ridden alone, without Marek sitting behind her. The horse's back felt long, all to herself.

They rode off into the wilderness, with no road to guide them, only the sun, the stars and the memory of a displaced Ilion.

* * *

Filip kept the Atrean Sea in the corner of his left eye as he led the rescuers southwest along the coast. The blue sky ahead was filling with tall, bloated clouds that promised rain, if not the spring's first thunderstorm, by the end of the afternoon.

After a day on the tiny boat, then two days in Damen's house preparing for the trip, the travelers needed plenty of space. They rode close enough to see each other but far enough out of earshot to avoid conversation.

He relished the chance to spend time alone with Alanka. Her deep, even breath and slack arms around his waist told him she'd dozed off. It was probably the closest he would ever come to sleeping beside her.

The salty wind scoured his face and tossed the horse's mane in black waves over her neck. The mare's hooves squished the soggy ground. Long, red-tufted marsh grasses brushed her flanks, causing her mud-brown hide to flinch and shudder as though she were besieged with flies.

"This place smells strange," the mare thought. "The grass itches, and my feet are sinking."

"The footing's fine," he murmured. "It's not so different from Velekos."

"What?" Alanka's arms tightened around his waist.

"Talking to the horse."

"Oh." She rested her forehead on the back of his neck and loosened her arms. As she drifted off again, they slid down to rest in his lap, inspiring a desire for something he couldn't have. He took her hand off his thigh and held on to it.

"Sorry," she mumbled. "Didn't sleep well last night. Or the three hundred nights before that."

He cleared his throat. "If you want, I have another idea about how to help you."

She lifted her head. "With my magic?"

"Yes. Remember on the boat when we spoke of purifying rituals? In my country, these rituals involve asking the forgiveness of those we've slain."

"How?"

"First we go to the temple of Rovas, the god of war, and pay a tribute for each soldier we've killed. The priest gives us a receipt, which we take—"

"A receipt? Like you get for buying eggs?"

"Precisely." He continued before she could laugh at the notion. "We take that to another temple, where a priest of Xenia, the death goddess, speaks to our fallen enemies on our behalf, asking forgiveness."

Alanka started and gasped. "Like a second-phase Crow."

"Yes." He clucked his tongue to soothe the pony, who had pinned her ears back at Alanka's sudden movement. "By reconciling with the dead, we find peace."

"Do the dead always forgive you?"

"In my experience, yes. They have nothing to gain in the afterlife by holding a grudge."

She snorted. "My father gains nothing by holding on to part of me, but he still does."

"Perhaps that's a different problem with a different solution."

"So Rhia says. Does your people's ritual work?" Her voice

quieted to a whisper as if she were afraid to utter the hope. "Afterward, you feel clean?"

"Yes." He stroked her palm with his thumb. "Pure."

"I can't imagine." She released a wistful sigh. "What about the nightmares and flashbacks? Will I stop seeing the faces of those men?"

"There's only one way to find out."

"I'll ask Rhia when we stop."

"You don't want to ask her now?"

She nuzzled his neck and looped her other arm tight around his waist. "No. I don't want to ask her now."

He smiled and lifted her hand to his lips. Alanka seemed the last woman in the world who would find him appealing. His people had destroyed her family and her home. Their deaths plagued her mind, awake and asleep. He should have been a painful reminder of all she'd lost, of all the deeds that brought her shame, however misplaced. Yet she seemed drawn to him almost against her will.

A dull chill slipped over Filip's neck. Perhaps Alanka was with him not despite his being a wounded Descendant, but because of it. Maybe she was using him to assuage her guilt over the men she'd killed in battle. He dropped her hand.

"Why do you like me?"

She stirred, almost sleepily. "What kind of question is that? I just do."

"What is there to like? I'm not kind."

"You're kind to me. And you're handsome and—and strong."

"I'm not strong. I fall down weeping over wounded animals."

"I find that sweet," she said. "Besides, you could learn to block animals' thoughts if you'd undergo the Bestowing."

"I can't."

"You can."

"I won't, and if you assume I'll change my mind, then you've misguided yourself."

She was silent for a moment. "I like the way you kiss me."

His arms jerked, causing the horse to stop. He imagined lying naked with Alanka in the grass that surrounded them, his wound bare to the bright sunlight.

No. He'd keep his legs covered somehow so she could see nothing but his face and neck and chest, which were whole and healthy.

But she'd want to see his leg. She'd be curious. She'd want to touch it.

"You want me because I'm your fallen enemy," he said. "Not because of the man I am."

"You think I'm with you out of sympathy?"

"It makes sense."

"It makes *nonsense*."

"I've seen battle shock in my troops. They go crazy—"

"I'm not crazy!"

"—and crazy people don't know what they want or why they want it."

She gasped, then her voice turned icy. "How dare you?"

"Admit it. I'll never be the kind of man you need."

Her silence deafened him, and he realized he'd gone too far.

"If that's how you really feel," she said, "there's nothing more to say."

He turned to her, to take back his foolish words, but she

was already sliding off the pony's haunches. Alanka stumbled when she hit the ground.

"I should speak to Rhia," she said, "about my soul retrieval, and about the ritual you suggested." She turned her face from him as she brushed off her trousers. "Thank you for the ride."

He watched her walk back to meet Rhia, who sent him a wary look as Alanka approached. Then he urged the mare forward, keeping the sea in the corner of his eye.

It was easier this way. Somewhere across those waters lay his home, his family, his reckoning. He should face it alone.

Rhia crossed the fog into the Gray Valley.

Koli's drumbeat kept her anchored to the world outside, which already felt less real than this wretched place. The light from the invisible sun bleached the rocks a pale yellow, while the dead tree looked darker than ever.

No one met her this time. She called the names of Razvin and Skaris, but only her own voice echoed back.

She noticed that the tree seemed to have grown—not taller, but wider. Its branches hadn't extended past the second pile of rocks the last time she was here.

She approached it, thinking of the dead tree Crow had revealed in a vision during her Bestowing. That one had been paired with a living tree, full of leaves, flowers, fruit and birds. The Gray Valley offered no such alternative.

As she neared the tree, one of its branches stretched to touch her. She gasped and drew back. It was alive after all. She waited for its twigs to bud leaves, but they remained bare and brittle. Any strength the tree pulled from the unforgiving terrain and sun was dedicated to extending its grasping limbs in a twisted parody of life.

"Pretty, isn't it?"

Rhia shivered at the sound of Skaris's voice, but she didn't turn to face him. He wasn't the one she'd come to see.

"Why, yes, Skaris," he answered himself. "It is quite pretty, just like me. And by *pretty,* I mean, of course, *ugly.*" He dangled the captured crow over her shoulder, swinging it by the feet. Its wings hung straight to the side, flapping feebly. Its black eyes had turned a dull brown, and it no longer tried to peck Skaris's hand.

She turned from the tree and brushed past the Bear to walk down the rocky valley, her feet feeling wooden beneath her.

He kept pace on her left side. "Look, I can make it talk." He grasped the crow around its belly and squeezed. It rasped a halfhearted caw. "Not as loud as she used to be. Are you, Rhia?"

She kept walking.

Skaris whistled a few notes of a Kalindon reel, as though they were two friends on a morning stroll. "You probably wonder what I want in exchange for this." He held up the crow.

"Razvin!" she called to the hills.

"No, that's not it. I want Marek dead."

Her pace faltered, but only for a step.

"Then he can join me here forever."

Rhia knew that wasn't true. When Marek died—many, many years from now, she prayed—he would pass to the

Other Side even if Skaris held a part of his soul. Crow didn't punish victims.

"We'll play with this bird, just me and Marek," the Bear said. "Won't be long now before I see my old friend."

Rhia wanted to run, but she knew it would encourage Skaris's taunts. She kept her pace steady and her face flat.

"Boring," he muttered. "Not like last time. That was fun."

A shout came from a high ridge on her right. A wolf pup was dashing down the hill, scattering dust and pebbles.

Razvin appeared at the edge of the ridge and called down. "Alanka, no!"

Rhia ran toward the pup.

"Where are you going?" Skaris jogged beside her. "Don't you want this?"

He tossed the crow on the ground, far to Rhia's left. She stopped.

Razvin chased the pup, who tumbled down the steep incline, paws over head, before regaining her footing. Dazed, she shook herself, then peered back at Razvin, ears tight against her head.

"Alanka!" Rhia took a tentative step forward as the crow fluttered and flapped in the corner of her eye, unable to take off.

She cursed Skaris under her breath, then squatted and pursed her lips to call the pup.

The little wolf wavered, then raced toward Rhia again, ears flapping, tongue lolling. Razvin was gaining on her, but his pursuit made her gallop faster. She leaped into Rhia's arms, a wriggling mass of fur and claws.

Rhia turned to run. In the distance, the bare black tree

pointed the way. It was too far. She'd never make it before Razvin caught her.

She faced him, the pup squirming in her arms.

"Give her back." The Fox's smooth tone had turned menacing. "This instant."

"No. She doesn't belong to you."

"She doesn't belong to you, either."

"I'm not taking her for myself."

He glared at the pup. "After all I've done for her." His breath faltered. "Doesn't she know how much I love her?"

"She knows it better than anything. It's killing her."

His dark eyes moistened. "But if she leaves, I have nothing."

"You have Crow. Go with Him." Her voice softened but stayed firm. "Find peace on the Other Side. I promise it's waiting for you there."

The sky darkened, as though a cloud had passed over the harsh sun. It wasn't a cloud, Rhia knew, even before she saw Him.

Crow alighted on the valley floor, wings scattering the dust into a thin yellow cloud. He ruffled His feathers, then stood up straight, taller than a man. The fear faded in Razvin's eyes.

"It is past time," Crow said to the Fox in a gentle voice.

Razvin turned back to Rhia. He lifted his hands as if to touch the pup one more time, then lowered them slowly. "Tell her I'm sorry," he whispered.

"Stupid girl," Skaris sang behind her. "You could have had this one instead." A strangled caw came from the recaptured crow. Rhia clutched the pup tighter, refusing to turn to see.

"This one angers me." Crow motioned to Skaris with His beak. "He mocks us, mocks the very idea of my realm. I have half a mind to annihilate him."

"No," she said. "Give me another chance. I couldn't live knowing his soul had been destroyed for my sake."

"Very well. Only say the word, and it would be my pleasure." He turned to Razvin and enveloped him in His glistening black wings. The ground trembled, then they disappeared in a haze of violet light.

Rhia turned and ran, hearing Skaris's long strides keep pace with her. Every step felt heavier and slower than the last, until she was staggering past the tree toward the fog.

"Rhia, wait." A vulnerable undertone in Skaris's voice made her stop, though she didn't face him.

"Save my mate, Lidia," he said. "Probably the only person who mourned my death."

Rhia remembered that Lidia had been taken from Kalindos in the invasion.

"Bring her home safely," Skaris said. "That's all I ask."

She opened her mouth to reply. Suddenly the pup twisted in her arms, scrabbling to get free. She grasped at the wolf and caught her back legs. The pup howled, yanking one foot free. Rhia leaped upon the creature, who snarled and snapped.

They rolled, wrestling, into the fog.

27

Alanka needed to run. Her muscles twitched and jerked, wanting to carry her far away from the pain.

The sea. She imagined its cold, dark peace. *The sea would end it all.*

Alanka tried to rise, but something slammed her onto her back. She shoved at it—hair, hands, a pale face.

"Get her arms!" shouted the face. It was the source of the sorrow. It wanted to give her more.

Strong hands pinned her shoulders to the floor. Fingernails dug into the skin of her upper arms.

"Alanka," the face-voice said. "It's me, Rhia. Please hold still."

Alanka snarled and tried to strike out with her feet. They met only air. A woman with hands to her own mouth bent over Alanka's belly. Warm breath flowed through her shirt over her solar plexus.

Alanka stopped struggling. A feeling as familiar as a childhood scent flowed through her. She whispered her own name.

"That's right," Rhia said. "Welcome home."

The hands at her shoulders—Koli's, she remembered—let go. Alanka touched her stomach, then her face. They felt like herself.

She sat up and looked at Rhia. "It worked, didn't it?"

"You almost got away from me at the end." Rhia let out a gust of air, and even in the tent's darkness Alanka could see the shadows under her eyes. "But, yes, it worked."

"You saw him, then? My father?"

Rhia touched her shoulder. "He went with Crow."

Alanka's numbness cracked. She jammed her hands against her eyes, but nothing could stop the wail building inside her.

"No…" Tears flowed down her cheeks and dribbled in a stream off her chin. "Papa…"

Rhia drew her close, and Alanka clung to her, though she was afraid the sobs racking her body would break the exhausted Crow woman in two. Koli rubbed her back and murmured soothing words of sympathy.

Even as her sorrow poured forth, a warm glow flickered within Alanka. She would sleep tonight, alone and whole. At last she would sleep.

Alanka couldn't sleep. Koli kicked and twisted the bedroll in her dreams, as though she were still riding a horse. Hard to believe she's a stealth master when she's awake, Alanka thought.

She crawled toward the tent door. A moment later, Koli rolled over into the space she'd left behind next to Rhia, whose extreme fatigue would no doubt keep them in camp another day. Alanka picked up her blanket and went outside.

At least the rain had stopped, and the light of the nearly full moon shone through a ragged layer of clouds. The ground near the doused campfire was damp but not soaked. She laid her blanket next to a scraggly tree and sat on it, leaning back against the trunk and facing the sea. Perhaps its distant waves would lull her to sleep.

No sooner had she closed her eyes than she heard a tent flap open. Her shoulders tightened.

Filip's voice reached her ears. "May I join you?"

"Yes," she said as neutrally as possible.

He laid down his own blanket and sat beside her, sighing. "Bolan snores."

"I'm glad."

Filip's mouth relaxed into a smile. "This is better, I agree."

She looked at his left leg. "Do you wear the prosthesis while you sleep?"

"No, I put it on to come see you."

"You didn't have to do that."

"The ground is wet. My crutches might have slipped."

She turned to face the sea so that the incessant breeze would blow her hair out of her eyes instead of into them.

"I heard you crying earlier," he said.

"I think the people in Leukos heard me crying. I was rather loud."

"It's nothing to be ashamed of."

"Did I say I was ashamed?" He was one to talk of shame, she thought, putting on his prosthesis just to speak with her, as if she would turn away in disgust.

Filip cleared his throat. "Forgive my harsh words earlier. I wish I could unsay them."

"I'll forgive you, but only if you admit I could like you for yourself, not for whatever you think you stand for."

"Perhaps."

"Otherwise you insult me."

"All right."

"Say it. Say that I like you."

He laughed softly. "You like me."

"And why is that?"

"Apparently I possess qualities you find attractive."

"Say it like you mean it."

Filip grasped her shoulders and turned her to meet his formidable gaze. He cupped her jaw in both hands and said, "I'm good for you."

"Prove it."

He gave her a deep, slow kiss that turned her insides to liquid heat. She slid her hands up his chest and over his shoulders, wanting to yank him on top of her and feel his body press the breath from her lungs. But she held back, hoping the kiss would make him want as much as she was willing to give. Which was everything.

When they stopped to share a shaky breath, he looked her hard in the eye. "Proven?"

She nodded. "I forgive you." She looked over his shoulder at the tents. "They can probably hear us, except for Rhia."

They took their blankets down the hill toward the shore, until they were out of sight of the camp. Alanka's heart thudded at the thought of being alone with him again.

They sat together on the sand. "How do you feel now?" he asked. "After the soul retrieval."

"Happy. Sad. Not numb anymore. I want things again." She cast him a sidelong glance. "Some things a lot. But I can't sleep, and my powers haven't returned. The thought of using a bow still makes my hands shake. I'll need to hunt soon to provide us with meat, and when I can't, everyone will know Wolf has left me."

"We're on the sea. We can fish." He lowered his voice. "Besides, I hardly eat meat anymore, since the day you shot that rabbit."

"Sorry." She stared out at the water, wishing it full of food. "I'd hoped my father was the cause of all my problems, but I guess it's more than that."

"Maybe it'll just take time."

"Rhia said the rest of me needs to get to know the old part all over again. *Integrate* was the word she used."

"Sounds sensible."

Alanka sat quiet for a moment, deciding how to articulate the change within herself. "I've always belonged to someone else—my father or a mate or my Spirit, or all three at once. Now, for the first time, I could be my own."

"Good."

She heard his trepidation and turned to him. "That doesn't mean I don't want to be with you."

"Good." This time he sounded as if he meant it.

The warmth in his voice made Alanka want to demonstrate how much she wanted to be with him, but she held back. "You told me once that where you're from, a man doesn't, er, do things with a woman he respects."

"Correct. In Leukos, we would have been married before our first kiss, maybe before we'd even seen each other, if we were from the best families."

"How sad." She stopped dancing around her real question. "Does that mean you've never had a lover?"

"I'm not a virgin," he said, "though I might as well be."

"I don't understand."

He looked out over the sea, but to the south, instead of straight ahead to the east. "When I turned seventeen, the night before I joined the army, my older brother took me to a brothel."

Alanka's eyes widened. She'd heard such places operated openly in Velekos and Tiros, and secretly in Asermos. Kalindos had largely eliminated the need.

"It was a festival night," he continued, "so most of the prostitutes were occupied. The only two available were my brother's favorite and a new girl, Palia. Palia was a virgin, and she hadn't been hired yet that night because her price was so high." Filip stopped.

"So what happened?"

He rubbed the back of his neck. "My brother paid it for me, even though the brothel owner thought it foolish to put me with her. She said I should have someone more experienced. But my brother acted as though he were giving me a special gift." Filip turned to her. "Are you sure you want to hear this?"

Alanka gnawed her bottom lip. "If you want to tell me."

He leaned forward, arms crossed on his knees. "I was nervous. She was frightened. I didn't want a woman who was afraid of me, so I offered to just sit with her until the time was up. She refused. She said there had to be evidence I had taken her virginity, or they would beat her. I offered to cut myself so there'd be blood on the bedsheets, but she said no. The next man would know, and if he boasted to his friends about getting a virgin at no extra cost and the brothel owner found out, Palia would be beaten. And besides, she said, the next man might not be so kind." He rubbed his knuckles over the faint stubble on his chin.

"So you did it, then."

"She took off her clothes, and I took her. I tried to be gentle, but I could tell she was in pain. I could tell she wanted me to stop." He put his head in his hands. "I enjoyed her, may the gods and Spirits forgive me. Afterward I was so ashamed I left without even looking at her.

"In the four years after that, there were countless times when I could have taken women in lands we conquered. But I kept seeing Palia in their faces—scared, helpless." He dug his heel into the sand. "With the wars, I had no opportunity to find what your people call a mate, and after my injury I lost hope of ever finding such a person."

She wanted to reassure him that she was that person, but something he'd said made her stomach quake. "If your army had won in Asermos, would the men under your command have raped me?"

He looked at her. "Possibly."

"And you'd have let them?"

"The enlisted aren't well paid. The spoils of war are the

only way to motivate them to fight. Like I said, I never took part myself."

"But you let them," she said.

"If I hadn't, they'd have killed me."

"You were their commander."

"I was a lieutenant. They respected me as much as they would a trained dog. Maybe less."

She felt sick. "What about the women your people took from Kalindos? My neighbors, my friends. Their daughters. What happened to them?"

"I don't know. It depends."

"On what?"

"On their ages, on their—suitability for various roles." He rubbed his knuckles together. "When I spoke of this in the hospital with your friend Adrek, he tried to kill me."

She scoffed. "Maybe I should have let him."

"Maybe you should have."

"Filip, I was only—"

"It was what I wanted."

"—joking." She stared at him. "What did you say?"

"I did it on purpose, said things to anger him, cruel things about what might happen to his little girl. Hoping he would end my life."

"He never told me what you said to set him off."

"That's to his credit." Filip turned to her. "I hate what my people do during war. But without the power of fear, our lands would be overrun, and we'd be the ones enslaved."

"We? They're still your people, then? After all this?" She gestured to the space between them.

He shook his head and looked away. "I spent twenty-one

years as an Ilion, and not yet a year as one of you. And in that year, only a handful of you have treated me as a friend. So I suppose I no longer *have* a people."

"You're with us now, trying to save Marek and Nilik. That means a lot."

"I hope I can be of worth." He joggled his left foot. "Even with this."

She touched his arm. "Whatever happens in Leukos, please believe that you're worth something to me."

He turned to her, and in the nearly nonexistent moonlight she saw him search her eyes for the lie that wasn't there. "I believe it," he said. "I don't understand it, but I believe it." He took her face in his hands and kissed her.

Alanka shivered, and not only from the strengthening breeze that warned of more rain. As Filip's warm fingers slid down her neck, she imagined lying underneath one of his men, fighting for her life in a field of dead warriors, or trapped in a Leukon brothel exchanging her body for the privilege of survival.

She broke away.

"What's wrong?" he said.

She looked at the sky. "It's about to pour again. I can smell it, even without my powers."

He took his hands off her. "The rain's not what bothers you, is it? It's those things I told you."

"I'm glad you told me. I want to be with you, but to do that, I need to see you clearly, the way I never seem to be able to see any man." She looked away. "But it hurts sometimes, like staring at the sun."

He sighed. "How do we make this work?"

"We can start by realizing we deserve each other. No more 'I'm not worthy of you' talk, all right? We're a couple of busted-up misfits, but at least we're equally busted up."

He stood and helped her to her feet. "It's a start."

They made their way back to the campsite, hand in hand, as the rain broke over them.

Filip ran.

In his dream the trees and trails of Letus Park flashed by faster than ever, blurring in the corners of his eyes. His brother was gone, and he ran with no man.

But not alone. He looked down to see that it wasn't his own feet running, but the hooves of the white horse. Her muscles strained and bulged under his legs as he rode without saddle, bridle or blanket.

They shot into an open field, too large to be part of the park. Its rolling hills of waving grasses undulated to the horizon. The rising sun shone behind them, so that Filip and the horse raced their own shadow. He held his arms out straight to the side, and the shadow grew wings. A long laugh burst from his lungs.

The horse stopped. Filip pitched over her head and landed on his back on the grass. The dream ground was soft and spongy, so he bounced and rolled without pain, but not without humiliation.

When he came to a halt, he lifted himself onto his elbows. "Why?"

The horse snorted and shook her snowy mane. "I told you, this magic isn't yours yet. You don't want it enough."

"I do." He got to his knees. "More than anything."

She stepped closer, her hooves soundless, and huffed a warm breath upon his forehead. "Prove it."

He woke to the patter of rain on the tent above his head, with Bolan's snores providing the storm's thunder. Filip reached over and nudged his shoulder.

Bolan jerked awake, then wiped an arm over his face. "I was doing it again, wasn't I?"

"Never mind that. I need your help."

Rhia's head felt as heavy as a rock. Hearing voices by the campfire and noises of breakfast, she tried to push the blanket off her body, but it tangled in her legs. She sank back to the ground, pulse pounding in her temple.

Koli appeared in the tent door. "I thought I heard rustling. Hungry?" She entered with a plate of food.

"It's late," Rhia said. "We need to keep moving."

"You're not going anywhere." Koli held out a slice of toasted bread, burned on one side. "That soul retrieval took all your strength, and then some. I wish we'd brought an Otter. When I woke up, I thought you were dead."

"I've been dead, and this isn't dead." Rhia tried to sit up. Every muscle felt like a tug-of-war rope. She hissed in a breath. "Although it's close."

"You have time to get your strength back. We're not leaving for a few days."

"Why? Is something wrong with one of the horses?" She wanted to throttle the Velekon stable master. "I knew that gray gelding wouldn't last cross-country."

"It's not one of the horses." Koli uttered a dry chuckle.

"Actually, it is. I'll get Filip, let him explain." She shoved the plate into Rhia's hands and left the tent.

Rhia picked at the bread and meat, hunger overcoming curiosity. A sharp, sudden memory of Marek's succulent poached quail eggs tightened her stomach and made her want to cry.

"Rhia," said Filip from outside the tent. "I wanted to tell you myself."

"You can come in. I'm dressed."

He flipped open the tent door but didn't enter or even look at her. Her father had told her Filip's sense of propriety was extreme even by Asermon standards.

"I thought about what you said last autumn." He glanced at her, then returned his gaze to the ground. "How Crow wouldn't leave you alone until you admitted your Aspect."

"Horse is following you?"

He put on a grim smile. "When I dreamed of Her in Asermos, I thought your father had planted it in my mind to convince me to help you."

"He's too honest for that."

"She came to me again." He looked straight at Rhia. "There's no honor in doing anything halfway. Either I become one of you, with my whole self, or I go my own way alone."

She lurched to the tent door, her head swimming. When she got there, she saw his pack sitting on the ground beside him.

"Filip, no. We need you."

"I'm leaving shortly," he said, "for my Bestowing."

She drew in a deep breath and grasped his arm. He seemed surprised by her touch.

"You won't regret it," she said.

He gave a quick nod. "Lycas insists that he and Bolan watch over me to make sure I'm not meeting a spy."

"The Bestowing should be a sacred time between a person and his Spirit."

"I can't blame his suspicion. He says they'll stay out of my sight to give me the illusion of privacy."

"Filip, you ready?" Bolan called from the edge of the campsite. Filip waved to him, then turned back to Rhia.

"We'll go to a cove up the coast a mile or two. It has shelter in case of rain." He stood carefully. "Thank you for helping Alanka. It reminded me who I need to do this for."

"For her?"

"No." He turned and walked away, shoulders squared like a soldier's. Exhausted from the brief conversation, Rhia sank back onto her blanket. Though Filip's Bestowing would cost them a few days' time, having him as a trusted ally—with complete control of his powers—would help them more in the end.

Rhia rolled over and withdrew a flat wooden box from her pack. She wanted to open it, hold its contents to her face and feel her husband close to her again. But the box had to remain sealed until they reached Leukos, so she clutched it to her chest instead.

"Hold on, Marek," she whispered. "We're coming."

28

Marek frowned at the ragged paper in front of him, on which he tried for the fourth time to write his name. The late afternoon sun angled through the sitting-room window, stabbing his eyes, which were already sore from squinting. His fingers felt huge and ungainly around the shaft of the feather pen. Black ink stained his palms and created hand-prints on the old, thick blanket Basha had draped over the desk to protect its wooden finish.

He grimaced as he ruined another letter with a hapha-zard slash at the end of its last stroke. Five days of this, and no progress he could see. His hands retained none of the steadiness with which they had gripped a bow and arrow. If Basha was ever going to let him outside the house, he would have to prove he could read and write at a basic level.

Marek glared at the wolf carving sitting on the green

marble table across from him, a table that seemed to have no purpose except to display one of the living room's many worthless objects. The wolf stared back at him, fierce eyes judging him and his circumstances.

You should be ashamed of yourself.

He shifted his chair so he couldn't see the carving, even from the corner of his vision, but could still keep an eye on Nilik's crib. The guard at the door watched him laconically.

Marek resisted the urge to stare at his son every moment. His fear of losing Nilik had diminished slightly, since Basha indicated that her mercy would hold if Marek didn't displease her. She even allowed him to speak before being spoken to, though he had to choose his words carefully to avoid her wrath. As long as she let him stay at his son's side, he would indulge her any way she wanted.

Almost any way. His Wolf senses hadn't completely died; he could feel her body temperature rise when she came near him. He walked a narrow path—making her appreciate him enough to keep him around but not enough to exact other ownership privileges. At least twice a week, some young man in Marek's slave quarters would be beckoned to her chamber late at night. The thought sickened him.

From his new vantage point at the desk he could see a collection of smaller animal carvings gathered around the base of an iron lamp. The fox sat on its haunches, facing away from the others, as if surveying the room. Its eyes gleamed with tiny pieces of silver stone.

He'd never trusted Fox people. Though they shared powers of stealth with Wolves, as well as enhanced senses of smell and hearing, Foxes always looked out for themselves first. Their magic supported the survival of the individual, not the pack. They'd tell as many lies as they could get away with, as long as it suited their needs.

His mentor, Kerza, had told him to learn from other Spirits, not just Wolf. But he was proud of his Animal and wanted to embody every quality: loyalty, honesty, bravery, protection of others. No compromises, not even for survival.

But in a place like Leukos, Fox's lessons might serve him better.

He stared at the fox carving until his eyes unfocused. *Grant me your wisdom. Tell me what to do to get out of here.*

Whatever it takes, came a voice that sounded like his own, and yet not.

"What a day!"

Basha swept into the room, uncoiling a pink silk scarf from around her neck. Petrop followed her and picked the scarf off the floor the moment it fell from her hand.

"How's my little one?" she said.

"He's asleep," Marek whispered. "At least he was."

She leaned into the crib and tickled Nilik. "Mother's home now. You don't want to waste time napping, do you?"

Marek braced himself for the inevitable screech, which followed a moment later. Petrop winced, as well, and shared a look with Marek that bordered on commiseration.

Undaunted, she lifted the baby into her arms. Marek had to grip his chair to keep from yanking his son away from her.

To her credit, she imitated the rocking motion Marek used and hummed an approximate version of one of Nilik's favorite songs. The boy's cries softened but continued.

"Your mother made a name for herself on the Senate floor today." She popped her eyes wide at Nilik the way he liked. "That's right! Politics are never boring when you have the proper flair. But those bad men won't let Mother run for reelection."

"Why not?" Marek asked. The Senate, from what he could tell, was a larger version of his own village's Council. A basic grasp of Ilion political factions could come in handy if he ever escaped.

"All because she's a woman," Basha said to Nilik, as if the baby had asked the question. "Women can finish the terms of their dead husbands or fathers but can't be elected on their own. We weak females aren't made for such taxing duties." She released a high titter, though Marek didn't understand the joke. Nilik let out a full-throated wail. "My reaction precisely!" she exclaimed, then turned a brilliant smile on Marek. "At least he knows I exist."

She waved her hand at Petrop, and he departed silently. Carrying Nilik, she shifted over to the wolf carving. "Do you like this one, Marek? You're a Wolf, right?"

He nodded, though now it seemed only a half truth.

"Which animal would I be?" she said. "If I had one of those Spirit Guards."

"Guardian Spirits."

"Don't correct me. Which would I be?"

He thought of a cockroach and stifled a bitter laugh. "If you're good at politics, you might be a Fox."

"I'm very good at politics. Recognizing who wants what and what they'll do to get it. People underestimate me because I'm young and female and pretty." She stroked the wooden fox's head with her littlest fingernail. "It's a useful weapon."

"May I ask another question?"

She thought for a moment, then tilted her head indulgently. "Speak."

He gestured to the artwork displayed around the room. "You seem to have a fascination for my people. Even though we're the enemy."

"Even though you killed my husband? I can't blame you for that. We invaded your lands—what were you supposed to do, welcome us with open arms and let us take everything you'd worked so hard for?" She tucked Nilik's blanket under his chin. "That whole campaign was ill-advised and undermanned. It was destined to fail. All the oracles said so."

"You consult oracles? I thought Ilions didn't have magic."

"The gods have magic, of course, and they lend a bit of it to their priests and priestesses. It's one way they keep Ilions in power, where we belong." She scoffed. "Some individuals are overly superstitious, though, and can't buy a loaf of bread without consulting the oracles. I like to use my own mind." Nilik's cries faded into coos at last. "My turn to ask questions. Did you fight in the battle at Asermos?"

"Not exactly. I was a—a scout." He decided not to mention how he'd decimated the Descendant cavalry by sedating their horses the night before the battle. No doubt his actions had made him infamous. "They captured me." He replaced the feather in the ink bottle to avoid snapping it in his fist. "They tortured me."

"Tortured you? How?"

He glanced at the guard standing by the door. "They beat me, left me in the sun."

"How long?"

"Hours. All morning."

"My healer said you had no scars. What did they beat you with?"

"Their feet and hands."

A high titter escaped her throat. "That's not torture. They just roughed you up and let you bake a bit. Torture is having your skin peeled off in strips or having your fingernails ripped out."

He gaped at her.

"There's much worse, I'm told," she said, "but not fit for a woman to hear, whatever that means. You're lucky they didn't deploy a torture detail in the Asermon campaign."

He ran his thumb over his fingernails and had to agree.

"How's your magic these days?" she asked him.

He didn't want to reveal any weakness, and since it was daytime, she couldn't ask him to turn invisible. "It's fine, though I don't have much use for it here."

"Interesting. What's my cook making for supper?"

A test. Marek sniffed the air but could only perceive a vague odor. "Meat."

"What kind?"

"Poultry," he said, keeping the uncertainty from his voice.

"Good. What kind of poultry?"

He guessed her favorite. "Duck."

"Sorry, it's pork. Your powers are fading, like some of the others. I wonder why?"

He shut his mouth tight against his own theory. "What do you mean, like some of the others?"

She shot him a sharp look, then stroked Nilik's hair as she regarded the boy. "I wonder if this one will grow up to have a Spirit Guard."

Marek almost corrected her words again, but stopped himself.

"Which one do you think he'll have?" she asked him.

"It's hard to say, in one so young." He wondered if news of the Raven prophecy had come to Leukos, if they knew what Nilik might be. "His mother's a Rabbit."

"No, she's not."

Marek's heart tripped. Basha had caught him in a lie.

"His mother's not a Rabbit." She smiled sweetly at Nilik, then nuzzled his forehead. "His mother's a senator."

29

Filip gazed up at the iridescent bird who stood twice his height as he knelt on the cold, sandy soil. Something told him that he shouldn't regard this creature, that he should prostrate himself as he would before a manifestation of the sky god, Atreus. But he couldn't look away.

"I thought I was a Horse," he whispered. "What Spirit are you?"

"You are a Horse," the bird replied in a low, feminine voice that danced through Filip's mind. "I am Raven, the Mother of Creation, the Spirit of Spirits. Though I belong to no one, I greet all of my people at the Bestowing."

He looked down, at the reedy grasses under his knees. "Then I'm one of them now." His chest ached with loss.

"You are unique," Raven said. "You keep one foot in each world, that of your birth and that of your future."

He frowned at Her word choice. "I only have one foot," he said bitterly.

"Exactly." She flapped Her wings, sending sparks of color through the crisp morning air. "Listen to your Spirit and you will be blessed."

She darkened then, to the color a raven should be. Her wings and feet straightened, then bent, and Her feathers turned to sleek hair. Ears and mane sprouted from the new body, and Filip watched it mold itself into the blackest, most beautiful mare he'd ever seen. Her coat, tail, and mane dazzled without the benefit of the sun, and Her dark eyes gleamed at him with an inner light.

"Good morning," She said at last.

"I—I—" His mind blanked. "I thought you'd be white."

"I am." She faded from ink-black through slate-gray to the pure, blinding alabaster of his dream horse, of his home city. "Better?"

He shaded his eyes. "Whichever you prefer."

She blushed into a rich chestnut-red, leaving a white star in the middle of Her forehead. The change in color didn't surprise him; nothing could after the past three days.

On the first day of his Bestowing, Filip had sat on the grassy dunes, counting the waves as they rolled into shore. His stomach began to growl near midday, then ceased its complaints by sunset, which was obscured by thick clouds. The fasting hadn't bothered him; army life had made him scorn the seldom-met needs of the flesh.

Something crept close at the fall of the first moonless, starless night. It watched him in the dark, and though it wasn't an animal—he couldn't hear its thoughts—it oozed the aura of a predator. Filip sensed he shouldn't show fear, so he kept counting the waves, by sound alone. To keep his breath from lurching into panicky gasps, he matched it to the rhythm of the sea.

The thing drew away at the scarlet sunrise, and only then did Filip begin to tremble, for he knew it would return.

The second day brought heat and delirium. Animals came from the sea, the woods, the sand, speaking like humans, in a way that his gods never had. He wanted to smash the statues of every deity in the Ilion pantheon to show their falsehood. In the next moment, he wished they were here to beseech, to help him make sense of all this.

But when night fell, the thing from the woods stole those competing urges. It stole everything. The living void seeped into his soul and expanded, squeezing out all he once thought belonged to him. For hours he balanced, un-made, on the blade-thin edge of life and death.

Compared to all that, and to the appearance of Raven, the Horse Spirit felt comforting, familiar. Yet part of him resisted. Like a journey off a cliff, the final step was the hardest.

"I wish to be left alone," he told the Spirit.

Horse sighed. "There's wisdom in setting oneself apart, but it's not my wisdom, and it's not your destiny."

"I don't believe in destiny. I want to make my own choices, determine my own life."

"When you were a soldier, did you determine your own life?"

"No," he admitted, "I followed orders. But it was my choice to join the army."

"Your choice. Living in a world where military service is

the only measure of a young man. Following in the footsteps of your grandfather, your father and your brother." Her nostrils flared. "How is this a choice?"

"Those things are all true. It doesn't mean I didn't want to do it."

"But when you were a soldier, you were part of a body, serving something larger than your desires. Why now do you want to go your own way?"

"When I joined the army, they beat out all sense of me as a separate person. It was necessary to maintain discipline and cohesion. But now that I can see my self again, I don't want to lose it." He shifted his left leg. "I've made enough sacrifices for the so-called greater good."

"And yet you're here. Because the others expect it of you?"

"No. It's for me. And You."

"We're both here," She said softly. "So what are you waiting for?"

Filip frowned. It was a fair question. He hadn't come this far just to hide and sulk like a recalcitrant little boy. It was time to be a man.

"Nothing." He got to his feet. "Now what?"

"Come and cleanse yourself."

They walked through the marshy grass to the center of the clearing, which was ringed with tall, whispering pines.

Filip saw no fresh water. He turned to the Horse Spirit. "Where do I—"

"Shh." Her red eyelashes blinked slowly. "Look again."

He turned back, and nearly fell over in surprise. A pool of glowing water rippled not five paces from where he stood.

"Get in."

Mesmerized by the tiny, bubbling waves, Filip took a step closer to the pool.

Horse snorted. "Undress first."

Filip hesitated. No one except Zelia the Otter healer had seen him naked since his injury. At home with Tereus he had undressed in the dark, as much to hide from himself as from the Swan.

But he was tired of being ashamed. If he couldn't reveal himself to his Spirit, he'd never be able to show Alanka, and their love would never be whole.

Filip peeled off his shirt, then undid his trousers. He sat on the ground to unstrap the prosthesis. It chafed his knee and the stub of his calf as it came off, for it had been left on too long. Once he'd retreated into his mind two days ago, he hadn't thought to remove it.

When his clothing was off, Filip edged over to the pool and dipped his right leg.

A fiery jolt shot from his foot into his hip, and he cried out in agony.

Horse murmured something he couldn't hear, but Her tone filled with concern and surprise.

"Is it supposed to hurt?" he asked the Spirit, panting through gritted teeth.

"When you submerge, the pain should stop."

He yanked his leg out of the water. "Put my whole body in there? Do you think I'm crazy?"

"The Bestowing requires a full commitment. Perhaps the water burns you because you're not yet one of us."

"If it's rejecting me, then throwing myself in seems like a stupid idea."

Horse took a step forward. "Who's rejecting whom?"

She was right. Halfway was too far, and not far enough. He launched himself face first into the pool.

The water sliced on impact. He pushed to the surface and drew his head out, expecting to see the pool fill with his own blood. It was as clear as ever.

Then the pain stopped. The sudden cessation almost hurt worse than the agony itself. He drew in several deep, rasping breaths. Within a few moments, however, he calmed himself. Wiping his eyes and nose, Filip noticed that the water was caressing him, searching him, as if it had a life and hands of its own. He submerged again.

He let his body sink, down, down. There seemed to be no end to this pool in any direction. He could swim forever, but where? Maybe the Spirits were dangling before him one last chance to leave this world. He searched for temptation within himself, and found none.

Filip broke the surface and gazed up at Horse. Her tail swished.

"For a moment," She said, "I thought you were going to disappear. Climb out now. It's time."

He clambered from the pool onto the grass, his skin humming. "Time for what?"

In the vision, as in his dreams, Filip ran. Not with two legs, not on horseback, but on four legs of his own, over an endless prairie. The herd pressed around him, heaving and grunting, hooves slamming the ground like thunder against clouds.

A few kicked and bucked and whinnied, but not Filip.

He wanted only to run, to feel the solid earth beneath his feet in a steady rhythm, to clutch this feeling of connection uninterrupted by falsehood, to sense the speed.

He edged around the right side of the herd and broke for the lead. The wind gusted into his nostrils and whipped his mane over his neck. A few threads of golden forelock danced over his right eye. Exhilaration and gratitude increased his speed until he neared the front of the herd, running on its outer right flank.

Then he saw it, in the distance. He angled his muzzle to get a clearer view, unaccustomed to having eyes on the sides of his head. Perhaps it was an illusion created by the long, dancing grass.

No. Close ahead, the world stopped. The prairie wasn't endless—it was a plateau, and the herd was about to run over its edge into a wide canyon.

His pace slowed a fraction, and he drifted to the right, ready to stop. He was the only one.

"No!" he tried to call in a trumpeting neigh. "Stop!"

They didn't listen. He ran faster, urging his body to the left to steer the other horses away. There was time to turn them back if they changed course now.

Rather than heeding his warning, the herd swept him along in a wave of legs and hooves and bodies, a wave that could no more be held back than those of the sea.

Filip was hemmed in by another horse to his right, enveloping him inside the herd. If he stopped now, they would trample him. His legs ached, and his left hind hoof jabbed a sharp pain up through his ankle into his cannon bone.

The cliff loomed closer. He strained his neck to search for an opening, any way to escape the herd.

A small gap opened to his right. He swerved in that direction, his front hoof clipping the heel of the horse in front of him. They stumbled, and one of Filip's knees brushed the ground before he regained his feet.

With his last fragment of strength, Filip leaped aside, far enough to let the herd pass. He skidded to a stop, sending a skewer of pain through his left hind leg.

Chest and flanks heaving too hard to give one last warning, he watched the herd barrel toward the cliff and over the edge. He turned away and waited for the screams.

Which never came. After a few moments, he looked back at the empty edge of the plateau. Nothing but dust moved there.

He hobbled to the cliff and peered over. The other horses were gone. Not piled in a bloody heap at the bottom of the gorge. Gone.

He thought perhaps the vision had ended, then realized he still had four legs, one of which was beginning to heat and swell. His sweat-soaked hide shivered.

The silence broke with the pounding of a hundred hooves. Filip stared across the canyon to see the horses reappear on the other side. They plunged forward as before, in a swirl of grass and dust, tails streaming behind them like soldiers' flags.

He looked down at the edge of the cliff, then ahead at the horses again. He put one hoof, tentatively, into the air above the gorge. It felt like air—insubstantial and mundane. It wouldn't hold him, wouldn't transport him into another realm from which he could reappear at will. He would fall.

He watched what had once been his herd fade into the distance.

Filip came back to himself, on his hands and knees. His limbs gave way, and he collapsed. The loneliness bore down on him; he drew up his legs and covered his head with his arms, as if such a feeble action could ward off the feeling of absolute abandonment.

A soft muzzle tickled his ear. "Would you still prefer to be alone?"

"What if I say yes?" Filip whispered. "Will you go away and send another Spirit? Or better yet, send no Spirit at all and let me go back to the way I was before I came to this godsforsaken land?"

Horse hesitated. "Yes."

He moved his arm to see if She was teasing. The dark eyes held only sadness.

"I will not only leave you Spiritless—I can restore your body to its original shape."

Filip sat up. "You can give me back my leg?"

"Your leg is gone, buried with all the others. But I could alter your false one in such a way that your people wouldn't notice the difference. You could return to Leukos with honor."

"Why would you do that for me?"

"To show you the mercy of the Spirits. Even if you reject us, even if you return to what you call home, you will remember how we didn't force you, that we let it be your choice."

"It's never felt like my choice," Filip said, then reconsidered. "Until now."

"You were the first among your people to find your way back to us, even though you weren't looking." She flicked one red ear. "Perhaps we put too many hopes into you."

"What kind of hopes?"

"Of reconciling all the people again, with us and with each other. When your ancestors rejected our ways, we may have been too hasty in taking away their magic. It left them with no choice but to build and conquer." Her flank shimmered as She drew a deep breath. "We will offer another chance, if it's not too late."

"You'll give my people magic?"

"Not all of them, not yet. They would only use it to rule others. Besides, the powers of the wilder Spirits are weakened in your city. Our strength comes from things of the earth, not things built by humans."

Filip contemplated how the Asermons had no temples for their rituals, how Bolan had told him that man-made structures separated them from the Spirits. It was so different from his people, who built elaborate temples to the deities.

His stomach sank, and he looked up at Horse. "Do our gods exist?"

"They exist." Horse swung Her head toward the south. "They exist because you created them."

"That's not what I mean." He put his head in his hands. "But they must exist, outside of our minds. They've answered my prayers. I prayed for speed to beat my brother in the Ilion Games, and it worked. During the drought I prayed for rain—we all did—and it worked."

"That's how you measure your gods' strength? By how often they do your bidding? What about all the times they didn't answer your prayers?"

"I hadn't made a large enough sacrifice," he said, "or I'd said the words in the wrong order. Or maybe it was just their will."

"Why do you make excuses for them? If they are true gods, they don't need your apologies."

Filip felt the last of his old faith fade within him, yet nothing settled in its place. "I can't worship you."

Horse snorted. "I don't want your worship. I want your honor and your respect. I want you to give that to every person and every creature you meet, but especially to me. I want you to hold my wisdom close to your heart, or your head, or whatever you use to make decisions, so that you can find it when you need it." She stepped back. "That's all. If you can accept that, if you can accept *me* as your Guardian Spirit, then rise."

Filip dug his fingers into the sandy soil, one last attempt at resistance.

But he wanted to cross the chasm, not stand on its edge and peer across, or gaze with longing at its rocky depths. Without his Spirit, he was alone. Without Alanka, he was lost.

He planted his hands on the ground and heaved his weight onto his foot. Then he stood, arms spread—for balance and to receive whatever entered them. "I'm ready."

"Close your eyes," Horse said softly.

Filip obeyed, then felt himself waver. He stretched his arms wider to keep his balance, but did it too quickly. His body wobbled and fell forward.

A soft, warm form caught him in time. He wrapped his arms around Horse's neck and curled his hands around the long, coarse hair of Her mane. He sobbed without tears over his lost home, his inability to turn back time.

When his breath came deep and even again, Horse spoke.

"Filip, the Spirits have given you a place of honor in their hopes. We expect much from you. In return I give you the power to live inside the minds of other creatures, to feel the ground beneath their feet, the wind through their feathers, the waves over their scales. With this power you shall connect to the land, the air, the water, as few others have." She grumbled. "I daresay, no one needs this power more than you."

A sudden warmth flowed through Filip, stealing his breath. His blood sang with freedom and power, cleansing him with every heartbeat.

"We will always be with you," She whispered. "Never forget that."

She was gone. Filip sank onto the grass and rolled on his back. He stared at the blue sky, his mind drifting with the clouds.

A vulture soared overhead, black-and-white wings catching the breeze like a sail. Filip closed his eyes and opened his awareness to the creature.

It was hot and bright up here, and silent except for the wind's low whistle. The vulture was hungry but not starving. The feathers at her wingtips rippled, letting her anticipate the slightest change in draft. The world below was tiny and passive, like a war map empty of soldiers.

Is that thing dead? the vulture wondered. *Saw it move a while ago. Down for closer look.*

Filip saw himself flap his arm to show he was alive.

He disconnected, then watched from below as the vulture sailed away.

The sun cleared the treetops, and he realized it would burn him if he didn't dress and return to the shade. Yet he lingered, turning his head to the side to shade his eyes.

A beetle crawled through the grass nearby, and Filip wondered what it would be like to have six legs instead of one. Cautiously, his mind reached out to the insect.

Green, everywhere, and huge. The world around the beetle teemed with life Filip never knew was there. Ants, the size of one of his six feet. Mites, smaller yet. He stumbled through the forest of grass, following the scent trail of a nearby female. Around the next blade, she waited, ready.

Filip pulled his mind out of the beetle's—out of disgust or decency, he wasn't sure. He sat up, head aching.

He dressed, beginning with his prosthesis. It reminded him of Horse's offer, to let him return to Leukos more or less whole, but without magic and without Alanka. In exchange for his acquiescence he'd been granted more power than most of her people normally received.

The Spirits wanted him to reconcile two populations with little in common. Did They want him to undo centuries of Ilion progress? Then again, if the accomplishments of Ilios meant disconnecting from the Spirits, maybe it wasn't progress after all.

Perhaps this voyage to Leukos would mark the beginning of a new era of peace, one in which his parents' people and Alanka's could learn from each other without death and captivity.

Or maybe it would be the next phase of war.

Marek lay awake, listening to the snores and sleep whimpers of his fellow slaves. Like every night, he willed his mind elsewhere, into the dark forest of his home, the place where he had lived and hunted, the place where he had met Rhia.

If he closed his eyes and clamped the thin pillow around his ears, he could pretend he was with her that first night, on the cold ground, with each other's bodies as the sole source of warmth. He'd been invisible at night back then, and she'd let him make love to her before even seeing his face. Somehow they had known, after only a few hours, that they belonged together.

He ached for her touch now. During the day he could occupy himself with his chores and caring for Nilik, but night brought loneliness and longing without relief.

A hand grasped his shoulder, and he stifled a yelp.

Petrop.

The butler, dressed in his nightclothes, whispered, "Her Honor wishes to see you in her chamber."

Marek froze. "What for?"

"Correction—Her Honor orders your presence in her chamber."

Marek sat up and reached for the shirt hanging over the foot of his bed.

"Don't bother," Petrop said.

Barefoot, Marek followed the butler down the dark hallway, lit by the torch the older man carried. Booted footsteps behind them told him they were well guarded.

Now Marek understood why he'd been given soap and a tub of hot water to bathe and shave with that evening, instead of the usual cold, damp cloth. He'd thought it a reward for some task well done, when in fact, it was preparation for a task ahead. His knees felt liquid.

Following Petrop past the top of the stairs, he came to a part of the house he'd never entered before. His pace slowed as they passed a closed door. Nilik was in that room, he could smell.

The next door was open and flanked by guards. Petrop led him through a small sitting room, past a table with a reflective glass. Marek stopped at the threshold of a bedroom, his eyes adjusting to the light of a dozen candles.

Basha lay in the center of a large bed surrounded by lush purple curtains. Red silk sheets revealed bare shoulders draped with golden curls. One thin eyebrow arched at the sight of him.

"Come." She beckoned with long fingernails. "I have a meeting early in the morning, so no time to waste."

Someone gave Marek a pointed shove between his shoulder blades. He crept forward to stand at the side of the bed. This couldn't be happening.

"My healer claims you are free of diseases," Basha said. "She also says you're well endowed for someone of your stature. So you may trade five days' kitchen duties for the privilege of serving in my bed tonight." She drew the sheets aside to reveal her naked body. "I assure you, it will not feel like drudgery."

Marek looked at the floor, searching for a diplomatic way to decline. "I'm truly honored," he said, "but I have a wife."

"Not anymore."

He swallowed. "We've taken vows."

"Look at me." When he dragged his gaze back to her face, she continued, "If you never come home, won't she marry someone else and have another baby? I know how your magic works. If she's ever to come into full power, she'll need a child she can be assured will grow up into a parent."

"But it's so soon." If he could get a reprieve, maybe she'd lose interest over time. "Only a month since I was taken. I need time to mourn before I can—serve you this way. Before I could do it well."

She looked past him at Petrop. "Is this slave attempting to negotiate with me?"

"It would appear so, Your Honor."

"Fascinating." She turned her attention back to Marek. "Before making your final decision, be aware that I have guards watching us." She twirled the end of a curl around her finger. "If you refuse me, they will kill you."

A shudder gripped his body. To betray Rhia this way

would sear his soul to ashes. He couldn't. The memory would be worse than death.

The Wolf inside him made one last stand. "Let them kill me."

Basha sat up and moved closer to examine his face. "You're serious, aren't you?"

He stared over her shoulder and said nothing.

"Then let's try again." She drew her fingernail down the center of his bare chest. "Refuse me, and I won't have you killed. I'll simply sell Nilik to the highest bidder."

He looked at her. "Like who?"

"Perhaps someone who loves children—" her hand drifted lower "—but in a different way than I do."

Marek's stomach lurched, from both the thought and her touch. "You wouldn't do that to him."

"Why wouldn't I? I'm not overly fond of him." She clicked her tongue. "He doesn't like me. All he does is cry. Perhaps I'd be better off with a more pleasant child. It would be best to make the switch now before I become attached."

"No."

"Is that a no? Or is that a yes disguised as a no?"

Whatever it takes, said the voice again, the voice that wanted to survive.

"I can't force you," Basha said, "the way I could if I were a man and you a woman." She untied his trousers. "But I can encourage you." She slipped her hand inside. He caught it.

"Please, don't."

Basha slapped him with her other hand. "No begging! Be a man, not a little girl."

Cheek stinging, he stared at her with a mix of horror and

a rising rage. She moved to strike him again, but he seized her wrist in time to avoid the blow.

She laughed. "That's right. I've heard you 'beasts' like it rough." She stroked him, hard. "So show me."

"No!" He shoved her away, and she fell back onto the bed, laughing.

He turned from her, but when he saw the door to the hallway, he remembered who lay in the next room.

Nilik.

Marek stopped. Two of his fellow slaves had been born in captivity, their bodies used in every way since childhood. If it had happened to them, it could happen to Nilik.

Basha waited behind him.

The choice should have been easy. It shouldn't have taken so long to turn back to the bed. But first his soul had to fly away to perch on the ceiling, where it could watch him undress and climb into the bed with Basha. It watched as he met each of her demands. It wept to see his body's willingness. It couldn't see his eyes, but it felt the vacancy within them.

Afterward, Basha stretched and nuzzled her pillow, smiling. "A good effort for a first time. A bit sloppy, though, like your writing." She trailed a finger in the sweat of his chest. "Don't worry. Experience will bring precision to both endeavors."

He stared at the ceiling, half-hoping his soul would stay up there forever. His body was no longer a clean place to live. But it came back, anyway, for Nilik, and with it an unsurpassable anguish.

Back in the slaves' quarters, the guards let him wash again. He rubbed his skin with bath salts until it bled, but couldn't erase her smell.

The next morning, Basha let Marek leave home to help fetch produce from the market. The guards watched every word and movement, but they couldn't stop his mind from storing the sights, sounds and scents of freedom.

Wolf had left him, but another Spirit had taken His place, one who would keep Marek's body alive and his mind scheming, even as his soul shriveled within.

Alanka walked with Filip along the sandy beach. She knew their journey was almost over, for they had turned northeast. Her eyes strained for Leukos in the distance, but the summer evening haze made the horizon hard to see.

Several times in the past two weeks Filip had guided their troupe inland to avoid small Ilion settlements along the shore. He'd shown them one, Marisos, from a nearby hilltop. From a distance it looked like Velekos, with the ominous addition of a large stone fort outside, flying the red-and-yellow Ilion flag. She'd shivered, hoping she wasn't looking into her own people's future.

In Leukos, Filip said, it would be easier to blend, as one of many anonymous peasants come to find work in the prosperous city. Bit by bit, the countryside was coming under the control of noblemen who evicted the peasants from their land, then replaced them with slaves. Even the richer farmers struggled to extract food from exhausted fields. No wonder the fertile hills of Asermos looked so good to the Ilions.

He let go of her hand and reached into his trouser pocket. "I brought you down here to the sea for a reason."

"A reason other than a romantic walk on the beach?"

"Two reasons, then," he said without smiling. He pulled his hand out of his pocket and opened it. A wooden bar the length of her little finger sat in his palm. It was painted with red-and-yellow stripes.

She picked it up. "What's this?"

"A ribbon. Every Ilion soldier who completes basic training receives this one."

She tried to bend the inflexible bar. "Why's it called a ribbon when you can't tie it?"

"These bars stand in place of the real ribbons, which are worn on parade uniforms. We wear these on our field uniforms here, in rows." He pointed to the space above his heart. "We can acquire others through service or valor." He chuckled. "We pretend we don't care about ribbons or medals, that all we care about is the mission. But secretly we keep score."

She had learned to ignore his habit of referring to the Ilion troops as *we*. Since the Bestowing, he was one of her people; someday she knew his words would follow. "Was this ribbon yours?"

"I got it from Adrek, your friend who tried to strangle me. He brought it from your village. It fell off one of the invading soldiers."

She almost dropped it, as if it would burn her, but then placed it carefully in his hand. "You kept it, so it must mean something to you. It's yours now."

"Not for long." He drew back his arm to throw it in the sea.

"No!" She caught his wrist. The ribbon fell to the wet

sand in front of them. She dashed to pick it up before the next wave rolled in.

"What are you doing?" he said. "I want to get rid of it."

"You can't throw away your past. It's part of you." She pointed toward Leukos. "It's a part we need if we're going to survive in your city. You have to act like them, talk like them, think like them." She held out the ribbon. "Horse wants you to be a bridge between our peoples. A bridge can't stand if it's not connected to both shores."

Filip stared at her for a long moment, then took the ribbon and tugged her into his arms. "You understand me better than I understand myself."

"It's because—" She stopped. Every other man had swept the words aside. "It's because I love you."

His body stiffened, and he pulled back. "I wish you hadn't said that."

Fear froze her muscles. "Why?"

"Because I wanted to say it first." He cupped her face between his broad hands. "I love you, Alanka. I promise I'll love you forever."

She took in a sharp breath. "What are you saying?"

"When we return home, I want to marry you." His thumb caressed her cheek. "If you want."

He kissed her, and she wanted to melt into his embrace and let him shield her from the pain of the past and future. But it felt like something someone else would do, not her.

"What if we never go home?" she said when their lips parted. "What if we stay here, even after we find Marek and Nilik? There are so many others from my village. They could be scattered around the country."

"I'll help you find them. If we stay here, we'll just be married between us. I'm legally dead as far as Ilios is concerned." His lips twitched. "At least I don't have to pay taxes."

"There is that." She raised her chin. "What are taxes?"

He laughed. "Taxes are when the people pay money to— Wait, you never answered my question." He looked as if he was trying to look amused. "Will you marry me?"

"Maybe." Her gaze dropped. "I'm not ready now. Not until my Spirit returns, if He ever does."

"Alanka, maybe Wolf hasn't abandoned you. Maybe you abandoned Him."

She pulled out of his embrace. "How can you say that?"

"I've offered ways to reconnect with Him, but you have an excuse for why each one won't work without even trying. It's as if you'd rather wallow in guilt than become whole again."

"I am whole again. Rhia returned my soul part."

"But you haven't listened to it. You act like your father's watching over your shoulder, judging your memories, calling you a murderer for defending your brothers' home." He stepped closer to her. "You have the chance now to help Marek. Wolf will be at your side. If the Spirits regret abandoning my people long ago, they won't be quick to do the same to those who've served them well."

She shut her eyes and turned away. "I don't know how to let Him back in."

"If you stop pushing Him away, Wolf will probably figure it out on His own." Filip put his arms around her from behind. They stood for a long time, listening to the waves. Suddenly he drew a quick breath. "Look."

She turned to where he was pointing. The haze had cleared, and the setting sun shone from behind them, glistening pink against a series of bumps on the distant horizon.

"What is that?"

"It's Leukos," he whispered. "We'll be there tomorrow."

31

Filip led the rescuers east along the coast, watching Leukos grow on the horizon. He tried not to remember the view of the sunrise from his old bedroom window. Countless mornings had found him regarding that red orb, contemplating the power it granted to his nation—long summers for growing crops, warm seas filled with food and rays that warmed their homes long after sunset.

He steeled himself for the first sight of an Ilion flag, bearing the same red and yellow that adorned his officer's uniform. It had been sliced off his body in the field hospital and discarded, probably burned. He wished he had even a scrap of it now.

Filip rubbed his chin for the hundredth time. His fair color and fine hair had made it difficult to grow a decent beard, which he needed as a disguise in Leukos. It had taken the entire month, since the day they left Asermos, to cover his chin. Leukon men of his class shaved every day, so with a beard he'd be looked upon—and ignored—as a ruffian.

Alanka craned her neck behind him to look ahead. "It's beautiful, in a strange sort of way." She slid her hand down his arm. "How does it feel?"

At first he couldn't speak, couldn't begin to answer a question that cut so deep. Finally he said, "I'd always dreamed of riding home a hero. Look at me now."

"I am looking at you," she said. "You have your dream."

He touched her hand in gratitude. "Not yet."

At Filip's suggestion, they slipped into the northwest quadrant of Leukos, one of the city's less savory and therefore less well-guarded sections. At least here he knew they could afford a room and a stable for the ponies.

Their drab, utilitarian Asermon clothes resembled those of the rural peasants, so there would be no need to buy new wardrobes, other than a few accessories such as red-and-yellow sashes, worn by men and women of all classes to signify their loyalty to Ilios. It pained Filip to think of wearing one as a mere disguise.

By noon they had procured two rooms at a plain but sanitary-looking inn. Filip paid for a week in advance, and the gruff proprietor asked no questions as he pocketed their money.

"That's the advantage of a big city," Filip told his friends as they walked, unaccompanied, down the inn's stone hallway. "It's easy to blend in. Besides, no one really looks at each other."

"Why not?" Koli asked.

He stopped outside their rooms. "Give someone an unfriendly eye—or a too-friendly eye—and they might pluck it out." He unlocked the men's room, handed the other key to Koli and realized he should have mentioned that sooner.

After washing up, Filip and Bolan knocked on the door to the room where the women were staying. Rhia beckoned them in and drew a flat wooden box from her pack.

"Take care of it," she said.

"We will." Filip took the box and slipped it into the inside pocket of his tattered vest.

Alanka approached him. "You'll be safe, right?"

"Of course. There's no law against petting stray dogs." He touched her warm cheek. "Don't go out without Arcas and Lycas. Better yet, don't go out."

He and Bolan left the inn and strode through the long shadows of the side streets toward the market. On the way there, he explained the city's layout.

"It's divided into quadrants. Right now we're in the northwest quadrant. Tawdry area, for the most part. Lower-class, manual laborers, a few craftsmen. Few slave owners, though, so I'd be surprised to find Marek here."

Bolan cast a wide-eyed gaze around him and said nothing.

"Don't gawk," Filip told him. "You'll call attention to yourself."

Bolan narrowly avoided bumping into a donkey cart. "Where are all the trees?"

"In the park."

"What's a park?"

"A place where they have trees." He breathed in deep through his nose, savoring the unique mix of salt air, rotting fish and horse dung, a combination he once found putrid. Now its familiarity made it painfully sweet.

On the outskirts of the bustling market block, they found their first target. A skinny brown dog lurked in a recessed doorway, ribs showing through its dull, shaggy coat. Filip and Bolan approached it from an oblique angle so as not to startle it. They leaned against the stone wall of the building. Bolan squatted with a chunk of bread, holding it out to the side without looking at the dog.

The animal, a female, slunk out of its safe place, nose straining forward, legs tense and ready to run.

"Come on, girl," Bolan murmured. "Early supper for you."

Filip took Rhia's wooden box from his pocket, and the dog backed up.

"It's all right." Bolan offered the bread. He pursed his lips to make a kissing sound, avoiding the dog's gaze.

She stretched out, snatched the bread from his hand and leaped back to gnaw it, dripping crumbs from the sides of her mouth. Her scrawny tail wagged weakly. Filip held open the box.

Bolan rolled his sleeve down over his hand and picked up Marek's scarf, the one Rhia had packed, the one they hoped held Marek's scent over a month after his disappearance.

Bolan held out the scarf in the same posture as the bread. The dog crept forward, curious. Filip closed his eyes and linked his mind with the dog's.

Hunger pinched her gut, and her mouth was raw and sticky with thirst. Tiny things crawled through the fur on her neck.

The man with the food held out something else. *Could it hurt me?* The dog stepped back. But his hand smelled of bread, and his mind made kind, soothing noises. *Safe.* She took a step forward on sore paws.

The scarf smelled of another man, and, more faintly, a woman. Food Man wanted something from the dog.

"Have you smelled this man?" he asked. Filip heard Bolan's words through the dog's mind. He opened his eyes to see her lick Bolan's fingers and risk a glance at his face. She wanted more food. No sign of recognition.

Bolan frowned. "Thank you, anyway." He reached in his pocket, the one that held the rest of the bread.

Filip stopped him. "We need that for the others."

"But look at her, she's starving."

"There are hundreds more like her. You can't save them."

Bolan stood and looked at the dog, who backed off several paces, ready to flee, though she didn't look as if she would get far on such shaky legs. "How can they let them live like that? Why doesn't someone take care of them?"

"Because they're just beasts. They don't have souls."

Bolan turned to him. "You know that's not true."

"Now I do, but how are these people supposed to know that? The Spirits abandoned them, left them not only without magic, but without wisdom, too." They walked on, and he lifted a hand to the tall buildings around them. "They made their own wisdom out of nothing. Can you blame them?"

"They abandoned the Spirits first."

"Maybe, but they're only human. What's the Spirits' excuse?"

"What about the gods?"

Filip stopped walking. They stood before a small temple, erected in honor of a god he'd never heard of, no doubt the protector of this specific neighborhood and its people. "I used to believe they gave us all this," he said, "that the city was sitting here waiting for our ancestors. Most Ilions believe that, especially here in Leukos."

"What do the others believe?"

"That our ancestors built it with the gods' guidance."

"And what do you believe now?"

Filip watched the worshipers file in and out of the temple, entering with offerings and leaving empty-handed. For one brief black moment, he hated the Spirits for tearing the veil from his eyes.

He turned back to Bolan. "I believe it's getting late. Let's move on."

They gave a final glance at the brown dog, who had returned to lie in her doorway. Her head rested on her paws, dark eyes following them. Filip shut his mind hard against the dog's longing, before it could break him.

They walked in silence down the street to the market. The dogs here were bolder and fatter, though still unkempt and uncared-for. As soon as they smelled the food that Bolan and Filip offered, they swarmed around the two men. As they ate, they sniffed the scarf but took no more than a passing interest.

By midday Filip and Bolan had moved on to the northeast quadrant, where most of the government buildings were located. Filip tilted down his face, on the slim chance he was recognized.

They reached the square across from the Senate building where the city's largest market served the politicians and their burgeoning staff. It was crowded at this hour, with the afternoon respite. Throngs of people massed into the shady areas, fanning themselves and sipping cold juice drinks or diluted wine. Filip's mouth would have watered if he'd had enough saliva to wet it with.

In the wide, sunny courtyard in front of the Senate, a war monument stood, a monolithic structure of dark gray stone. It absorbed and radiated the sun's heat. No one stood near it on a summer day unless he or she had to.

He had to. He crossed the street, avoiding a train of noblemen on horseback.

Bolan hurried to follow. "Where are you going? The dogs are all back there."

"I have to see." He strode to the monument, feeling its heat oppress him from a hundred paces away. He reached its left side, then walked along its flank, careful not to step on the red and yellow roses strewed along the base. He trailed his fingers along the polished marble, touching the names of those who had lost their lives generations before his birth. So many wars, so many dead, so many sacrifices to keep his people free.

Around the last corner, on the side that had been blank the last time he was here, a new section was carved. At the top read Asermos.

Filip's hands shook as they caressed the stone, searching down, near the end, at waist level, for the last to die. He found the names of the six enlisted men shot by Bobcats outside the hospital.

And right before them, his own name.

Kiril had made it home after all, and reported Filip's demise. He was truly dead to his countrymen now.

His finger, no longer trembling, traced the letters of his first name, the stone's heat nearly burning his skin.

"Is that someone you knew?" Bolan said over his shoulder.

Filip nodded, then moved his hand to his second name. He heard Bolan sound out the letters, then gasp.

"It's you." He reached to touch the F. "I can't imagine…"

"No, you can't."

"And who's that?" Bolan pointed to Filip's last name. "Kal-Kalo—"

"Kaloyero. It's me. It was me. My family name." He looked up the stone, among the mass of men, some of whom he fought side-by-side with, some he'd only heard of. "It's the same as my brother's." He traced the outline of *Fedor.* The corners of his eyes felt heavy and thick.

"Your family thinks you're dead," Bolan whispered. "How horrible."

"No, it's good," he said vehemently, then wondered whom he was trying to convince. "It means I'll be remembered with honor. It means my family was well rewarded." His false foot shifted the stem of a red rose against the base of the monument. "Sacrificing both sons to Ilios would not have gone unnoticed. They'll be rich forever."

"It doesn't make up for losing their children."

"True, especially since no one lives to carry on the name.

But with that kind of money, they can pay a very nice dowry for my sisters, maybe enough to let one of them keep our name." He slid his finger across *Kaloyero*. "If she has a son, it will live on."

"A name is that important?" Bolan asked.

Filip turned from the monument and gazed across the street at the market, for a moment unable to remember why they were there. Who was he? Only Filip, or maybe no one at all.

A dog scampered off to the left, shooed by an irate butcher.

Filip pointed at it. "Back to the mission," he said to Bolan.

They started across the courtyard, slowed by the weight of the afternoon heat. Filip let himself look back once, and not at the monument itself, but at the roses left by those who loved the fallen. They may have been fresh this morning, but now they lay limp and wilted in the sun.

Their scent lingered in his memory, to haunt him the rest of the day.

32

Rhia leaped to the door when she heard the knock. She threw it open to reveal Filip and Bolan, sweaty and red from the day's heat.

Filip entered and handed Rhia the box with Marek's scarf. "Your husband's in Leukos."

Alanka gasped and hugged him. He winced as she scraped her arms over his sunburned neck.

"I'll get the others." Koli brushed past them into the hallway.

Rhia opened the box to see the scarf, dotted with dust and dog slobber. "You're sure?" She looked at Filip, then Bolan. "What about Nilik?"

They shook their heads. "We don't know," Bolan said. "I'm sorry."

Rhia wanted to hurl the box against the wall. Then she

remembered Marek's message. He would watch over Nilik, whatever it took. If Marek was alive, they must be together.

The others entered. "You found him?" Lycas said.

"In the northeast quadrant, the government district." Filip took a long sip of the water Alanka offered him and Bolan. "Several of the animals—dogs, horses, even a stray cat—recognized his scent. They remembered him fondly because he petted them."

"When was he there?" Rhia asked.

"Impossible to tell exactly," Bolan replied. "But some of them remembered it as a sunny day, while others remembered rain, which means that he didn't just pass through on the way to somewhere else. He's been on the streets more than once."

"I asked around," said Filip, "and it rained the day before yesterday."

Rhia's logic tried to quench her excitement. "How do we know the animals were remembering that storm and not another?"

"It must be," Filip said. "It rarely rains this time of year."

"So he was there only two days ago." She paced, turning the box over in her hands. "If he goes to that market regularly, then he must live nearby."

"How large is the northeast quadrant?" Arcas asked Filip.

"It's enormous. There's no way to know exactly where he is unless we're lucky enough to spot him."

"Then we'll go to the market tomorrow when it opens," Rhia said.

Filip nodded. "It's our best lead. But if he belongs to someone now, his presence at the market will be at his owner's whim. Going out in public is a reward for household slaves who behave well."

Rhia shuddered at the idea of someone owning Marek. He would never stand for it.

She noticed Filip giving her a chilling look. "I need to speak with Rhia alone for a moment," he said.

The others went to the next room to figure out what they needed to make dinner. Filip closed the door behind them, then sat in the rickety chair by the bed. She could see the exhaustion in his red-rimmed eyes.

"What is it?" she managed, her heart pounding.

"You remember how my Spirit gave me unusual powers for a first-phase Horse. I can not only hear an animal's thoughts, but I can connect to its mind—see what it sees, hear what it hears, smell what it smells."

She nodded. "Go on."

"I sensed something troubling in the animals who met Marek."

Rhia held her breath. "What was it?"

"They smelled him, of course." He looked at her with dread. "He smelled like fear."

The next morning Rhia was at the market the moment it opened. She tried to appear unassuming as she walked past the blocks of merchant stalls with her friends, but her gaze darted in all directions. Filip's findings had fed her worst suspicions. Marek was held against his will. He suffered.

Koli pinched Rhia's arm. "You look suspicious. We're here to shop, remember?"

"I don't want to miss Marek."

"There are seven of us. If he's here, one of us will see him."

Rhia nodded. They had split into three groups—Filip and Bolan, Lycas and Alanka, and she and Koli with Arcas.

She faked a casual glance at the nearest stall's produce. Some she didn't recognize, including a fuzzy blushing fruit whose heady scent she could smell from where she was standing. Curiosity overcame her, and she reached for it.

"First of the season," said the proprietor, a plump man with curly blond hair. "Everyone's asking about them—I'm the first to sell them. Come back in an hour, they'll all be gone."

"How much?" she asked, wanting to appear normal.

He told her the price, and she haggled him down by half, as Filip had instructed, taking two for the price of one.

She caught up to Arcas and Koli at a flower stand. Many of the blooms she recognized—lavender, chamomile, purple coneflower, but the larger ones she couldn't place.

Rhia examined a container of red flowers. Their smooth petals clustered in a velvety embrace. Like the fruit, their scent was cloying, overpowering. She ran the back of her finger against a petal. Its softness made her ache for Marek's touch.

"She likes them." The merchant, an old woman with sharp blue eyes and several missing teeth, smiled at Arcas. "Buy one for her. Why not?"

"What do they do?" Rhia asked.

The merchant looked confused. "Do?"

"What ailments do you take them for?"

The old woman chortled. "Nothing but loneliness." She

waved her hand. "Silly girl. The herbals are over there. These flowers are all for decoration." She raised her eyebrows at Arcas. "Or love."

Arcas started. "Oh, she's not my—er, not anymore."

"Maybe it was lack of roses that did it, heh?"

Rhia realized she meant the flowers. Next to the container with the long-stemmed flowers sat several pots containing soil and rose shrubs. One of the homes they'd passed on the way to the market had displayed these in a window box.

"Why spend money on something so useless?" Koli murmured. "That wouldn't impress me at all."

Arcas bought a red one and handed it to Koli, who promptly changed her mind about the utility of a rose.

Something hit the back of Rhia's leg. She looked down to see a pebble bounce near her shoe. She ignored it, assuming it had been kicked by a passerby.

Another, larger pebble hit Rhia's calf. She turned to look across the street. A man with light brown hair slipped back into the shadows behind a row of fish vendors. Her breath quickened. Marek? She started forward, then remembered Filip's warnings.

She tapped Koli and motioned for her and Arcas to follow.

"There's the signal." Lycas squeezed Alanka's arm so hard it hurt.

"I didn't hear it."

He jerked his thumb over his shoulder. "This way." He hurried down the street toward the fish merchants. She had to jog to keep up with him.

Rhia was waving at them from the head of an alleyway, obviously trying to subdue her excitement.

"They found him?" Alanka couldn't keep her feet from running.

They entered the alley. Halfway down, Rhia, Koli and Arcas surrounded a man sitting on a crate. Alanka didn't see a child in his arms.

Rhia stepped back.

It was Adrek.

He stood to greet Alanka, thinner than ever. A beard covered his face, and his hair fell ragged over his forehead, but beneath the mess his green eyes glistened at the sight of her.

"You're alive!" She ran forward and hugged him hard. His sharp collarbone dug into her neck, and his shoulder blades seemed covered only by skin. "I thought you died."

"Some of us did."

"Oh, no." She drew back to look at him. "What happened?"

"We were ambushed near the second battalion's base, east of the city." His shoulders slumped. "Some died in the fight. The rest were taken captive."

"What about you?"

"They put me and the other men to work clearing rocks for a new army camp near Surnos."

"You were a slave?" She touched his cheek in sympathy.

"I escaped two months ago and came here to look for Daria." His gaze dropped. "No luck yet."

"Where's Marek?" said a voice behind her.

Adrek looked up and snarled. "You!" He hurled himself at Filip, who dodged his attack and sent him sprawling on the ground.

"Adrek, stop!" Alanka rushed to quiet him, worried he'd draw the attention of the police. "Filip's one of us now."

Adrek rolled to his feet with no trace of his usual agility. "What do you mean, one of us?"

Rhia stepped forward. "He's had his Bestowing. The Horse Spirit claimed him."

Adrek turned an incredulous gaze on the rest of them, settling on Lycas.

"I couldn't believe it myself," the Wolverine said, "but I saw it happen."

Adrek gaped at Alanka's hand, wrapped around Filip's. "Makes no sense." He rubbed his head, then looked up at Rhia. "I saw Marek."

Alanka's heart leaped. Rhia jumped as if she'd been shocked.

"Where?" they asked in unison.

"In the market a few days ago," Adrek said. "That's why I was here today. Hoped I could signal him."

"Was he with anyone?" Rhia asked.

"Guards, six of them, and two other slaves."

Alanka's throat thickened with tears. Her Wolf-brother had lost his freedom.

"What did the guards look like?" Filip said.

Adrek angled a suspicious gaze at him, then spoke to the others. "They wore the insignia of the Senate on their shoulders."

"Then he's owned by a senator." Filip scraped his beard with his knuckles the way he did when he was deep in thought.

"But how do we find out which one?" Rhia asked. "What if his owner never lets him come back to the market?"

"We could follow each of them home," Lycas said.

"And ask the animals nearby," Bolan added.

"I have an idea." Filip paused. "I saw the war monument in the Senate courtyard yesterday. My name was on it. Everyone in this city believes me dead."

Alanka felt her eyes soften. She touched his arm. "I'm sorry."

He gave her a tight-lipped smile. "It helps us, because I can walk about without being recognized. Also, the monument reminded me of something else." He looked at the others. "Once every ten days the homeless are permitted to beg in the Senate courtyard. They're not allowed to speak or look at anyone, but they can show their presence. The law is meant to keep the politicians aware of how far anyone can fall." He took a deep breath. "Many of the homeless, unfortunately, are wounded veterans who can't find work. Often their families abandon them out of shame if the injury occurred in a military defeat." His voice quieted. "It would've been my fate, most likely, had I returned home."

"I see now why you couldn't," Lycas said. "But what does this have to do with Marek?"

"I know." Alanka gazed up at Filip, her heart heavy. "You mean to beg in the courtyard yourself, to overhear information."

He nodded. "It's a prime place for gossip. They would speak freely in front of a beggar. No one's more invisible to them, except perhaps a slave."

"I'll go, too," Adrek said. He met Filip's startled gaze.

"The more ears, the better. Besides, I can't let you be the only hero." He winked at Alanka.

"We'll all do it," Lycas added. "The men, at least. The women should patrol the market, in case Marek shows up again."

Filip's jaw dropped. "Thank you. It would be most useful." He let out a long breath and seemed to search for his next thought. "According to the calendar, tomorrow is the next legal begging day."

"Good," Adrek said, "because it's not only Marek we have to save. When I was clearing the land near Surnos, I overheard the soldiers say it was for the children. Maybe they're bringing the Kalindons there. Maybe that's where Daria will be."

"An army camp for children?" Rhia said. "Are you sure?"

"That's what I heard, and out there I still had my sharp senses."

Alanka jolted. "What do you mean, *out there* you had them?"

"My magic is mostly gone in the city." Adrek looked at her and Lycas. "Yours will both disappear, too. The wilder Spirits have no power here."

"Cougar has abandoned you?" Alanka said.

Adrek shook his head. "I can feel Him. He's with me, but doesn't have much to give. I've got half the stealth and night vision I did when I was first phase." He rubbed his thin arms. "Strength and jumping, next to nothing, like I'm thirteen again. But I feel more connected to Cougar than ever. He's all I have left. Until now, anyway."

Alanka felt a pang of sympathy and admiration for her

former mate. Unlike her, he'd kept his faith, even after suffering more than any of them.

Except perhaps Marek.

Marek took Basha hard and rough—because that was the way she demanded it, but also because it was the only way he could channel his hatred. When his mouth pressed against her neck in what she called passion, he had to stop his teeth from tearing out her throat.

As soon as it was over, he turned to leave the bed. She grabbed his arm.

"Wait," Basha said. "Stay awhile."

He lay back down and regarded the ceiling. He couldn't look at this woman who had robbed him of everything he'd ever cared about—except Nilik—without wanting to kill her.

"You've been so quiet lately." She turned on her side to face him. "More than usual, that is."

He said nothing.

"You may speak."

He said nothing.

"By the gods, don't be so sullen." She trailed a finger down his arm, and he wanted to bite it off. "I only see light in your eyes anymore when you're holding Nilik." Her nails tickled the palm of his hand. "Or holding me, but that's a different sort of light, isn't it?"

He heard her raise herself on one elbow. "Look at me." She leaned in closer and turned his chin to face her. Her eyes sparked with fear and she let go of him. "On second thought, don't look at me."

Marek expected to be dismissed, but Basha spoke again.

"I'd rather you not dislike me too mightily. It makes me feel like a tyrant. Just because I own you doesn't mean I don't respect you."

Marek laughed out loud, then covered his mouth. He'd be punished for sure.

"Respect your people, that is." Basha went on as if he'd had no reaction to her last statement. "I find your culture fascinating. It's so different from ours, I doubt you'll ever be assimilated the way our other conquests have. Not by force, at least. I keep telling my colleagues that, but they won't listen to a woman, not even me."

He felt the Fox inside him prick its ears, and he realized his opportunity. Self-pity would paralyze him. If he was to survive and escape one day, he needed information.

"If not by force," he said, "how will you conquer us?"

She bit her bottom lip as she smiled. "Ah, you can form words after all. I thought perhaps my body had rendered you speechless."

He waited for her to answer the question. She stretched and turned onto her back. "Some want to mount another invasion, but I suspect that's to save face. They lost so pitifully at Asermos, they want to avenge that humiliation. But such a deployment would be futile and expensive, especially when the tensions among the cities are so high."

"There's internal strife?" His own lands had experienced it more than once, which partly explained his village's historic mutual hostility with Asermos. Kalindos had never been foolish enough to wage outright war against the larger village, but skirmishes had occurred, causing bad blood to simmer down through the generations.

Basha's expression grew guarded. "Nothing Leukos can't handle."

He turned to her, which made her face light up in surprise.

"You say my people fascinate you," he said. "Is that why you wanted Nilik? To have a piece of that culture?"

"You're half right. Nilik's a baby. He has no culture. He'll be raised as an Ilion citizen, as a Leukon, and he'll have my dead husband's name. As far as anyone, including him, is concerned, he's my son."

Marek tried to keep his voice steady. "Then he'll never know who he really is?"

"You see, that's the mystery." She rolled over to face him and whispered conspiratorially, "We want to see if your people will gain magic when they come of age, if any Spirits will take them on, and if so, which ones. We have our theories."

"What theories?"

"That the Spirits' real power lies in the wilderness. People like you, whose animals need lots of space and have no tolerance for human interference, your powers fade in the city. But others, we've noticed, do not."

"Which others?"

"Those with animals that can live alongside humans, who survive in the city, even if it's in the park. Horses, Goats, Spiders. Bats and Foxes, to a lesser extent."

He shuddered at the last Animal—was that why it felt as if Fox had taken over his soul in the absence of Wolf? Was She even now helping him find a way to escape? If anyone was a survivor, it was Fox.

Basha counted off on her fingers. "What else? Rats, of course. Several birds—Swans, Sparrows, Mockingbirds."

Crows? he wondered. Of course. They were everywhere.

"You see, Marek, that's why you're half correct. I wanted Nilik because he was Asermon, but not to add him to my collection of quaint, rustic works of art. It's to find out if I'm right."

"Right about what?"

"That your people can be conquered without force. To do that we need to know everything about your powers. These children, especially the newborns, are a perfect experiment." She smoothed his hair back from his face and curled her finger around the ends. "You will all fall before us, be assured. Everyone does in time. But I'd prefer to do it later and overwhelmingly, rather than sooner and sloppily. It's much more humane that way, don't you agree?"

Marek felt as if his head were caught in a vise.

"Perhaps you don't agree," she said. "So I'll tell you there was a third reason for wanting Nilik." Her gaze dropped to the space between their bodies. "I was lonely. I had lost so much."

And gained only a Senate seat, he thought.

"I know you mourn your wife," she said. "I understand, because I think of my husband every night and every morning. That's why I ask others to share my bed."

Ask? She must be joking.

Her eyes turned pensive. "I wonder sometimes when I look at Nilik, if my son would have done the same things he does. Like the way he stretches out the fingers of his right hand when he yawns, as though he's drawing in breath through them." She imitated the motion. "Do other babies do that?"

"They each have their own gestures, like older people."

She smiled sheepishly. "Obviously I haven't much experience with infants. I was the youngest child in my family. I preferred playing with anything other than dolls—toy animals, even my older brothers' little soldiers, when I could steal them. Until I was pregnant, the idea of being a mother never appealed to me." Her smile faded. "But when the baby died, it was all I could think about." She brushed his cheek with the back of her fingertips. "You lost one, too. You understand me."

Marek did not answer. He hoped he'd never understand her, never understand how she could treat him this way and pretend it was nothing remarkable, how she could plot to use Nilik's powers against his own people. Even if she released them both tomorrow and put them on a ship to Asermos, he'd never forgive her.

"I should go." He sat up. "With your permission, that is, Your Honor. It's getting late."

"Stay." She put a hand on his chest. "I want you again."

He froze. "I don't think I can."

"It's a challenge I'd like to accept." She drew him down beside her. "Kiss me."

He withheld a sigh of disgust, seized her shoulders and pulled her into a hard, brutal kiss. After a moment, she pushed him away.

"Not like that this time," she whispered, her eyes wet. "Kiss me like you don't hate me."

He hesitated. How could he?

A voice whispered in the back of his mind. *You have her.*

Basha's eyes screamed her need for something to fill the space her loss had left behind. If he gave it to her, she could be influenced, even by a mere slave.

Whatever it takes.

He lowered his head to brush his lips against hers, softly. She moaned.

"Yes." Basha took his hand and drew it up her waist, over her breast. "Touch me like you don't hate me."

Though Marek thought his hands would burn her with loathing, he obeyed, banishing his soul where it couldn't crumple in her hands like a sheet of discarded paper. Without it, his body could do what it had to do, could respond to her touch as if it didn't repulse him.

When he was ready to enter her, she stopped him. "One more thing." She gazed up at him. "Tell me you love me."

He rolled off her as tears swelled his chest and eyes. "I can't do that. It's the one thing I can never do."

"Please." Her voice stopped short, as she must have realized she'd never spoken that word to him before. "I'm so alone."

"I don't love you."

"Of course you don't. Just let me pretend."

Pretend, he thought, and it came to him, the secret he'd been missing. He would pretend Basha was Rhia. Though her hands, legs, voice and scent were different, maybe his mind could fool his senses long enough to fulfill this task. If he could give Basha this, she would be his, and he could find a way to escape.

He turned back to her, and it was Rhia's skin he touched and kissed, Rhia's mouth on his neck and shoulders, Rhia's hands stroking him back to readiness.

It was in Rhia's ears he whispered, "I love you," but as soon as the words left his mouth, they lost all meaning.

33

Using his crutches, Filip hobbled to his place at the foot of the stairway to the long stone Senate building. He sat next to one of two small shrubs flanking the stairs. Their shiny leaves were the only green he could see, though they looked black in the dim predawn light.

He placed his begging bowl on the white stone pavement and waited. Everything about this endeavor felt wrong, down to his core, but he told himself his unease came from the preconceptions of his youth.

Soon dawn leaked blue around the buildings and over the white courtyard. The war monument stood as a dark void, a reminder to all who passed of their countrymen's sacrifices.

They would get a few more reminders soon. Adrek, Arcas and Lycas had spaced themselves around the square, along with about a dozen regular Leukon beggars.

The clear sky blushed pink and orange, and the tops of the buildings glowed. He watched as his city came to life. Soon the streets bustled like anthills. Senate staffers in blue uniforms, most a few years older than Filip, hurried through a side courtyard to his left, ready to prepare the building for another session.

He spotted the first senator crossing the street from the market, a few hundred paces away. He was dressed in the goldenrod robe of his office, a red sash at his waist, and looked to be in his late fifties. He used a wooden cane, favoring his right side.

Filip sat with his back to the wall, his half leg extended before him, with the empty part of the trouser tucked under his stump so that there could be no mistaking what had happened to him.

His mouth went dry at the thought of his countrymen seeing him like this. They would wish he'd hide himself like a proper man. No, a proper man would have died in battle or ended his own life rather than continue this way.

The senator hobbled across the courtyard, on a path that would take him past Filip. Surely this man would understand what infirmity meant. Upon closer look, he looked more like sixty or sixty-five years old. Lines etched his face like a map of the Four Rivers region. The metal tip of his cane clicked against the stones as he approached the building. Then Filip saw a blue patch on the man's shoulder, signifying that his wounds had been garnered in victory. He leaned around the small shrub to get a better glimpse.

The senator stopped at the foot of the steps and looked

straight at Filip, who stared back. For one moment, they were brothers-in-arms.

Suddenly the older man roared and waved his cane at him. Filip's stomach twisted. After telling his friends, "Don't look at them," he'd forgotten the rule himself. He dropped his gaze to the pavement in front of him.

"I ought to have you arrested." The tapping came closer, louder. "It's bad enough we have to see human garbage like you every tenth day, but to have one of them look at us, judging us?"

"Forgive me," Filip whispered, "I meant no—"

"Do not speak to me!" The cane whistled through the air, missing his left shoulder by less than a handspan. "If there weren't laws against beating you myself, I'd bash in your skull. Think I'm too old and feeble to do it?"

Filip trembled with rage at having to beg for the chance to beg. He imagined the surprise that would paint the senator's face if he grabbed the cane, turned it around and plunged it into his gut. Then the man would see that a warrior lived in him still.

His imagination would have to suffice. He kept his gaze on the ground. An ant wandered in the mortared crack between the flat stones.

"Spaneas, what's the matter?" Another man approached on lighter footsteps—another senator, judging by his yellow hem, the only part Filip dared to regard.

Spaneas snorted. "This hoodlum had the temerity to look at my face, even speak to me. We should fetch the police."

"Later. Come, the chairman needs to speak with you before the meeting." He tossed a coin into Filip's bowl before taking the older man away. Filip was so surprised, he forgot to nod his gratitude.

As the sunlight on the buildings changed from orange to yellow, other senators filed past, ignoring Filip in their hurry to get inside before the session started. Though he wasn't watching their eyes, he sensed their indifference and understood what it was like to be invisible.

A bell gonged, and the courtyard fell empty and silent. Filip looked across at Adrek, Arcas and Lycas, each at other corners of the square. None of them signaled success.

Perhaps this plan was idiotic, he thought, as the late-morning sun grew hot and merciless. He'd overheard nothing before session besides the ramblings over political minutiae. A new bridge in Thalassia, a law forbidding the sale of slaves under a certain value on holidays, the trading of votes on various issues.

At one time it would have fascinated him. He'd hoped to run for office when he was older, be elected by the people, unlike his plodding bureaucrat of a father, slavering at the feet of politicians.

The Spirits had other plans for Filip, as did the gods, if they existed.

When the sun had reached its zenith, another higher-pitched bell sounded, and within moments the enormous front doors of the Senate building swung outward. Senators, staffers and other officials streamed out, each trying to be the first across the street so he or she wouldn't have to stand in line at the market stalls.

To Filip's left was an area of shade, provided by a large canvas awning. It soon filled with those returning from the market with their meals. A few tables and chairs sat there, but most people mingled on their feet, cradling their food and drink as they moved from one high-powered acquaintance to the next. Filip's father had told him that more government work was accomplished in this one hour than in the entire remainder of the day.

Several of the senators and their staff made the rounds of beggars, tossing coins into each one's bowl as if throwing bread crumbs to pigeons. They chattered about political and social gossip, but nothing that seemed relevant to Marek or Nilik.

Suddenly a familiar voice came from his right. His breath seized. It couldn't be.

"My testimony wasn't terribly pedantic, was it?" the man asked his companion.

"Certainly not. Everyone enjoys a detailed account of the sewage system."

They passed in front of him, discussing the merits of a public-works bill, and Filip was certain. The skin on his nape seemed to crinkle and crawl.

His own father was within arm's reach.

"One moment." Filip's father turned and walked back toward him, his footsteps slowing. He stopped a few paces away, then dropped several large coins in Filip's bowl, murmuring a prayer to Rovas, the war god. In a moment the other man joined him. Together they cast a shadow over Filip, whose neck cramped with the effort to keep his head down, his gaze on the ground where it belonged.

"Feeling generous today, Kaloyero?"

Without moving away, Filip's father spoke solemnly. "My two sons died almost a year ago in Asermos."

"Ah." The other man tossed in a coin of his own. "I am very sorry."

"My family—my wife, my daughters and I—we miss them horribly. We feel like we'd do anything to see them once more."

Filip's fingers tightened on the fabric of his trousers. His throat ached. If he looked up, his father would know his eyes, would see through the beard and the mud to his son beneath. He would take him home, hold a celebration feast in his honor, maybe give him money to buy Marek's and Nilik's freedom. The relief and joy would overcome his shame at his son's condition.

Filip began to raise his eyes.

"But now I remember," his father said, "it could be worse. My boys could have ended up like him."

Filip's gaze stopped, having risen as far as the monument. He dropped his chin, eyes burning.

"True," the senator said. "To have both sons' names engraved on the memorial—such a loss brings pain but also great honor. There are fates worse than death."

They spoke as if he had the ears of a potted plant. Did they think he couldn't hear them?

His father scoffed. "Honor, yes. If only honor could banish the silence of an empty home."

Filip turned his face away, wrenching his mind from the images of his family. Derina would be sixteen now, ready to choose a man brave enough to spend his life listening to bad jokes. Little Kiniska, only twelve—Filip wondered if she'd outgrown her bug collection yet. And his mother…he couldn't think of her at all.

A woman with a low, strong voice passed by, speaking to her companion. "It's a waste of money and lives," she said, "all to satisfy men's sense of revenge."

"Arvano, who is *that*?" Filip's father asked.

"Senator Basha Mylosa. Myloso's widow."

"I hadn't known she was so young and…"

"Pretty? Don't be fooled. She's as shrewd and cutthroat as any of us. Has a predilection for the Asermons, though. She wants to conquer them without force."

"That's ridiculous."

"She puts forward innovative arguments. I, for one, will be sorry when her term ends. We need fresh ideas in this staid old building, not to mention a voice of moderation against the rise of the military." Arvano's shadow moved, and he lowered his voice. "Some say her baby is actually an Asermon boy, not the son of her late husband."

Filip dragged his mind out of its pool of misery to listen.

"They say she miscarried Myloso's child and found this one to replace it."

Filip's father laughed. "Who are 'they' who say such things, Arvano? Is it the voices in your head?"

"You know how it is. Slaves talk to other slaves. Information is the one commodity they have to sell. I admire her audacity, if it's true."

"It can't be true."

"She never went in public during her time of mourning, which was proper. There was time to make the substitution. It sounds far-fetched, but if you could hear the way she speaks of Asermos on the Senate floor, you'd change your mind."

Filip heard his father clap his companion on the back. "This has been an edifying and, er, entertaining respite, but I must be back to work. I trust my testimony will prove useful."

"Certainly. You'll find a token of our appreciation in your next payroll."

"I'll look for it. Thank you."

They moved away, but Filip's father stopped and turned back after a few paces. "Be well, young man," he said to Filip in a low voice. "I shall pray for you, today and always."

His footsteps receded. Filip sat for a long moment, then scratched a shallow hole in the sandy soil beneath the shrub. He took the red-and-yellow ribbon from his pocket, pressed it into the hole, then covered it with soil until it vanished.

At sunset, Rhia joined Alanka and Bolan to meet Filip at the rendezvous point in an alleyway several blocks from the Senate courtyard.

"Did you hear anything?" Rhia asked him, her stomach roiling.

"Perhaps."

Alanka and Bolan eased him to sit on an empty crate. He glanced toward the street, then spoke in a hushed voice.

"A senator named Basha Mylosa has a child. Rumor says he's an Asermon baby she's passing off as her own son."

"Her own son?" The news was what Rhia had most hoped and feared. "And what about Marek?"

"Adrek and Koli are following her to see where she lives. Maybe they'll find signs of Marek. Lycas and Arcas are following them for protection." He wiped the sweat from his ruddy face and glared at his crutches. "I did all I could."

"You did plenty." Alanka handed him a water skin and smoothed the damp hair from his brow. "You might have saved Marek and Nilik."

He took a long gulp, then shook his head. "We still have to get them out of there. Senator Mylosa will have a well-guarded house. We'll know how well guarded after the others return."

Alanka opened the long bag she'd been carrying. "I thought you might want this." She handed Filip his prosthetic leg. "So you wouldn't have to crutch all the way back to the inn."

"Thank you." He took the leg. "Very much."

Rhia walked with Alanka and Bolan to the end of the alley, giving Filip privacy and blocking the view from the street.

"Don't worry," Alanka said. "We've slipped Marek out from under armed guards before. We can do it again."

Rhia thought about how she and Lycas and Alanka had crept into the Descendant camp to extract Marek. It had been a trap, though, set by the Descendant colonel to obtain a more valuable prisoner—namely, Rhia. Marek's powers of invisibility had saved them, along with the speed and grace of Colonel Baleb's horse, Keleos.

The key, though, had been Baleb's arrogance in allowing them to enter the camp. Perhaps Basha had a similar weakness.

Filip joined them, and they headed back toward the inn. Rhia heard him speak quietly to Alanka as they walked side-by-side behind her and Bolan.

"With the money I made today," he said, "I can purchase a room for the two of us for a night. If you want."

Rhia could hear Alanka's smile in her voice. "I'd like that."

When they returned to the inn, Filip washed the grime from his face and hair, then went in search of the proprietor to rent a room.

Alanka watched him stride down the hallway, then closed the door and turned to Rhia. She seemed to be trying to restrain the joy in her eyes.

"I'm glad to see you happy again," Rhia said. "You finally have someone worthy of you."

Alanka's face relaxed into a grin. "And an Ilion, no less."

"After all he's done for us, it's hard to think of him as one of them."

"True." Alanka drew in a sudden breath. "Should I shave my legs? The women here do that, I've noticed."

The door swung open, startling Rhia.

Lycas swaggered in, followed by Arcas, Adrek, Koli and Bolan. "Sorry about not knocking," her brother said. "We found them both."

Rhia gasped and felt as if she could jump to the ceiling.

Adrek sat on the bed beside Alanka with a self-satisfied sigh. "Once it was dark, Koli and I were able to sneak right up to a window."

"It's strange," Koli said. "The room we saw was filled with Asermon art—carvings, sculptures, tapestries. Not like this inn, or the other buildings we've seen in Leukos."

"But what about Marek and Nilik?" Rhia's heart pounded. "How did they look?"

"We couldn't see Nilik inside the cradle," Adrek said. "Marek seems well-fed, with no injuries. But—" He stopped and looked at Koli.

"He wasn't doing anything," she told Rhia. "He just rocked Nilik in his cradle, not singing, not speaking to him, nothing. He looked…dead."

"Until someone passed by," Adrek said. "When Marek heard them coming, he jumped up and backed away like he thought he was in danger."

"But nothing happened." Koli fidgeted with the end of her braid. "Eventually he sat down at the cradle again. No one came in, so he must have heard someone in the hallway. Skittish as a yearling."

"That's not like him at all." Rhia sat in the chair, trying to calm the storm in her mind. She had to think clearly. "We need to get him out of there."

"And soon," Lycas said. "Before we lose our powers. My hearing's already not what it was yesterday, and the run across the city actually winded me." His face contorted in disgust.

Rhia turned to Arcas. "What about you?"

"My Spider powers feel normal so far," he said.

"Good." Rhia stood. "You'll be needed next."

34

Filip unlocked the door for Alanka and let her precede him inside. She cried out when she saw the full tub of steaming water.

"This is ours?" She dashed to the side of the metal tub. "We don't have the wrong room?"

"I ordered it for us." He looked around the room. It was small but clean. The proprietor had left a lamp burning on the bedside table. A plate of fruit and bread sat beside it, as well as a pitcher of wine. A bar of soap and a shaving kit lay on a small shelf attached to the tub.

She dipped her hand in the water and yanked it out again. "Too hot." Alanka angled her head to look at him from under her dark eyelashes. "But it's big enough for two."

He gave her a smile he hoped hid his nervousness. "It might be." He scratched his chin. "First I need to shave."

"I'll do it for you." She drew a chair next to the tub. "Sit."

He obeyed. Using a pair of scissors, she trimmed his beard close to his skin. Then she wet a small cloth with the hot water and held it against his face. The steam released the tension in his jaw and temples, and he sagged against the back of the chair.

Alanka dipped the small basin into the tub to fill it with water, then handed it to him to hold. "Aren't you worried people will recognize you without the beard?"

"I'm more worried they'll recognize me with the beard, as one of the beggars in the Senate courtyard. I was around a lot of people today—not that many of them actually looked at me."

She took the cloth away and rubbed lotion on his face. "It must have been hard."

He mused on this word, *hard*. Where Asermon swords and arrows had failed, his own countrymen, his own father, had succeeded. They'd turned him into nothing.

But after a day of feeling like a clod of dirt, he had come back to Alanka, who had treated him like a hero. Not a fallen hero, like the version of him etched upon the monument, but a man who could still fight for something larger than himself. In her eyes, he knew, he would never be nothing.

"Yes, it was hard," he said finally.

She picked up the razor and began to shave him, tilting his head to the side to reach under his jaw. Each touch of her fingers on his face and scalp left an imprint of sensation. He gripped the chair's arm as an impatient passion woke within him.

She noticed the gesture and misinterpreted it. "Don't

worry, I won't cut you." She swirled the razor in the basin. "I used to do this for my father every day."

He remained silent. The less he spoke, the faster she'd shave, and the sooner he'd feel her skin against his. His pulse throbbed in his throat.

"Will you grow your hair?" she asked when she was nearly finished.

"It depends if we stay in Ilios. Long hair is a status symbol here, only for military officers and noblemen."

"You're plenty noble for me." She wet the towel in the tub and wiped his face. "There. A month's work undone."

He stroked his chin, which felt like his own again. His cheeks tingled and smelled of mint. He hoped she liked the scent.

"Thank you." He stood and set the basin aside. When he turned back to her, she looked at his face and tittered. "What's so funny?" He swiped at his nose and ears. "Do I have lotion on my—"

"No, that's not it. I'm not amused." She stepped within the reach of his embrace. "I'm just happy."

He bent his head to hers. "So am I."

Her kiss felt cautious, as if she feared she'd scare him away. He pulled her tight against his body so she could feel how much he craved her. She moaned and snaked her arms around his neck, drawing him into a deeper, harder kiss.

He untied her shirt, and she lifted it over her head. A tight sleeveless garment lay underneath, covering her breasts and the top of her belly, displaying taut nipples. He bent to suckle one through the thin material, caressing the other with his thumb. She shuddered.

In a moment the undergarment was gone, and he tasted her perfect round breast, salty with sweat. Alanka moaned again, making his blood pound so hard, it seemed to fight the confines of his veins.

"Filip?"

He pulled away. "What's wrong?"

"Tub."

"Right." He stripped off his shirt, while Alanka stood before him and undid her trousers.

Her dark eyes glittered at him. "Help me?"

"Yes." He slid the trousers over her hips, along with the soft undergarment, and knelt to remove them. He reached to touch her naked body, but she stepped back.

"I'm taking a bath. Will you join me, then?" She put a foot in the tub and almost yanked it out. "Still hot." She stepped into the tub, wincing and gasping. He would have laughed at her bulging eyes had her body's beauty not stolen his breath.

Alanka sat down and exhaled heavily. "I think they want to cook us for dinner." She reached back to pull out the tie from her braid.

"Let me do that." He moved to stand behind her.

"No. No more touching me with your clothes on." She looked up at him. "I can shut my eyes if you want."

He almost agreed, then realized it wasn't what he wanted. He wanted her to see him, finally.

Filip unfastened his trousers and undid the straps of his prosthesis. He sat on the bed and removed his shoes and socks, then the false leg, setting everything beneath the bedside table. He slid his trousers over his hips, then his knees, where he held them for a long moment.

Alanka's eyes met his, and the desire to touch her burned away the last fragments of fear and shame. He let the trousers fall to the floor.

She looked down where his left leg ended, then back at his face. A smile crinkled the corners of her eyes. She regarded the dark gray drawers that covered his hips.

"Almost done now," she said.

Filip let out a deep breath, wondering why he had ever worried. He leaned back on his elbows and lifted his hips to remove his drawers. He sat up and dropped them to the side.

Alanka drew her knees up to give him room. "You're too beautiful to hide."

His face heated, and not from the billowing steam. Using the table for support, he moved to the tub, sat on the edge and swung his legs over in a smooth motion. He thanked every god and Spirit that he didn't lose his balance and fall in. The water came to the top of his waist and soothed his aching limbs.

Alanka turned around in the cramped tub and shifted herself between his legs. "Now you may undo my hair."

The feel of her skin, slick and hot against his, sent the blood racing through his body, hardening him against her back. His hands trembled as they unwound the soft, dark strands. When her hair was free, she slid down to submerge herself, her head nearly reaching his lap. He groaned and reached for the soap, needing a distraction to maintain what little control remained.

She murmured with delight as he worked the soap through her hair, massaging her scalp.

"Does everyone in Leukos have a bathtub?" she asked him.

"Most use the public baths, but many have movable tubs like these. The wealthiest have permanent tubs in their homes, made of tile."

"Did your family have a tile tub?"

"No. We had one like this."

She grew quiet.

"What is it?" he asked her.

"Sitting here, I finally understand why people want to be rich. Makes me wonder what I'd do to have a hot bath every day."

She submerged again, running her fingers through her hair to rinse it, creating a mass of floating black strands. He gazed at her body beneath the ripples and wanted to give her a thousand nights in a row like this one. She had suffered so much. She deserved a life of comfort.

Alanka came up from the water and turned to face him, kneeling between his legs. "Will you wash the rest of me?"

He covered her shoulders and breasts with the rich suds that slicked her skin and made her sigh. She tilted her head back, parting her lips, and he wanted her now, fast. But there was one thing he needed her to do first. One thing he couldn't ask her to do.

As he washed her, Alanka's fingers stroked his thighs, then descended lower, to his knees. She opened her eyes and looked at him. "Do you want me to touch it?"

He swallowed. "If you like," he said, though he longed to tell her yes.

"I want to touch all of you." Her hand slid down behind his left knee until it reached the hard, blunt stump. She caressed it cautiously at first, then firmly, her fingers exploring the ridges of scars. Instead of feeling numb, it felt alive and exquisitely sensitive. He let his head sink back onto the edge of the tub as his hands spread the lather over her smooth belly.

"Do you like that?" she said.

"Yes." His breath came faster. "I didn't think I would. But it needs your touch." As did a hundred other places on his body.

"It doesn't feel like an absence," she said. "It feels like you."

Suddenly she stopped and gazed over his left shoulder, head tilted, eyes unfocused. "Do you hear that?"

He held his breath. In an apartment down the street, perhaps a block or two away, a fiddler was practicing. It sounded like a slow waltz. It was so faint, he wouldn't have discerned it without his enhanced Horse hearing.

Which meant…

"I can hear!" Alanka drew in a quick, sharp breath. "I can smell!" She moved her head from side to side, a smile daring to creep across her face. "One moment I could only smell the incense and the soap, but now I smell everything. Outside, inside…" She looked at Filip, then leaned over to inhale the air above his shoulder. "You smell wonderful."

"Your powers have returned?" he said, though the answer was obvious.

"I think so." She gripped his shoulders. "Dance with me, to celebrate." She pressed herself close, straddling him. He looped his arms around her body, slippery with soap. They swayed together in the tight space of the tub.

"How is this?" he said.

"It's perfect." She slid down against him. "You're perfect."

Alanka took Filip inside her, and they cried out. He held her face between his hands and kissed her, savoring the wetness within. Her tongue teased his, and he tried to thrust upward, deeper inside, needing more. With her knees outside his hips, the confines of the tub held them fast.

Alanka looked down. "This could be better."

"Should we move to the bed?"

"Not until we're cold and wrinkly." She lifted herself, then turned to face away from him, on her knees, resting her forearms on the other end of the tub. Her hips were out of the water, dripping, beckoning. "Try now," she said.

He hesitated. He had taken Palia at the brothel this way, from behind, so he couldn't see the pain on her face, so he could pretend her cries were ones of eagerness.

Alanka looked over her bare, glistening shoulder at him. "Now, Filip."

Water splashed from the tub as he shifted to kneel behind her. He entered her, deeply, and all memories fled. They moved apart, then together, sliding in a quickening rhythm that tore a groan from his throat. He placed his hands over hers on the side of the tub, intertwining their fingers. Her moans grew in pitch until she uttered a breathy scream.

As he marveled at her pleasure—how he'd caused it wasn't clear to him—he felt his own rise, overpowering his control in the span of a breath. He surged within her as the world went bright and hazy.

The man he had been was gone, smashed to pieces, but the man he would become had just been born, whole and healed at last.

Alanka sagged against the side of the tub. Her knees ached, but her blood sang.

Filip draped over her, panting. With a groan, he sat back in the tub. She turned to watch him dunk his head underwater, then come up wearing the broadest grin she'd ever seen on his face.

He moved forward into her arms. "That was…"

"That was to calm us down. The night's barely begun."

She reached for the soap and lathered him up, relishing the hard muscles beneath his skin.

He closed his eyes and sighed. "Renting this room was possibly the best idea a human being ever had."

She laughed. "Don't expect an argument here. Turn around."

With some effort, he shifted in the narrow tub to face away from her. She gasped. Except for a small round scar on his right shoulder, his chest had been smooth. The skin on his back, however, was puckered with long, crisscrossed lines.

She drew her finger down one of the scars. "How did you get these?"

"Basic training."

"They whipped you?"

He shrugged one shoulder. "Not just me. Everyone."

"Why?"

"So we could learn to ignore pain."

She thought of the Ilion soldier who had kept charging her even with two arrows sticking out of him. "Your men fight bravely, even insanely. Kind of like our Wolverines."

"But our soldiers don't have magic to boost their imperviousness. We get tough the hard way." He turned his head to the side. "Do the scars bother you?"

"No. They're part of you." She leaned forward and kissed each one. Then she washed his back with the same tenderness as if they had been fresh wounds.

By the time they were clean, the water had cooled. Alanka stood and wrung out her hair, watching Filip watch her. A new light was in his eyes; she hoped it stayed there forever.

She wrapped a towel around her body and stepped out of the tub. Before she could offer Filip help, he had followed her, grabbing his own towel. It surprised her how nimble he was on one leg.

"I'm starving." She padded over to the small table. Filip stretched out on the bed. She sat beside him, placing the plate of fruit between them. "I don't even recognize most of these."

He picked up a chunk of deep pink fruit. "This is watermelon. They don't grow up north." He offered it to her.

"What do I do with the seeds?"

"Spit them out, or swallow them." He pushed it against her lips. "Don't be scared."

She laughed and gingerly bit into the fruit. Juice spurted down her chin and onto her neck, making her laugh louder.

He leaned forward to lick the juice from her collarbone before it dripped under the towel. "Do you like it?"

"The watermelon or what you just did?"

"Yes."

"Yes, I like it."

Filip smiled and reclined on the side, head propped on his hand. He took a bite of the fruit, chewed carefully, then picked a seed out of his mouth and laid it on the edge of the plate.

"You don't eat them?" she said.

"When I was a boy, my brother convinced me that if I ate a watermelon seed, a watermelon plant would grow in my stomach and eventually devour me from the inside out. As revenge."

"You don't still believe that."

"Of course not."

"Then why not eat them now?"

He shrugged. "Habit."

"I dare you to eat one." She picked up a fat black seed and held it out between her fingertips.

He looked up at her, down at the seed, then gave her a heavy-lidded gaze as he slowly stuck out his tongue. She felt her body turn to liquid. Despite his lack of experience, an instinctive power of seduction lurked within him, a power she planned to enjoy.

She placed the seed on his tongue and watched it disappear into the wet darkness of his mouth. "How is it?" she whispered.

He swallowed, never taking his eyes from hers. "I'm cured."

She leaned forward and gave him a long, deep kiss, a promise for the rest of the night.

As she poured their wine, she noticed that he hadn't covered his legs, either with the towel or the blanket. That he trusted her enough to expose himself made her glow inside, even before sipping the wine.

He savored the drink, eyes closed. Then he looked at her, his face serious again. "You have your powers back."

"They're not as strong as they used to be, I guess because we're in the city. I can feel Wolf's presence, like Adrek said about Cougar. It's faint, but it's there now. I don't know what I did to deserve it."

"Remember what I said before? How you couldn't make peace with yourself until you made peace with your enemy? By accepting my wound, you've done that." He stroked her arm. "In your eyes, I'm a hero, and in mine, you're a warrior. We only had to learn to use each other's eyes to see." He touched her chin. "Do you still think you're a murderer?"

She stared at a blank space on the wall and remembered the battle. The faces of those she killed dredged up a skewering sorrow, but not guilt, not anymore. "No. I had to do it." She heard a new strength in her voice. "And I'd do it again."

"You may, indeed, if Rhia's plan gets us into the senator's mansion."

Alanka thought of Marek sitting in that room, drained of all fierceness. She'd get him out if she had to shoot everyone in the house.

Calm down, she told herself, drawing a deep breath to dissipate the rage. Turned inward for so long, it begged for a target outside her.

"You never had to do anything to deserve Wolf's favor," Filip said. "You just had to forgive yourself."

She watched his hand glide over her waist and wondered if she could ever be as gentle with herself as he was with her. Perhaps he could teach her.

"Yes," she said, "I'll marry you."

Filip stared at her, and for a moment she thought he might take the offer back. Maybe his respect for her had vanished the moment they made love. His people's strange ways could be seeping back into him now that he was home.

"Let's do it now," he said.

"Get married? At this hour?"

"Right here. We can't do it legally in Ilios anyway so we might as well take our vows now."

"What vows?"

He squinted at the ceiling. "I think they're mostly about property. We can eliminate that part, since we have none."

"What else do your marriages mean?"

He laced his fingers with hers and pressed their palms together. "Loyalty. Above family and place of birth. We become a nation of two." He quirked an eyebrow. "And eventually three, four, five…"

"Two is fine for now," she said.

"Two is perfect." He kissed her. "What about Kalindon weddings?"

"They're short and rare. We pledge in the name of our Spirits to love each other forever. It's a hard thing to promise."

"I promise to love you forever," he said quickly, then added, "in the name of Horse." He thought for a moment. "That wasn't hard at all."

She laughed, then couldn't stop laughing. She'd dreamed of her wedding day since she was twelve, and now it had come in the depths of her enemies' city, lying naked next to a plate of strange fruit.

Filip waited patiently. "It's good to hear you laugh, Alanka. But you could have chosen a better time to recover your sense of humor."

She rubbed her face and became solemn again. "Filip, in the name of Wolf, I promise to love you forever." She kissed him softly.

He gazed at her, as if sealing the moment in his memory.

"What do Kalindons do then?" he asked.

"Everyone eats and drinks until they pass out, then they wake up and eat and drink some more. Then comes the orgy."

His eyes widened. "You're joking."

She giggled. "Not a formal one—it's just how things usually end up. It's good luck to conceive a child on a wedding night—your own or someone else's." Filip looked at her belly, and she added, "We won't tonight. I've been taking wild carrot seed for months."

"Why?"

"I was in no shape to have a baby. Even now, I want to wait until we have a home where we can raise it in peace." She frowned. "I don't know if that day will ever come."

"Let's not worry about that day." He reached across her for the bread-and-fruit plate. "Let's finish our wedding."

They drank enough wine and fed each other enough food to stuff their stomachs and weight their eyelids with drowsiness. Then they made love again, with a slow heat that gave them hours to find every inch of bliss on each other's bodies.

Alanka fell asleep in their entangled embrace, feeling pure contentment for the first time she could remember. Her Spirit and her beloved were with her at last. Tomorrow she would return to her mission, with more power and strength than ever.

But tonight she would rest.

35

Marek walked behind Basha, his gaze on the pale gray stones beneath his feet. He barely noticed the market crowd jostling around him. It was larger than usual on this holiday honoring some god who existed only to make the temples rich. Two guards kept close to him. The short swords in their belts squashed any thought of escape he might entertain.

He felt the midday sun sear the back of his neck, the lower part of which was bare. Basha wanted his hair to grow long again. He wished for a knife to cut it short, though he was no longer sure if he'd use it to slice only his hair.

Nilik gurgled and cooed in the carriage pushed by Petrop. Basha laughed with delight. "Demedor, you love a crowd, just like your mother."

Marek's stomach felt another pang. He'd eaten and slept little in the past several days. His body seemed to rebel against itself, perhaps in retribution for the things it had done with Basha.

He saw her embroidered boots near his feet. She took his hand and pressed a coin into it.

"Marek, fetch me one of those fried breads with the fruit on it." She scrutinized his face and clicked her tongue. "Get one for yourself, too. You look positively skeletal. People will talk." She looked at his guards. "Go with him."

The fried-bread line was endless. The treat was one he'd always looked forward to at the midsummer Fiddlers Festival in Velekos, but now his gut heaved at the thought of the sweet, oil-soaked flour.

While he waited, he explored his new powers. Fox had taken him under Her care, enhancing his hearing and night vision, though his sense of smell was diminished from that of a Wolf. He wondered if he had the second-phase Fox power of camouflage—blending into his background by remaining motionless—or if he would start over in the first phase. None of his people had ever changed Spirits midlife.

He couldn't test his camouflage, since he was never alone, not even to bathe or piss. Basha said he was so valuable, someone might try to steal or harm him. He wondered if she sensed that Marek posed the greatest threat to his own life.

If it weren't for Fox, he would have found a way to die by now. Even his son wasn't enough to live for anymore. As soon as Nilik reached the age when he could understand who his real father was, Marek would be sent away or killed. Basha couldn't take the chance that he would tell his son of his identity. It would ruin her experiment.

A Wolf would have chosen the noble route, to perish rather than betray his beloved Rhia, to put honor before life. Fox had saved him, but for what?

A stone rolled near his feet. He glanced at it, then froze.

It was tied to a crow feather.

He lifted his head and looked behind him.

A young man stood in a vendor's stall across the street, perhaps twenty paces away. His dark brown gaze bore into Marek, cutting through the air like a hurled dagger.

Arcas.

Marek turned back to the fried-bread stand to keep his guards from getting suspicious. His mind reeled. Why was Arcas here, his old rival, the man who'd once held a blade to Marek's throat for "stealing" Rhia?

Marek pushed back his shoulders in a long stretch, feigning stiffness in his lower back. As he did, he let his glance trip over the crowd, back to the stall.

Arcas was surrounded by wooden carvings. A sign read Custom Designs, from what Marek could tell. The Spider looked at the other side of the street. Marek followed his gaze.

Basha.

His mind made the connection with a sudden spark.

"Your order!"

One of his guards jabbed him in the back. He turned to the fried-bread stall, where the vendor was glaring at him. "Hurry up," she snarled. "There's people waiting."

He stepped forward and ordered as Basha had instructed, one for her and one for himself. His stomach twisted again, but from excitement now instead of dread.

He and the guards found Basha, who was contemplating the purchase of a new decorative plant.

"There you are," she said. "I thought I'd have to call the police."

"My apologies, Your Honor." Marek handed her the fried bread. "There was a long line."

"Yes, it's dreadful how they let anyone come to these festivals. You'd think they'd have a special day for the worthwhile families to attend without having to mingle with the rabble. Maybe we should pass a law to that effect." She turned away from the plant, apparently forgetting it in the excitement of a new policy initiative.

"Your Honor." Marek tried not to sound too eager. "There's an artist whose wares you might like to see."

"Hmm?" She gave him a distracted glance. "What kind of artist?"

"From Asermos. He makes carvings like the ones you have in your living room." Marek took a calculated risk. "But these are better."

"What?" Her voice went shrill. "Impossible. Show me."

They went to Arcas's stall. The Spider was the only person within the shade of the small tent. He displayed an ingratiating smile at their approach.

"Good afternoon, my lady." He glanced at the patch of red and gold on the shoulder of her white dress. "Forgive me—I mean, Your Honor."

Entranced by the array of carvings, she waved off his apology. "Are you the artist or just the vendor?"

"Both. I'm independent."

"I can tell." She shoved her plate at Marek for him to

hold, then picked up the wolf and examined its many teeth. "These are unlike anything I've seen. You have your own style." She pointed to the carved wooden spider around his neck. "I see from your fetish you're an artist by Spirit. Your magic is obvious."

"Thank you, Your Honor." He bowed. "I am humbled by your appreciation."

"Yes." She set the wolf down. "Are these for sale or merely samples?"

Arcas swept his hand over a table of wood carvings. "For sale, Your Honor. These are all the animals I have here in Leukos." He looked at Marek, down at the table, then back at Marek, who caught his meaning and stepped closer.

On the table sat a group of exquisitely carved animals: a wolverine, a bat, two horses, a wolf, a cougar, a spider, and—*great Spirits, yes*—a crow.

Besides Rhia and Arcas, it must be Lycas, Alanka, Koli and perhaps Adrek—but who were the two Horses? It took a moment to remember the name of Arcas's friend Bolan. He was probably represented by the placid grazing horse.

The other Horse could be Filip. Had a Descendant come to help him? It would give them an advantage none of the other rescuers had possessed.

Marek indicated the rearing steed carved from a light-colored wood. "This one looks new."

"It is." Arcas pointed to the west. "Its material comes from this region, in fact."

So it was Filip. If he had Arcas's signal right, they were staying somewhere in the western part of the city.

"How lovely," Basha exclaimed. "An amalgamation of

the two cultures. Symbolic of things to come, I hope." She ran her finger along the blue cloth that covered the table. "Hmm. No foxes."

As if the word had awakened that wily part of him, Marek conceived an idea. "May I suggest that you commission this artist to make you one?"

Her face lit up. "Yes! But bigger than that little thing I have now. Life-sized." She held her arms far apart.

Marek held back a derisive laugh. "Your Honor, with respect, real foxes aren't that big. They weigh as much as a large housecat."

She furrowed her brow. "But I want a big one."

"He could make you a larger one, perhaps even human-sized." He looked at Arcas. "Right?"

Comprehension dawned on the Spider's face. "Certainly. There's enough driftwood scattered about the beach to make a human-sized fox."

Basha's eyes narrowed. "When could you have it ready?"

Arcas made a show of consideration. Marek hoped it would be soon, but not so soon as to rouse Basha's suspicions.

"Seven days."

She scowled. "I'm hosting dinner on the festival's final night. That's in four days. To have this to show my rivals— it would make them remember what they're dealing with."

"Four days?" Arcas feigned dismay. "Perhaps, if an extra fee were involved."

"It shall be." She waved her hand and started to turn away. "Petrop, negotiate a price and give him a third as a down payment."

"Half, Your Honor," Arcas said. When she turned back

to him, wide-eyed, he added, "If you don't like the final product, I'll give you a full refund. No other artist would guarantee his work that way."

Her lips pinched together. "Half, then. But I want it on the morning of the fourth day, first thing."

Arcas bowed. "I shall work day and night. Tomorrow morning, plus three days."

"See you then." As she walked away with Marek, she said, "Thank you for alerting me." Her voice went sultry. "You shall receive a special token of my appreciation tonight."

Marek glanced back at Arcas to see if he had heard. The Spider's narrowed eyes and furrowed brow told him he had. Would he tell Rhia?

No. If Marek ever saw her again, he would confess and beg her to forgive him. Then he'd spend the rest of his life earning that forgiveness.

36

Marek awoke to his son's wails. He lifted his head from the pillow.

Impossible. Nilik slept in another wing of the building, too far for his cries to reach Marek's ears. He looked at the dark window of the slaves' quarters.

Perhaps he had dreamed it. Yet he could barely sleep knowing that Arcas and the others would arrive in a few hours. The Spider still looked strong, and his Bear training would help him overcome the guards, if he could get inside the house.

Then there was Lycas. Marek's Wolverine brother-in-law could drop a man just by looking at him, it seemed, and was nearly impervious to weapons himself.

Marek's ears strained for Nilik's voice again, though he couldn't go to him in the middle of the night. He couldn't leave the room unless Basha summoned, which she hadn't done since the night after the market.

It should have been easier to couple with her that evening, knowing that Rhia was coming to release him. But the numbness had vanished, and when she had finished with him, he'd fled back to his quarters to vomit. He'd wished for the torturers to flay him, to tear off every bit of skin that smelled like Basha.

Marek stared at the window now, waiting for daylight and the liberation it would bring.

Petrop shook him awake at sunrise. "Go to her," he said, as brusque as always.

Marek hurried to dress, then followed the butler across the wide house, into the residential wing. As he passed the top of the stairs, he heard Basha crying.

"What's wrong?" he asked Petrop, who did not reply.

The door to Nilik's room stood open. No sound came from within. Marek ran into the room, ignoring the shouts of his guards.

He dashed to the crib and looked inside.

Empty.

"Where is he?" He tried to rein in his panic. Maybe the wet nurse had taken Nilik to feed or bathe him.

"Marek!" Basha's shrill voice came from the hallway. She rushed into Nilik's room, face drenched with tears. "Marek, they took him."

"What? Who?" Maybe the Asermons had rescued Nilik. "Kidnappers?"

"No, the army." She grasped the front of his shirt. "They took him away from me."

"What army? I don't understand."

"They took him." She uttered more words, but they were lost in the waves of sobs, all but the phrase *my baby*.

Basha pressed her wet face against Marek's chest. Dazed, he let his arms drift around her back. This wasn't happening. He'd had worse nightmares. Soon he'd wake from this one.

She pulled away and turned to the guards, who stood awkwardly by the door. "Leave us."

They hesitated. Petrop stepped forward out of the hallway. "Your Honor, do you think that's wise?"

"Leave us!"

The butler shooed the two guards out of the room, but left the door open. Basha charged after him and slammed it shut, then locked it.

"What happened?" Marek's heart slammed his ribs.

She picked up a white cloth from a small table by the door and wiped her eyes with it. "They said they had to take him away." She choked out another sob, then swallowed hard. "Into the wilderness, so his powers could rise when he grew older. They said the city wasn't the right place for such an experiment."

Marek's gut twisted. "He's gone forever, you mean? Never coming back?"

"They've made a camp for all the children, out west, near Surnos. They'll raise them to be loyal to Ilios, use them to create a magical fighting force to conquer your people." She dragged the cloth against her cheeks again. "It was my idea.

I thought I was so clever. How could I have known they'd take my own son?"

He grasped at one last hope. "If you let me go with them, I'll watch over him for you. You'll know he's safe and happy with me."

She shook her head. "They left before dawn. You couldn't go, anyway. They want no influence from your people on the children."

He sank onto the window seat, pulled one of Nilik's plush toys into his lap and clutched it close. His chest felt as if it would rip apart, straight down the middle.

"What can we do?" he managed to say.

"Nothing." Her voice hushed. "I'm so sorry, Marek."

He looked up at her. She'd never said those words to him before.

It didn't matter now. Nothing mattered. Even if he were rescued, his promise to Rhia was broken. They couldn't go home without their son.

But if he escaped, they might be able to find the children in time, if they knew where to look. Though his heart was shattering, he had to keep his head, ask careful questions.

"What's this place like, this—"

"Surnos?" She sniffled. "It's a stupid little town, surrounded by forests and mountains and other such useless things. Just the sort of place your people would enjoy."

"Have you been there?"

"Not since I took office. It's too far—over two days' ride—and I have too many duties." She breathed a mournful sigh. "But it seems I have one fewer duty now than I did yesterday." She put her face in her hands. "Hold me."

Her voice was so pitiful it took Marek a moment to realize it was an order. He went to her and enfolded her in an embrace, careful not to squeeze the last breath out of her as he wanted more than ever to do.

She clung to his waist and released a fresh sob. "At least this time I have someone to share my grief."

He wondered how real her grief could be, after she had threatened to send "her baby" away to get Marek to do her bidding.

"I never knew until now," she said, "how much I needed him."

Marek looked at the window, where the morning light was streaming in. If he could get closer to the front door…

"Let me fetch you some food," he said. "You need your strength."

"I'm not hungry. And I'm canceling tonight's celebration. I can't go through with it. Soon everyone will know Demedor wasn't truly my son." She drew away from him. "I need to send word to the artist not to come." She moved toward the door, and he stepped into her path.

"Are you sure? You loved the idea."

"It will only remind me of the child. Besides, if I display that carving, they'll all laugh at me. They'll say I was the one outfoxed this time, and I was." She wiped her nose and reached for the doorknob.

"Wait."

She turned to him, looking surprised at what sounded like an order.

"Send me to tell the artist," he said. "Maybe I can convince him to return your deposit. He might listen to one of his own countrymen."

Her lips twisted a sad smile. "That's very sweet, but I don't care about the money. And you're not going anywhere."

A shiver snaked down the center of his back. "I don't understand, Your Honor."

"I need a child of my own. You'll give it to me." Her bloodshot eyes held a cold blue gaze. "You won't leave my chamber until I'm pregnant."

He gaped at her, certain he'd heard her wrong. "Me?" He fumbled for a way to show the absurdity. "I'm a slave. It would dishonor you."

"No one will know. My mourning period is over, and I shall find a husband soon. I have several suitors, any of whom would marry me tomorrow. That day won't arrive until I'm carrying my very own Asermon child, one they can't take away." Her fist clenched around the tear-soaked cloth. "One I can watch forever, whose power I can share when he grows up."

Marek's breath grew quick and his mind more desperate. "But I'm not Asermon. I'm Kalindon."

"Beasts are all the same." To his stare, she replied, "Don't give me that look. Only a beast could betray his wife with another woman as readily as you did."

His lip curled. "I did it to save my child."

"You did it to save yourself. As you will continue to do. At least now you won't have to wear one of those lambskin sheaths when we do it. You can enjoy it even more." She unlocked the doorknob. "The guards will take you to my room."

She opened the door and gasped.

The hallway was empty.

Blood spattered the walls and painted the floor in two trails that led into Basha's room.

She turned her wide-eyed gaze up at Marek. Her astonishment turned to fear.

"No…" She opened her mouth to scream, but he grabbed her and covered it with the palm of his hand.

"Do as I tell you and you'll live," he hissed.

He dragged her into the hallway, then the outer room of her chamber. Lycas stepped from the shadows, hands covered in blood. Basha struggled and kicked at the sight.

The Wolverine withdrew a dagger from his belt. "This the one who owns you?"

Marek looked down at Basha, then held out his hand for the weapon. "Not anymore."

Lycas hesitated, then slapped the hilt into his outstretched palm. "Be quick and quiet about it."

Marek held the blade to Basha's throat. "Let's go, Your Honor. Make a sound and I'll cut the living breath out of you. Understand?"

She nodded quickly. Grasping her by the base of the neck and holding the tip of the blade under her ribs, he guided her ahead of him out into the hallway and turned for the stairs. Lycas followed.

"Where's the boy?" he asked Marek.

"Gone, but we can catch them. She'll show us where they're going." He shook Basha's shoulder. "Won't you?"

"I won't betray my country," she said.

"Who else is with you?" Marek asked Lycas as they neared the top of the stairs.

"Arcas is downstairs, and—"

"Lycas, hurry!"

In the foyer below, Arcas was holding two guards at bay with a Descendant military sword. They swooped around him, holding shorter swords of their own, trying to move within striking range.

Basha shouted to the guards, then raked her foot behind Marek's ankles. He felt himself lose his balance, and he clutched the only thing within reach—Basha herself.

They tumbled down the stairs together, bouncing off the wall and the banister. Marek's elbows and knees yelped in pain as they banged against the stone. Basha screamed all the way down. When they reached the bottom, her cry cut off.

Dazed, Marek felt Basha lying under him, coughing, and saw someone leap over their bodies from the stairs. More shouts and clangs of steel echoed off the walls. His hand was warm and wet.

He rolled to his knees, searching for the knife before it could be used against him. He turned back to Basha.

Her stomach was soaked in blood, where the black hilt of the dagger appeared. He gasped and backed away, feeling his own blood drain from his face.

"Marek…" Her eyes rolled white with pain, and she grasped at the knife handle. "Marek, what's wr—" Her voice pitched higher. "Can't. Br—"

"Marek!" Arcas was struggling with his opponent near the front door. Marek's gaze darted around the foyer for a way to help him.

In the sitting room beyond the fighters, the wolf carving watched him from the green marble table. With a leap and a roll, Marek ducked the swordplay and landed in the sitting room. He grabbed the wolf by the hind legs. It felt heavy as stone.

He strode toward Arcas's opponent, who glanced back a moment too late.

Marek dashed the wolf against the side of the guard's head. The man lurched, falling against the table. Arcas swung the curved blade to slice the guard's throat. Marek leaped back from the fountain of blood. Without hesitating, Arcas turned to the other guard and slashed him in the side. Lycas moved in for the swift, silent kill.

Marek ran back to Basha, who had managed to pull the top half of her body to rest on the lowest stair. The red pool expanded around her.

"Don't. Leave. Me." She coughed a mouthful of blood.

He knelt beside her and stared into the eyes he hated, wondering how fast she would die.

A shout of rage came from the dining room to his right. He looked up to see Petrop running toward him, wielding a cleaver high above his head. Marek stood to leap out of the way.

Basha seized his ankle with a weak grip, enough to make him stumble and fall to his hands and knees. Petrop was only a few steps away. Marek twisted into a desperate, dodging roll.

A *crack-twang* came from behind the butler. His eyes went wide, and his feet tripped over each other. He fell forward, landing next to Marek, the cleaver clanging the stone floor less than a handspan from Marek's head.

A vibrating arrow jutted from the center of Petrop's back.

Soft footsteps padded closer. Marek sat up to see Alanka running toward him through the dining room. He staggered to his feet and embraced her.

"I'm sorry I let you go." She clutched him so tightly he couldn't breathe. "Where's Nilik?"

"Gone, but we'll get him back."

"First we have to get out of here." Lycas pulled a brown cloth from his belt and quickly wiped his hands and weapons. "We've barred the doors to this part of the house, but it won't hold them long, especially after all that shouting." He handed the cloth to Arcas to clean himself. "Let's go."

"How will we get past the outer gate?" Marek asked. "It's well guarded."

"The same way we got in," Arcas said, "thanks to your idea." He pointed to a wooden pallet lying in the back of the foyer. It was connected to two horizontal poles for carrying. A large dark brown blanket lay rumpled upon it. "On the way out, you can play the human-sized fox sculpture, the way Alanka did on the way in."

Marek turned to her. "What about you?"

"I'll find my own way out."

"No." He took her arm. "You don't want to be caught by these people."

"I won't be. We have a plan."

"Which is working so far," Arcas said. "Except for that." He pointed to Basha. "We hadn't planned to kill the senator."

Marek turned to her. Her golden eyelashes fluttered, and her breath came in short, shallow gasps. Slumped on the bottom stair, she gazed into a distant horizon. He wondered if she watched the approach of Crow or one of her gods.

"A knife in the gut's survivable," Lycas said, "depending where it goes in." The Wolverine pulled out a longer dagger. "She's seen us. We should finish it." He took a step toward her, then stopped. "I've never killed a woman."

"Give it."

Lycas looked at Marek's shaky palm, then placed the dagger in it. "Under the ribs and up, left side." Marek switched the dagger to his other hand, and Lycas added, "Her left, not yours."

"I know."

"And keep your grip far back on the hilt. If you cut yourself and bleed, it'll be harder to hide you."

Marek turned to Basha, avoiding Alanka's eyes. He heard the Wolf woman stifle a whimper of protest. She didn't know he was no longer her Spirit brother.

He put his foot on the bottom stair next to Basha so that he crouched over her body. With a sudden calm, he placed the tip of the dagger under her ribs, against the pink silk of her nightgown. He'd peeled this gown off her three times. He'd torn it once, on her command.

She stirred at the prick of the blade. "M-Mar—"

"Don't speak to me." He grasped her bloodstained chin and forced her to look at him. "Even at the end you tried to trap me. But I'm free now. If they catch me and hang me in an hour, I'll be free of you forever."

He tightened his grip on the dagger. Basha's blue eyes sparked fear, then triumph. She let out a faint gasp and fell still, her gaze blanking.

"She's dead," Alanka whispered.

"What?" Marek put a finger to Basha's neck. "She can't be." He dropped the knife and shook her shoulders. "Basha!" His vision reddened with rage. She'd escaped.

"That solves things." Lycas picked up the long dagger. "Grab the one out of her stomach. We might need it later."

Marek grasped the short dagger and twisted it hard as he withdrew it. Though her body jerked, it was only from the motion itself, and her face held no reaction.

He was seized by the desire to pierce her unbeating heart, to carve out a space as big as the one she had made inside him.

Arcas took the weapon from his hand, replacing it with a clean brown cloth.

"Come," the Spider said. "It's time to go."

Marek wrenched his gaze from Basha's corpse. When he stood, Lycas grabbed his elbow and led him to the pallet. Marek knelt upon it, making himself as small as possible, grateful for once that he and Alanka were so close in size. They draped him with the blanket.

Arcas lifted the cloth and placed the weapons beneath it. "Be ready to use these if anyone discovers you."

A soft hand touched his shoulder. "See you soon," Alanka said.

The pallet tilted as Lycas and Arcas lifted it. Marek concentrated on staying motionless. He held down the long dagger with his right hand and the Descendant fighting sword with his left, the short dagger tucked under his knee. Though he'd never been trained for combat, the solidity of the weapons, as well as the anger pulsing his blood, assured him he could thwart any enemy. It was delusion, a part of him knew, but a calming delusion.

They reached the rear courtyard, where the sun beat hard on the dark blanket. Marek licked the sweat from his upper lip and prayed they would make it past the gate.

"She didn't like it?" came a voice he recognized as one of the exterior guardsmen.

"A bit wild for her tastes, I'm afraid," Arcas replied. "She paid me in full, though, so I can't say I care. Artists can't afford to be too sensitive if they hope to eat."

The guard chuckled. "Good way to think of it. Mind if I take a look? Maybe I'll buy it myself." He touched the edge of the blanket. Marek's hand tightened on the sword.

"No." Arcas's voice deepened in warning. "She ordered me to burn it, said no one was to see it."

"Why?"

"How should I know? Maybe she's embarrassed by this passing fancy. But if she found out you'd had a peek—you know how she is."

Just then, a swelling cacophony of caws arose above.

The guard stepped back, boots clicking the pave stones. "What in the name of Atreus?"

Marek felt the sun's glare soften, as though a cloud had passed before it.

"A bad omen," the guard muttered. "You two, get out."

"Good day," Lycas told him as they passed by. "And good luck."

They hurried onward, down the street, and Marek felt his lungs expand.

He was free.

The surrounding light darkened further. Arcas and Lycas set the pallet down carefully.

"Be quiet a while longer," the Spider whispered. "It won't be easy."

Marek pushed off the blanket. They were in an alley. He looked up to see hundreds of crows pass through the narrow piece of visible blue sky.

Whispers came from behind a large flat piece of wood that stood on its end. He approached slowly, taking care not to kick any of the refuse strewed about the alley.

A woman knelt on the ground, hair covered in a gray cowl. He couldn't see her face, but he knew the hands that were raised in supplication.

Rhia.

Arcas held him back. "Don't interrupt."

"What's she doing?" he whispered.

"Saving Alanka."

37

Filip flew with the crows.

Sitting at the edge of an alley across the street from the senator's mansion, he let his mind flit from one bird to the next, until he was dizzy with flight. He broke the connection, opening his eyes to regain balance. The iron fence surrounding the mansion was lined with a hedgerow more than twice his height. No one could see in or out.

He looked at the roof of the mansion. Gods be blessed, a crow sat on the corner. He reached out.

Through the bird's eyes he saw the expansive front garden. Colors flared sharp and bright, and every distance came into focus at once. The garden held mostly ornamental bushes, some of which could provide cover for Alanka as she made her way from the living-room window to the outer iron fence. Adrek waited in a tree that grew over the fence. Koli sat within his line of sight a block away, within her hearing distance of Bolan, who stood across the street from Filip. They all waited for his signal.

The crow showed him the guards patrolling near the window, then it shifted its gaze to watch the rest of its incoming flock. Filip cursed and searched for a better-positioned candidate.

One of the birds glided from the roof of the house to the top of the gazebo, which was barely visible over the hedge row. He checked the crude map in his hands, the one Adrek and Koli had constructed from their spy mission. The gazebo was about halfway between the window and the tree.

Filip's mind reached out again. The crow eyed the ground below it, looking for food or shiny objects to collect. A movement caught its attention—the guards were running for the front door, from which shouts emerged.

The bird's gaze swept the garden for its mate. No one but crows as far as Filip could see. The yard was empty, for now. He lifted his hand and gave the signal.

Bolan responded with a softly whistled tune—nothing that would garner attention, but one that Koli's Bat ears would pick up immediately, though she couldn't see him. She would send a signal to Adrek, who would beckon Alanka to run.

Which she did. A glint of metal caught the crow's eye, the shutter swinging outward. Alanka climbed out of the window, then scuttled low to the ground toward the tree. Filip switched back to the rooftop crow.

Guards were coming around the back of the house. There wasn't time for Alanka to make it to the tree without being detected. Filip held up his hands, and Bolan stopped whistling. The gazebo crow saw Alanka dive behind the small structure.

He let out a breath and rubbed his temples, which throbbed from wielding the power for so long in such a jerky manner. He hoped it would last without breaking his mind.

"Please," he whispered to the Horse Spirit, resisting the temptation to pray to one of the gods. "Just a little longer."

He reconnected with the rooftop crow, who watched the guards approach the gazebo, swords drawn.

Alanka held her breath when she heard booted footsteps. She couldn't shoot both in time, and with Adrek's fading powers, he might miss if he tried.

One of the guards cried out. She peered around the edge of the gazebo to see the man fall, clutching his leg, which held an arrow. His companion stopped, and an arrow whizzed over his head. He ducked, and she saw her chance.

Alanka sprinted across the open grass, straight for Adrek. A shout came from behind, then the thump of boots against grass as the other guard pursued. There was nowhere to hide now.

Adrek dropped his bow and crouched down, hands extended toward her.

My first flight, she thought.

She leaped into his arms, and he launched her straight up, using her momentum and his own strength to throw her into the tree.

Her shoulder slammed the thick branch, but she wrapped her arms around it, then heaved a leg up and shimmied toward the trunk, awkwardly, to get out of Adrek's way.

She looked down. Adrek had looped the strap of the bow over his back and was ready to jump. With the guard ten paces away, Adrek would have one chance, with diminished powers, to reach the limb.

He bent his legs and jumped. His palms met the branch, then slipped, until he was holding on by his fingers.

"Adrek!"

"Go!" he said.

She stretched forward along the branch.

"Don't." The Cougar's face was red from the strain. "Branch'll break. Save yourself."

"Shut up and hold on."

She slid forward on her stomach. The branch cracked. She froze. It held, for now.

In the front garden, more guards ran over, brandishing short swords. If Adrek slipped, he'd be killed—or worse.

She scooted out farther onto the branch. More creaking of wood. Adrek's fingers were slipping.

She lurched forward and grabbed his forearm. Her legs twisted tight around the branch, summoning all the strength in her body.

She couldn't lift him, but her grip gave him enough leverage to get a better hold of his own. Adrek flexed his arms and flung a leg over the branch—a far cry from his usual graceful vault. She slid down the limb to the trunk, bark scraping her stomach. Another crack, the loudest yet.

Alanka leaped to the next branch, facing the street. Her foot slipped, and she tumbled, bouncing from limb to limb. She fell on the sidewalk in a bruised, scratched heap.

Adrek grinned at her from the tree above. "Pure grace as always."

She glared at him, then grinned. "Get down here so we can run away."

He leaped to the ground, stumbling a bit on the landing. A shrill whistle cut the air.

"Let's go," she said.

When Rhia heard the whistle, she opened her eyes and lowered her trembling arms. She released the crows, ending the chant of beckoning.

Someone whispered her name, and the haze left by the chant made her think, for a moment, that she was dreaming.

She shoved back her cowl and looked up.

"Marek…"

He fell to his knees beside her. She touched his face, his hair. Her vision blurred with tears.

"It's you," she said.

"And you, too." He pulled her into his arms, and she closed her eyes, savoring the smell of his skin and the feel of his body against hers at last. For a moment, it was enough.

She opened her eyes to look at her brother and Arcas over Marek's shoulder. "Where's Nilik?"

Marek let her go. "They took him away this morning." He held a finger to her lips. "We're going to get him back."

"When?"

"Today." He stood, holding her hands. "If we leave now."

Lycas stepped forward. "We'll split up like we planned and rendezvous with the others back at the inn."

Rhia and Marek ran down the alley into the street, dodging carts and other pedestrians. Everyone else was running toward the senator's mansion, captivated by the sight of the crows and the sounds of chaos within the iron gates.

"Rhia, wait." Marek pulled her to a stop as soon as they left the northeast quadrant. He took her face between his hands and touched his forehead to hers. "I just want to look at you for a moment."

But his eyes were closed. His hands crept over her face, outlining her nose and jaw. One of them smelled of blood.

"Marek—"

"I'm sorry." His breath came hard and sharp. "Rhia, I'm so sorry."

"It's not your fault they took Nilik." She stroked his hair. "I swear, I'll never blame you. I love you." She pressed her cheek to his, both of them wet, then moved her mouth to kiss him.

He turned his head away. "I can't."

Her heart twisted. "Why not?"

"Not until I tell you. Not until you know what I've become."

"Marek—let's get our son, then we'll talk."

"You're right." He took her hand. "Let's go."

They raced back to the inn. No one was in the room Rhia shared with Koli and Alanka. She knocked on the men's door.

Adrek opened it and threw a shout of delight when he saw Marek. He hugged Marek hard and dragged him into the room. Alanka jumped up to join the embrace.

They both sobered to hear the news of Nilik. "If only

we'd done this a day sooner," Alanka said, "then you'd both be here."

"You had no way of knowing." Marek touched her shoulder. "Thank you for saving my life. It was a well-timed shot."

The corners of her mouth drooped. "No, it was far too late."

While they waited for the others, Alanka told Marek how she had lost her Wolf powers. "You lost yours, too, didn't you," she asked, "because you were in the city? Don't worry, they'll come back once we get out into the wilderness."

Marek's gaze dropped to the floor. "We'll see."

He looked so broken. Rhia moved to put her arms around him.

Just then the others entered, Arcas first, out of breath. "Good, you made it," he said to Marek, who stood and embraced him.

"I'll never forget this," he said to the Spider. "I didn't deserve your kindness."

Arcas scoffed. "You're not sorry you stole Rhia from me." He winked at her. "And neither is she."

"And you." Marek approached Filip. "You had every reason to hate me, and no reason to help me. Why did you do it?"

Filip looked past him at Alanka. Marek turned to her, then glanced between her and Filip.

"I've missed a lot, haven't I?" Marek said.

Lycas hugged Marek and said, "I'm getting really tired of rescuing you."

They all shared an uneasy laugh. Then Marek explained the Descendant army's plans, which made Rhia quake inside. If Nilik were to die in Velekos, as she and Damen had foreseen, it could be as part of a Descendant invasion. He could slaughter and be slaughtered by his own people.

She might never see him alive again.

Filip led the mission out of Leukos and forbade himself to look back. He knew his city would be gleaming in the midday sun.

With the money Senator Mylosa had given Arcas in advance for the nonexistent carving, they had bought two more horses, bringing the total to seven. Filip had sent Koli ahead on the fastest steed to act as a scout.

Alanka sat with him on the other Ilion horse, arms encircling his waist. "You think we'll catch them by nightfall?" she asked him.

"They'll be traveling slowly—one, because they have children with them, probably in carts, and two, because they have no reason to suspect they're being pursued. We'll have surprise on our side." He touched her knee. "Are you ready?"

He heard her pat the bow strapped to her back. "Ready to kill again," she said with false cheerfulness.

"It's the only way. We can't let any go free to send a warning. Besides, we won't kill everyone. The wet nurses can go back to Asermos as prisoners. The Council can decide what to do with them, maybe send them home."

"Maybe?"

"Alanka, this is war." He heard his own voice harden. "They've invaded your lands, taken your villagers, and now they want to raise your own children to destroy you. Your survival trumps the fate of a few soldiers and wet nurses."

"They're still people."

"They're not people. They're the enemy." He shut his mouth tight, knowing he'd said too much again.

Her arm tensed around his waist. "That's what you thought of us before you invaded, wasn't it? That we were beasts?"

"Yes. It was necessary." He turned his head so he could see her face. "I've chosen my side, and it's with you. Forever. But it doesn't change what I am, and what I am is exactly what we need to rescue Nilik."

A cloud of dust appeared on the distant hillside. Filip shaded his eyes to see a dark chestnut horse galloping toward them.

"It's Koli." He waved his arm. She returned the signal, then slowed the gelding to a trot to start its cooldown.

The others dismounted and led their horses into a cover of trees by the side of the road. Koli rode up, her mount dancing under the restraining reins, his neck arched and his hide spotted dark with sweat. She dismounted and let Bolan take the gelding for a hot-walk.

"That horse," she said, panting, "he doesn't like stopping."

Filip offered her a waterskin. "Fast, though, right?"

She widened her eyes and nodded, then took a series of greedy gulps.

"It's two carts, with two guards each on horseback," Koli said. "Looked like soldiers driving, so that's six total."

"How many children?" Rhia asked.

"Twelve, plus four wet nurses. I didn't recognize any of the women, so they could've been Ilion or Kalindon." She looked at Adrek.

The Cougar shifted his feet. "Was there—a young girl, maybe three years old, dark curly hair?"

Koli nodded. "That sounds like one of the older children."

"Daria." Adrek clasped his hands together and closed his eyes.

Koli continued. "There were four baskets, which I assume contained babies. Two of them were crying." She closed her eyes and recited the rest of the details. From the description of the caravan guards' uniforms, Filip surmised they were cavalry officers, possibly even his own former comrades.

"Will that make it harder for you to kill them?" Alanka asked with a directness that never failed to stun him.

"If anything, it will help. I know how they fight."

Filip took a long stick and scratched a plan in the dirt. "We'll follow Koli's path to pass them by nightfall, then wait in ambush under the cloak of the woods. When they arrive, first Bolan and I will drive the soldiers on horseback away from the caravan so that Adrek and Alanka can shoot them without endangering the children."

Bolan cleared his throat. "You want me to attack cavalry officers?"

"I want you nowhere near them. Use your powers to frighten their mounts. If it becomes necessary to engage them one-on-one on horseback, only I will do so. Understand?"

"I have no problem with that," Bolan said.

Filip focused on his stick sketch again. "As the guards peel off, Arcas and Lycas will dispatch the drivers. Rhia and

Koli will grab the reins to make sure the cart horses don't bolt."

"What do I do?" Marek said.

"Make sure no one carries off any of the children. It'll be after dark, so you can pursue them invisibly."

"No, I can't," Marek said.

"But we're out of the city," Alanka said. "My powers are back to full—so are Adrek's and Lycas's."

"You don't understand." Marek looked at Alanka, then Rhia. "I'm not a Wolf anymore."

Rhia felt the world tip as she stared at her husband. "Not a Wolf?"

"It was part of what I tried to tell you before. Wolf couldn't help me in that place. So another Spirit claimed me."

Her mouth went dry. "Which one?"

He faded. She watched him melt into the background— not invisible, but camouflaged. Everyone gasped but Rhia, who couldn't find the breath.

Then Marek shifted his weight and reappeared.

Her husband had become a Fox.

"I don't understand," she said.

"I didn't want to live." His eyes filled with agony. "The things that happened to me, the things I did—I thought my soul would leave forever. Fox showed me how to survive, and I'll always be in Her debt."

Rhia stepped close to him. "Marek, what was so horrible?"

He looked at the others and said nothing.

Filip pointed downhill into the trees. "There's a stream not far away. Let's water the horses before we go on."

When they were alone, Rhia took Marek's hands. "What is it?"

"Don't touch me." He pulled out of her grip. "I'm not clean anymore." He covered his face and sank to his knees. "Forgive me."

"For what?" She lifted his chin. "Whatever it is, I'll understand."

The shadows beneath his eyes seemed to stretch over his cheeks.

"I've betrayed you," he said. "My owner made me—do things."

"What things?" Her voice rang hollow inside her head.

His gaze wavered beyond her shoulder, but came back to her face. "Some of the slaves, the men she liked, she—we—"

A cold fist closed over her heart. "Marek?"

He shut his eyes. "I'm saying this wrong. No one forced me. I could've died instead. I would've rather died, I swear to you." He looked at her. "But she said she'd send Nilik away if I didn't—serve her in bed."

Rhia let go of him and took a step back. She wanted to turn away, wanted to run and hide under a rock. But if what he said was true, it sounded like…

"She raped you," Rhia whispered.

"It's not that simple. She couldn't have forced me." He covered his face again and looked as though he would claw away his own skin. "Rhia, I lost my soul. It was the only way."

"No…" She dropped to her knees, tears clouding her eyes. "I still see you. I feel you." She held his face in her hands. "You're here. All of you."

He grabbed her wrists as if he wanted to push her away. "Forgive me."

"Shh." She swept the hair off his forehead and kissed it. "There's nothing to forgive."

"Do it anyway."

Rhia looked into his eyes, though the pain in them sliced her. "Marek, I forgive you. I love you for what you did. You did it to save Nilik." She clutched his face. "Please don't let this destroy you."

Rhia kissed him, and his mouth pressed back hard. She tried not to think where that mouth had been, of the skin it had tasted. The ferocity of Marek's kiss told her that Wolf lay waiting to take him back, the moment he was ready. But she didn't care. Fox or Wolf, he was Marek, and he was hers again.

They parted, and she traced the corners of his lips with her thumb, wondering if they would ever rise in another smile or smirk. A sudden rage curdled inside her. "Where is this woman?" she said. "I'll kill her."

"I already did."

She thought she saw a pang of regret in his eyes. "Good."

"It was an accident, though for weeks I dreamed of nothing else. I wanted to kill her almost as much as I wanted to live."

"You sound as if you're sorry."

"Rhia, I've killed three people this last year. Maybe they were justified, but I can't forget the light fading from their eyes."

"I know." Though she'd never taken a life, she'd felt Crow carry more souls from this world than she could count.

"They each leave a mark. This war's deaths will haunt us long after it ends—if it ever ends." Rhia stood. "But now it's time to add a few more."

38

Alanka pressed her forehead against the back of Filip's shoulder and waited for the signal. In the cover of the dark woods, they sat astride the black mare, who shifted her feet impatiently. Filip murmured a series of indiscernible words, and the horse quieted.

Alanka's stomach somersaulted at the thought of riding into battle, though she knew she fought for her family, her people, her land. She wouldn't let them down.

Filip reached back and rested his hand on her knee. She covered it with her own.

Ahead through the trees, the road to Surnos glistened gray in the twilight. In the woods on the opposite side, Adrek and Bolan waited on the dark bay pony, whose white star and stocking had been covered in pitch to blend with the darkness. Marek, Arcas and Lycas lay in a ditch on the other side of the road.

She and Filip heard the wagons at the same time, judging by the way his shoulders tensed. The children's whimpers could be heard over the squeaking cart wheels and the clopping of hooves.

Far to their right, Koli and Rhia turned onto the road, their horses ambling toward the wagons.

Filip took his hand out of Alanka's and sat up straight. She could feel the energy spark from him. Slowly, quietly, he unsheathed his sword.

The wagons appeared to the left. Alanka's mouth went dry.

From the right, Rhia and Koli hailed the wagons, which stopped directly in front of Filip and Alanka.

"Step aside," the lead guard shouted. Filip cocked his head at the sound of the man's voice.

"We're lost," Rhia said. "Can you help us?"

"No, we're on a mission."

A baby in the first wagon began to cry.

"Is this the road to Leukos?" Koli asked.

That was the signal. Alanka squeezed her legs tight around the horse's flank as Filip urged the mare forward with a shout. They galloped forward, Filip brandishing his sword high and hurling a war cry he'd learned from Lycas.

Alanka nocked an arrow against her bowstring, trying to keep her balance long enough to get off a shot.

Just as the attackers reached the wagons full of screaming women and children, the guards recovered from their shock and drew their swords. Suddenly the four cavalry horses reared, their eyes showing white rims of panic. They reeled away from Bolan and Adrek, who were approaching from the other side. Whatever Bolan had said to them, it had sparked a primal terror.

The lead guard's horse crashed into Filip's, spilling Alanka from the black mare's back. She eased into a roll, ending up on her knees next to the first wagon.

"Are you all right?" Filip called to her. In response, she nocked the arrow and shot one of the fleeing guards in the back.

Before she could lower her bow, something hard and heavy landed on her. Alanka heard the faint zing of a blade withdrawing from a sheath. She kicked out, and the weight disappeared. She rolled to her feet to see Lycas atop the wagon driver, who had been a moment away from killing her. Over the shrieks of the frightened children and horses, she heard the man's skull crack against the road.

Hooves pounded, fading into the distance. She looked ahead to see Filip in full pursuit of the lead guard. They disappeared around a bend.

Two Ilion horses trotted past her, riderless. Another *crack-thwong* sang through the air, and the fourth rider, heading back toward Leukos, fell from his saddle. Adrek let out a whoop from the other side of the wagon, where he sat on his horse behind an alarmed-looking Bolan.

Alanka ran to Koli, who was bending to grasp the reins of the second wagon horse. Its driver was lying lifeless under Arcas.

"Lend me your mount," she told Koli. "I have to help Filip."

The Bat scoffed. "You'll never be able to handle this one."

"But he's the fastest."

Koli groaned and dismounted. "Good luck." She offered Alanka the reins, then cupped her hands to boost her onto the horse's back.

Alanka guided the dark red gelding in front of the wagons, onto the open road, then gave the horse his head. He swerved under her and took off.

She clutched his mane and leaned low over his neck, riding a wind she didn't know how to stop.

Rhia slipped off her horse into the wagon. "Nilik!"

Five small faces stared at her, red and strained with tears. Two frightened young women hunched over the infants in their laps. Rhia recognized them, but her mind couldn't bring up their names, not until she'd found her son.

A hearty wail came from a large white basket near her feet.

She knelt and lifted the basket's cover. The world melted away.

Nilik.

She reached in, carefully, and took him in her arms. He was twice as heavy as she remembered, with twice as much hair, but he was her son.

"Nilik…" She couldn't breathe. Tears welled up inside her, but her eyes refused to release them. She would never cry, never be unhappy again. She brought her face close to his, to kiss him, smell him, make him hers again.

"Daria!"

Tucking Nilik against her left shoulder, Rhia turned toward the second wagon. Adrek held a three-year-old girl high over his head, then pulled her into an embrace. The girl's mother, a young Kalindon Spider named Nelma, beamed up at him, an infant in her arms. The size of the bundle made Rhia fear Nelma had become pregnant here in Ilios.

Adrek rubbed noses with the curly haired girl in his grasp. Daria scrunched up her face, then clutched his hair so tight he yowled.

Rhia tore her gaze from the happy reunion to search for Marek. He had sacrificed so much to be able to hold his son whenever he wanted.

Bolan appeared at the back of the wagon. "Everyone all right?"

"Where's Marek?" she asked him.

"He went after a woman carrying a baby." He pointed into the woods. "She started running as soon as we rode up, probably thought we were bandits." The Horse climbed into the wagon, sat down between two crying children and lifted them onto his knees. "Guess where we're going?" he asked them. "We're going home." He opened a small bag tied to his belt. "Who wants cake?"

The children's sobs turned into shrieks of delight. Koli covered her ears as she passed, leading a dead guard's horse. One of the wet nurses, an Otter woman Rhia recognized from Asermos, laughed, then began to weep.

Rhia's eyes strained to see who else was missing. Alanka and Filip. She glanced at the darkening sky and hoped for their quick return. They needed a head start to outrun the Ilion army, which would no doubt send a search party when the children failed to arrive at the camp tomorrow.

She lowered Nilik into the crook of her arm. He wasn't safe yet, not by a long way.

Marek crashed through the woods after the woman and child. "Wait!" he called. "We're from Asermos!" Her steps slowed but didn't stop. "And Kalindos!"

She halted and turned to him. As he drew nearer, he saw her pale face and light brown hair in the dim light. A young Bobcat he'd known since childhood. Skaris's mate.

"Lidia?"

She crept toward him, clutching the baby to her chest. "Marek? Is that you?"

"It's me." He half turned away toward the others. "And Alanka and Adrek and—"

She struck him hard across the face. "That's for killing my mate." She spit on his feet. "I'd give you worse if it weren't for the child." She hunched her shoulders over it and glared up at Marek.

He rubbed his cheek. "I hope you'll forgive me someday. In the meantime, let us rescue you."

She gave him a guarded look, as if she didn't dare believe her captivity was over. He knew the feeling.

"We're here to take you home to Kalindos," he said. He motioned for her to precede him down the path back to the others. As she passed him warily, he looked at the baby. It was hard to tell its size from the bundle of blankets around it. "That's not Skaris's child, is it?"

"No. If he'd been second phase when you fought, it'd be

you lying at the bottom of that gorge." She stepped over a fallen branch. "I don't know who the father is. I was a slave in Leukos. A couple of men...had me."

He found the strength to say it out loud. "Me, too."

She stopped and stared at him. "You, too, what?"

"I was a slave in Leukos until this morning. My owner also—she threatened my son if I didn't."

Lidia let out a long breath. "Why did they do this to us?"

"They want to conquer our people completely. They would have used these children to build a magical army loyal to Ilios. They would've killed you or sent you away once the children grew old enough to understand who they really are."

Her eyes formed slits. "I believe it." She began to tremble. Marek held out his arms, and she let him take the baby. They walked on, Lidia kicking every stone in their path.

"Thank you for saving us," she said finally.

"I only saved myself. They did the rest." He gestured to the road, which had become visible through the trees.

"Who's 'they'?"

He shook his head. "You won't believe it."

Filip's enemy fled before him. He wore the colors of one of his brothers-in-arms and the rank of a captain. It should have felt strange to want to slice through the red-and-yellow uniform Filip had once borne so proudly. All that mattered now was the heat of the hunt.

As soon as his steed's black head stretched past the left hindquarters of the Ilion's dappled gray, Filip raised his sword and swung.

The blade reached the uniform's material, tearing a hole in fabric but not flesh. The other rider jerked his mount hard to the right. Filip cursed. He'd struck too soon.

To his surprise, the guard pulled to a halt and drew his own sword. Filip stopped and turned, staying in the shadows of the overhanging trees. The Ilion and his horse glowed in the blue summer twilight.

The officer's steel helmet covered his face, all but his eyes and mouth. Filip reached into the mind of the gray horse. Battle steeds were acutely tuned to the moods of their riders. This man was excited but far from nervous about this confrontation. Perhaps he'd been yearning for a good battle after playing babysitter.

"Come out of the shadows and fight," a familiar voice inside the helmet called.

Filip stayed where he was, blocking the escape route. The sword he'd ached for lay light and elegant in his hand, ready to sing at a flick of his wrist.

"Come and get me," he said.

The captain rode forward—not in a rush of attack, but a steady walk. "Sir? Is that you?"

The voice sounded boyish now, and even more familiar.

"Kiril?" Filip uttered the name with disbelief. Of all the people, in all the places. The Ilion who would have been a Firefly, the one man to escape Asermon captivity alive and whole. "What are you doing here?"

The rider halved the distance between them. He took off his helmet to reveal the gleaming brown eyes and shoulder-length dark hair Filip had seen every day for three years. "I think that's my question for you."

"I asked first."

"Right." He seemed to defer to Filip out of habit. "When I came home, they asked which Asermons were pregnant, so I told them of two women I'd heard Zelia discuss with her assistants." His voice faltered a fraction. "The third child was a lucky find. They heard about him after arriving in Asermos."

"For this they promoted you to captain?" Kiril had been a second lieutenant when he escaped Asermos. Progressing two grades of rank in less than a year was unprecedented.

"I was due for first lieutenant before I got home. Because of my time in Asermos, they assigned me to this— project." Filip thought he detected disgust in Kiril's voice. "I helped set up the camp," the captain continued, "and got a field promotion two days ago when I agreed to lead this mission."

"You've done well for yourself."

Kiril scoffed. "By some measures."

Slowly, Filip rode out of the shadows. "You told everyone I died."

"As promised."

"Thank you."

Kiril stared at Filip's rough clothes. "Your turn. Why are you dressed like a peasant and attacking convoys?"

"The third child. His parents are…friends of mine."

"Ah, you've become one of them." He shook his head sadly. "Still talking to animals?"

"Yes. Your saddle is too tight at the withers, by the way."

Kiril slid his fingers under the front of his saddle. "Feels fine to me."

"You're not the one wearing it."

Kiril broke into a smile, which Filip couldn't help returning. "It's good to see you, sir."

"Filip is my only name now. Besides, you outrank me."

Kiril shifted in his saddle, leather creaking in the silence. "I need to go."

"I can't let you."

"Then we shall fight, to the death, I suppose."

"It doesn't have to be that way." Filip dared to ride a few steps closer. "Join us."

Kiril laughed. "Why in the name of all the gods would I want to do that?"

"Because you miss the magic."

Kiril's laughter faded abruptly. "How can I miss what I haven't lost?"

"You still have it?"

"Not still. Again. When I was in Leukos it went away, but they sent me out here and suddenly—" he spread his hands and puffed out his cheeks "—I can't control it. The others laugh at me."

"All the more reason to join us. We can show you how to connect to your Spirit and develop your powers."

"I don't want them to develop. I want them to go away."

His words sounded painfully familiar. "I know you do. But you can't imagine what it's like to have a Spirit who accepts everything you are, who grants powers and asks for nothing in return but respect."

"You're right. I can't imagine that, because it's a lie."

"It's the only truth. The Spirits want us to bring the world together again."

Kiril sat up straight. "That's what this camp will do. These children will conquer their own homeland with magic. Then we'll all be united under the Ilion flag."

Filip uttered a sad laugh. "Don't you understand? These children will grow up with power they can't control, like I was, like you are now. You'd end up killing them for your own protection." His voice hardened. "How does that sound? A decade from now, exterminating a generation of twelve-year-olds?"

Kiril frowned and threw a glance toward the convoy of children, miles behind them. "I have my orders."

"Only if you wear that uniform."

Kiril scoffed. "You want me to be a scruffy rebel like you? What would my family think?"

Filip had no answer. For Kiril to turn traitor would be the epitome of dishonor. He had no right to ask his friend to make that choice. Not voluntarily.

"A proposal." He raised his sword. "Join us or die."

"Assuming you can beat me."

"I've always beaten you."

The captain raked a derisive glance over Filip's prosthesis. "That was when you were a man."

Rage and shame flickered inside Filip, but only for a moment. "We'll fight on foot."

Kiril raised his eyebrows. "So be it."

They tethered their horses on opposite sides of the road, then met in the center, ceremonially. Before fighting, they bowed, then crossed swords and grasped each other's left hand. As he stared into the eyes of his battle brother, Filip tried to turn him into just another faceless enemy.

"I don't want to kill you," he told Kiril. "If I win, you join us."

Kiril hesitated. "Agreed. If I win, I take you prisoner."

"I won't leave my wife. If you win, kill me."

The distant sound of hoofbeats came from Filip's left, from the direction of the convoy.

Kiril's posture stiffened. He heard it, too.

They each took two steps back, Filip testing the ground beneath his false leg. It provided a firm, even surface. He circled to his right to get a glimpse of the oncoming horse. Its color and speed told him it was Koli's mount, but it was swerving in an odd manner.

Before Kiril could attack, Filip backed up and opened his mind to the chestnut gelding, for just a moment.

In the brief flash, he knew something was wrong. The steel bit pinched his mouth from reins held too tight. His mane was yanked from side to side by someone fighting not to fall off. The rider's voice yelled in his twitching ears.

Alanka.

"Wait," he told Kiril, but the captain lunged at Filip's good leg. Filip twisted in time to block the blow with his sword, then slammed his shoulder hard into his opponent's chest.

Kiril stumbled back, a look of astonishment on his face. In the distance, the hoofbeats halted.

Filip threw his sword aside. "Get down!" He flung himself at Kiril, tackling him as a loud crack snapped the air. They crashed to the ground. Kiril slammed Filip's ribs with the hilt of his sword, but Filip slipped around his back to maneuver him into a headlock.

"If you won't listen," Filip said, "then look."

He turned Kiril so he could see the arrow sticking out of the ground a few feet away, the arrow that had almost killed him. Kiril uttered a crude oath, then went limp.

Alanka rode closer, shouting Filip's name.

"Don't shoot!" he called. "It's all right." He let go and helped Kiril to his feet.

The man's expression was a mixture of relief and mourning. "You saved my life."

"I did, didn't I?" Filip stepped into the road to stop Alanka's horse before it could bolt again. He murmured soothing sounds to the creature, whose mind was a cacophony of complaints.

When he had hold of the horse's bridle, Alanka slumped in the saddle with relief. "What's going on?" she said. "I thought he was the enemy."

"Not anymore." Kiril walked forward slowly, holding the hilt of his sword out for Filip to take. "I owe you my loyalty now, brother."

Filip accepted the weapon and inserted it into his own sheath. "I have an idea how you can repay the debt."

Kiril nodded reluctantly. "Somehow you managed to give me the only honorable excuse to help your cause."

"You were looking for one?"

Kiril gazed past them, up into the trees. Filip turned to see the branches full of light. Hundreds of fireflies winked on and off, creating a shifting tapestry of yellow-green dots.

"It's beautiful," Alanka whispered.

"Yes." Filip helped her slide off the horse into his arms. He pulled her close, glad to be alive. "It certainly is."

"So where do we go from here?" Alanka asked Filip as they rode back to meet the convoy. He wore both his own sword and the Ilion's. She rode his black mare, to her relief, and he somehow restrained Koli's chestnut gelding while holding the reins of the horse Kiril rode.

"We'll go wherever you want," Filip replied.

"I want to stay in Ilios until every Kalindon and Asermon goes home."

"That could take years."

"We could start with that children's camp. They're bound to bring more babies soon, right?" she asked Kiril.

"That's the plan," he replied. "I can't say I'd be sorry to see that place destroyed, despite my hard work in creating it." Kiril brushed the dirt from his uniform sleeve. "Does being a rebel pay well?"

Alanka laughed. "No, but you meet more interesting people."

He gave her a crooked smile. "Including women?"

"Other women, yes," Filip said. "Specifically, the ones who aren't married to your commander."

"I thought I outranked you."

"Not anymore." Filip sidled his horse closer to Alanka and spoke to her in a low voice. "There's just one thing. Playing renegade in the wilderness will make it hard to start our own family."

She frowned. There'd been a time when all she wanted

was a man who wouldn't leave her, a man to give her children and a stable life. "We have time for that later," she told him. "This is more important."

He nodded. "After a year we'll reevaluate."

"Five years."

"Three."

She chuckled. "Three years."

Soon they met the wagons, which were already rolling in their direction.

Lycas met them at the head of the group, dressed in the too-tight uniform of one of the dead soldiers. He drew a long dagger from his belt when he saw Kiril. "Who's that?"

"Our newest comrade," Filip said. "He's bound to me by a warrior's honor. And he has his very own Aspect."

The Wolverine narrowed his eyes. "You must be joking."

Filip turned to Kiril. "Show him."

The Firefly raised his hands, cupping them into an empty sphere, which a moment later filled with a yellow-white light.

Lycas's jaw dropped. "That will come in handy. But keep an eye on him. He gets no weapons."

The group moved as quickly as they could through the darkness, with Kiril providing light when he could, and Adrek and Lycas leading the way with their night vision when he couldn't.

In a few hours, they reached a crossroad. They turned right to head north, away from Surnos and toward the lands of their people.

At first light, they found a place in the woods to pull far off the road to hide and care for the children.

All day they kept a keen ear out for travelers on the road. Each time horses were heard, the troupe fell into total silence. It pained Alanka to see how acutely even the youngest children sensed the mortal danger.

As soon as the sun descended behind the forested hills, they prepared to set out again. Alanka looked at Filip. "It's time to tell them."

They went to Rhia, who was lifting toddlers up to Nelma in the wagon. She turned when Alanka approached.

"What's wrong?" Rhia asked. "Your face is sad."

Alanka touched her friend's shoulder. "I'm here to say goodbye. We're staying in Ilios until we find the other Kalindons and Asermons."

Rhia smiled, even as tears filled her eyes. She embraced Alanka tightly. "I don't know what to say, except that I'll miss you. And thank you."

"A Horse and a Wolf against the Ilion army?" Arcas appeared from the other side of the wagon. "You'll need help."

"Are you volunteering?" Filip asked.

From across the camp, Koli shouted, "Not without me!"

A grin spread across Arcas's face. "Consider us a team. We can divert any search party looking for the children, too."

"Thank you." Filip took Alanka's hand, looking stunned. "That makes four, five including Kiril."

"Six." Lycas approached them. "As soon as I get them safely to Velekos, I'll come back and meet you in Surnos."

"What about your daughter?" Alanka asked.

"I want to be with her." Lycas fingered the red lining of his uniform. "But I want even more to protect her future, make sure she has a free land to grow up in."

"I'll watch over her as best as I can," Rhia said, "as well as Mali will let me."

Someone touched Alanka's hand. She turned to see Marek, then reached to hug him hard. Her throat tightened almost too much to speak.

"I just got you back," she whispered. When she let go of him, she stroked his cheek. "You'll be a Wolf again someday."

He nodded, though the sadness in his eyes said he didn't believe her. "Bring them all home, Alanka. Bring Kalindos back to life."

39

Marek stared down at the Marison River, sparkling in the light of the waning crescent moon. The clear, shallow waters marked the north-south border between Ilios and the lands of the Reawakened, as he had come to think of his people.

He was free, at least on the outside.

His arms ached from lugging restless children. Their group had abandoned the wagons two weeks ago so they could leave the road and avoid detection. Their escape route had led through mosquito-filled woods, far to the west of Ilion coastal settlements.

Behind him came the light tread of Adrek's footsteps. Marek unslung the bow and arrows from his back. The Cougar came to stand beside him at the top of the hill.

"Sorry we have to share." Adrek looped the quiver's strap

over his shoulder and adjusted it for his thinner frame. "Wood around here's too brittle for bow making."

"It's good to have it again, even part of the time. I'm glad Alanka brought it."

"Guess she always knew they'd find you."

Marek shrugged. "Or she wanted a spare."

They stood listening to the chirps of the summer's first cicadas, never taking their eyes off Ilios. They hadn't shared stories of their enslavement, but when they'd washed in the river, Marek had glimpsed the scars on Adrek's arms and back.

"My watch now," Adrek said. "Go sleep. If you can."

Marek gave Ilios one last, long stare. Tomorrow when they continued north, he wouldn't look back.

As he approached his family's tent, Nelma came out with Nilik in her arms.

"Feeding time." She glanced back at the tent. "Rhia asked me to keep him for an hour or so afterward."

His stomach fluttered at the implication. "No, you're too exhausted."

"It's no trouble. He usually falls asleep in the middle of eating, anyway. This way, I won't have to wake him." She reached to pat Marek's arm, then seemed to think better of it. "I'll see you at daybreak." She headed for the tent she shared with Adrek.

Marek wiped his clammy palms on his trousers.

"Are you coming to bed?" a soft voice asked from within.

He swallowed hard and entered the tent. Rhia lay on her back, her hair spread loose and soft on the folded blanket they used as a pillow.

Marek sat next to her. "Everything's quiet out there."

"And in here, for once." She smiled, briefly, as if testing the expression. "I've missed you, Marek."

He lay on his side but didn't touch her. "I was only gone a few hours."

"You know what I mean."

He did, and wanted to run.

Her hand crept forward, cautious as a stray dog, and touched his cheek. He steeled himself to keep from flinching.

"I won't hurt you," she whispered. The pain in her voice twisted his gut.

"Of course you won't." With every muscle in his face clenched, he leaned forward and kissed her. Her hand slid behind his head so that he couldn't pull back without an effort.

Fighting the urge to draw away, he wrapped his arm around her waist, pulling her body tight against him. She uttered a soft moan and slid her tongue between his lips.

His insides froze. He let go of Rhia and turned his face away. "I can't. I still can't."

"I'm sorry." She took his hand. "It's too soon. I shouldn't have—"

"No, it's not too soon." He sank down on his back and pressed his other hand to his temple. "I don't think I ever will."

Rhia's silence rang louder than any cry of protest. When she finally took a breath, she said, "Because of her. Because of what she did to you."

"Feels like she still owns me. Like she's clutching a piece of my soul."

"Maybe she is."

He looked at her, not daring to hope. "Ilions can be soul thieves, too?"

"It's not about magic. It's just power, something anyone can take." She laid a soft hand on his shoulder. "Come with me, and let's get it back."

Rhia watched her brother Lycas strike his flint to light the small bundle of thanapras. He placed it in the clay pot she'd brought.

"Be careful this time," he told her. "Tereus will kill me if anything happens to you."

Marek turned to Rhia. "Is this dangerous?"

"Crow will watch over me," she said. "Lie down."

Rhia knelt on the blanket next to Marek and chanted— silently, so as not to wake the camp's children. Her lips moved, and her throat strained, but no sound echoed outside of her own head. She knew Crow would hear it anyway.

Rhia finished the chant and lay on her back, her shoulder and hip touching Marek's.

Lycas tapped a small chunk of wood, a near silent version of the ritual drum. Rhia's breath grew deep and even as she stepped through the fog into the Gray Valley.

It was night. The sky stretched black, starless, but the rocks sparkled as though they lay dusted with snow under a full moon. Even the dead tree glowed white, its branches a lustrous marble.

Rhia waited, but no one appeared. For the first time, the Gray Valley felt like a place of fragile peace.

She turned left to search a part of the valley she'd never explored. No wind tossed her hair or rattled the tree branches. Though she walked softly, her footsteps thumped loud in the utter stillness.

A growl came from behind, then a metallic bang.

Rhia faced the dead tree. A golden-haired woman crouched in its hazy shade, her back to Rhia.

"Were you Basha Mylosa?"

The woman stood with dignity, as if receiving a guest. Her curls fell below her shoulders, glistening in the light of the invisible moon.

"I will always be Basha Kantera Mylosa."

At her feet sat a blanket-draped cage. Something inside it yipped and howled.

"Hush!" Basha slammed her heel against the cage.

The heat of wrath crawled over Rhia's scalp. She drew a deep, ragged breath and tried to steady her voice. "The Other Side is beautiful and peaceful, much better than this place. But you can't go unless you give him up."

"How do you know what it's like?"

"I've been there."

"And you came back?" Basha started forward, eyes gleaming. "I want to come back, too."

"You can't."

"Bring me back and you can have him."

"I wouldn't even if I could." Rhia forced her feet to stay put. "Give him to me."

Basha stopped and laughed, tilting back her head. The mirthful titter descended into a threatening chuckle. "No one gives me orders, especially not my murderer's little bitch."

"I know how you got that." Rhia pointed at the fox's cage with a trembling finger. "I know what you did to him."

"But you don't know what he did to me." Basha came closer, swaying her hips and swishing her long white skirt. "How he made me scream his name night after night."

"Stop it."

"How he showed me new worlds of brutal pleasure I didn't know existed."

"Shut up." Rhia's voice cracked.

"He loved it!" Basha's eyes gleamed like a young girl speaking of her first sweetheart. "And he loved me." She stood close to Rhia and examined her without lowering her own chin. "I set free the beast in him, the one he could never show a delicate creature like you." She plucked at Rhia's sleeve.

"Enough." Rhia shoved Basha's hand away, then realized it was the first time she'd touched one of the dead souls. She shuddered. "Give him to me," she said, too forcefully, "or I will end you."

"Sorry, that won't work." Basha flicked the fingers Rhia had touched as though they had filth stuck to them. "I'm already dead."

"Not as dead as you could be." Rhia sensed Crow nearby, waiting for her decision.

Basha's eyes narrowed. "You're as poor a liar as you are a lover. According to Marek, at least."

Rage burned Rhia's gut, begging her to do something she'd regret until the day she crossed the Gray Valley herself.

"I think I'll stay." Basha returned to the cage and sat on it. She crossed her legs and leaned back on her hands. "I'll watch your dog of a husband wither in your embrace. I'll watch your marriage become an empty, passionless shell.

And I'll watch your only child slaughtered at the hands of—"

"Stop!" Rhia lifted her hand to signal Crow.

Wings rushed forth, but when she looked up, it wasn't the night-black of Crow's feathers that filled the sky.

Raven flew to her.

Rhia dropped to her knees and covered her face. Icy shame coursed through her at what she had nearly done.

"Rhia, look at me," said a voice that flowed like water. "There is something you should know."

She dropped her arms to regard the every-color bird.

"This woman stole Marek's soul part because someone else has a piece of hers." Raven's head dipped. "You may end her if you wish. Or help her."

Rhia looked at Basha, who stared slack jawed at the Spirit of Spirits. The fox in the cage had fallen silent behind the drape.

"Help her how?"

"Find her missing piece and bring it to her."

Rhia looked around the valley. "I don't see anyone else here."

"He hides. He cannot speak."

Rhia gazed at the cage. It would be so easy to annihilate Basha.

Easy the first moment. Then would come the other moments, lined up in a row until her own death, living with what she could never undo.

She turned her back on the tree.

"Be warned," Raven said, "the place you go is farther and harder than any other. You risk your own life in this venture."

Rhia stopped. Perhaps she could come back another time, when she was stronger. Marek could wait.

No. She'd seen the dead look in his eyes. She had to get her husband back before Basha holed up in a far-flung place in the Gray Valley where Rhia could never find her.

Rhia took a step forward, then another. The rocks all looked the same in this direction, too.

Then the valley curved to the left, taking her around a bend, out of sight of the barren tree.

Her skin jumped. A dark void lay ahead of her, carved from the pale rock like a wound. A place to hide.

She walked to its entrance and extended her hand within. It disappeared. No light penetrated the cave even an inch. She pulled her hand back, fingertips tingling with a reborn fear of the dark, the fear that Marek had once helped her conquer.

She held her breath and lifted a foot to step inside.

"Rhia, wait," came an all too familiar voice.

Her jaw clenched. Skaris was the last person she needed to see right now.

"I have something you need," he said.

"Leave me—" She cut herself off. His voice had lost its mocking lilt.

She turned to him, hoping it wasn't another trick.

Skaris stood behind her holding the crow. It no longer dangled from his hand, but sat upright and alert on his wrist.

The Bear lifted his arm, and the crow took off. Its strong, lustrous wings thumped the air as it flew to her. It alighted on her shoulder, and though it had no weight, its presence seeped into her, calming her nerves like a warm bath.

"I'm sorry," Skaris said. "For everything. Thank you for saving Lidia."

She peered past him. "Where are Zilus and the others?"

"Moved on. Guess they felt like they were leaving the world in good enough hands. I was waiting to thank you for saving Lidia, and to give that back to you in person." He gestured to the crow. "Figured it was the least I could do."

"Thank you," she said, two words she never imagined giving the Bear.

They watched as the Crow Spirit swooped from the sky. Skaris suddenly turned to her, brown eyes shadowed by the night.

"Don't wait," he said. "Hurry."

She ducked into the cave before her fear could rise again.

Blackness surrounded her in every direction, even behind. She spun in a circle, searching for light, and lost her bearings. Panic squeezed her throat.

The crow grabbed a lock of her hair and pulled hard to the left. She turned in that direction. The crow let go, and Rhia began to walk.

Forward, forward, she chanted in her mind. Her pace quickened. The cave narrowed and its ceiling lowered, until she was crawling on all fours through a tunnel not much wider than herself. At least now she wouldn't overlook the soul thief, as there was no room for him to run past her.

The terrain sloped down steeply, requiring all her strength to keep from tumbling forward. She stopped to rest for a moment, stroking the soft feathers of the crow's neck to reassure herself.

Rhia had no idea how long she'd been crawling; Marek

must be worried by now. Lycas's faint tapping on the block of wood was a tenuous tether to the world she'd left behind. He would have to stop one day, and she'd be lost in here forever. The cave would swallow her present, her future and eventually her past.

Then she heard it, below her brother's rhythm. Liquid, sloshing. The sound reminded her of a boot popping out of thick, wet mud.

Forward, she reminded herself, and kept moving. Her hands and knees grew numb against the cold, hard surface. Suddenly the cave widened in all directions. She sat up and stretched her arms; they touched no walls.

The sucking sound echoed in the total blackness. At last she'd come to the end of the cave and was sitting in a room. She reached forward along the ground in front of her, searching for a person.

Her fingers slid into a moist mass. She stifled a scream and jerked back her arm.

"Who are you?" Her voice thundered in the tiny room.

The floor oozed and squished as if it were alive. She touched its surface and felt warm, pulsing muck.

"I don't understand." Basha's soul thief wasn't a man, but an unformed, unconscious being.

A chill slithered down her spine.

"You were never born," she whispered.

He didn't reply. He couldn't reply. There would be no reasoning with him.

She put her hand in again, cringing at the membrane curling around her fingers. "I'm sorry. Please let me help your mother."

The mass seemed to groan. She thought of Nilik, how she had struggled for nine months before his birth to keep him alive. Would he have gone to a place like this, holding a part of her forever? How many more almost-children lived here?

The answer came to her, and she nearly withdrew her arm.

All of them.

Tears spilled from her eyes. Her hand swam through the mass, searching for something whole.

Legs. Talons. She grabbed them and yanked, expecting hard resistance. The thing popped free so quickly, she pitched backward, knocking her head into the cave wall. She sat up, woozy.

Rhia's fingers examined the bird in her hand. The size of her forearm from elbow to wrist, it fluttered its wings in what felt like indignation. She stroked its head and felt tufts of feathers sticking up like ears on a cat.

The bird let loose a high-pitched descending call, like the whinny of an alarmed horse. Basha was an Owl, a screech owl in this case. Marek might be amused someday, if she could ever get back to him.

A wave of fatigue swept over her, and she leaned back against the cave wall. The room now seemed like a warm, secure place to spend eternity. For these never-to-be-children, it wasn't a barren exile, but a haven. She could rest here, just for a while. Her eyelids grew heavy. Rhia let them sink, ignoring the crow that tugged at her hair.

Pain spiked her hand, wrenching her awake. The owl had chomped the tender webbing between her thumb and forefinger. Rhia rubbed her eyes hard, then fumbled to find the room's entrance. This part of Basha had just saved her life.

But not yet. With the owl tucked under her arm, she crawled back up the tunnel on her knees and one hand. The room had weakened her, and every exhale seemed to transfer her strength to the cave itself. Every time she stopped, the crow urged her on with a tap to the back of her head.

What seemed like hours later, she emerged from the cave, gasping for air. She collapsed on the cold, rocky ground.

A pair of embroidered boots and a white skirt appeared before her. She looked up to see Basha gazing down. The fox's cage sat behind her, still draped with a blanket.

Rhia opened her parched mouth to speak. "Your son gave me this." She lifted the screech owl with both hands. Basha reached for it. Rhia pulled it back. "Give me my husband first."

Basha frowned. "How do I know that's really me?"

"Look in her eyes."

Basha turned her sharp gaze on the owl, whose heart tripped against its soft breast. Basha's face softened. "I'm her home." She looked at Rhia. "What happens next?"

"Crow takes you to peace."

"And then what?"

Rhia had no answer. "That's it."

"It sounds boring."

"And this place amuses you?"

Basha pushed out her lower lip. "I didn't say that." Her fist twisted in her skirt. "I want to live."

"I know."

"There were so many things I wanted to do. I was going

to help your people. Who knows what my country will do to you now?"

Rhia felt the rage rise within her again. The crow uttered a soft *grok* in her ear to calm her. She gave it a grateful glance, then spoke to Basha in a firm voice. "We'll find a way to manage without you."

"You think so, but you don't know them." Basha sighed and stepped away from the cage. "I'm through with you all. Take it. It's yours."

"No," Rhia said, "it's Marek's."

The crow alighted on the corner of the cage closest to Basha, as if to guard it from further treachery.

Rhia held the owl in her hands, knowing she could yet take vengeance. Basha's eyes filled with fear, and Rhia relished the sight for one long, sweet moment.

She released the owl. It flapped its gray-streaked wings and landed on Basha's shoulder.

A shadow blacker than night appeared next to them. Crow bent to touch Rhia's forehead. "Raven said She will not forget this day. You will see Her again, when the end seems nigh."

He enveloped Basha in his wings. Her pale face turned rapturous as they faded together into violet light.

A growl rumbled inside the cage, sounding unusually menacing for a fox.

The crow lifted the edge of the blanket. Gray fur glowed in the night.

Not a fox. A wolf.

Yellow eyes of pure wildness peered through the bars. A dripping pink tongue lolled between long white fangs.

"You're coming with me," Rhia said. She staggered to her feet and grabbed the cage's handle to lift it. It wouldn't budge. She yanked on it with both arms but couldn't slide it more than a handspan.

She squatted next to the cage. "If I let you out, will you run away?"

The wolf licked his chops. She groaned. She had nothing that could act as a leash, no way to confine or control him until they reached the fog.

"Either way, you can't stay in there." Rhia unlatched the cage and opened the door. The wolf shot out, then turned to regard her. "Please stay," she said.

At the sound of her voice, the wolf loped away, down the valley toward the tree. She tried to chase him, but her legs grew heavier with each step.

The dead tree glowed white ahead of her. She kept her eyes on it as her feet shuffled over the rocky ground. By the time she reached it, the wolf was gone.

Rhia dropped to her knees. She had lost Marek.

The air itself seemed too heavy for her body to hold up. She crawled forward a few more steps, then collapsed onto her stomach. The crow nudged her arm, then her head, uttering concerned clucks deep in its throat.

The valley floor was cold against Rhia's face, and the chill soaked into her body. Soon she would freeze to death like she did on Mount Beros. But this time she would be alone. This time, no one would bring her back. Crow would come, shaking His head in disapproval, wishing He'd called someone stronger. She hadn't even the strength to cry.

A warm breath blew against her ear, followed by a short

huff. Something wet slid over her cheek and under her nose. Sputtering, she lifted her head.

The wolf stood over her. He pawed her shoulder and whined like a dog begging for its morning meal.

"I can't," she whispered. "Not by myself."

He sidled closer. She pushed herself to her knees and looped an arm over his thick, furry shoulders. The wolf grunted, and for a moment Rhia thought he would bolt.

Step by laborious step, they left the tree behind, the wolf on four sturdy legs, she on one blistered hand and two aching knees.

Just when she thought her strength would fail, they entered the fog, together.

40

Marek clutched his wife's limp body. "Rhia, come back," he whispered, his breath threatening to turn to a sob. "Come back to me."

"What's happening?" Lycas asked. He looked as if he wanted to reach for his sister.

"Don't stop drumming," Marek told him. He rocked Rhia and shouted a plea to Crow in his mind. He couldn't lose her. "Rhia, leave me there if you have to, but come back."

Her hand twitched against his shoulder. He gasped, then held her out to examine her slack face. Perhaps he'd imagined the movement.

She moaned. "Marek..."

"Yes!" he said. "I'm here. Come to me."

She opened her eyes, slowly, as if their lids were made of stone. "I got it."

Lycas stopped tapping. "Thank the Spirits," he grumbled. "Now what?"

"She has to return my part," Marek said. "Hold her up."

Once Lycas was supporting Rhia's weight, Marek lay down beneath her. He took her cold, limp hands and cupped them to her mouth. She leaned over and breathed against his solar plexus.

A hot jolt seared through Marek, racing to the end of his fingertips. He cried out in near anguish.

Something inside him had shifted to make room for a fierce, strong presence.

He was Wolf again.

He reached for Rhia and took her gently from her brother's arms. Her skin was warming, but the heaviness of her limbs told him her strength was spent. She sank against him.

"I'll get the Otter," Lycas said. "She'll know how to help her." He left the tent quietly.

Marek stroked Rhia's hair. "Thank you. I can never repay you."

"Be here," she whispered against his chest. "That's all I want." She dragged her hand up to rub her cheek. "That and some food, honey water and three days' sleep."

He chuckled. "I don't suppose anyone packed a secret stash of meloxa, did they?"

She tilted her chin to look at his face. "How do you feel?"

"Like a man whose wife almost just died, but didn't. Relieved. Happy. A little angry that you risked your life."

"I didn't know it would take so long." She tugged his shirt. "What I meant was, how do you feel with your soul part back?"

"Like a Wolf." He closed his eyes and inhaled hard through his nose. "But I can still feel Fox. I don't want to let Her go. She saved my life, and probably Nilik's, too."

"No one's ever had two Spirits at once. But Crow said things are changing."

"For the better, I hope."

She was silent a moment. "Eventually."

He held her tight until the Otter woman came to the tent. As she ministered to Rhia, Marek stepped outside to speak to Lycas. The eastern sky held the first blush of dawn.

"Thank you for helping us," he told his brother-in-law.

Lycas nodded, then opened his mouth as if to speak. He shut it again.

"What is it?" Marek said.

The Wolverine rubbed the back of his ear. "When I was in the hallway at the senator's mansion, dispensing with those guards…"

"Yes?"

"I heard what she said to you."

Marek's face heated. His wife's own brother knew he'd been unfaithful. "I'm sorry."

Lycas held up a hand. "If you ever apologize for it again, I'll punch you so hard you won't wake for a week. What that woman did to you…" He ground his fist against his palm. "It's why I stopped myself from killing her. I thought you should have the privilege."

As odd as the statement sounded, Marek knew that from Lycas it was a declaration of absolution. He'd needed to hear it from someone besides Rhia, someone who didn't desperately want him to be whole again.

He let out a deep breath. "Thank you."

"You're welcome." Lycas patted his shoulder.

Marek picked his way over the rocks and shrubs toward Nelma and Adrek's tent. He needed to see his son.

The wounds Basha had dealt him would take years to heal. The memories would last forever. But perhaps he could take what he'd learned in Leukos to help his people resist the inevitable Ilion aggression.

Whether Raven bestowed Her Aspect in the next generation or the next or the next, the Reawakened would fight.

Rhia gasped at the crowd awaiting them at the edge of Velekos. Though Bolan had sent a pigeon days before with news of their return, Rhia hadn't expected the entire village to greet them. Their cheers echoed off the cliffs near Prasnos Bay, where the water shimmered and sparkled in the late-morning sunlight.

Her pony balked at the oncoming crowd, causing Nilik to squirm in the sling against her chest. Behind her, Marek squeezed her waist and pointed ahead to the left.

"Look," he said, "in front."

Rhia shaded her eyes and squinted into the sun. A wide smile stretched her chapped lips. "Father!"

"Let me take Nilik while you run ahead," Marek said.

"No, we go together." She clicked her tongue to urge the pony forward.

Tereus reached her first as the crowd swept among their troupe, hugging the adults and cooing at the children. He helped her and Marek dismount the pony and took his grandson in his arms.

"He's so big." Tereus's face pinched, then he bent to kiss Rhia's cheek. "I knew you could do it."

She gazed at her father with blurry eyes, then heard a familiar voice call her name.

Damen was rushing toward her. She hugged him hard enough to make him gasp, then drew back. The dark circles under his eyes might be a good sign.

"Your son," she said. "Is he—"

"On his way." He stood on tiptoe to look behind him. Nathas led Reni through the crowd, pushing aside those who would jostle her. The Squirrel woman held a bundle in her arms.

Rhia let out a tightly held breath. "That's why you've lost sleep."

"Sleep?" He rubbed his eyes and looked at the sky. "I remember something called sleep."

Marek sprang to their side and wrapped Damen in a Kalindon-style bear hug. Rhia turned to Reni and Nathas as they approached and remembered to greet them before gawking at the baby.

"His name's Corek," Reni said. "In memory of Coranna."

Tears slid from Rhia's eyes, unbidden and unexpected. Marek's and Nilik's disappearance had overshadowed Coranna's death. Now that they were safe, she could finally mourn her mentor.

Damen slid an arm around Rhia's shoulder. "There's a feast waiting in the town hall," he said gently. "That's the best part, heh?"

She wiped her eyes and nodded. Only a fellow Crow could understand the consoling power of food.

They headed for the village, where more people waited in the streets. A large open tent had been set up outside the Velekon town hall. Rhia's stomach growled at the savory smells, and she wished the crowd would let them pass more quickly.

She looked at Marek. "I was going to ask if we could wash up first, but now that we're here…"

He smirked. "It would be impolite not to eat a little."

"Just a little."

They ate and drank all afternoon, fitting in bites and sips between visits from total strangers who wanted to welcome them and meet Nilik, who slept through most of the chaos.

Finally, after dinner, she was able to speak with Damen alone about the cave in the Gray Valley. He rubbed the corner of his jaw as he listened, tensing at her description of the oozing, sucking mass.

"Should we move these unborns," he asked her, "and if so, where?"

"I don't think they can be moved. They seemed like a part of the land itself. And they didn't feel unhappy to me. Not happy, either, just—there." She shifted her feet under the table. "It's hard to explain, but they didn't feel like people."

"How could the senator's son steal her soul piece if he wasn't a person?"

"Maybe she gave it to him. Maybe she thought it would keep him alive."

Damen ran his teeth over his bottom lip. "I think I would've done the same for Corek. Not consciously, of course."

"We all try to bargain with Crow, whether we mean to or not."

Damen swished his drink. "And it never works." He took a long sip and set the empty mug aside. "Next time either of us speaks to Him, we'll have lots of questions."

The fiddlers struck up a reel, and Rhia felt a hand squeeze her shoulder.

Marek kissed the top of her head. "I insist you don't dance with me."

She laughed and stood to join him, despite her drowsiness from the food, ale and traveling. At first it felt strange to dance, to move with no purpose other than joy, but the music injected her feet with an energy she hadn't felt in months. They danced the first song together, then switched partners with every new tune, according to Kalindon custom. The Velekons were confused at first by the irregularity, but soon caught on.

As evening fell, she sat with her family and Damen's, devouring the last of the berries and cream. Lycas was telling their escape story to another group of curious Velekons. With each mug of ale, the events grew larger and wilder.

"...and then the crows themselves carried us away," he told an astounded group of listeners.

"How could they do that?" asked a gray-haired woman with a skeptical regard.

"They grew wings the size of horses, of course," Lycas said, "and wrapped us all in a giant blanket made of—of rose stems. So they could grab hold." He nodded solemnly.

"What are roses?" another voice asked.

"Hideous plants," Marek said, "with thorns that leap out and cut you, like snakes from a hole." He exchanged a grim look with Lycas. "It was a painful journey in that blanket."

When the Velekons wandered off to spread the story, Lycas and Marek shared a long laugh.

"That ought to keep people talking awhile," Lycas said as he finished his dessert.

"When will you go back to Ilios?" Tereus asked him.

"Right away." Lycas's gaze tripped over the crowd again, as if expecting Mali and Sura to appear. Tereus had told them that when Mali found out Lycas would be leaving again, the Wasp refused to bring their daughter to see him. Rhia planned to have some words with her old nemesis, the kind of words she wouldn't utter in front of her own father.

Tereus nodded. "I'll help Adrek and Nelma take the children back to Kalindos."

"And see Elora while you're there," Rhia said.

Her father gave an embarrassed smile, then sobered. "It will be hard for her to hear her children are still missing."

"They won't be for long," Marek said, "if Alanka has anything to do with it."

Rhia looked at Nilik, who slept in an open basket beside her. On the other side of him, Damen's son, Corek, stretched and cooed in Reni's arms. From the corner of her eye, Rhia saw the rest of the table watching the babies, as well. She knew what they were all thinking: which boy would become Raven?

"I think they should arm wrestle for the Aspect," Marek said.

Damen set his elbow on the table and pushed his plate out of the way. "Maybe their fathers should act as stand-ins, heh?"

Marek rolled up his sleeve. "Agreed, Crow man. Let's see whose son gets to save the world."